DEAD MOON RISING

a LAST STAR BURNING *novel*

CAITLIN SANGSTER

SIMON PULSE
New York London Toronto Sydney New Delhi

This book is a work of fiction. Any references to historical events, real people, or real places are used fictitiously. Other names, characters, places, and events are products of the author's imagination, and any resemblance to actual events or places or persons, living or dead, is entirely coincidental.

SIMON PULSE
An imprint of Simon & Schuster Children's Publishing Division
1230 Avenue of the Americas, New York, New York 10020
First Simon Pulse hardcover edition November 2019
Text copyright © 2019 by Caitlin Sangster
Jacket illustration copyright © 2019 by Isaac Yeram Kim and David Field
All rights reserved, including the right of reproduction in whole or in part in any form.
SIMON PULSE and colophon are registered trademarks of Simon & Schuster, Inc.
For information about special discounts for bulk purchases, please contact Simon & Schuster
Special Sales at 1-866-506-1949 or business@simonandschuster.com.
The Simon & Schuster Speakers Bureau can bring authors to your live event.
For more information or to book an event contact the Simon & Schuster Speakers Bureau
at 1-866-248-3049 or visit our website at www.simonspeakers.com.
Series designed by Jessica Handelman
Jacket designed by Heather Palisi
Interior designed by Mike Rosamilia
The text of this book was set in Venetian 301 BT Std.
Manufactured in the United States of America
2 4 6 8 10 9 7 5 3 1
Library of Congress Cataloging-in-Publication Data
Names: Sangster, Caitlin, author.
Title: Dead moon rising / by Caitlin Sangster.
Description: First Simon Pulse hardcover edition. | New York: Simon Pulse, 2019. |
Series: Last star burning ; [3] | Summary: "There's only one thing strong enough to unite people
who have been fighting for years, and Sev holds the key to it inside her mind. If she can't reach
the cure in time, there may not be anyone left to save"—Provided by publisher. |
Identifiers: LCCN 2019010270 (print) | LCCN 2019012905 (eBook) |
ISBN 9781534427860 (eBook) | ISBN 9781534427846 (hardcover)
Subjects: | CYAC: Epidemics—Fiction. | Fugitives from justice—Fiction. |
Survival—Fiction. | Fantasy.
Classification: LCC PZ7.1.S263 (eBook) | LCC PZ7.1.S263 De 2019 (print) |
DDC [Fic]—dc23
LC record available at https://lccn.loc.gov/2019010270

To B. W., A. Z., A. J.,
and Dr. Jones

CHAPTER 1
Sev

THEY SAY TO FIND A HERO YOU CAN'T LOOK TO the past. Heroes from stories aren't real anyway, and that's what the past is, right? A story told by whoever had the biggest gun. Instead, we're supposed to find heroes around us.

I have nowhere to look, though, because my body *won't* look. It's made of ashes and wind and dead things, nothing but an echo of a heartbeat left inside me. My life has turned into a dream, every moment I'm Asleep making it harder to remember what it was like to be awake. If there was a hero next to me I wouldn't know, because all I can see is the dark side of my eyelids, feel the grainy sheet on the bed underneath me. The only things that change are sounds. Temperature. Right now I'm cold. I can hear the steady *plink, plink, plink* of fluid dripping to my IV.

The door hinge squeaks, and cool air washes over me from the hallway like a breeze from the ocean, vast as a year and deep as the sky. If my body could tense, it would, but instead I'm curled up inside my mind, waiting for whoever it is to poke or prod me. To pick up my dead weight and throw me in a burn pile, mutter ugly things into my dead ears, or touch my dead body because I can't stop them. Whoever it is stays quiet, lurking near my bed.

You are alive, not dead. It's a whisper at the back of my mind, crumpled like a wet sheet of paper. *Just like the princess in our story. Asleep until someone kisses you awake.*

I wish I could grimace, because that's not the only ending I've heard to the sleeping princess's story. Also, I don't want anyone in Dr. Yang's base to kiss me, thank you very much.

The person prowling in my room sits in what I think must be a chair, the legs squeaking under their weight. I hear quick, nervous breaths that are free of a gas mask's rusty tang. The bit of me that's still awake braces for violence or worse. No mask means SS now, and SS is a beast that I don't have the muscles to fight anymore.

"We've done everything you asked." A muffled voice filters through the closed door. *Helix*, my brain supplies. *The Menghu who killed June's father.* The person invading my room bolts up from the chair, footsteps padding to the far side of my bed away from the door. "There isn't enough Mantis to last us much longer." Helix's voice grows louder, though it's still attempting a respectful tone. "You *promised*—"

"Don't argue with me, Captain Lan." That's Dr. Yang. The door opens again, his footsteps tapping in, probably here for my weekly checkup. I think it's weekly. Maybe it's daily, and I've only been lying here for two days. I can't tell.

He pauses inside the room. "Aren't you supposed to be sending orders to Dazhai?" Not speaking to me, because he knows I cannot answer.

The intruder by my bed doesn't move for a good thirty seconds. But then the sound of army boots on concrete rings out as they leave my side and walk out the door.

Eight years my mother survived this. Eight years she *listened*, keeping her mind awake so she'd be able to pass on the possibility of curing SS. I'm like her, I guess. Dr. Yang put me to Sleep for knowing the truth too. That the note Mother left me in the device we found at Dazhai wasn't gibberish. It was a clue telling me where to find the cure.

"Medicine is an exact science." The doctor is speaking again, vague amusement at my unauthorized visitor melting away to leave only clinical precision. "You'll have to trust me, Helix. I promised you a cure, but you and your soldiers will have to be patient."

He can't get the cure. Not unless I tell him where Mother hid it. The tiny living part inside me raises her head, listening to Helix's silence. It's heavy. A waiting silence that could end in death or destruction or maybe a cup of tea. It's hard to tell. All I know is Helix doesn't ask any more questions.

CHAPTER 2
Tai-ge

THE COT FEELS LIKE SOME KIND OF CANVAS. ROUGH grain, stretched tighter than I'd expect. Of course, all the missions I've participated in with the City up until now required specific flight plans, an eye on the clouds, and exactly zero cots. Maybe cots have been this way all along, and I had to sleep on one to know the way the fabric scratches at my skin.

Voices outside my tent draw my spine straight. Each time I inhale, it strains through the filters of my mask, so loud I have to hold my breath to listen. Three voices, coming from the direction of the Chairman's tent. Female. Two I don't recognize, harsh and precise as they issue through gas mask filters. The third voice, however, is familiar as the raw-scrubbed lines of my knuckles even through the rasp of a mask.

When the voices draw close, the two unfamiliar ones pass by, leaving a shadow waiting outside the tent flap. I stand, waiting to see if she'll finally come in. Wanting her to. But not wanting to face her.

An arm pushes aside the untied tent flap, General Hong's

polished boots all I allow myself to look at once she steps inside. The air between us seems to be filled with nothing but disappointment.

"I have an assignment for you, Son."

I chance raising my eyes past her knees, almost to her belt buckle, the City seal a proud falcon and beaker etched into the metal. Silence is respect. I wait.

"It's a chance to alleviate some of the difficulty in which we find ourselves." She sighs, bending until her face comes into view, forcing me to break the boundary between our stations and look her in the eyes. "I'm proud of what you did, Tai-ge." My chest lifts, some space finally opening inside it, only to turn back to stone when she continues. "It just wasn't enough."

Failure. I got into Kamar when it was supposed to be impossible for a Second. I got the device Sev's mother left behind. And then I let Menghu take it away from me.

"Do we know where they took the cure yet?" I ask, knowing better than to voice the other question that's been burning inside me since Dr. Yang's Menghu flew me from Kamar to Dazhai camp, leaving me on the dead airfield and taking everything of value with them.

It's been two weeks. Two weeks of measuring the gap between my tent and the next. Of eating exactly what I'm rationed and hanging my uniform coat so the wrinkles left from being stuffed under my mother's bed will smooth. Two weeks of disappointed silence.

"No," Mother finally responds. "We don't know where the Menghu took the device you found in Kamar. Dr. Yang has been quite communicative about progress, though." She sighs, her tone a familiar frustrated cadence. "After Jiang Sev killed her mother with anti–Suspended Sleep serum, apparently the setbacks seemed insurmountable. But, now that he has this new data, Dr. Yang is optimistic we have what we need to cure SS."

"Sevvy—Jiang Sev—didn't hurt her mother on purpose. Dr. Yang told her—"

Mother frowns over my slip using Jiang Sev's nickname, but mercifully doesn't comment. "There are other patients in a similar state, and he's had success waking them when using the serum correctly, Tai-ge. That girl never was much for listening. There's a proper procedure. A dosing schedule. You can't give it to a patient all at once. If it wasn't on purpose, then it was incompetency."

I lick my lips, letting her finish. She's right about Sevvy. Rules seemed an annoying itch to my friend as we got older.

"Apparently, Jiang Sev can read the data contained on the device, but she won't cooperate." Mother's eyes narrow. "I have no doubt the obstacles will be worn down soon, though."

Worn down. I keep my eyes focused on Mother, refusing to blink. It doesn't stop the terrible images that crop up in my head, the tingles of pain that streak down my arms and back that make me wish I hadn't been a part of putting Sevvy in a cell. But I push that thought aside. Sevvy should know better than to hold back now. We need the cure. The whole world does. We can't be picky about who is in charge if there's nothing left to be in charge of, but still it sits wrong in my stomach that I'm here in this tent and she's being . . . worn down.

"Is Dr. Yang allowing First and Second involvement?"

"There are Firsts from the Circle, who are being asked to help, but the Chairman won't relay any details. It is my belief that Dr. Yang isn't allowing him to do so. The information you brought me before going to Port North regarding Dr. Yang's true loyalties and Chairman's actions . . . You were correct. He has been compromised somehow by Dr. Yang. We have to forge forward ourselves."

"If Dr. Yang manages to develop a working cure . . ." I pause, not sure how to phrase what we must both be thinking. "How long do we have before he stops pretending to be a loyal City comrade? He'll use the cure to compel Seconds and Thirds to support his Menghu forces."

Mother walks over to my cot and sits down, the frame squeaking. She gestures for me to sit next to her, a smile touching her lips at my automatic hunch. My head higher than hers makes me uncomfortable. "Dr. Yang says he wants to unify us, but I am afraid you are right. He means only to take what we have. I have great admiration for what you were able to accomplish, as I said before. But without the device we need a way to fight. Which brings us to your new assignment."

Fight? I hold the word inside. There was a time when I could say some of what I thought to my mother. When I could tease her and deviate from what she wanted without repercussions. That was when we had beds, pillows, wooden floors beneath our feet. Walls that isolated our family enough to allow us to be mother and son when no one could hear. Now she's stepped into Father's shoes and we live in an open field where every moment we are made from gas masks and metal stars. The fate of the City has slipped from the Chairman's shoulders to settle on Mother's.

The Chairman. Anger churns inside me, my teeth clamping so tight my jaw begins to ache. I've seen him here in the camp, waving, encouraging. Serving the Seconds and Firsts with a stalwart firmness, a determination that's meant to be inspiring. As if rationing isn't a direct result of him handing our supplies to

Dr. Yang. Without Chairman Sun, the Menghu would never have invaded the City. We never would have ended up in this cold-water camp, biting our tongues as he opens the gate and lets gores in one by one.

He and Dr. Yang together have much to answer for. But Mother and I are the only ones who know.

"We need to have another way to fight SS until we can take the cure for our own, Tai-ge." Mother pats the cot next to her again, and this time it's an order, so my knees bend. "Masks break every day, and we have no way to fix them or build new ones. The Mantis stockpiles are growing thin, disappearing into Menghu camps. The moment Dr. Yang has a working cure, it will be loyalty against an empty stomach and compulsions. Our soldiers and workers will become his slaves." She touches my shoulder, pushing my hunched shoulders straight. "You remember the medic we sent with you to Kamar who was so easily swayed into betraying you? I doubt we can expect better from most of our ranks. They are frightened."

My chest clenches over the memory. Xuan tried to kill me. He told Sevvy . . . I don't know what he told Sevvy, exactly. Something that made her set him free and turn me out for the gores . . .

I mean, I do know what he must have said. That I was working with Mother to get the cure. That I meant to take it back to her, to people who could analyze it, reproduce it, and actually use it to save us all from SS. But the way he said it must have cast me as a villain because he didn't care about saving anyone. All Xuan wanted was to escape from his duty. His expertise was supposed to get us into Kamar's main city, onto their island, so I could disable the weapons they used to shoot our helis out of the sky. Instead, he left. Landed us all in Kamari jail cells.

Xuan is the reason I failed Mother. Failed my people. Failed Sevvy.

I blink the thought away before it can take over. I don't owe Sevvy anything. She's the one who wouldn't listen to reason. And excuses are for the weak. For those who refuse to take ownership of themselves and their actions. My failures are mine, no matter who else contributed. It was *my* failing to place trust in Xuan.

Mother leans forward, fingering her mask before letting her hand fall. For a moment I think she means to put a hand on my knee. A comfort. Instead, she stands. "We must be able to protect our people, to give them an alternative to capitulation." She touches my shoulder, her hand perfectly positioned as if she thought out all the angles and pressure before moving. "So I'm sending you back to the City."

I push myself up from the cot. Back to the City? We abandoned the City, its labs, and its factories to SS, the disease spreading too quickly to do anything but run.

Lagging a respectful two steps behind my mother, I square my shoulders and follow her out of the tent. The light seems bright outside, cheery after the two weeks of gloomy waiting for judgment inside my tent. I may have listened to Sevvy during the invasion, dirtied my boots with the spoiled world Outside, then failed at the task Mother set me after I tried to make amends. But now I can make up for it.

All the muscles tensed along my shoulders loosen because I'm back where I belong: two steps behind the General. Whatever it is Mother has for me to do, whether it's in the City, in the camp here, or at the center of the Earth, I will do it if it means she trusts me again.

* * *

After the the official meeting with what's left of the First Circle, my fingers drum against my hip as I walk toward the heli-field. My assignment feels like an anchor in my head, holding me steady. Mother's at my side, I have something worthwhile to contribute to City objectives, and in just a few minutes I'll be back in the air where I belong.

The craft set aside for me is a smaller model than the one I flew with Sevvy. Room only for a pilot and a few passengers crammed in behind. To one side there are piles of boxes laced into the harness that will hang beneath the aircraft as we fly. Supplies.

The pilot, copilot, and three of Mother's entourage stand at attention just outside the door, waiting for Mother and me to climb in. A girl my age is situated closest to the ladder and sneaks a look at me as I ascend, not the least bit embarrassed when I catch her. She's got two stars on her collar, but the state of her uniform tells me she's from the outer circles of the camp where supplies are stretched thin. She has dimples and no gas mask.

The lack of mask is jarring at first glance, but then a pleasant change. Even if it does mean she's a drag on our Mantis supply, it's been two weeks since I've seen someone's face. Two weeks since someone has smiled at me. She looks nice.

That's what Mother always wanted: to find a nice Second to add to our family, someone we could train, *groom* to stand next to me when I took over Father's place as General. I always smiled back when they appeared across the dinner table, knowing no matter how hard I looked at Sevvy, her traitor scar would never go away.

Only, this girl's smile brings Sevvy to mind. The way she grinned when she got me to laugh. Or her hidden smile that appeared when the laugh was going to be a surprise. Or at my expense.

The way she screamed at me not to touch her. To get away.

The butt of a Menghu gun connecting with her head, and the way she crumpled to the ground.

Not all my failures are irreversible. I want Sevvy to see that I was right, that the City isn't broken. Since she's most likely wherever the cure is, that isn't going to happen until I've done what Mother has asked in the City. Once we have a way to fight Dr. Yang's SS bombs, we'll be able to launch a mission to take the cure. I will be a part of that mission, and I'll save Sevvy.

It's the only logical path forward.

Mother and I sit down next to each other in the heli. As I reach for a headset to protect my hearing from the sound of the heli's propellers, the girl with the dimples pushes by, knocking my hand aside. She doesn't apologize, just settles in the seat directly behind me. Mother's eyes narrow, but she doesn't say anything, pulling my headset from its tether and handing it to me. After we lift off, I can't keep my eyes from the pilot's hands. Watching every button she pushes, every correction she makes. Clouds whip by my window at one hundred knots, the air pressure gauge dancing back and forth, and I find my hands clenching in my lap. It's hard to watch someone else's hands be responsible for keeping us in the sky.

By the time Mother touches the crook of my arm, we've been flying for quite some time. Her fingers press a button to isolate the connection between our headsets. "There are a few things we couldn't speak about at Dazhai." Her voice crackles over the connection between us. "The Chairman's cronies were listening, so we couched this as a mission to bring food and order to those still trapped inside City walls. To attempt to salvage resources . . . You know. You were in the meeting."

I nod, staring straight forward as I listen, my chest hollowing as the pilot adjusts the rotors. Why is she even using them? This craft isn't optimal for gliding, but the weather outside would have made it a perfect solution to the fuel gauge ticking closer and closer to "empty." Using the main propellers makes us faster, I suppose, but it seems a waste of fuel.

"I could only persuade the Chairman to send a small unit to scout ahead. They landed three days ago and are clearing a safe place for you to set up a command center. You will need more Seconds to accomplish our true purposes, of which there are three. First, clear and secure a path to the main gates. Once you've done that, there are two Red platoons close enough to the City you could request their help without using the broader radio relay system. That way the Chairman won't know you're moving them, and he won't be able to report it to Dr. Yang. Bring in as many as you can."

Though Mother looks perfectly at ease, I can almost feel the tension—the *fear*—causing her to fidget. "Second, you'll need to secure the mask factory. I'm afraid all the Thirds who evacuated were stationed in the upper quarters, so we don't have any workers who will know how to restart production. I'll be looking for Seconds who were stationed down there. Keep me posted on your progress, and I'll send everyone I can find. Once the factory is secure, your last objective will be to clear out one of the Mantis manufacturing labs. I'm afraid that will be the most difficult task, as our information says the First Quarter is where the highest concentration of infected are. We'll have to use Second medics who trained in the First labs to get things up and running." She turns toward me, pulling on my arm until I look at her. "Seconds are the backbone of the City. We were everywhere, saw everything."

I nod. "And the infected? What strategy do we have for helping—"

"Captain Bai, your second-in-command, has specific instructions. We don't have Mantis to spare at the moment, but hopefully once you've accomplished your objectives, that will change. The moment you've made progress, notify me over the secure link I've given you." I feel the press of the little device in my pocket, uncomfortable knowing that once I'm in the City, it will be our only reliable way to communicate without being overheard. "We'll begin hiding raw components and stashing them in supply runs to the City to facilitate successful Mantis manufacture."

"Which will allow us to have some autonomy from the Chairman and, therefore, Dr. Yang. You've thought of everything." I say it quietly.

She smiles patiently before turning straight-ahead again. "There's one thing I couldn't help." Her mouth hardly moves as she speaks, almost as if she's humming to herself. "Dr. Yang is very suspicious of this venture. He doesn't believe our comrades trapped in the City deserve relief. When I insisted, he allowed the Chairman to relent. However . . ." She picks an imaginary speck of dust from her sleeve, rubbing it between her fingers. "The next day, Chairman Sun insisted on providing you with proper support."

"What do you mean?"

"A handpicked assistant. A specially trained Second to represent his personal stamp of approval on the effort to save the people trapped inside City walls."

Saving people who are trapped. What would Sevvy think of that? It's difficult to feel the glow of being right, because she isn't here to see that her ridiculous fears about the City leaving behind anyone who will be a drag on our resources were unwarranted. But it does make me feel a little bit of pride in the midst of our awful situation in this war. I am the hands of the City, and I will do what it takes to rescue anyone who still has enough left of them to save. I was right about that at least, whatever Sevvy might think.

Or whatever Howl *taught* her to think. After all, Xuan wasn't the instigator of Sevvy turning traitor.

Mother's words sink a layer deeper. A handpicked assistant from our Chairman, who is under Dr. Yang's thumb. I can feel the girl behind me staring into the back of my head, her attention like the brush of a razor against my skin. She doesn't fit in with Mother's people. I definitely didn't ask her to come. Which leaves one empty space for her to fill. I'm suddenly glad for the heli propeller roar, keeping this conversation private. "My assistant is the Second sitting behind me, right?"

Mother nods.

"She's . . . Menghu?" Hot anger floods my throat, folding in on itself over and over. Menghu destroyed the City. Menghu slaughter us, steal our food, our masks, our Mantis. Menghu are Dr. Yang's bloody fingers disassembling everything in the world I love.

Mother's miniscule nod confirms my suspicions. "I'd bet my favorite star pins on it. You can't let Captain Bai know. . . ." I nod, unable to hear the words just as much as Mother can't bear to say them. If our soldiers knew the Chairman is dancing to an Outsider's tune, that would be the end—or, perhaps, a very bloody beginning, and we aren't ready for either of those outcomes. "You need to take care of her," Mother's gas-mask whisper rasps through the headset. "Before she sees what we are doing, but after you've found her method of communicating and can mimic her."

My stomach clenches. *Take care of her.* A dome of rock appears through the cockpit window, an island of stone floating in a sea of cloud, smoke still billowing up from it in ugly charcoal streaks.

My home, polluted by SS and Menghu filth. The pistol holstered under my coat presses into my side, begging to be set free. We could take care of this right now.

I can feel the girl shift behind me, all of my muscles tensing in response. A softer thought comes underneath, though. The Menghu have Sevvy and everything she knows about the cure. That's the battle coming next, the one that's going to matter.

Is there a chance this girl knows where Sevvy is?

"I can trust you with this, can't I?" Mother looks over at me, her expression etched in steel, and it kills me that she feels the need to ask, as if I'm a young child who doesn't understand the importance of this task.

"Of course you—" The heli drops, taking my stomach with it. I glare at the pilot as she fiddles furiously with her controls until we're out of the updraft she should have seen coming.

Mother puts a hand on mine as a sort of reassurance, and shame blossoms inside me. She thinks I'm scared, not indignant the General of the People's Army is stuck behind an inferior pilot. I pull my hand out from under hers, collecting myself.

"I can do this, General." The staccato rhythm of my heart quickens when her steely expression doesn't change. As if she handed me Father's boots and has already decided they're too big. "I won't make any more mistakes."

CHAPTER 3
Howl

THE WORLD IS GORE-HOLE BLACK AROUND ME.

I have cause to know just how black that is. Of course, I don't mean the hole most people think of when you say "gore hole." I'm unfortunately acquainted with the mouth and throat portion, but I've been lucky enough to stay away from the other end.

Taking a deep breath through my nose doesn't do much to calm the steady *thump* of my heart. *Where am I?* The room is too quiet, no buzz of electricity waiting to be used, no whine of air through a duct. It's as if I've been completely disconnected, put in a not-place in a not-world where there isn't anything but the mat I'm lying on.

Pain from my shoulder bites through me and down my side. My fingers slide across the raw wound over my collarbone and the thick string threading it together, as if I somehow got switched with a Jiaoyang mending project and the kids sewed me up instead of old Menghu uniforms.

Broken collarbone. Gore bite. The thought comes with unwelcome memories: the smell of death enveloping me, teeth fencing me in.

Of June, tears streaming down her face, her mask lying next to her on the floor. Sev pressed up against me, stone dust falling around us as the walls tried to shake themselves apart. Luokai with his teeth bared. The island, Port North, surrounded by waves, the whole world pulsing as a heli falls from the sky. The cure, on a paper that we sent to Sole . . . something about a device with more information. Sev climbing.

I sit up, ignoring the pain and the wave of nausea that sweeps over me. Sev left me. I mean, of course she did. I couldn't climb, and we had to get up to that tower to find some device her mom left to make sure we got everything Jiang Gui-hua recorded about the cure.

Rolling onto my knees is difficult, and I have to hold my arm close against my ribs, the sling Sev made for me gone. But once the pain dies down, I begin pulling at the rough braids of the mat until the itching, straw-like strands unravel. I break the strands into six-inch pieces, then tightly bind them so the sharp, severed ends stick out at either side.

Not much of a weapon, but enough to surprise someone if they think I'm unarmed.

Just as I'm finishing, there's a stone-on-stone *click*. Light makes a line on the floor that expands as a door slides into the wall, the person who opened it casting a shadow into the darkness of the room.

Surely no one here is dumb enough to walk into a dark room without backup. My muscles tense, ready to launch myself at the stranger. Just as it becomes apparent that this person *is* that stupid, light blasts from every direction, blinding me. I throw my arm over my eyes.

"You were going to stab me?" A voice asks. "With *straw*?"

My brother Luokai's voice.

"It seemed better than trying to strangle you with the blanket." My shirt would have made a better strangulation device, but strangling people isn't very useful if there's more than one to fight.

I let myself slump down to the ground, willing my eyes to adjust to the light as I hold my injured arm close. Pain stabs through me over and over, but I don't let go of my bunch of straw. The last time I saw my brother, he was trying to take a bite out of my leg, and the only reason he stopped was because I gave him the bruise still shadowing his temple.

And then he apparently locked me in a room underground when I was supposed to be escaping with Sev. *Where is she?*

I hold still, waiting for the adrenaline surge to calm before I say anything. If I can't control the information I give by regulating my tone of voice, then I cannot afford to speak.

By the time my eyes are properly adjusted, Luokai is standing above me, his face bled dry of any feeling. "Feeling a little better, I think?"

"Where's Sev? And June? Is she awake yet?" Swallow. Maintain eye contact. Watch his hands, his feet, his eyes . . .

"June's safe. Jiang Sev is . . ." His eyes narrow a fraction. "Gone. I would have told you sooner, but they were keeping you under until they were sure you were stable."

"I've been *drugged*? When did Sev leave?" I catch myself leaning forward and force myself to slump back, adopting a calmer tone. If Luokai knows what matters to me most, he could use it to take more from me than he already has. "How long have I been down here?"

"A while." He smooths his robes across his knees. "And our deal is at risk of not being fulfilled."

"Our *deal*?" This time my hands clench down to keep me from doing something I'll regret. "The one where you infected my friend in exchange for giving Sev the cure her mother explicitly set aside for her?"

"It wasn't the cure. At least, the notes I gave you weren't." Luokai puts a hand in his pocket and draws out the link he took from me, hesitation a heavy weight on what he's about to say. "Sole says the formula we sent was something to do with long-term Sleep."

"Why am I down here, Luokai?" I'm out of patience. "Where did Sev go? Was the cure on the device?"

"I sent Baohujia—our soldiers—to find you once the bombs stopped. Both of us are down here because Gao Shun—the Baohujia leader—knows we were exposed to contagious SS."

"I'm immune!"

"Yes, well, Gao Shun isn't willing to take chances. She wasn't happy about me setting the two of you free the day the Reds came since you both were exposed to me when I was contagious. The *right* formula for the cure had to have been on the device Jiang Sev was supposed to get from her."

I go up on my knees, anger poking through the holes pain is making in my wall of self-control. *"Where is Sev?"*

Luokai licks his lips, slipping the link back into his pocket before meeting my eyes. "Soldiers from the helis took her. And the device."

The words sting inside me, numbing everything so I can't speak, can't think.

"From what I gather, there was an incident up in the tower—" Luokai's still talking, but the words fall flat in my head, meaningless in the face of the plans I need to start making.

"*Who* took her? Menghu? Reds? Which one?"

Luokai takes being cut off gracefully, merely inclining his head. "By the time Gao Shun woke up, there was no one left alive to identify the aggressors. They were definitely not from our island, but they were all dressed like Baohujia."

The hairs on my arms stand up. Using enemy uniforms in order to access a secured place sounds like a Menghu tactic if I know anything. Dr. Yang announced the mission to invade Port North to a bunch of Reds, but there's no way he sent just Red soldiers here. He has only managed to keep Reds in check because he has some kind of hold on the Chairman. It was that hold that allowed Menghu to invade the City, that allowed them to take masks and Mantis directly from Red camps after contagious SS began to spread, all because of some picture.

A picture that makes Chairman Sun obey Dr. Yang. It could be anything. A past indiscretion, a medical implant waiting to kill him—it could be a picture of his dead wife in the ground for all I know. The days when I could have snooped until I found the answer then used it as leverage myself are long gone.

Dr. Yang must know that whatever his hold is on the Chairman, it couldn't possibly be absolute. If, during the invasion, Red soldiers managed to get the cure to Chairman Sun or General Hong, it probably would have destroyed any power Dr. Yang had over City forces. My guess is the doctor sent Menghu in to make sure that wasn't a possibility.

So Menghu probably have the cure. They probably have Sev, too. The information sits like a bomb inside me, fuse already ignited and burning fast.

"As I said, our deal is in jeopardy." Luokai's face is closed enough I can't read it. No convenient eyebrow furrows or looking away from eye contact. No fidgeting or adjusting his position. Is it possible this man has no tells? "We need to get you out of here as soon as possible to recover the cure."

"Just so we're clear. You're saying if I don't bring a cure back to you, you're going to hurt June?" I watch him. Wait.

Luokai doesn't break eye contact, sitting up straighter if anything. "I am not a monster, Howl. But without a cure, she's probably better off here with people who know how to take care of her."

"I want to see her."

Luokai shakes his head. "I can't facilitate that. I'm sorry."

My hands twitch toward my side as if there's a weapon I can use to persuade him, but all I have is straw. "You touch a hair on that girl's head and you won't live to be cured."

The corner of Luokai's mouth curls into a smile. "We're clear, Howl." He pulls himself up from the floor and goes to the door. "There's a group of Islanders that set out for the mountains this morning. If you can walk, you should be able to catch up with them and get into the thick of things quicker than you would be able to alone. Sole is still holding out under the Mountain. If you go to her, I'm sure she'll help you find where they took the cure, and then we can get it back."

What's the likelihood that Sev and the cure are in two different places? The thought feels almost like hope. *Jiang Gui-hua wanted Sev to find the cure. It's probably coded for her somehow. Dr. Yang has to be trying to force Sev to work with him.*

I sit back, trying to think through the gaps. To find reasons why I could be wrong. But it's the only information I have, so there isn't much else I can do but hope I'm correct and act accordingly. My mind begins worrying on the next question: the quickest way to Dr. Yang and, probably, Sev. Attempting to join an Islander caravan could help—then I wouldn't have to scavenge for food or wander through territory I'm not familiar with. But that plan comes with problems. "You think they'll just welcome me into their group?" I put my hands up, showing him my First mark. "I don't know about you, but I tend to be choosy about the people allowed near me while I sleep."

He smiles. "You will be exactly what they want. You can't tell them you came from the island or quarantine. About me. But if they believe you to be a First who is sympathetic to the island, then they will take you exactly where you need to go."

A wave of nausea pulses from my core to my throat as I push myself up from the ground on shaky legs, but it doesn't have much to do with the pain. If the Menghu really do have Sev, this isn't going to be pretty.

We've lived very different lives. Had very different choices. Sev said it before she left me to climb up the island, helis buzzing in the sky. She stopped me before I could tell her the rest, what Sole and the rest of the Menghu believe of me. That I didn't just kill Reds. That I'd destroy anyone who rubbed me the wrong way, friend, enemy, or anything in between.

I trust you, Sev said.

Taking a deep breath doesn't help, the words like a knife in my brain. *I trust you.*

I knew the things the Menghu said about me, but I never countered them. I never told them that Tali was killed because of a sniper hiding in a tree, not because we argued two nights earlier. Or that Gaohua made the mistake of going off alone and was cornered by gores. That Helan, who told everyone he was as good as dead after I disagreed with him rather violently about tactics, went down under a *Red* bullet. No odd circumstances, any of them, and yet somehow their murders belong to me.

I didn't do it. Not on purpose, in any case. But I let everyone else believe it, even Sole. When the other Menghu thought I was someone to fear, there weren't any sideways looks, no references to where I came from. The Chairman and I shared a *name*. My reputation made me more than my dead parents. Dangerous. In control.

I had to be a gore, I thought, to survive.

A memory of a little girl bleeds up into my mind. No, not the girl, but the husk I left of her, blood-splattered hands still clutching her doll. I take a long, deep breath and then another, trying to make it go away. To somehow make it not true.

Luokai's face is blank, watching me impassively.

Two years in the City taught me to see more than uniforms when I looked into a crowd, that people weren't bad or good or enemies or friends just because of the insignia they wore. But right now those same people, no matter what it is they believe, have Sev.

Where does that leave me?

The air inside me is the only thing holding me up. I know what it means to go up against Menghu, and if it means Sev gets to live, then that's what I'm going to do. I know how to be a gore.

"I can walk." My legs shake under my weight, but I tell myself it's the truth. "Let's go."

CHAPTER 4
Tai-ge

WHEN THE HELI LANDS, I FIND MYSELF LISTENING
for the Menghu girl behind me, keeping track of her without
actually *watching* her. But the moment I climb out of the heli, all
thoughts of Menghu blow away in a swell of smoke. The market,
a warren of wooden dens and stalls—a place I'm accustomed to
elbowing through the crowds, weaving through lines of workers
waiting to exchange their ration cards—is nothing but charred bits
of kindling. The square above it is white with ash, right to the
base of the only thing that remains upright—Yuan Zhiwei's statue
at its center. It's dusted over with the tiny particles of ash, the
marble scorched by flame. Up the hill, where the City Center once
stood, there are only blasted remains, stones blackened and strewn
in every direction, though the Arch still stands.

Every swallowful of air feels as if it should burn, but my mask
keeps the taste of chemicals and death out. It's as if I'm here, but
not here at all, removed from this place that used to be my home.
Whatever caused the fire must have started on the southern edge
where the damage is worst, eating through the booths only to lose

its teeth the closer it got to the wall dividing the Third Quarter from the Aihu River and the Second Quarter beyond. There are still ghostly remains of structures on that side, the wood cracked and teetering as if it means to give out at any second.

Mother is silent next to me, her eyes on my fingers as they tap against my leg. Waiting to see if I fold or hold strong.

"What happened here?" I ask.

She shakes her head. "Is that the first question you should be asking, Major Hong?" Mother's eyes weigh on me until I realize she's talking to *me*. Major? A ripple of alarm finds my chest, but I smooth it down. Major. I can do this.

A man in full Outside patrol fatigues detaches from the line of soldiers waiting at attention between us and the ashy remains of the market. "This is your second-in-command," Mother continues. "Captain Bai."

Captain Bai gives an exact bow, head still and low until Mother nods, releasing him from the subservient pose. "We've secured the square and a ring of buildings beyond." He keeps his eyes politely lowered as he speaks. "As advised by the Firsts, we first cleared a cannery and used the chemicals to make torches. They'll keep back anyone lacking a mask."

Something moves just out of my line of sight, a feeling rather than something I can see. The dimpled Menghu is just behind me. "Good work, Captain Bai. I look forward to working with you. Shall we debrief—"

Mother clears her throat, and I pull back, waiting for her to speak. "You've done an excellent job, Captain Bai. You will find the resources you requested here." She gestures to the pallets of supplies we brought along with us. The boxes seem too small to shore up our cover mission to help the people stuck here in the

City. "I have all confidence you and my son will get the situation here under control."

Again, a deep bow. "For the City, everything is possible, General."

"I'll expect a full report this evening." Mother walks back to the heli and boards without looking back.

The Menghu girl eases over to stand directly at my side. "I'll be your contact point in consulting with Major Hong." Her dimpled smile seems sharp, cutting between me and Captain Bai.

Inwardly, I roll my eyes. How am I supposed to pretend that this girl is my assistant or anything other than what is glaringly obvious: a gore attempting to fit into a City uniform?

What does she know? I can't help but think it again. *Does she know where Dr. Yang's base is? Where they took Sevvy and the device?* If only I could *reason* with this girl. Then this whole war could be different. No scrambling to manufacture masks or reopen Mantis labs, for starters.

I focus on Captain Bai. "It won't be necessary for you to communicate through my assistant, Captain. I'd like a full account of what we're up against here."

Captain Bai's face doesn't move as he speaks, every word perfectly square. "Yes, sir. I'll take you to the building we've cleared for headquarters."

The Menghu sticks close behind me as I follow Captain Bai. When we get to the building he's chosen, I can't help but want to laugh. Or cry—it's hard to tell which as the orphanage's thick windows stare down at me. Sevvy's old home.

"Is there a problem, Major Hong?" Captain Bai keeps his eyes averted.

I inhale, imagining the ash-soaked air scrubbing clean through my mask filters. "No. It's a good choice, Captain."

The door used to sag to the side, rattling with every gust of wind, but it's been replaced with what looks like a factory door: heavy wood that turns easily on thick hinges. Captain Bai leads the way inside. The polished-cement floor is still cracked down the center, and the low desk and locking cage of a door installed just behind it are exactly as I remember. There's no reason it would change, I suppose, but without orphans or nuns—and with the market square a pile of ash and the City an SS bomb waiting to explode—somehow I expected this to be different too.

It just feels empty.

"The cafeteria on floor one is large enough for briefings. And there's a smaller office just next to it that will do for strategy sessions and any of your other needs." Captain Bai opens the grate that blocks access to the stairs, waiting for me to walk through. "We thought quartering you on the third floor would be safest."

Of course that's where he wants me. Maybe he'll read into my past somehow and suggest I sleep in Sevvy's room, in her old bed. Her last ugly look of betrayal still sits in my brain as she fought to get away from me. Blamed *me* when it was Menghu who came for us. Acted as if I weren't trying same as her to get the cure to a safe place. A place were we could all *use* it.

I shake my head, wishing I could control her touch on my thoughts the same way I can control the number of wrinkles in my uniform coat. Even with reality laid out clear before her, Sevvy didn't want to give me the device. Didn't trust me to know the difference between right and wrong when it was obvious she was the one who hadn't properly evaluated the situation.

The things Sevvy said to me feel like scars now. She practically accused me of being less than human, unworthy of her friendship or love. But scars are what they are, fading over time.

I know I chose the right thing, whatever she might have thought. And so I keep walking, refusing to let this place hurt like an open wound.

When we get to the third floor, I stop at the fourth door down, feet stalling out of habit before Sevvy's old room. There's an orphaned shoe on the ground in front of it, laces undone.

Captain Bai stops at attention by the door, taking the pause as my choice of rooms. Inside, the room is worse than I expect. White plaster. Bare floor. Naked mattresses on battered wooden frames. No chests full of possessions, no shoes or coats, no clothes hanging over the bedposts or from the hooks on the walls. I walk into the room and lower myself onto the bed that used to be Sevvy's, the springs squeaking under my weight.

What was I expecting? That finding something of her here would smooth out my memories of her? So many of her smiles have now been painted over in my mind to be a gritting of teeth instead.

There's not so much as a strand of hair in this room to say Sevvy has ever been here.

"I'll take this one." The Menghu sits on the other bed, crossing her ankles.

"Sir?" Captain Bai asks.

"That will be fine." If Dr. Yang wanted me dead, he would have told his soldiers to kill me back on the tower in Kamar. If the Menghu's here, I'll be able to watch her just the way she's meant to watch me.

My skin prickles as I look her over, wondering where this girl's bloody set of bones are—Menghu wear the trigger fingers of those they've killed like jewelry, according to Sevvy. She smiles at me, kicking her feet from her seat on the bed because they don't quite reach the floor. She doesn't look like a killer. But a face does nothing but shield the truth of a person.

Captain Bai's surprised expression at the unconventional sleeping arrangement makes me squirm inside as it occurs to me what he must see. A young man less than half his age. A Major, though he's done nothing to earn the station except be related to the General. Sharing a room with his pretty "assistant." A mockery of everything a Second should stand for.

I close my eyes for a second, wishing I could take back letting the Menghu stay in here, but not sure how to fix it without losing face.

Captain Bai keeps his eyes respectfully lowered. "General Hong mentioned that you've only been given our primary goals. Her specific implementation plans are below, and there is some urgency in beginning our—"

Just as I bring up a hand to stop him, the Menghu interrupts. "You'll have my things brought up with his? And I'm thirsty."

"I'll take care of my own things, and so will she," I answer before the captain can respond. "As for orders, let's talk downstairs. Could you give me a few minutes and I'll meet you in the cafeteria?"

He gives a gruff sort of nod, lowering it into a bow at exact regulation angles before backing through the doorway. Once he's out of sight, I turn to the girl, my fingertips brushing the gun holstered at my side. "If you want to play a convincing Second, I'd start with—"

The Menghu springs off the bed, and I barely have time to pull my gun before her knife presses into my collarbone through my thick winter uniform. We stand there staring at each other, her knife at my throat, my gun pushed up against the fabric over her heart.

"If you want to play a convincing Second, I'd start with at least pretending to respect people who outrank you," I finish. My voice sounds much steadier than I can account for. "And you can get your own water."

Her full mouth widens into a smile, her dimples a sharp slash across each cheek. "You think *I'm* the one alienating Captain Bai?" The edge of her knife clicks against the two metal stars pinned to my collar. "Can't you see how much he hates that Mommy sent you here to temper-tantrum at him when there's real work to be done?"

"I don't think—"

"You've probably never *had* to do any real work before. Lucky for you, I'll be here to help you get through it. In all your meetings, every mission. Every meal. Every moment." She leans a hair closer. "I'll be right by your side, just like the Chairman asked."

I edge back from her knife, keeping my gun firm against her coat. "If you're going to make an attempt on my life, get on with it. You might get to see some of my blood, but it'll be the last thing you do."

She presses against my weapon, as if she's daring me to fire. "You kill me, then my friend bunked with the Reds downstairs will kill you back. You do anything but what I say, this whole unit will be dead."

I pull the gun away from her, letting it hang by my side. She doesn't move the knife, so I swat it away with the flat of my hand. "Want to try this again? I'm Major Hong." The title hangs crooked when I say it out loud. "What's your name?"

"Mei." She relishes saying it, licking her lips and watching me closely, as if it's supposed to mean something to me.

Clearing my throat again, I occupy myself with holstering my weapon. "What can I do for you, Mei? There's a pressing need for food outside this safe zone, and I'd like to get started distributing it." I take a step toward the door, pausing with my hand against the frame. "Unless you were hoping *I'd* be the one to fetch your water?"

Mei's smile never detaches, scarred into her face as if she couldn't let it slip if she wanted to. She folds the knife up into her coat sleeve and laughs, one hand brushing the hair out of her eyes in a horrifyingly girlish gesture. "That would be nice, but I'm getting a when-the-sky-turns-to-flame sort of vibe. I was expecting to sneak a little more. For you to pretend you didn't know where I came from and for me to pretend you're worthy of being spat on."

"I trust you have adequate Mantis supplies?" I ask, when it seems she doesn't have anything else to add. At least she isn't trying to pretend she's civil. "We don't have any for you to steal."

The laugh slides right out from her throat, her face going hard. "You came to help the infected trapped here but forgot to bring Mantis?"

"There's only so much we can do with Dr. Yang redirecting most of our stockpiles toward Menghu." I rack my brain, thinking of all the other things Captain Bai is probably waiting to discuss. Things we won't be able to say if Mei is standing at my shoulder, not unless we want Dr. Yang to stop this mission before it starts.

"It gives you all a taste of your own medicine." She smirks. "Or the taste of no medicine, I guess."

"Let's make this easy. What is it you want? I'll do my best to be accommodating. No one wants a repeat of what happened at Dazhai." The massacre. Menghu running with their guns drawn through a Red camp.

"I want the first fifteen years of my life back, *Major* Hong."

The way she leers over my title makes it plain she means to pay no respect. "That, or I want to watch the pedestal you're standing on crumble."

I try to keep my teeth from clamping down together, the muscles in my jaw sore. Perhaps this is the beginning of my newest failure. Not doing exactly as Mother said and finding she was right after all. I should have waited, watched, and then taken care of this girl. I never much understood spies and lying, though. It doesn't fit together in my head, because the world is made up of truth no matter how much you try to twist it into something else. It never even occurred to me to do anything but confront Mei. People who lie hardly seem like people at all, as if they exist on some other plane where reality depends on the way you word it.

The thought smolders for a moment in my mind because it's not true. I know how to lie. I lied to Sev about what I really wanted to do with the cure. It was necessary. There was no other way she'd let me stay with her. She was being unreasonable, twisted by the Outsiders she'd fallen in with.

Does that mean lying is all right so long as the end in mind is worth it? I'm not sure.

I step into the hall, ready to be done talking. "You're welcome to watch whatever you like. But Captain Bai is waiting for me, so you'll have to do it at a quick walk."

Mei gives me a nose-wrinkled smile, full to the brim with disingenuous excitement. She has freckles all across her nose.

CHAPTER 5
Howl

THE SHORES OF THE ISLAND SEEM TO BE MADE from broken tiles and crumbling stone. There's a heli lying on its back like a dead fly just outside the doorway from which we emerge. Luokai eyes the aircraft as we pick our way around it, our pace much slower than I'd like. Unfortunately, I'm the one who's slow. Luokai found me a sling, so moving I can handle, but everything still hurts. At least the bite has healed over. Luokai called in a medic to cut out the stitches outlining gore teeth in my shoulder, leaving nothing but scabs and ugly red lines to remember.

"There are still Reds in the settlements rounding people up." Luokai's voice is soft as he leads me down the steep switchbacks toward a long white bridge that spans the distance between the island and the beach. "We haven't had any on the island itself in about a week—"

"A week? How long was I out?"

Luokai licks his lips. "You weren't . . . out exactly. 'Subdued' is more like it."

"That's right. You said they drugged me."

"For your safety. Your wounds broke open while you were trying to help Sev find Gao Shun."

"You sure it wasn't because I had to fight off a compulsing
Seph?" I give Luokai a pointed look.

Which he misses completely because he's watching his footing.
Still, he nods in acknowledgment as if fighting him off that night
was an unfortunate given. "The medics worried you'd break them
again if you woke up confined."

"How long have I been *subdued*, then?"

"Twenty-three days."

"Twenty . . ." The number won't even come out of my mouth,
stuck inside me. The whole world could have burned in twenty-
three days. Everyone I know could have gone out in one violent
flash. Twenty-three days is a lifetime that I've just *lost*.

"Keep your eyes open out there." Luokai is still talking, as if he
can't see what the medics—no, what *he* has done to me. "You'll be
an asset to Reifa's team."

He's so calm. Ruining lives, condemning civilizations as if
the ground under him is solid enough he'll never fall. Shaking
my head, I try to concentrate on what he's saying. Reifa. The one
leading the group of Islanders I'm supposed to catch up with.
"What am I supposed to say to her again?"

"I think you will find your connections to the Mountain and
knowledge of Red camps will be a good start."

I try to quicken my pace as we negotiate a set of stairs, but
still have to take them one at a time like an old man. "How's Sole
doing?" I ask, eyeing the pocket where Luokai stowed the link
after telling me the cure we sent her was bad.

"I don't know. She thinks I'm you, and I don't know how to
ask questions the way you would."

"You haven't told her who you are?" The words come out sharp as knives, and I have to bite the rest back. Losing my temper won't help anything. Just think of the last time. . . .

But then I do think of the last time. Sev all curled in on herself, her eyes wide and scared as if she was waiting for my head to split in two, for the gore she was sure lived inside my skin to come out. I swallow the thought back, continuing down the stairs.

When we get to the wide bridge that links the island to where the settlements lie empty up the shore, Luokai stops, handing over the rucksack he's been carrying. I can only carry it on one shoulder because of my wounds, so I'll be sore by the end of the day, but if it comes down to a choice between a sore back and an empty stomach, I'll always choose food.

"There's some medicine in the front pocket to fight the bacteria from the gore bite. Not the same kind they were giving you in quarantine. I couldn't take that without anyone noticing." Luokai points at the battered bag. "It's stronger, I think. Take the pills twice a day. We can't have you relapse out there."

My hand absently touches the pocket he indicated as I look out at the bridge, the stone bright white and exposed in the sunlight. Anyone on the other side will be able to see me as I cross. When I was with Tai-ge, Sev, and June in the heli, it took us, what, ten hours to fly here? So, at the roughly fifty-five-knot speed Tai-ge had us gliding at, the old farm from where we took off has got to be at least six hundred miles away. Which means walking back there will take approximately the rest of my life.

My foot catches on the ground, and I stumble forward. A month of walking, maybe. *If* I find this Islander group and we make good time. Manage to find food along the way and don't get completely lost. Six hundred miles in a heli could be twice as long on the ground, accounting for mountains and rivers. Gorges and cliffs. Soldiers and gores.

Sev's a prisoner somewhere. I need to be there *now*.

Hefting the rucksack, I look back at Luokai. "There's a lot riding on me finding her and the cure."

"Yes."

"Not just your sanity. Not just June's. If Dr. Yang has the cure, he's going to come root out the last person hiding here. He'll take control of everything."

Luokai nods. "I wish it were not so."

I point to the bridge. "Is this the best you can do? Doesn't this place have helis, soldiers, food reserves . . . *You* know the way to the mountains, but you're sending me alone?"

Frowning a little, Luokai takes a step closer to me. "There's not much I can do, Howl. I have to take care of June until you return."

June. Her name on his lips makes my blood begin to simmer again, as if he weren't the one who turned her Seph. I turn back to face the bridge, afraid if I look at Luokai anymore I'll hit him. It's been a long time since I've fought someone just to make myself feel better. Doesn't seem smart at the moment, especially going after an infected person who a) won't remember that aiming for a snapped collarbone is fighting dirty, and b) might eat the broken pieces if he wins.

So instead of hitting Luokai, I start walking. There's wind skimming my ears, the crash of water below me, bits and pieces of broken stone that skid under my feet across the white of the bridge. A long shadow from the statue that stands at the bridge's head stretches over me, Luokai's hidden inside it, the two of them darkening my path across.

He doesn't speak again, not enough left between us even for a good-bye. There's a hole in my chest where I've kept my brother all these years, hoping he was out here. That one member of my family hadn't melted away, unable to survive the heat of a life at war like the rest. But now I know the truth, and I don't look back.

I find new tracks from the bridge easy enough, a small group that passed through within the last few hours, one with a shaved heel that sticks out like strawberries in winter. It gets more complicated as I creep through the structures lined up beyond the beach, their stone walls scorched and the ground saturated by many, many booted footprints. It's not long before I have to take cover inside one of the little stone houses, a heli buzzing overhead. The bite in my shoulder throbs.

Sheltering under the eaves, I pull out the bottle of medicine Luokai left in the rucksack. Twice a day, he said, so I put one white pill in my mouth, hoping it kills pain *and* gore diseases. My collarbone isn't grating painfully the way it was when I first woke up with Sev, but it still hurts.

Once the heli is gone, I manage to find prints from the shaved heel again and follow it into the trees. The tracks aren't too hard to follow in the tall grass, and I'm beginning to wonder how helpful traveling with this group could be if they're leaving such obvious trails for Reds to find, when a voice stops me cold.

"This way. Looks like there are five, maybe. Four?"

Creeping into the shelter of a tree trunk, I listen for a moment before I move closer. Not that it matters. The two men ahead of me are making so much noise themselves, there's little chance they'd hear me even if I were kicking my way through the dead grass like a little kid. When I'm close enough to see the City's falcon and beaker emblazoned across their backs, I let myself lag behind, listening for evidence of more soldiers. No other tracks mar the ground this way, so they must have been scouting and happened upon the same Islander tracks I've been following. The next time the two Reds pause, I get a good look at their guns, a nauseous revulsion swirling with an awful kind of longing inside me. If I had a weapon, all this would be so much easier.

A gun.

The little girl I killed skips across my thoughts, the memory of her cracked and torn at the edges from years of trying to repress it. I haven't shot a gun since . . .

I jam a different image in front of that bloody little girl: Sev, tied up in Dr. Yang's lab. If these two Reds are trying to shoot up the Islanders who are supposed to get me back to Sev, then I *have* to take this situation in hand. I made mistakes before, yes. But if I let my past dictate what I can and can't do, Sev will be sitting right next to that little girl in the dark recesses of my mind, peering at me whenever I close my eyes. This is an emergency.

I crouch, touching the damp ground next to one of the Islander boot prints, trying to decide how fast they were moving and how long ago it was they passed. But, as I lean closer, everything in front of me blurs. My mind seems too heavy, sliding this way and that, threatening to tip me over onto the cold ground.

One of the Reds looks back, his hands idly touching the gun as he scans the trees around me. I dig my fingers into the grass, command every muscle of mine to freeze, to become a blade of grass, a bit of bark, but my lungs turn slick and wet, refusing air.

He takes a step in my direction, craning his neck as if his mind can sense something amiss, but his eyes can't see it. I can't spare a thought for shoddy training practices in the City, though. My body is trying to slip apart into bloody pieces right here, to do this man's job for him.

Breathe. In. Out. But the air won't come, and my eyes go gray, blocking out the trees, the grass, even the Red and his gun. *What is happening to me?* A voice inside me screams. Panic, every soldier's most familiar enemy.

A mouthful of air finally slides into my lungs, and the world around me snaps back into focus. The Red has already turned away and is following his partner into the trees.

What was that? I creep up from the ground, gauging my balance, my body, and what it is or isn't capable of at the moment. Take a step. I can walk, but fuzziness still lurks at the edges of my vision. Whatever it was, I don't have the luxury of time to be sick right now. I need to find these Islanders now. Before the Reds do.

Legs shaking, I follow the Islander trail a little farther, look-ing for a good spot to break away so I can get around the Reds, when my eyes find another broken path through the grass. A gore trail.

It crosses the line of broken grass stems left by the Islanders, then continues into the trees in a different direction, but there's something funny about it, some of the grass bent in places a gore wouldn't have touched. . . .

A slow smile pulls at my mouth. I switch to following the gore track, nose almost to the ground until I find it. A footprint, the heel worn on one side. I start moving faster, and the fuzziness swirling at the edges of my vision turns to darkness. *Overtaxed,* I tell myself. *First time up in weeks; it's no wonder I'm a little shaky.* I take off down the trail, dull panic unfolding inside me as every step gets harder.

By the time I find the Islander camp, twilight makes it hard to see—at least I think it's twilight blurring the two tents ahead into one brownish smudge. Based on the way my legs are shaking, I've maybe got an hour before I go from impaired to unconscious. I prop myself against a rock shielded by a bush and blink until my eyes clear enough to case the campsite. I don't recognize any markings on either tent. No numbers, no City mark, no hammocks.

Also, no lookouts.

I scrub my good hand through my hair. *This* is the group Luokai seemed to think will get me to the mountains safely? They might have done a good misdirect back there, hiding their trail in the gore track, but whatever advantage it would have given them has been destroyed by this campsite. There's a fire. With *smoke.*

Making a mistake like that in the mountains would be asking for a knife between your ribs. Here with Reds prowling, *looking* for people to take away in their helis? I shake my head, wishing it would stop spinning. I can't risk my life, Sev's, June, *the cure*, on the chance that no one else has noticed these idiots are here. I can, however, take any supplies they have to offer. Namely food, water purifiers, a hammock. Maps, maybe.

A weapon.

Two men emerge from one of the tents, the first with many years of good food evident on all parts of him. He stops at the edge of the fire to prod at the steaming packets nestled at the base. The second man is closer to my age, his eyes scanning the darkness beyond the camp. His eyes stop on the bush blocking me, but he turns away, not experienced enough to know that when you have a gut feeling you're being watched, you either find the person watching you or run. Two others come out, but I don't stop to watch them. There were tracks for four. That means no one is in the tents.

I slide my weight from behind the cover of brush, circling around until the Islanders are hidden by canvas walls. Out of sight, I crawl to the back side of the tent they've just emptied.

Stay out of the tent. Maybe if I wish it hard enough, some god of nature will hear me and keep them distracted. *Keep poking at that fire and planning for whatever it is you're doing out here.*

If you stay out, I won't have to kill any of you.

The tent base doesn't connect to the walls, so sneaking in is easier than boiling noodles over a fire. Packs sit just inside, a long knife that looks as if it has seen a century of wear sitting on the ground next to them, but the edge is sharp.

A glance inside the first pack gives me a little more hope, familiar shapes of dried fruits and vegetables as well as something that looks like protein rations packed together inside. Just as I persuade my shaking fingers to clench around one of the straps, footsteps swish through the grass outside toward the tent door.

Sweat from my hand slips between my fingers as I grip the knife.

The flap opens, light streaming directly into my eyes. The shape in the doorway could only belong to the wary young man, the moment of shock at finding a stranger where a stranger shouldn't be, freezing him in place. It's the breath between finding the world is much more dangerous than you thought and a scream. An old friend of mine.

I drop the pack and dart toward the young man, but every movement oozes as if I'm stuck in mud, squelching through every moment in slow motion. The long knife feels like confidence in my hand as it catches on something, tearing like material instead of flesh. But I can't see—I can't *see?*—anything but what's directly in front of me.

And what is directly in front of me? Nothing. My knees are in the dirt when I should be on my feet. Time seems to have skipped over me, because the young man is already outside, calling for help.

The ground feels too dusty and dry when it hits my cheek, though I can't remember the time between kneeling and falling. My brain doesn't blank out, though, letting me feel every moment as four people crowd around me, the knife I'd held coming to rest on my neck.

CHAPTER 6
June

THE WORLD IS SUPPOSED TO BE A CIRCLE AROUND me. Above the circle, there's sky and clouds and sometimes stars, and then inside of it there's mountains and hills and maybe some water or we'd all be thirsty. And inside those mountains and hills, there's birds and trees and people and rocks. But instead of being up there in the circle where I belong, I'm Underneath.

It's sure as a day's worth of sun. I know how long it takes for people to wake up from SS, and my eyelids are stuck tight. Sun, moon, and stars'll come up over and over like they always do, and I'll just be down here waiting for my bones to rot.

Do bones rot? I think back to the bodies I've seen, but my memory feels too sticky to be sure.

"June?" Warm air brushes across my face, the sound like an erhu. I try to turn my head away from the man's breath, but my body doesn't much care what I want. Another voice, different from the first, says, "We'll tell you when she wakes up, Speaker Luokai."

"How much longer do you think? She still has a chance?"

Luokai. The man who looks like Howl but old and sad, and also evilish. He made me take off my mask. Once again, I tell my head to move, my arms to push me up from this bed, my legs to *run*. It's because of him that everything inside my circle—the sky, the mountains, the whole world—is now nothing but a tiny, black cave.

"Could you give me a moment alone with her?" At least I think that's what he says. They speak funny, like the people in my memories. He sighs as the other men go, and it seems to hover over me, condensing down by my toes, making them tingle.

"You have to wake up," Luokai whispers. It's almost as if I can feel the shape of him, even without eyes or a face or body or the rest of it, trapped the way I am in my brain. "I'll never forgive myself if you don't."

"Your friends are . . ." Luokai's pause is enough to tell me what he's got to say is either bad or a lie, maybe both. I try to jerk my hands up again, to move my head, maybe swing my foot to kick Luokai in the head. The thought stirs the tingles in my toe, and they race up from my feet into my legs and then to my stomach and chest, battling across me like ants on dead meat. Dad used to call that feeling "fishing for spears," and he laughed when he said it, but I still don't know why.

By the time I was old enough to ask, he was too dead to tell me.

"Howl left just this morning." My ears open at the sound of my friend's name. "He's better than he was before. He's going to help your other friend, Jiang Sev, because the helis took her. Hopefully, they'll both be back soon."

The helis *took her*? I knew Howl and Sev weren't supposed to be here anymore. We'd all still be locked in Luokai's prison cell of a sleeping room if I hadn't taken off my gas mask and let him infect me. But the blood and spit and fear gummed up around those words—they *took her*—fill my lungs with an inch more of water. Every bit of my new family, the ones who can't get sick so they can't forget that they like me. Gone.

Then my toe twitches—and every inch of me freezes, more freezing than SS could ever do to me. My toe moved because *I told it to.*

The tingling passes my torso and sneaks into my heart. Then past my neck, all the way to my face. And suddenly I realize that moving might be a possible thing, at least a little, if I wanted to.

It's the choice of it that lets me stay still. I *could* move—but I won't, not yet.

Open your eyes. There's a voice in my head, and it sounds like a gore, but I ignore it. *Not yet,* I repeat to it. I know how to stay still even if the gore inside me doesn't.

"I'm going to take care of you, June. You'll be safe until they get back, I promise." Luokai must be bored. Winding down a conversation he didn't mean to get into with a person who can't talk back. That was the same before he breathed SS into my mouth and locked me away. People forget you're there, get bored, and wander away when you don't talk back. Luokai's knees crack as he stands. *Not yet.* He takes three steps to the door, each *swish* of his robe like thunder in my ears. *Not yet.* A faint *hush* when the door begins to slide open.

Now. I roll off the table and am out the door before it can shut again.

The blanket I have clutched around me wards off the wind pushing behind me as I run—*try* to run, my legs shaking like new workers at a City farm. Light is like a knife in my eyes. *You're going to fall,* the gore howls inside me. *They'll catch you, and you'll be stuck here forever.* Staying isn't an option, so I *make* my legs move, my feet dragging sideways across the stone. Hands grab fistfuls of my blanket, so I let it go, sending one of the Baohujia off-balance, the others stumbling over him.

Which lets me run. Toward the brightest, glaring light. A window.

Luokai's erhu voice shouts, commanding me to stop or someone to stop me, though I sort of think if he wanted either of those things to happen, he'd probably do better trying them himself. I climb up on the windowsill, no glass to keep me back. Escape sings in me like the sun about to rise from behind the mountain in the air. But then my fuzzy eyes manage to focus on the ground. Fifty feet below. Jagged rock cut into tiered paths that promise no soft landings. No reliable handholds until at least fifteen feet below the window.

Footsteps behind me, my whole body tense as a gore ready to pounce. *You'll die either way.* The gore doesn't seem very concerned about this. *Die on the rocks or locked in a room by a Seph.*

The thought seems to go clear in my head like good bottle glass. I can't be trapped again. Not by someone with SS. I can still feel water closing over my head, cold as a snow angel's bum. Dad's fingers pressing hard into my shoulders as he held me down.

Everything around me seems to fade: just me and the drop below.

My foot skids across the stone windowsill, the rest of me following, poised over the drop like a boulder at the top of a cliff that you just want to push. *JUMP*, something inside me says. It's a *new* voice, one that sets the gore's hackles up inside me. *JUMP*, it says, taking hold of my muscles. And while I usually ignore the gore, this voice seems to know about life and the circle and things. It's showing me the path I can run, the way out of this trap, the way to safety, never mind the drop. So I jump.

CHAPTER 7
Tai-ge

WATCHING CAPTAIN BAI'S FACE GO BLANK—HIS opinion of me sinking with every word that comes out of my mouth—is almost physically painful. He agrees to take me on a tour of the perimeter instead of briefing me on Mother's specific plans. Despite the urgency of the situation. Despite direct orders.

Every time he begins on that subject, I interrupt, trying not to acknowledge Mei listening intently at my elbow. The buildings feel so close together in the Third Quarter, clustering like comrades at the end of a factory shift. It makes it difficult to see the physical boundary of the area Captain Bai has cleared—torches set in concrete-filled buckets that form a line between us and the infected—until we're right on it, the smoky blast from the torches an instant change from clear air to poison.

Mei draws in a shaky breath, her uncovered nose twitching.

Putting a hand on Captain Bai's shoulder, I keep walking, focused forward as if I can't see her struggle to inhale.

"I need . . ." She gasps, wet, ugly sounds that shake her solid frame. "Major Hong, *give me a . . .*"

I wave at the two soldiers trailing along behind us to pull her out of the gas cloud—"Find her a mask, would you?"—even as I push Captain Bai around the edge of the building where the torches start, each about ten feet apart.

"It's unwise to bring your assistant any closer—" Captain Bai shuts his mouth when I put a hand up, leaning to peer around the old bricklayer housing to check that she can't come any closer. Mei resists the soldiers, her eyes furious as she tries to follow us with an elbow shielding her nose and mouth. She stumbles to her knees, coughs racking her chest.

"I'd rather keep the General's orders between the two of us." I turn back to him. "Tell me the details of the directives she gave you. I want to *start* with distributing supplies, because I feel coordination with the people stuck here will be better facilitated if—"

Captain Bai's head gives a jerky shake. "They didn't send us supplies to feed anyone but ourselves, Major Hong." He looks out at the buildings, everything beyond the torches that I can see silent. Waiting.

"What do you mean?"

The captain abruptly pulls his gaze back from the street winding between the crumbling brick of the buildings and stares fixedly at my collar, his eyes a little too hard.

The change is so abrupt it has me searching the worn cobblestones for an assailant or something that could elicit such a strong reaction from a hardened patroller. All I see is a bit of torn fabric on the street. Something black and fuzzy mixed with red . . . it takes a moment before my eyes sew the pieces together, the bits all that's left of a doll. A comrade in uniform, the same ones factories turn out by the hundreds.

How did such a thing come to be shredded just on the other

side of the torch line? I look back at Captain Bai, his eyes still focused on my collar, my stars. "What is it the General asked you to tell me?"

The Captain draws a heavy plastic envelope out of his coat, almost like a packet of water purifier but as long and wide as my hand. "Open it. But be careful not to get it on you."

I turn it over, looking for a way to open it, but it's sealed on all edges. The captain waits a moment before impatiently taking it back and pulling a knife from his coat pocket. "Don't you have a knife? Standard issue for patrollers."

Yet another thing wrong with me. I think back to the knife Sevvy and I passed around in the heli. I gave it to her when we were young as a way to defend herself. Back then, she treasured it because it was something of mine. I look down, forcing myself to focus as Captain Bai slits the envelope, then holds it open to reveal the brown powder inside.

The next time I saw that knife, it came out of *Howl's* pocket. At first I'd thought he took it from her. That it was one of the reasons he frightened her. But after a while, it was apparent that she'd given it to him. Allowed him to swap out the unassuming blade to turn it into a true weapon. Something that had once been mine, and he made it his.

Sevvy was also mine, or so I'd supposed.

What does that even mean? Mine. I'd always thought the expression was supposed to be sweet, but maybe it never was.

"What is it?" I ask, watching the careful way Captain Bai holds the package.

"Growth regulators, sir."

I rack my brain, trying to understand. The weaker variety can be used to ignite an explosion when paired with heli fuel, as I did back when Sevvy and I were breaking into the camp at Dazhai. But one explosion wouldn't . . .

But then it hits me. In concentrated forms, growth regulators combined with water form a toxic gas cloud. Death within twenty-four hours for anyone who breathes it. "Growth regulators?" I almost can't say it. We're here on a mission to help people, and Mother sent me with poison?

"They're diluted. Only enough to cloud a few blocks at a time. We're meant to put them at strategic positions down the Aihu River, which, with our gas masks, will give us a clear path to the wall. Once on the wall, we can secure the gate. Then, after we've radioed for extra units to come, we'll use the torches to push out from the river to enter the mask factory." Captain Bai blinks a few too many times. "If we don't contact the two units within range within the next forty-eight hours, they could move too far for us to reach. General Hong has, understandably, not shared our plans with anyone other than me."

My mind spins, remembering the inadequate-looking piles of boxes we brought with us under the heli. Poison. It's fast. Efficient. But my chest seems to clench at the thought of using it on infected here in the City. The people I came to help.

"Let me think." I look back out into the quiet buildings past the torch line. Isn't staff part of what we need? Thirds who know what materials are required to make masks and how to use the equipment in the mask factory? "Have you had a chance to communicate with the people here? There must be someone out there of rank who could help us coordinate clearing a safe pathway to the gate. They're *our* people."

Captain Bai's sigh is a little tired. "Perhaps if we had more time. There's some organization out there. A leader. He approached us when we first landed, but the directives we've been given leave no room to help."

"But there *is* some kind of structure. A way we'll be able to coordinate relief efforts after . . ." After what? After we gas entire blocks of people?

Taking a step back from the torch line, Captain Bai puts a hand to his forehead, rubbing it across his eyes. He looks down at the doll, torn and dead on the cobblestones, and a shadow passes across his eyes. But then his expression hardens, a shield sliding in place across his face. "You're young, Major. It isn't our job to choose who lives and who dies. Which life is more important. That's why leaders who can see the whole picture are the ones giving orders." He raises his eyebrows, the shadow of disgust returning to his face. "You think your mother handing you that title made you smarter than the rest of us? That we can just discount the General's weeks of strategizing because you don't like seeing the results up close? That's treason, Major Hong."

He's gone too far, and he knows it. I can see it in the way he tucks his chin under, as if he expects an angry radio dispatch from Dazhai once I've had time to whine over the link about the way he's treating me.

One word he said really sticks, though. Treason. It shivers through me.

"Give me another way, Major Hong, if you've got one." Captain Bai's teeth sound gritted even through his mask's filters, and there's a vein bulging in his forehead. "Give me another way, and I'll take it."

That night, it's well past midnight when Mei finally goes to sleep. At least, I think she's asleep. She's still fully clothed, a threadbare blanket pulled over her head. But her breaths have finally slowed, rasping out from under her covers in even lines.

If the snoring is any indication, she has a cold. Or maybe the torches have long-term effects on one's sinuses. When Captain Bai and I retreated from the line of chemical torches, she was standing there waiting for me, eyes murderous, nose running.

Before we were within earshot, I warned Captain Bai to only use soldiers he knows well as he prepares the growth regulators. We only have twenty soldiers here, but he did mention that some of them were new to him. Hopefully we can keep whoever it is Mei is working with in the dark about what we're doing tomorrow morning.

Morning. I roll to my back, eyes tracing the ceiling. I have until morning to think of a way around gassing my own people that will still get us the gate within the forty-eight hours. There are cracks in the ceiling plaster, lines to mark the hundred years this orphanage has been standing just off the market center. I didn't truly believe Sevvy when she told me Outside patrollers would use chemicals to clear whole areas of the forest around farms, choking the life out of everything left unmasked for miles around. Now, though . . .

Shifting to my side, I put the information into a box in my head, looking at it from all angles. I suppose if the only other people Outside are enemy combatants—or at least people who could very easily become enemies the moment a thought strikes them—it makes sense to use the biggest weapon you can afford. Cost-to-benefit ratio. Kill five to save a hundred.

Mei stirs, and the muscles in my neck contract in response, pinching down my back and into my arms, leaving me stiff until she rolls to face the wall.

Is the cost-to-benefit ratio here too high, or does this just seem so untenable because I've never been the officer making the decisions? Sacrificing a few comrades to ultimately give the rest of us a chance against Dr. Yang seems like it should be an acceptable bargain, but I find myself thinking of the doll I saw in the street, what was left of her hair caked with mud.

We can't even explain fully to the soldiers what it is we're trying to accomplish without reports going straight to Dr. Yang. What will they think tomorrow, cleaning bodies out of the buildings that line our route to the City gates? Looking for familiar faces as they drag the dead away to be burned. My chest tightens, each inhibited breath coming too slow through my mask.

Pulling myself up into a sitting position, I place my feet on the cold floor, my skin feeling raw everywhere my gas mask rubs: against my chin, across my cheekbones and nose. There is no relief from it.

I creep over to Mei's bed and pull her pack out from underneath. Inside, there's only a pair of dirty socks. Where would she have hidden her things? She must have clothes, at the very least. A link to whomever she reports. Mantis.

Pushing the pack back under her bed, I study her. She's still covered with a blanket from the crown of her head to her calves, her grimy boots making a speckled halo of dirt on her mattress underneath them.

I know this orphanage inside and out. Sevvy and I hid things for each other—notes, food, gifts—in all the nooks and crannies of this place. Wherever Mei's hidden her things, they have to be close, somewhere easy to access without calling attention to herself, or she wouldn't be able to take a consistent Mantis dose.

Unless she's got a bottle hidden on her person.

With the link I'm supposed to take. A link that might point me toward a Menghu base. Toward Sevvy.

I put a hand out, hovering just over where her shoulder must be. The blanket balloons out over her face as she exhales. If I pull back the blanket now, unzip her coat—

"If you touch me, I *will* kill you." Her voice is a muffled whisper. "Why don't you go back to your own bed like a nice little boy?"

Stepping back, I sit down on my bed and lean forward, elbows on my knees. "Do you know where Sevvy is?"

She pulls the blanket away from her face, blinking at me. "What?"

"Jiang Sev. It was Menghu who took her. Do you know where she ended up?" I look down. "I'm . . I'm worried about her." It's not a lie. But not the whole truth.

Mei watches me for a beat longer than seems called for, the words setting something off in her brain. But then she just sniffs. Turns over toward the wall and pulls the blanket back over her head. "What kind of a nickname is *Sevvy*? It's longer than her real name."

"Have you made any headway on the cure? Mother said Sevvy wasn't being cooperative when they opened up that device."

"Not like they need her to cooperate." Her voice is muffled by the blanket.

Fear stabs like a frozen knife in my stomach, the stories Sevvy told me about her time with the Outsiders crackling like a fuzzy radio channel at the back of my head. "What do you mean? Dr. Yang's not still telling you people that she's the cure, is he?"

Mei sits up in one graceful motion, the puffy hood of her

jacket standing out like wings from her shoulders. But she doesn't say anything.

I press a hand to my cheek, trying to think. "We found a device with the cure on it at the island. Your friends took it right out of my hand. That's what Dr. Yang wanted, isn't it? The cure? That's why he made Reds invade Kamar." Mei still doesn't respond, her eyes thoughtful.

We stare at each other a minute longer before I give up. "I'm going to get a drink of water." I push myself up from the bed. "Would you like one?"

She shakes her head.

Stepping into my boots by the door, I shoulder my way into the hall, frustration a steel trap around my jaw. The cafeteria is dark, so I walk past it, wondering if some fresh air will help me solve the growth regulator problem. Outside, everything looks wrong; the lights that used to dot the City at night extinguished. I look up the mountain toward the Second Quarter, wishing for something familiar, something to tell me what to do.

I freeze when my eyes find a light. No, more than one, all congregated together near the center of the district, close to where my home is. Where it *was*, I suppose, the thought an uncomfortable ache inside me. Our family compound is empty now. Empty of my family, the Thirds who cleaned and cooked for us. Empty of anyone but the sick and the dead.

This whole city will be nothing *but* dead men, women, and children unless I do something.

I give the lights a hard look. Then go inside for a coat.

CHAPTER 8
Howl

MY HEAD SWIMS, MOLD-LACED DIRT FILLING MY nose every time I try to breathe. Rough hands haul me up from the ground, the knife sharp against my throat.

Four Islanders crowd around me in the tent like kids on their first encounter with a dead body. Words fly back and forth, all of them passing straight through my ears without making an impression—Port Northian, I hope. The alternative—that I'm so sick I can't understand speech—is too horrifying to contemplate.

The man who took the knife isn't one of the two I saw before. He wears Baohujia robes like armor, making a barrier between me and an old woman, the fourth of the group. The other two—the portly one and the thin one I attacked—hang back, watching.

When the Baohujia pulls my bag from my shoulder, he doesn't seem to notice pain hissing out from between my teeth, and tears open the pockets one by one. He takes out the bottle of pills Luokai gave me, squinting down at them for a moment before handing them to the old woman.

Next, he searches my person. This is when I should jump up,

kick the soldier in the head, grab one of their packs, and run, but instead my body sways from side to side, my arms like rubber snakes.

The Baohujia's hands stop when they get to my wrists. He turns to the old woman, speaking softly. She raises her eyebrows, fixing me with a curious stare. The momentary reprieve doesn't last long, though, because the Islander hands the old woman the knife, then pulls a thin, plasticky cord from one of the packs. He uses it to tie my hands and feet, wrapping it tight enough that my fingers immediately begin to swell.

They're not going to kill me. The thought registers too slowly. *Why aren't they killing me?*

Once the Baohujia is finished tying me, the old woman raps out a set of what sounds like orders that result in the Baohujia and the overeater exiting the tent, leaving her alone with me and the young man I attacked. When they're gone, she settles on the ground directly in front of me, carefully arranging the knife I was holding minutes ago in plain sight on her lap. The young man stays by the door, his breaths still coming too quickly, his hands clenched around the long slash I made in his coat.

Alarm beats in my chest, my brain ticking off a list of considerations. Wrists bound. Ankles tied, though the Baohujia did it over my boots, so I might be able to do something about that. The long knife is accessible, gripped only between an old woman's wrinkled fingers, though it's countered by a flash of gunmetal gray at her hip. I could throw one of the packs behind me, lob a fistful of dirt into their eyes even with my hands tied.

But the list flickers down to one solitary item: I still can't move.

I can't even see more than fuzzy outlines, and the floor seems to be spinning. The woman hefts the knife, leaning forward to examine the single line carved into the spot between my thumb and forefinger, the same spot the Baohujia paused to look at while tying me up. My First mark.

She turns to the young man, making an impatient gesture with her hand.

"Why did you break into our camp?" he asks.

"Why did . . . ?" His language is perfect, not choppy and squeezed the way every word Luokai said was, as if he'd forgotten the words he was born with. "I was hungry. You have food."

His eyes skate down to touch the First mark carved into my hand, his fingers white as he clutches at the tear in his coat. But he turns to the old woman, speaking to her in Port Northian. A translator. The woman, her shoulders hunched and her neck bowed, seems to be just a bit of skin wired to a frame, her movements pained. She speaks for a moment, then pulls my shirt collar back to show the scabs stuck to my skin like leeches.

"You are important, and yet you have gore teeth in your shoulder. You're miles away from a place sanitized and safe enough for your rank . . ." The young man takes a shaky breath, his shoulders hunching as he speaks. "She asks if you are thirsty."

I lick my lips, dry from my sprint to get to the Islanders before Reds found me. "Yes, I am thirsty."

The young man's lips purse into a grimace before he shares what I've said with the old woman. She nods and jerks her head at him as if he doesn't even deserve the effort it takes to say out loud what she's asking for. The young man stands, goes to one of the packs, and comes back with a waterskin. Hesitating a moment, he opens it and holds it out toward my mouth, but I don't drink.

Sitting forward, the woman runs a finger along the edge of

the long knife I held only moments ago. As she speaks, the young man translates. "What are you doing so far from your guards? Your camps?" She holds up the bottle of pills. "Injured, no less. I've never seen someone survive a gore bite like that."

I shrug, the word still spinning around me in a drunken swirl, words limping along inside my mind when I need them to run. Now that there's water right in front of me, all I can think is how dry my throat feels. "I . . . didn't like what the soldiers were doing. It was my first trip here, and I didn't realize . . ."

"If you lie to me"—she interrupts the translation with a flood of Port Northian, the translator licking his lips as he switches from Port Northian to my language. The old woman leans forward to press the point of the knife to my sternum with a little smile—"I will split your heart in two and make Song Jie eat it."

I look away from the knife to eye the interpreter, the knife's pressure too soft to be much of a threat. "Song Jie? Is that you?"

He keeps his eyes down as if looking at me while also listening and speaking simultaneously would make something in his head explode.

The knife creeps back to my collarbone, pain twinging through me as she once again examines the red, raised skin. Song Jie takes a moment to listen to what she's saying before passing it on to me. "She wants to know what you're running from."

"I'm not running from anything. I'm trying to get back to the mountains." Why didn't I walk into the camp first? Luokai said they'd welcome me if they knew I wasn't on the Reds' side. That they needed help . . . Scrunching my eyes together doesn't help dispel the way everything seems to be out of focus.

But there's something else funny happening in my head. A crackling sound, like boots on grass. The guards outside?

Suddenly, as Song Jie begins to speak again, a sound I know all too well clicks through my brain, all of my muscles tensing in response.

The metal *click* of a soldier pulling open the slide on his weapon to check there's a bullet in the chamber. It takes only a second to skip through all the members of the group. The only gun is the old woman's, and she's sitting right here in front of me.

"Run." I look at Song Jie. "We all have to run."

Song Jie blinks, his mouth hanging open midsentence, as if he can't quite process what I'm saying.

"They're outside. They're coming in right now." I pull against the ties the Baohujia used to restrain me. "Untie me. They'll probably concentrate fire on the south side because your tents are—"

"*Who* is outside?" Song Jie cuts in.

The old woman looks from me to the interpreter, her brow drawing down farther every moment Song Jie doesn't translate.

"Your guys outside might already be *down*." I lower my voice to a whisper. "Maybe not if they're trying to cart you off to a farm. Maybe they'll try to take us alive." Pulling against the ties sends stabs of pain through my shoulder. I can't move. Can't fight. Can't run. My eyes go to the hint of metal in the old woman's sash, the gun just out of reach. "Untie me *now*."

Song Jie says something to the woman, who goes to the tent door and peers out at their bright fire, smoke like a signal in the trees. Panic sweats out of me every moment they stand here doing nothing.

This can't be how I finally go. With my head down and my hands bound.

Wrenching up from the ground with a gasp, I barrel into the tent's central pole, pushing until the stakes wrench up from the ground and the whole thing tumbles over. Toward the spot the stupid smoking campfire should be.

Song Jie, so reedy and small, slams into me as the canvas falls down over all of us, taking me to the ground. Pain strips me down to the basics, nothing left inside but needing to escape. My elbow jams into Song Jie's chest, and even though it isn't a good hit, he recoils.

A shout sounds from out in the trees. I squirm free of the tent's folds just as flames begin to lick at the canvas. The old woman and Song Jie are yelling to each other as they extract themselves. Charred canvas smell chokes my throat. Fire might be distracting enough for the Reds to miss one or two of us running free. Frantically pulling at my bootlaces, I curve on the ground and loosen the ties as best I can with my one good hand, but I can't slip my feet out. "*Untie me,*" I wheeze. "If it was a scout, then the rest will be here soon." My brain goes to where it's most comfortable, the many times I've seen Reds attack, the times I've attacked Reds. "We have maybe a minute. They'll hit this side of your camp, circle around if they haven't already . . ." My eyes are dimming again, my balance all off, nothing but pain inside me. "Please, cut me loose."

A blast of light ignites off in the trees, the sound of gunfire like nails pounding into my ears. The old woman yells something, and someone—the big Baohujia?—hefts me over one shoulder. Bones press painfully into my stomach as he runs, and all I can see is fire, impressions of the Islanders scurrying to grab things like shadows lurking at the corners of my eyes.

My collarbone is a solid white light of blinding agony, and it isn't long before even those last shadows fade to nothing.

* * *

When I wake, my body is cocooned in fabric. The hammock—long bamboo poles thrust through the fabric on either side of me to hold it aloft—bobs and sways sickeningly, a figure shouldering the two poles just behind me as he walks. There must be someone in front, too, but I can't muster the energy to look. My eyes drift closed again. Every part of me aches and my mouth tastes of sick, like acid and decay both at once.

A creaky old voice speaking nonsense eases the silence, the old woman's shadow falling across me as she walks alongside me. "You're awake," a lower voice interprets. Song Jie. He's the one carrying the back half of this makeshift litter.

I groan, holding my arm close to my chest, though no matter how I adjust, the persistent ache in my shoulder won't quiet as she continues to speak. When Song Jie translates, his voice is flat. "You saved us."

Opening my eyes hurts, but I do it, straining to look up at her. "If they find me, they'll . . ." Kill me probably. If Dr. Yang or the Chairman haven't ordered their soldiers to torture me first. But I can't tell these people that. It's like Luokai said—this old lady is interested in my First marks. "If they find me they'll take me back to the City. There's someone who needs help far away from there, and if I don't get to her . . ." The words boil in my throat, too desperate, too sick. Sev's face is like a stone in my head, weighing me down. "I need to get back to the mountains."

"She says the medicine you brought with you is making you sick." Song Jie grumbles it, adjusting the pole on his shoulders. "That it's poison. Enough to kill the bacteria the gore left in you, but only barely enough not to kill *you*. Whoever gave it to you didn't expect you to run away. Or meant for you not to."

I twist to the side, some choice words brewing in my mouth.

Seph-eaten Luokai. The cure, Sole's life, June's life, *his* life are all riding on whether I can get the cure from Dr. Yang, and Luokai gives me *poison*? What a complete—

"Reifa says we need your help. Maybe as much as you need ours right now." A frown touches his mouth, and for a moment I think he's going to go back to fingering the slit I made in his coat.

Reifa. That's what Luokai called the leader of this group. I try to raise my head to look at her. "Unless you can get me back to the mountains within a few days, I'm not sure you *can* help me." I let my head sag back against the hammock, too tired to continue thrashing. "What were you hoping I could help you with that was worth carting my dead weight away from that camp?"

"I *don't* think it was worth it to carry you. . . ." Song Jie's mouth presses into an ugly line as Reifa hisses something in his direction, but after a moment, he translates what I've said. I think. Reifa laughs, skimming a hand across the hammock as if she'd like to pat me on the head and can't reach. I count myself lucky she isn't still clutching that knife.

"We know how to get to the mountains," Song Jie translates. "But not what lies inside them. We need help filling in the blank spots on our map. Where the farms are. The City itself." He pauses, grimacing over my weight.

"And . . . you want me to tell you where to find the best grub?" I snort, wondering if it would even hurt anyone to give up that information to this crew. That's what Jiang Gui-hua was supposed to have done—given up the City's coordinates to Kamar, that nonexistent enemy the City's been using as a scapegoat for the horrors necessary to keep their workers in line.

Only . . . Kamar is a story. The island, *Port North*, where Sev's mother was born, is real enough. Just without the teeth and claws the First Circle wrote in. I attempt to focus on Reifa, wondering what she is even trying to accomplish.

Reifa speaks again, Song Jie listening very carefully, his face a little too blank when he finally translates. "We don't just need help filling in our maps. You're highly ranked. You'll be able to show us how to get into the City. Smuggle us in, even."

The beginnings of curiosity bud up inside me. "Why would you need to get inside the City?"

Song Jie stalls over this answer for a moment, finally contenting himself with, "We need a miracle. We need to find your Chairman's son."

CHAPTER 9
June

WHEN I WAKE, MY WIND IS HOLDING ME. SHE'S been with me since a heli came to take Mom. Maybe Mom sent me a little bit of herself so I'd have someone to hug me close after Dad couldn't, to find me places to hide and to tell me when to run. Sometimes she even jabbed at me when my stomach was too empty for me to move so I'd get up to find food. Just now she's a pillow, though, even if I can feel the stone under my head right through her. There's blood on the rocks and scrapes across my arms and legs. My shoulders and left arm hurt, one knee bloodied. But my ribs obey when I breathe.

My head's the real problem. It's still attached after jumping out the window and everything, I guess. But my head's what made me jump. I should be dead. The fifty-foot drop is more of a fifty-foot steep hill now that I see it from the bottom, dotted with bushes that must have slowed me down. I didn't know that when I was looking down, though, and still I jumped.

I'm broken inside. Like Dad.

No use crying, little girl. You have to take life or it will take you, just like

Aunt Tian said. The gore. Awake and tearing at me even as my head spins. He's speaking like Luokai now, tongue frayed into Port Northian. Like my dad when he still had a tongue to speak. *Tears are for people who are already dead.*

I take one more breath, then wipe the wet off my cheeks. The bright drowns me as I try to take stock of my surroundings. All I can see are the outlines of bushes, a rough stone path. Shading my eyes helps a little, which is when I hear it.

The rush of waves. Water.

My insides dry out, the feel of fingers bruising my shoulder hot inside my head.

Then a bigger problem. Footsteps coming my way.

I roll over onto my side and push myself up from the ground. Here's what I have to do:

Step one, hide. My feet are silent, years of sneaking enough to make me invisible. I follow the path I fell onto, the way twisting back and forth down the rocks until it turns to steps, wall on one side and a cliff on the other. Pebbles stick in my feet as I turn the last switchback, only there's no more path on the other side. My stomach flops as my feet say hello to a drop straight down to gray-blue water.

Whoever those footsteps belong to, I don't want to be found. They'll probably drag me straight back to Luokai.

Luckily, hiding is what I do best. There's a little cave carved into the stone wall, a statue inside—a rock lady with rock clothes and rock hair. I duck behind her, accidentally tipping the plate at her feet, spilling rotted starfruit and pears and old incense onto the cave floor.

Instead of running straight over the cliff like I almost did, the person following me stops inside the cave's mouth, his long shadow creeping up to sit next to me on the floor.

"June?"

An erhu for a voice.

"Are you hurt?"

The words are like stones plunking into a river. An obstacle to flow around. Except I never did much like water after what happened with Dad. Fire was better, because it never looked safe. It never made promises about keeping you alive only to stick its slimy arm down your throat.

"No one can survive compulsions alone, June." Luokai's voice sounds like Howl, but it's not the same. With Howl, both of us understood that he was saying the right words—the words that would get us to where we needed to go—even if they weren't the truest ones. The only thing I know Luokai wants is a hostage. Still, he talks, solemn and quiet like a prayer to the stone lady hiding me. Her hands stretch out toward him, a lantern hanging from one of them as if she means to use it to clock him over the head.

I'd be okay with that.

My wind brushes by me, pulling fingers through my hair just the way Mom used to. Shivers poke up like little barnacles on my skin. This cave is too much a memory—like those old temples Dad used to take me to, no matter how much Uncle Parhat complained about the climb. He'd leave fresh pears and water, kneeling in front of the statues inside as if they were made from more than rocks. Ask for help to find Mom. They never did make her appear. I'd much rather have eaten the pears.

Parhat, Dad's brother, didn't have anything left to wish for, so when SS took him, it wasn't hard for what was left of him to be pushed aside. Dad held tight to two things: finding Mom and protecting me.

Until he didn't anymore.

I push away the memories, the things I can't go back to change. Dad might have forgotten to protect me, but Sev and Howl never once did. They're my family now.

"Your friends will never find you if you run away," Luokai says, as if reading my mind. "They wouldn't even know where to look for your body."

There's maybe something to what Luokai is saying. But not enough to listen, really. Sev's too soft to make it back here alive anyway, and Howl's too good at running. He'll either run straight into something or run straight away, and neither of those things will bring him back, no matter how much he wants to come.

They're the rest of my list.

Number one was hide. Done, but not really, since Luokai knows exactly where I am, even if he isn't trying to grab me.

Step two is get off the island. And step three is to find Sev and Howl before they get themselves killed because I'm not there to tell them to be less dumb. Step four is maybe to make sure that cure thing is real and then to stick it in my head before any more compulsions come.

That's the problem with all of these steps. I know what compulsions do to Sephs who don't have any help. Closing my eyes tight, I press my fingers hard into my arms, the thought of compulsions shivering just under my skin.

"June." Luokai hasn't come any closer. "I can help you. I know you're scared of SS."

COMPULSIONS. THEY'RE INSIDE ME. My fingers are pressing so hard. It's not the gore's voice I hear now but a twisted version of my own. GET THEM OUT.

You can't get compulsions out, the gore hums. They're in your blood *now.* I run a hand down my arm before I can stop myself. *COM-PULSIONS IN BLOOD. GET BLOOD OUT.*

The gore starts to howl in protest as my fingernails dig into my arms, looking for the sickness inside me. My wind swirls in close, frantic to stop what's happening, but my muscles and skin and eyeballs—it's like none of it belongs to me anymore. Like up on the window before I jumped. All I can see is my fingernails, raggedy like dandelions, my skin turning red as they press into my arms, the sound of my blood inside like a rumble in my ears.

Hands jerk my jagged fingernails back from my arms, then pin them tight against me, arms holding me still as worms inside me try to squirm through my skin. *SS. GET IT OUT.* My heel slams into Luokai's shin. *I WANT IT OUT.* I tear at his arms, slam my head into his chest. I'm watching from above, my body trying to escape so it can bleed the sickness away.

Breaths coming quick, the voice in my head starts to sound more like a question. *SS OUT?* And then it only sounds like a horrible memory as my body lets me back in and I'm able to remind myself that my blood is better inside me. My arms relax, my ribs feeling bruised from SS fighting against Luokai.

Even after I go limp, Luokai doesn't let go for a moment. But he doesn't fight me when I squirm out of his grasp. Only, I can't run away, because that's when the shaking starts. Sinking to the floor, I wrap my arms tight around my ribs, shaking, shaking, shaking, until I'm afraid my body will break into little bits. A little pile of June.

"It's okay." Luokai stays where he is, his arms limp as yesterday's fish. "You're okay."

CHAPTER 10
Sev

"HERE AGAIN TO SEE YOU, SEV." DR. YANG'S LIGHT tenor voice. "Your color is good. Vitals are hard to read, but that's normal for Suspended Sleep. You're not going to be gaining any weight on liquid meals, but you haven't lost *too* much yet."

His fingers press into my wrist, then fiddle with the tube biting my arm. I will everything inside me to jerk my arm away, to stop him touching my skin, but, as always, my body can't hear me.

"Things Outside are getting quite . . . interesting." His voice sounds amused. "Refugees flooding in this direction are getting picked off by scavengers. SS is spreading nicely. It'll only be a matter of time before the whole world just shrivels up. Except for me. The soldiers who follow me. The farms we've managed to keep control of. I think we could survive *without* the cure if we needed to."

Monster. The word tastes like gore teeth in my mind. *Watching people die all around you.*

"That isn't the ideal, though. I know there are people you care about out there. Tai-ge and his family. Howl, wherever he's gotten to. The little Wood Rat girl the Menghu found prowling around Dazhai right before that map key disappeared. Your friend, I believe? I don't know why I was surprised. Blind trust runs in your family."

And now the monster is in me, a growl boiling deep inside with no way to get out. Eight years. Eight years he left Mother paralyzed like this, rotting away in her little glass cage, hoping the right moment would come to bring her back so she'd tell him where to find the key to his new kingdom.

"There are already hundreds, maybe even a thousand who have died now." He pauses. "I don't want anyone else to die if they don't have to. Is hoarding the cure for yourself really worth their lives, Sev? Just think of how many more will go if you have to Sleep another month. All you have to do is tell me where the cure is and they'll be saved."

I wish I could breathe enough to scream. Wish I could ball his collar in my fist and tell him exactly how many people out there have SS because of me: none. He's the one who made it contagious. He's the one who spread it.

He's the one who can still move, the one who's still a living creature, not like me.

The last bit of me left curls up tight inside my head, trying to count through all the people who were relying on me to bring them the cure. June. Peishan. Mei. Luokai. Sole.

Everyone. Hoping the dead girl will come.

CHAPTER 11
Tai-ge

I CAN FEEL SOMEONE FOLLOWING ME TOWARD the lights in the Second Quarter before I get to the Aihu Bridge. The ashy remains of the market square booths sift over my boots as I walk, an abandoned coat button crunching beneath my weight. The charred remains of a cat. I stop watching the ground when my boots kick over a blackened bone too large to belong to an animal.

It isn't so much sound or movement that persuade me that it's Mei shadowing me. The feeling in my gut—dread? Revulsion?—matches her exactly. Gripping the small canvas bag I found as I prowled through likely hiding places on the way up to getting my coat, I walk faster, almost at a run by the time my boots hit the Aihu Bridge. The new timbers still smell of wood and pitch. The torch line is just on the other side, smoke already curling around me, rebuffed by my mask. Mei probably won't even be able to set foot on the bridge.

An opinion I immediately revise when someone crashes into my side, shoving me into one of the bridge's massive supports. My hand clamps down on my mask, keeping it tight against my face as

I dodge, hoping to avoid another blow, only it doesn't come.

Mei stands between me and the torches, a mask hastily pulled over her nose and mouth, hair sticking out at odd angles from the crown of her head. The half-amused, confident expression that's been splashed across her face since I first saw her has fled, something wild taking its place.

"What in rotted Sephdom do you think you're doing?" She hardly looks at my hands, one of which should be holding a gun, but I can't risk dropping the canvas bag where it's huddled under my coat.

Can't risk her seeing that I have it.

"I'm here to help people." I point up to the Second Quarter, the lights from before now hidden by the buildings standing shoulder to shoulder uphill from us. "Those people. Which one of my soldiers did you condemn by stealing their mask?" I told the soldiers to get her one, but I didn't really believe Mother had sent extras with the supplies.

Continuing across the bridge means pushing by Mei when she doesn't move. She's solid, twisting to trip me when I attempt to use my weight to get by.

"*I'm* condemning people, Major Hong?" Mei spits my name as if it's a curse. "If you were trying to help people you wouldn't have brought only growth regulators and enough food to feed your team. We both know why your mother sent you here. Going out there just to keep up appearances is worse than stupid."

The sanitized air sucking in through my mask seems to stop entirely, leaving my lungs suctioned empty. She knows we're after the mask factory? The Mantis labs? Or just that we're after *something*? I keep walking.

"It's too dangerous to go past the torch line." She doesn't

follow me, halted at the center of the bridge. Not the smoke, but some other invisible barrier stopping her advance.

"You wouldn't go out to help Menghu who were trapped?" I point to her mask. "You can now. I've got the reports that say there *are* Menghu stuck here, but since you're not moving, I guess I know the answer to that question."

Mei's eyes narrow. I don't claim to be good at reading faces, but Mei has the talent for exuding pure hatred in a way I've never encountered before. Perhaps I'm not the only one here who has trouble masking my thoughts. "It's not a matter of not *wanting* to help. I *can't* help anyone out there, and neither can you."

I step through the line of torches. "I don't believe that."

"This mission isn't worth getting garroted over." She puts her hands up in frustration and takes a step back from the line of fire and chemicals, me on one side, her on the other. "Not for me, anyway."

"My life is the City, Mei. Their lives *are* my life." It's in the pledge I said every morning before starting my shift in Father's office. *Together we stand, united to find the cure to SS.* I just have to figure out how to keep my comrades past the torch line out of harm's way so they live to see the cure. "That's the difference between the City and the Mountain, I guess." I take a step back. "I am a part of this place, and the people out there are a part of me. You are just one girl, ready to run the moment your own life is in danger."

"Didn't you run when we came for the City?"

I swallow, failure a coppery taste in my mouth.

"What about your General? Your *Chairman*? Why aren't they the ones walking into a food-deprived, Seph-infested neighborhood?" She points to the dark buildings. "Or is it just *your* life that's equal to all the expendable Reds they abandoned here?

What about the people who slave away on your farms? Are you equal to them?"

Her voice isn't just a combination of disbelief and annoyance now. Every word means to stab, as if this is somehow personal. But I grew up knowing that Outsiders would say anything to tear down the City even as they tried to get in.

"I'm doing what I think is right." I take another step back from the torch line.

"I thought obeying orders was all you were good for, Major Hong."

The words wilt something inside me. Not only because of the intended insult. There's nothing wrong with following orders if you trust the person giving them. But she's right. What I'm doing is in direct conflict with what Mother has asked me to do. That's why I'm *here*. To show I'm worthy of her trust. To follow her.

Is walking past the torch line treason, the way Captain Bai said?

I stare down at Mei's boots, the toes muddy, laces frayed. Perhaps I stepped too far outside the lines when I followed Sevvy. Maybe I broke something in my brain, making me wish for solutions to problems that are unfixable. To find hope where there is none, as if I can save the world just because I want to, not because it's possible.

But then I think of Captain Bai staring down at that ruined doll.

If there's a way to keep from killing our own people that Mother hasn't seen, it'll help her cause, not hurt it. Part of being a leader is being able to adapt if a situation isn't what you thought. Even Mother would try to piece another path together the way I'm trying to. It's like the City pledge, like *Sevvy* said: We're all people. We all belong to each other in the City, no matter what scars we have.

I turn away from Mei. "If you're too frightened to follow me, then I hope you come up with a good filler report. You can tell Dr. Yang we played weiqi and that you lost." In more ways than she realizes just now. I press the little canvas bag stashed under my heavy coat tight against my ribs, wondering how long it will be before she checks the spot under the stairs where she stashed it.

When the sun rises and it's time to take her Mantis, I'd guess.

I can feel her eyes on me until I turn up the road toward my family's compound. The shadows seem thicker on the other side of the torch barrier. This road which I know so well—down to the oddly shaped ring of cobblestones in front of the Huang's gate, the glass lantern missing from over Captain Chen's family compound—looks alien. Walking slowly, I freeze when a flurry of movement ignites just to my left.

It's a paper-cut lantern, the intricate knot and fringe at the bottom shivering in the wind. As I walk faster, the silence seems to come alive with whispers, twitches of movement in the curtains overlooking the street, shadows stretching longer than they should, turning to follow me. I count at least six people hidden in courtyards, peering through the geometric cutouts in a wall, sitting against the buildings, but none of them move. They watch, only their eyes following me.

If there is some kind of leadership set up here as Captain Bai seemed to think, they'd choose a location easy to defend with access to food storage. My guess is the Second Quarter cafeteria, only a few streets away from my home.

I turn onto the cafeteria's street and am rewarded by the golden glow of torchlight. It falls on a shoulder-high barricade, a woman stationed at a break between broken chairs and dresser drawers. Just as I'm about to step into the light, the woman screams.

It's a high, keening wail, at least ten decibels louder than any normal reaction to pain, surprise, or fear. I clap my hands over my ears, the scream uncomfortably loud even from twenty feet away.

A woman and a man burst out from behind the barrier. The woman—too pale to be a City dweller—slips a hand over the woman's mouth, careful not to let her fingers poke between the screamer's teeth. Her other arm goes around the woman's waist to steady her. A Menghu?

The man hangs back for a moment as if evaluating for damage before joining the first in holding the woman up. It seems to go on forever, the high-pitched scream petering out and then coming back full force once the woman has gasped down a breath. Finally, the sound dulls down to a stricken sort of silence. The screamer puts a hand to her throat and crumples, held up only by the two who came to help. They stand there clinging to each other, the man hesitantly asking a question too low for me to hear—probably too low for anyone to hear after that scream.

What sort of thought causes a compulsion to scream like that?

The three look up when I step into the light, the bleach-skinned woman narrowing her eyes when she sees my mask. She's definitely not from the City.

"What in Yuan's name are you doing here?" the man growls, stopping my advance. "Bringing more fire? More bombs?"

"I'd like to speak with whomever is in charge."

"Outsiders have done less to hurt us than your helis." It's the screamer who answers, her voice a damaged rasp.

The pale-skinned woman—the former *Menghu*—looks at me appraisingly. "What do you want?"

"We have to clear a safe path to the South Wall Gate." I step closer, the light too bright in my eyes, feeling exposed because they can all see me when I can't quite see them. "I was hoping to coordinate relief efforts—"

"You can't start by killing people only to expect us to step out of your way the next day," the man interrupts. "My daughter was in the square when it went up." His voice cracks on the last word, and it's a moment before he can continue, the two others reaching out to comfort him. "I should have been with her."

"Killing . . . who? I haven't killed anyone. The square burned during the invasion, didn't it? The soldiers who came—"

"He said he came to help," the Menghu interrupts. "Have him explain it to Lieutenant Hao."

"Fine." The man gives my mask an ugly glare, as if my wearing it is some kind of affront. "Come on."

The outer hallway looks dirtier than I remember, the wall's plaster riddled with cracks and holes where it used to be smooth. We go to the stairs that lead to cafeteria administration offices, the steps barricaded about halfway up with metal grates and broken furniture, though the checkpoint is devoid of guards. My guide stops at an open door near the end of the hall. "Lieutenant Hao?"

There's a man inside sitting at a table. He glances up from a pile of documents. "What do you need? I . . ." His eyes catch on my mask, and he stands quickly, pulling a gun out of his coat. It's semiautomatic. Typical Outside patrol issue.

A shiver runs down my spine as the barrel twitches toward the City seal over my heart.

"What is this, Feng Liu?" Lieutenant Hao growls toward my guide.

"I can speak for myself," I interject. "The General wishes to mitigate the damage done here. You are Lieutenant Hao, I presume?" I hold myself straight, not bowing an inch. No matter how long this man was with the patrollers Outside, I outrank him, and acting any other way will lessen what little control I have here. "We need to coordinate the best way to help you and the survivors left here in the City."

Lieutenant Hao lowers the gun a fraction, candlelight sinking into the jagged holes left in his collar where his star pin should be. I glance toward the man who led me here, Feng Liu, finding his collar empty as well. "*Coordinate?*" Hao finally asks. "I think I've seen enough *coordination* from you who left the City to know it isn't in our best interest." He doesn't incline his head the way he should.

"My soldiers need a clear path to the South Gate Wall in order to get more supplies into the City. We mean to restart Mantis production." I reach for the canvas bag concealed under my coat.

Hao tenses, once again taking aim with the gun. "Don't move. Take your hand out of your coat, or you'll be doing nothing but rot for the rest of this war."

I slowly withdraw my hand, then hold it up where he can see it. "I don't want anyone to be harmed. We've taken precautions with the torches to keep the uninfected here safe, but you can still help us move our mission forward." I clear my throat. "We'll bring you food. Supplies. *Mantis.* Whatever happened during the invasion—"

"It wasn't the invasion that has me worried. No masks for us, no place in the helis." He shrugs. "Not ideal, but understandable. No, what had me scared was our own people burning the market square a week ago so you could land your helis. It was *your* scouts who cleaned out the surrounding buildings one by one, then burned the bodies. You didn't even ask us to move before you started shooting!"

The scouts? They killed people in the square? My throat clenches, wondering if that doll was more than I thought. Perhaps Captain Bai saw it drop from its owner's fingers, a body he couldn't bring himself to burn.

No. It couldn't be. "You must have misunderstood. There are still invaders in the City, and they must have taken control of some helis. . . ."

"The invaders? They were left behind too." Lieutenant Hao's forehead creases deeper. "Never thought there'd be a day finger stealers would be easier to trust than my own leaders."

My mouth seems to be glued shut. Everything feels too tight, my mask digging into my jaw, my coat stretching across my shoulders and chest. It's not outside the realm of possibility that Captain Bai was ordered to burn and clear out the square. My own orders have been just as emergency-driven. Extreme resolutions in our extreme situation. But that's what I'm trying to temper. "I don't know anything about what happened in the square. Only that I need your help now to keep worse from happening."

"You don't deserve our help." Lieutenant Hao's voice rises. "I've seen enough in the last week to know exactly how much my life is worth to the new General, and I . . ." He bites his lip, the hand with the gun beginning to shake.

The hairs on the back of my neck rise as the man's gun arm sags to the side then snaps back up to point at Feng Liu next to me.

"Yuan's dirty unders," Feng Liu swears, dropping to the floor.

I follow his lead, plunging down as Hao discharges his weapon into the ceiling, then again into the wall behind me with wild, poorly aimed shots. I bolt for cover under the table, dropping Mei's bag to pull the gun from my coat. Lieutenant Hao slams into my back before I can get it all the way out, locking one arm around my neck, his other hand clutching at my mask's tubes, attempting to tear them from my face.

Slamming my elbow into Hao's stomach doesn't stop his hand groping for my mask, not until I squirm out of his grasp, then launch myself toward him, the close quarters under the table not ideal for any kind of fight. My knuckles catch on Hao's uniform buttons as I grab hold of him, using my weight to slam his head into the table leg.

Feng Liu springs to his feet, blocking my retreat. Going for my gun again, this time I get it free of my coat and slam the handle into the outside of his standing leg, just above his knee.

Feng Liu drops with a yell, and I scramble out from under the table to put my back against a wall, not sure who is still compulsing or how long it will last, my hearing nothing but a high-pitched squeal. But when I find my balance, the room seems calm.

No one seems to have noticed the noise, or perhaps they decided to stay out of it after the gun fired. Feng Liu is where I left him on the floor, clutching his leg. Hao is still under the table, his feet sticking out, limp, though I didn't hit him that hard. It takes me a few moments to catch my breath before I can bring myself to edge around the table to look closer. Lieutenant Hao puts his hands up, coughing as he rolls to his side, his nose bloody. I kick the gun away from him, keeping my own aimed at his chest.

Moving to where I dropped Mei's bag, I roll it toward him, the rattle of what's inside lost in what's left of my hearing. My voice sounds too loud in my ears, as if I'm yelling into a void. "A peace offering. I don't want to kill my own people. But killing is what will happen if you don't help me." I point to the bag. "Whatever the army was doing before, I'm in charge now. I can promise this. And more. We're not just here to make more masks."

Hao sits up and pulls the bag into his lap, his eyes bulging when he finds the Mantis bottles inside.

CHAPTER 12
Howl

REIFA WANTS TO FIND THE CHAIRMAN'S SON? IT'S
not a miracle she wants. It's a fairy tale.

Luckily, I'm really good at fairy tales. I *was* one for about two years, pretending to be the Chairman's son. The story Reifa is asking for isn't so different. I just can't deliver in the same way.

The old woman decrees that my next day will be spent soaked through, rain pouring directly from the sky into my hammock as Song Jie and one of the others carry me. My head is mostly clear by the time Song Jie gives a panicked command that sends us moving in a new direction just before twilight, landing us in a shallow cave with trees as cover. There are more Reds nearby, it seems.

Song Jie and my other carrier—the big Baohujia, Telan, as I've heard Song Jie call him—set me down on the cold dirt floor, leaving me to extract myself from the hammock's folds. I'm not shaking the way I was before, but my head still swims with the medicine Song Jie gave me, so I only sit up to take stock of our situation.

The cave is only deep enough to shield us from the rain, the trees outside creaking and shifting. Every foresty moan has my good hand groping my side where a gun should be, but there's nothing to grab. We're shielded from sight for the most part, so unless the group left tracks deep enough to withstand this rain for the Reds to find, we should be all right. I hope.

Reifa and Telan begin fussing with the bags, the portly fellow, Gein, sitting back to watch. Song Jie is the only one who seems to know how to do anything helpful, covering the entrance to the cave and pointing Telan to the bunches of wood they gathered throughout the day.

I slide over to sit by Telan after he's done stripping away the wet outsides of a few of the smaller branches and has begun piling the bits of wood into an unlikely-looking tower. Taking some of the smaller pieces, I start a new little tower on the dry, bare spot of ground, one that will actually catch fire. Telan watches me for a moment before he tips his own creation over in my direction, pulls a firestarter from the pack and places it near my feet, then gratefully backs away.

Gein sits on the ground next to me as I set the firestarter to the kindling, pawing through the pack Song Jie carried throughout the day as if it is his own. Song Jie lowers himself next to Gein, speaking in quiet, respectful tones. I watch the two of them from the corner of my eye as I blow softly on the little flare of fire, coaxing it to catch onto the larger branches. Reifa's in charge. Telan's their muscle. Song Jie knows where they're going and must have been the one who orchestrated that misdirection with the gore trail. Gein, though . . . There's nothing *wrong* with him that I can see, only that he seems *useless*. I look down as he laps liquid from his waterskin like a puppy, spilling it all over Song Jie.

Song Jie looks quite murderous but does nothing. He even cleans and stows the waterskin when Gein is finished, Gein hardly seeming to notice someone else is doing work for him.

An interesting choice for this trek toward enemy territory.

"Isn't there any Junis out there?" I ask, pushing aside the pine twigs Telan left. "This'll smoke."

"Junis doesn't grow on this side of the ridge." Song Jie pulls out a knife and begins carving away the wet outsides of some larger branches. "We'll have to put it out before long so we don't have a repeat of last night. Maybe move as soon as we're done cooking?"

"We're sheltered enough here there's a chance we'll be safe. Maybe just post a lookout?" I pull the last of the smaller branches closer, though the wood I've assembled is already a good start for a cooking fire. Reifa sits next to Gein on the other side of my tower, the old woman not quite making eye contact as Song Jie says something to her in Port Northian. She pulls a handful of small metal-laced cloth packets from her pack—the ones they were cooking food in when I first discovered their camp—and shoves them at the tracker without even speaking.

It's almost . . . dismissive. Interesting. The one person here who can speak two languages, read a map, and lead them to wherever they are going is the worst-treated one of the bunch.

Gein says something, punctuating the sentence with a grating guffaw. Reifa laughs too, and it seems genuine. I try to find some kind of resemblance between the two, because shared blood might explain his presence here, but all I can find alike are the Baohujia tattoos reaching out from under their ears.

"So, tell me more about getting into the mountains," I say. "How long it's going to take. And . . ." I force my voice to crack, the very picture of a comrade contemplating treason. "And . . . this miracle you need."

Song Jie barely glances up from the packets, pulling things from his pack: crackers, condensed protein rations that are in packaged brown bricks, root vegetables still sporting a coating of dirt, and some long, flat-leafed onions I recognize from the animal trail we've been following.

Reifa swats at his shoulder when he doesn't answer me, jabbing her finger in my direction. He bends his neck, voice respectful when he answers. A translation of my question, I assume, because Reifa turns back to me and speaks while looking me straight in the eyes, more acknowledgment than I've gotten from anyone since she ordered them to carry me like a fat pig on the way to its slaughter.

"What did she say?" I look toward Song Jie.

"She said we have another day or so." Song Jie moves his knife to the onions and roots he's harvested.

"Ambitious." By my count, at our pace, it should take nearly two months. Either Reifa knows something I don't about walking or Tai-ge took the long way when we flew here in the heli. Which, as it happens, is not possible. Looking around, I take stock of what they managed to salvage from the camp. Three packs, it looks like. Some food, waterskins, extra clothes. My eyes go back to the gun tucked into Reifa's sash, my insides like steel.

I need to get to Sev now. Or as close to now as possible. The likelihood that this group is going to make it through the night regardless of how well sheltered this camp is seems abysmally small.

I'll need to take their things before I go.

Gein abruptly stands, his voice too loud for the small space as he goes over to where Telan is sitting, and the two begin a game involving hand signs and loud grunts.

Maybe when the sun's completely down. They probably all sleep like the dead. Even if they set a watch like I suggested, it won't be hard to sneak away with the tools to survive. And, if they wake up, I can make myself pull the trigger again. I think I can. I'll have to.

Setting the firestarter to a new spot in the branches, I watch as the flames take to the wood, slowly turning it to char.

"Why do you want to get into the City?" I ask.

Song Jie rolls his eyes but interprets. When Reifa speaks again, he keeps his attention on his knife and the vegetables as he speaks, shrinking away from Reifa even as he tries to ignore the fact he's talking to me. "The Chairman's son is what kept the balance between our island and your city. If we find him again, perhaps a peace can be struck again."

"Do you really believe the Chairman will stop his helis just for one boy?" It's the question they must be expecting, the one I have to ask because it's what any soul-sucking First would say. The beginning of an analysis of perceived value, actual value, cost, and potential gains. Reifa nudges Song Jie until he translates, her dark eyes glinting as I feed the larger pieces of wood Song Jie stripped of wet bark into the fire.

"She says . . ." Song Jie clears his throat. "She says you know why. You have family or you wouldn't have run."

"What is that supposed to mean?"

"It's about more than war." Reifa sits forward, Song Jie translating as she speaks. "My guess is you had someone taken from you. Or had to leave someone behind? You have to get to the mountains because if you don't, something in you will break."

Something in you will break. Sev's face wells up in my head like blood in an open wound.

The old woman smiles, taking my silence for an answer. "If you have family, then you know what it is to fear."

It takes me a moment to find the right expression, the bland combination of words that won't give me away. But my pause is enough to tell her I'm listening a little too hard. "I thought family is what makes you happy, not afraid."

"Family is what you hold deep inside you." Song Jie's translation dulls as he continues to assemble dinner. Reifa's hand presses into her chest as she speaks, knobbly fingers tangling in her robe. "It's your children's faces you look for when the bombs start falling."

Gein lets out a loud guffaw, and Telan groans, the two ducking their heads when Reifa glares at them. They resume their game, casting furtive looks in the old woman's direction.

"I don't have children." I look down into the fire, the flames licking merrily through the wood, trying to hear in Reifa's voice why she's decided to share this with me. All I can see are her eyes, the way she leans forward, but Song Jie's translation makes me feel deaf to all the cues I should be able to gather from the way she speaks. "I'm not old enough."

"Everyone has children." Song Jie snorts at the words, as if they don't translate well. "Reifa says she did not carry any little ones inside her, but when your life is filled up with another, their life takes the place of yours, and it doesn't matter whose blood runs in their veins. They belong to you and you to them."

Light from the fire crawls up the side of Song Jie's face as he speaks, leaving his expression dark. Reifa, though, is watching me. "You ran from your own people," he says. "That is why Reifa let you come with us. Not many leave what they know unless they mean to save what they love. Was she wrong?"

"That I left the army to . . . to save my children?" Thinking of Sev as my child, even with Reifa's justification, is just a little too messed up for me. Smoke from the fire stings my eyes, only rain covering the sight of it from predators out there. The way Reifa looks at me crawls under my skin. It's too calm, too earnest. She's handling me, just like I've handled so many people over the years.

My eyes catch on the bulge in Reifa's sash. The gun.

She points at my shoulder, Song Jie translating. "I've never seen anyone survive a bite like yours, slaver. There's a lot in you that wants to live. But there's even more that wants someone else to keep breathing."

The words hit me in the gut as I she says them. It's a change, having more than just me I'd prefer to keep alive. It's easy when it's just you because you can control where you are, what you say, what you do. Surviving is a matter of making the right decisions at the right time. Adding other people . . . The thought of Sev, wherever she is—not *knowing* where she is. It's like a physical ache in my chest, making it hard to breathe.

"I hope whoever it is you're looking for is dead." Song Jie's voice surprises me from my thoughts, not a translation from Reifa. These words are his and his alone. Gein and Telan's game begins to get loud again, and Reifa hisses at them in Port Northian.

"I hope your whole family has been killed, just like you've killed so many of us," Song Jie continues. "Reifa doesn't believe me, but you know and I know. I can smell the dead all over you. You're a killer just like everyone else who came on the helis."

"I haven't killed anyone from your island," I reply.

"I would have been your first murder?" Song Jie cocks his head to one side, his mouth hard as he waits for me to confirm it.

Only, I can't, and it echoes inside me. Like the argument I had with Sev in the cave. Asking me how many people I've killed, that awful fear in her eyes as she watched the knife in my hand. "Look." My lips feel dry, and licking them doesn't help. "I'm sorry about what happened when I first found you guys. With the knife. It wasn't personal."

Song Jie's face creases into an enraged silence that conveys his thoughts without a single word.

Death is always personal when it's happening to *you.*

"You are only still alive because I can't lead them as far as they want to go." Song Jie can hardly breathe through each word, each one whispered louder than he could yell. "I hope Reifa sends you in first when we get there. I know what City-folk do to traitors."

"What *my* people do to traitors?" I wait until he looks up, his face murky. "How's it feel to lead this group? Feeding them, keeping them"—I shrug—"*mostly* safe, I guess. And still Reifa and the others treat you like something smelly they stepped in." My eyes find his naked cheek. "Is it because you aren't Baohujia?"

He picks up a waterskin, taking a long drink. "My father was a hostage from the City. Sorry, a *diplomat.*" The word feels arched and venomous, a scorpion about to strike. "My father is the reason the island started requiring hostage trades be younger. Father was old enough when he arrived that he *felt* like a hostage, like an outsider. Old enough to hate living on the island. To hate the language, the people. Everyone knew."

"And you don't feel the same way?"

"I am my own person. I'm an Islander." Song Jie glances toward Reifa and Gein. "But not everyone sees things that way. Every raid that happened, every time we saw red stars, their perception of me got worse. I hadn't set foot on the island for years, until the invasion." He drinks again, dribbling water down his chin. "But I'm not like him. I'm not a slaver like you."

So, Song Jie is a puzzle piece that wants to fit, that would do anything to prove he belongs, even enduring Reifa's distaste, the other's eyes skating over him as if he doesn't exist. I can understand the disgust in Song Jie's eyes as he looks at the City mark on my hand. Hatred, the need for revenge . . . It's like looking at myself three years ago.

That's what I was before. An empty vessel with no family, no friends. Willing to do anything to tip the world a little in my favor. And Song Jie can see it because it's in him, too.

Have I changed? How long did it take before I found all the weapons, before I decided my life was more important than any member of this group? Even now I can feel the gun in Reifa's belt calling to me. And, next to it, I can feel the warm blood of a little girl, the doll in her limp hands.

Song Jie goes back to staring at the fire, his last words muttered. "I hope everyone you have left is dead. That everyone in the City rots from the inside for what you've done to us."

That isn't who I am anymore. Someone who hurts other people.

Or is it?

When the fire dwindles and Song Jie goes out for the first watch, I lie down on the hard rock. And, though I know I should pull myself up the moment Gein starts snoring, that I should take the gun, the food and water, that I should put a bullet in Song Jie's forehead because he's the only one capable of following me, I don't.

Because I don't want Song Jie to be right.

CHAPTER 13
June

"YOU'RE COMFORTABLE ON A BOAT, I ASSUME?"
Luokai steps up to the craft, throwing one of the bags he brought
over the railing, which makes it bob unsteadily in the water. Another
pack full of food and two sleeping bags we dragged through the
tunnels above sit next to him on the worn planks of the little dock.
He turns to me, toeing the water-worn wood when I don't answer,
the clammy smells of cave and salt water and resin dripping into
my nose.

He says he can keep me safe from compulsions. Teach me to let
them pass. I don't believe that really. The important part is Luokai
knows where Howl and the others were planning to go. If I get to
them, then I'll be safe. They can take care of me until all that cure
stuff is figured out. Until then . . . I clench my fists, holding my
breath as if I can hold in the stuff that made my dad bad.

"You *haven't* ever been on a boat?" Luokai asks, studying
my face.

I know boats. Every time me and Tian and Cas and Parhat and
Dad went anywhere, it was either on our feet or in a boat. Just not

one like this. This one has a high back as if it means to keep its hindquarters dry, and there's a woman painted there, her hands raised to keep the water back. I step closer to run a finger across the hem of her robe, curls of paint crinkling off to fall in the water. She looks like the rock lady up in the cave, just peelier.

Long poles are tied to the side of Luokai's boat, one of five moored in this cave. There's a long metal thing that extends into the water at the back, making the boat tip and sigh with the weight. The middle of the boat is covered with a metal canopy bent into a tube, the end plugged with a rusty wall and a door. Past the covered part, there's enough space to walk a few steps, and then two benches to sit on at the boat's pointed nose.

"You don't need to know about boats. Just stay back from the edge and you'll be safe. We'll take it down the coast to a river, then cut inland," Luokai says, throwing another bag over the railing, then climbing in to stow it through the door of the enclosed portion of the boat.

I pick up the sleeping bags one by one and throw them in. The boat looks easy enough to escape from if I need it. Except boats sit on water, and water is an enemy I can't afford to forget. This close to the water, the gore inside me whimpers, ducking his head. He remembers why we don't like water even better than I do.

"I'm sorry for what happened before with Jiang Sev and Howl." Luokai's voice stalls. "I didn't *want* to infect you. But silence won't change the past or that we're working together now."

I gnaw on my lip, petting the boat's nose, as if it will sprout fur and lungs and ears to scratch like one of those pet rats people had in the south. Giving the boat one last pat—and offering a silent plea for it to stay above the water rather than underneath—I close my eyes, lift a leg over the railing, and spill myself into the boat.

Luokai sighs, a frustrated thing that tells me he's used to being obeyed. The meat on his bones is enough to tell me what sort of life this man has led. "I just want to get you back to your family. To Howl and Sev and . . . I'm trying to make up for what I did, even if it was necessary."

My nose wrinkles at the lie. Some lies are like food—you live off them. This lie doesn't help anyone but Luokai, maybe to feel better about himself. We both know he just wants to keep me close by so Sev and Howl will give him the cure.

One point in his favor, I suppose. That means he'll want to keep me alive.

I drag one of the bags filled with food and a waterskin to the front of the boat, along with one of the sleeping bags. It doesn't quite fit under the bench, but it will once I've repacked it. Luokai takes one of the long poles and slips it into the cave's gray water, pushing us away from the other boats. Once we're clear of the cave mouth, he straps the pole back into place at the side of the boat, ducks into the closed portion of the boat, then appears on the raised platform at the back. He fiddles with the metal parasite sucked onto the wood back there until it chokes and sputters, jolting us forward in the water, turning my stomach over and over with it. An engine of some kind, then, to push us faster.

That's good. Faster.

The air brushing my cheeks stings like ice melt, the salted ocean smell pushing against my eyes and nose, but I don't go inside the sheltered part of the boat. It's not just me who has a monster inside them on this boat, and I'd like to sit where I can watch for signs Luokai's monster is going to come out.

I know what it means for Sephs to take care of other Sephs.

I lean against the railing at the boat's rusty lip, and a strip of metal snags my coat. Wrapping my hands inside my coat's cuffs, I brace myself against the bench, then pull on the metal until it screeches free, leaving me with an arm's length of weapon. A rusted, semipliable excuse for a weapon, but, with a Seph, I'll take anything before I settle for nothing.

CHAPTER 14
Tai-ge

AN ESCORT FROM THE SOLDIERS UNDER LIEUTENANT
Hao is the only reason I don't end up in three other compulsion-
induced fights as I walk back from the Second Quarter to the torch
line. The infected soldiers check twice to confirm where we'll be
posting comrades on my side of the torches to allow hand signal
communication between us and Hao's people. Once everything is
set, I slip between torches and walk to the orphanage. Mei's asleep
when I get back to the room, her blanket once again pulled over her
head. I almost feel sorry at what she'll find in the morning: her bag
full of Mantis pills missing.

When morning light wakes me, Mei's not in bed anymore. Something buzzes inside me as I sit up and tie my shoes, check the
clasps on my mask. Will Mei appear from around a corner, a knife
in her hand? Is she looking for the Mantis I took? Thinking about
her makes me feel unsettled, as if there's a gore loose in the compound and I'm not sure where it is.

Unless she's already told Dr. Yang enough to do us damage

here. Maybe he's sent orders for my team to be eliminated. My head weighs down until it's flat against my palms, my elbows digging into my knees. Failure. It's right there, waiting to say my name again.

Failure seems like it was built into this mission. Why did Mother send us with gas instead of Mantis in the first place? It's messy, I suppose. A resource we can't make more of until we take back the City. Perhaps it was a gamble she wasn't willing to take, and yet here I am, disobeying her. Maybe I'm too weak to do what's required to be a leader. Too weak to be her son.

I get up and go to the wall where I hid my link, wondering what I should say. Tell her the risks I'm taking with these soldiers' lives? Wait until the results are nailed to the ground and she can crow victory along with me? Or, if it doesn't work, allow her the freedom to turn her back on the ashes of what's left of us?

But my fingers find nothing but the pinch of cold cement inside the crack where I hid the link. It's gone.

Panic stabs in my chest as I feel inside the crack again, and then again. Mei wasn't as good as she'd thought at hiding her things. Perhaps I wasn't as crafty as I'd thought, either. But without the link, Mother might think I'm *dead*. That I made it less than twenty-four hours in this steel trap. The room feels too hot, even as my skin breaks out in goose bumps.

"Sir?" Captain Bai's voice makes me jump. "Are you all right?"

When I turn to face him, it isn't concern lining his face. Every inch of him is wary. Finding your commanding officer tracing cracks in the wall when nothing stands between you and SS but a bit of plastic and metal would disconcert the best of us.

"I didn't sleep well," I say, stealing another look at the wall.

"We're ready to move, sir. The regulators are all portioned and prepared to go in the river. We just need your command to get into position and . . ."

"No!" The exclamation sets a hard look on Captain Bai's face. But I continue. "No. I . . ." I try to think of the best way to explain what I've done, remembering my conversation with Lieutenant Hao the night before, but it brings another thought to mind. "The market square . . . was it your soldiers who burned it?"

Captain Bai's cheek tics. Then his shoulders sink an inch. "No, sir. But we did the cleanup after. Clearing the buildings."

Every inch of the man seems to be made from brick and stone, but I'm not sure what's holding the pieces together. Years Outside. Years of following orders. Only to be asked to kill his own people. I can see the percentages flashing in my head. Kill a few to save the rest.

"You are a loyal man," I say quietly, not sure if I like the word.

Captain Bai straightens his shoulders. Looks just south of my eyes as a good Second should when talking to a superior. "I believe in my General."

"Believe in me now, then." I put a hand on his shoulder. "Last night I secured a safe path to the gate from the market square instead of having to follow the river. It'll take us directly past the mask factory. Lieutenant Bai promised the buildings along the road we're using will be as clear as the infected can make them."

Captain Bai's eyes dart to meet mine, and I hold them. For the first time since I set foot on the City's familiar paving stones, I see a glimmer of hope in this man's eyes.

Mei doesn't appear at breakfast or when we line up in ranks to clear the streets. Her absence is like needles in my skin, stabbing every moment I don't know where she is or what she's doing.

Perhaps losing her Mantis made her crumble into whatever it is Menghu are made of. Tarnished blades and stolen bullets, or maybe just a waft of bad-smelling air.

It smells bad enough down in the Third Quarter to be plausible. The whiffs of burning and chemicals I get as I adjust my mask match the layer of grime that seems to coat everything past the torch line. Captain Bai and his team seem to be walking over coals as we push toward the South Gate. We only have to clear the buildings lining the road and set torches on the other sides of them, protecting our people from Sephs who could shoot at us from above or jump from windows into our midst. Lieutenant Hao's promise holds true, though. The buildings are mostly empty along our path.

Mostly. We uncover a few infected stragglers who either did not know to leave or could not obey. None resist being moved outside our path, fleeing the moment the torches' chemical burn hits their lungs. We don't have to shoot anyone. And, judging by the slightly easier set to my group's shoulders, I'm not the only one who is grateful.

All the soldiers tense when I give the order to clear the mask factory, the darkness inside hiding the corners and ceiling when we walk in. My eyes catch on a flutter of movement above us just as a bloodcurdling scream erupts overhead. The sound echoes off the ceiling like a hundred brutal murders are happening right over us. The man next to me pulls his gun, pointing it toward the sound, but I put a hand on his arm.

The screaming cuts off as quickly as it started, and a pair of beady eyes peers over the edge of the catwalk. It's an old woman.

Captain Bai nods to a pair of soldiers, and they go carefully up the stairs to the catwalk, approaching her slowly. I can't help but tighten my grip on my weapon as they draw closer, hands up and open, as if she's a wounded animal.

"Are you here to help me?" she whispers, loud enough it echoes through the whole factory.

I breathe out, proud as one of the soldiers extends a hand and says, "I'll help you, Grandmother. You don't need to be afraid."

After checking things over and securing all the doors, my team heads out of the building. I hang back a step, watching as the soldier who brought the old woman down from the catwalk helps her up from a chair by the door and leads her outside. Now I've only to keep the promise he made her. That there's no need to be afraid.

I promised Lieutenant Bai we were on the same side, and I don't break promises. Looking around the shadows of the factory floor, hope feels like a space empty of weight. I need Thirds who know how to work these machines. I need Seconds humble enough to learn from them. Materials to replace the mess left here by Menghu and Sephs. Food and Mantis enough to keep all of us sane.

We can do this. We're going to do it.

I nod to the empty room before turning toward the door. But before I can follow my team, a hand darts out from the shadows and pulls me in, a finger snaking between my chin and my mask. "You yell, and you'll have so much SS inside you that there won't be room for anything else."

Mei. I hold extra still, letting her back me into the wall as I snake one hand up to press the mask firmly against my nose and mouth.

"Where is it?" she hisses. "You took all the Mantis I had."

"If you want to know, I'd suggest getting your fingers out of my mask."

There's a moment where we're stuck in the flash between pressing the trigger of a gun and feeling the bullet leave its chamber. Then she withdraws her finger. "What do you want?"

"I don't want anything. I didn't particularly want to kill you myself, so this seemed a better alternative." I try to move away from the wall, but she slams her weight against me, pressing my shoulder back against the bricks. "Are you going to kill me now, Mei? Or is it your *friend* who's going to do it?" If she really had a friend bunking with the other Seconds, I would have seen blood by now.

Mei swears. Or I think she does. It's hard to tell when everything that comes out of her mouth seems as if it's meant to offend. "I need Mantis, you dirty Red."

"Yes. That was the point. Should have thought of that before hiding it in a building I know like the back of my hand."

"I'll . . ." She chokes on the words, taking in a ragged breath through her stolen mask. No one has complained about their mask going missing, so we must have had one to spare. "I'll give you anything you want. I'll walk out of here. I'll leave. Just give it back."

"You'd give up your mission and run away? For Mantis?"

A rusty gush of air issues from her mask. It takes a moment before it registers that she's laughing. "Last night I thought you were being brave. Going out into the open with all the Sephs."

"I . . ."

"But now I see that you're just too stupid to know what it is you're up against." Mei pulls back a step, letting her hands fall. "You don't know what it's like to have SS lurking inside you. Waiting to take your hands or move your feet. That fear makes it worse. It gives you bad thoughts." Her hands twitch.

A rumble of dread rolls through me before I can quash it. "I guess you chose the wrong side. If you can't imagine a world where your superior officer is willing to risk his life for you—"

"I'll do anything, Tai-ge." Her use of my first name itches, an irritating flouting of convention. "I'll tell you where the Menghu in the City are hiding."

I step toward the door.

"I'll tell you where the camp I was based in is. The orders I was given, what I was after here. How Dr. Yang wanted me to handle sabotaging you if your purposes here conflict with his." Her voice rises as I get to the doorway. "I'll tell you where they took Jiang Sev."

My feet stop.

A choked laugh comes from behind me. "Out of all the things I just said, that's what you want? To know where Jiang Sev is?"

"Yes." Unease unfurls inside me, because if she doesn't know why finding Sevvy would be important, then maybe it isn't. I turn slowly to find her staring at me, something charged in Mei's eyes that I don't understand. "I might be able to help you if you tell me where she is. As soon as we get more Mantis, anyway."

"What did you do with mine?"

"I made a deal." I gesture to the factory, empty of everything but potential. The street outside, bare of fighting, gas, bodies. Mei's eyes narrow.

But then she nods. "You're smarter than I gave you credit for."

"Not so dirty as you thought?"

Mei laughs again, but if there was any warmth in it, it's sucked out by the filters of her mask. If she's telling the truth, that she knows where Sevvy is, it could be everything I hoped for yesterday. The end of this war we've been fighting for so long. The end of Lieutenant Hao's shaking hands, the torches, the City's broken promises to protect its comrades.

It would be easy for Mei to give me coordinates that I could pass to Mother, but if I'm going to make sure this isn't yet another failure on my part, I'll have to do the footwork myself. The payoff, if what Mei is saying is true, is too good to let go of.

I square my shoulders, look her straight in the eye. "I'm not dirty. Or dishonest, or a killer, or whatever else it is you believe about Reds. I came here to save people, and I'm doing the best I can. If you want Mantis, I need two things."

"Coordinates to your little traitor slave aren't enough?"

"Sevvy was my best friend."

"Some friend you are, letting her live the way she did up here. Letting Dr. Yang take her."

I swallow, echoes of Sevvy's voice loud in the open room. The way her face crumpled when I carried her up the stairwell at Port North, and how she screamed at me to get out of the heli when she realized I was . . . the same thing I've always been. A Second. A patriot. A soldier. A good son. Breathing deep, I find my center, my control. Arguing with Mei isn't going to help anything. She doesn't understand any more than Sevvy did. "I'll get you Mantis. But first I need my link back. And coordinates aren't going to be enough. I want you to walk me straight to wherever she is and let me in the front door."

Mei's forehead wrinkles, her mask twitching over what must be a snarl. But then she gives a slow nod.

"My life for Jiang Sev's? I think we can work that out."

CHAPTER 15
Howl

I TRUST YOU, SEV SAID. I TRUST YOU.

The night is too cold, and somehow morning light doesn't bring any warmth, as if this whole world has been sucked dry of hope. I stand, my feet steady under me, even if my shoulder is stiff, pain jabbing under my collarbone whenever I move my arm.

I wish *I* could trust me. How can I live with the nagging doubt at the back of my mind that I'm doing the wrong thing? Not because I'm choosing wrong, but that somehow I can't see what is wrong and what is right or if there's an in-between.

Song Jie catches my eye as he packs the last of Gein's things but drops it quick. *Would I have been your first murder?* It feels like blood in my mouth, coppery and begging to be spat out.

I *would* have stabbed Song Jie if I'd had to. The knife was in my hand, and Song Jie has the tear in his coat to prove it. What else was I supposed to do?

But now I'm standing in the middle of an empty cave trying to find a different reality. Sev always seemed to see something more than the plans that leave me alive and everyone else around me dead.

I shiver as Song Jie, Reifa, even Telan and Gein look at me sideways as we begin to walk, as if they can see straight to my core. Those years in the City cured me of wanting revenge, but here I am again, thinking in knives and blood as if there isn't any other way to survive.

But how *do* you grow new eyes to see the world? I can't be a liar. A killer. A *survivor*. I don't want that, if that's what I was before.

Just because Sev believes there is always a nonviolent solution to every obstacle doesn't mean she's right. The thought burrows out from inside me, as if somehow I can justify the hollow shell of a person I feel like I need to be in order to get to her. *She needs me.*

It's easier than admitting that it's me who needs Sev.

If I'm next to Sev, then that means someone loves me.

And if Sev's the one who loves me, that means I'm not a pox on what's left of the human race.

We set out into the trees uphill, my calves stretching and complaining after lying so long in quarantine and then in the hammock. The air feels like ice inside my lungs, carving away the last bits of fuzziness clinging to my brain.

If that's even when my fuzzy-headedness started. Can't say attacking the gore that charged Sev was one of my most clear-headed moments. If I'd been sensible that night, I would have pushed the stupid medic into the gore's mouth instead of offering myself up.

The memory is still sharp in my mind: Sev crushed into the ground underneath me, the knife in my hand scraping as it hit bone inside the gore's mouth. I shudder.

I didn't make an active decision to step between that thing and Sev, and I don't regret it.

I'm not sure which of those things is more frightening. Both more terrifying than the beast itself, for sure. Worse, because I know what I'm doing now—heading straight for Dr. Yang with the idea that I'm going to pry both the cure and Sev from his corpsified fingers—is about as smart as sticking my arm shoulder-deep into a gore's mouth.

That means I've changed, doesn't it? That when Sev said she trusted me, it was based on us, on what we'd done together, not dreams and lies. But as I think it through, it almost feels worse, as if the only thing that tethers me to humanity *is* Sev. And if I stomp back onto Menghu ground with blood in my mouth and a gun in my hand in order to get her out of there, she'll take one look at me and cut the cords between us. I'll fall.

I don't want to fall.

I don't want to just survive anymore.

Survivors are alone.

Gein jostles my arm, and I have to bite back some choice words about Yuan Zhiwei's extended family before I can turn to him with less-than-violent intentions. He's holding a roll of paper, lines marking mountains and hills, valleys and rivers. The southern half of the map is blank. Extending it out in front of me as we walk, Gein flaps the corners like bird wings, pointing at various spots in the area blank of notations.

My home.

"He's asking where we'll find the highest population concentrations." Song Jie clears his throat. "That's where the Chairman is going to be, correct? And his son."

"Yes. Definitely." Maybe they're trying to kidnap the Chairman himself. That would make more sense, even if it wouldn't be very helpful—just give Dr. Yang another reason to solidify the Reds behind him, leading them to avenge their beloved leader.

I can't stay with these people, tramping through the woods just hoping that somehow the promise of arriving in the mountains within days will happen. They're making a target of themselves. Eyeing Song Jie's pack over the top of the map, I bite down hard on my lip, the skin breaking. *Sev wouldn't know. She's not here to judge.*

It doesn't matter if Sev sees, the rational part of me counters. The part that hoped along with Sev that I can be better than I was before. *Attacking these people and leaving them to die would make you less.*

And suddenly it feels like a choice. An easy one. Not Sev watching me to make sure I'm not a monster inside. Not Sole shaking her head and saying I can't help it. Not Jiang Gui-hua looking down at me with pity or Dr. Yang choosing carefully his every word, knowing each one will twitch my arms and legs like marionettes on a string.

It's not Sev's opinion or anyone else that matters. It's my choice what I do next. And I don't want to harm anyone else.

I take half of the map and point generally to where the City sits, Gein squinting down at the paper. "When we get closer, I'll give you coordinates."

We walk until the trees around us grow so closely they seem to link arms, every inch of the forest so tightly knit that visibility is almost zero. Reds must still be tailing us, and every step I take blind feels like asking for a bullet to the head. Song Jie leads us down a balding ravine that screams *shallow grave*—anyone at the top will be able to see us and there's nowhere to run. Telan shifts uncomfortably ahead of me in our line as if he can feel it too, but he keeps his back to the trees until we get to a clump of boulders, as if pretending the threat isn't there will make it go away.

The boulders are apparently interesting enough to stop and stare at despite our precarious situation. Telan and Song Jie set

their shoulders to the smallest of the rocks wedged in the bottom
of the ravine while Gein watches, twitching when a fly lands on his
sweaty face. The two Islanders pull together until the moss begins
to tear, the rock underneath groaning as a section of it slides away.

There's a hole behind the rocks. A tunnel.

Reifa's face is a full moon, smiling as if Guonian's holiday
dumplings came early. Did we already pass Guonian and I didn't
even know?

It seems like a pathetic thought to be having at this
moment, waiting for the shots from above that will puncture
my head or heart if the sniper is good. A lung or major organ,
leaving me to bleed out if they aren't. Guonian dumplings are
something I've always eaten alone, watching other families and
wondering where I fit. For some reason I thought this year I'd
be with Sev. With June. Maybe even Kasim and Sole. With
Luokai even, both of us attempting to rediscover what it means
to have a brother.

Instead of making dumplings with Sev or getting into a glue
fight with June and Kasim while papering my door with red, I'm
being forced by a muscly Baohujia onto my knees to fit into a hole
that seems a place for the dead if I ever did see one.

Crawling through the tunnel is a lopsided affair with me holding my bad arm tight against my stomach, Reifa's backside only
inches from my face. When we finally emerge into open, black
space, I reach out to the sides to stop vertigo from setting in.
Based on the way our breath echoes, the cave has to be at least
fifty feet high and I don't know how wide.

A light flickers into existence just behind me. I look back to
find Song Jie's fingers leaving stripes of shadow across the little
globe painting the ground around him gold. The depths of the

cave seem to swallow the glimmering ball, bulky shapes crowding the space like gores in a predatory slumber. Helis.

The cave is an aircraft hangar built into the hill, each heli shrouded in silk. The shape and lines of them are familiar, but somehow off, the limbs and guts of the helis all in a slightly different place than I'm used to.

"*This* is how we're going to get to the mountains?" I ask Song Jie, who is igniting more of the little lights and handing them out, sickness a flower unfurling inside me. "The Reds out there . . . Were they after you or after *this*?" I gesture hopelessly at the hulking shapes.

"Stay out of our way." Song Jie brushes past me, following Reifa to the closest aircraft, the two of them holding their lights up to the propellers as Telan pulls the tarp away from its body.

The metal is painted black, guns huddled under its nose like a particularly lethal mustache. It's like nothing I've seen from the City. Hibernating since before the Influenza War, sick with sleep like the rest of us.

Telan and Reifa start testing the hatches, the windows, the wings. They follow *Gein*, of all people, as he shakes his head at the heli and moves farther down the line, then points to the next craft with a satisfied grunt.

"What's Gein saying? What's going on?" Only Song Jie hangs back, fishing in his pack for another light. The floor is dyed red under our feet, and when I follow the color over to where the helis sit, I can see a hint of yellow stars on the floor, like the Core at the Mountain. This must be a military base from Before.

"Gein found the one he's best equipped to fly." Song Jie goes down to his knees, digging into the pack. "Go. You can steal the best seat."

As Gein and Reifa pull open their chosen heli's hatch, I take my time walking over. My eyes find a long glass window set into the hangar's stone wall to my left, about fifteen feet up, and a doorway set into the rock just under it. Next to that, there's a cutout section mostly cluttered with shadows, but combined light from Gein, Reifa, and Telan is enough to see outlines of fuel tanks and long tubes. . . . They almost look like pre–Influenza War bombs. Piled together, as if there's no harm to be had from them.

Telan stops me before I can get too close to the heli, as if he's afraid I'll somehow alert the Reds outside to what we've found in here. He points to the ground, speaking in Port North's odd combination of sounds before going back to help Gein balance the heavy stairs that pull free with the hatch. I'm supposed to stay here, I guess.

Once the stairs are down, Gein climbs into the cockpit and settles himself on the other side of the cockpit window, which finally makes me understand. Reifa dragged Gein all the way out here because he's a *pilot*. I don't know how I would have been able to tell. Calluses? Maybe an extra lift to his walk? All the pilots I've ever known have looked like Tai-ge: ready to flap their arms and keep a heli in the air on pure muscle should the propellers fail.

"How did you know these were here, Song Jie?" I ask, unable to muster more than a whisper, as if these old creatures are worthy of reverence. "Why hasn't the island been using them to fight . . . ?"

I look to where I last saw him by the tunnel mouth. It's dark, as is the cave everywhere except where Telan and Reifa are using their lights to inspect the heli. Gein comes back down the stairs, growling at me to get out of the way. I duck under the propeller to check the other side, and my adrenaline is surging by the time I get back to where I started.

Don't any of them see that Song Jie is gone?

The realization only has a split second to settle before the *shing* of metal on rock echoes up through the cave, a sound I've heard too many times. My body moves before the rest of me can think. I bodycheck Gein, pinning him to the ground so we're both shielded behind the heli when the world explodes around us.

CHAPTER 16
Howl

EXPLOSIONS DON'T SPEAK IN A PARTICULAR LANGUAGE. They're a universal understanding that erases the need for words. It only takes a fraction of a second, and it changes your whole world.

It isn't a fire-and-shrapnel explosion, thank Yuan, but a wash of hot air and an ear-killing *boom* that knocks me off center. The heli rocks to the side, the force of the blast knocking Telan to the ground, his light skittering across the floor. Even with my eyes and ears covered and the heli to block the worst of it, I'm still surprised to find myself all in one piece. Gein, underneath me, looks blankly up at the heli propellers shaking overhead, his eyes unfocused. Ducking out from the heli's protection, I kick the light Gein was holding toward the tunnel we came from. Dragging the pilot out from behind the heli's bulk takes almost all my strength, and the pain tearing through my shoulder makes my arm feel like it's going to fall off. Gein's limp, but I can feel his pulse racing.

What do I need to get out of this? A pilot, for sure. Every step seems unbalanced, as if the floor is waving this way and that underneath me. Definitely the work of a flash-bang grenade. Whoever is out there must know what's in here: lots of combustibles. They're not going to use bullets unless they're sure of what they're shooting.

As I drag Gein toward the wall where I saw the door, I trip over a set of legs. Falling to my knees, I find long braids and slack, old-person skin—and a pulse. Reifa. She's alive.

Her gun is lying just next to her on the floor. Picking it up it feels wrong, as if taking her weapon means I'm taking her life. And worse, as if touching the weapon will bring back everything inside me that might be crooked. But I take it anyway, thrusting it into my waistband, where it pokes into my ribs. If not to use, then at least no one else will be able to use it on me.

In another life I would have left Reifa where she lay. In this one, I help her sit as Gein wobbles up from the ground, holding his head. Grabbing Gein and supporting Reifa, I shuffle both unbalanced Port Northians to the wall where I saw the window. Just as my fingers find the cracked wood door, a metal-on-stone *clunk* echoes throughout the hangar, telling me we have seconds before we're either dead or stunned. The doorknob won't turn, but it does splinter with my first kick, then cave with the next. We fall through the opening in a muddle of limbs and terror just as a second detonation roars by in a hot rush of air.

Pain in my chest turns everything white, the set of stairs inside the doorway a blurry impression of sharp edges. Gein gives a yelp, and Reifa buries her head into my bad shoulder, but we're shielded from the worst of it. "Follow me!" I yell, but I can't hear even my own words. The two Port Northians don't need the direction because they follow me up the stairs, Gein pausing to retch about halfway up. At the top there's the glass window I saw from outside. Controls decorate the wall and the long desk that's built in directly beneath the window, but they're all dead, not a flicker of light to be seen.

There has to be another way out of here. The helis didn't squeeze in through that tunnel. I just have to find where. Once I know where the exit is, I can shatter the window and pick off the assailants from up here with Reifa's gun, then get out before the rest of their group gets inside. Provided I don't run out of bullets before I run out of assailants. I don't know how many bullets are in her magazine, and I don't want to stop just now to check.

Swearing, I push one of the chairs toward the stairwell, wondering how long we'll last trapped up here. Maybe the desks can be moved and we can barricade ourselves in, but that would only extend our lives by minutes at best.

Gein and Reifa huddle against the wall on the top step, and I have to drop my chair to pull them out of the way, but somehow they pitch me over instead. My brain seems to blank out, nothing but the sure knowledge that we have less than a minute before whoever it is out there finds us up here and that *Song Jie*—that little Seph-eater—is probably hiding behind one of the grenade-wielding grunts down there.

Song Jie hated Reifa and the others. I could see it in the line of his shoulders every time he had to bow and cook and carry. Did he plan this, letting the Reds corner us in here where we wouldn't be able to find him? I believed him when he told me *I* was the murderer. Anger churns inside me. *He was right to be afraid of me.*

But that thought turns my chest to ice.

Afraid like the little girl I shot, her parents already dead bodies lying broken in the tent right in front of her. Afraid like Sev when we were in the cave, waiting for me to kill her, too.

I am not a murderer. But if I can't fight, then I might as well lie down here on the stairs with my hands over my head. Kind of the way I am right now, stuck between Reifa and Gein. If I can't fight, I'm choosing to die.

I don't want to die. Is it a choice between those two with nothing in between? Murderer or gore meat?

The door below cracks open, a yellow quicklight zinging through the air to hit the wall, then land at my feet. I don't see the soldier until he's right on top of us, yellow light hitting the stars pinned to his uniform and glinting down the barrel of the gun pointed at my chest. He says something, but I can't hear his words over the ringing in my ears. Hands above my head, I feel the gun I took from Reifa pressed into my ribs.

I explode up from the floor, kick the soldier's gun hand to the side. Grab hold of his wrist and slam his elbow into the wall, breaking his arm. His gun clatters to the floor as I pull Reifa's weapon from my waistband and point it at his head. The soldier crumples a little, holding himself together as he clutches his broken arm to his chest. He says something, the sound filtering in and out of my damaged ears, but his eyes meet mine and hold. *I didn't shoot you,* he seems to say. *I didn't want to kill you.*

My finger on the trigger presses hard without actually pulling it, the two of us staring at each other, two people on opposite sides, but for what? I doubt he wants to be here any more than I do, and it's my life against his. My life and Reifa's and Gein's. Is that an even trade?

Before I can press the button on this man's existence, a gunmetal *crack* fills the tiny stairwell. The man jerks forward, blood blooming across his chest in a violent spray. He falls forward, bullet wounds dark and wet in his back.

Below him on the stairs stands Song Jie, a gun in his hands. Where did he get a gun?

My hearing is still full of nothing but bullet holes, Song Jie's lips moving extra slow as if it's supposed to help. He lowers the gun, his steps exaggerated and deliberate. The same way you to talk to a feral dog with its hackles raised, ready to shoot if it goes for your throat.

Pointing purposefully toward the other Islanders behind me, he waits until I lower Reifa's gun before he brushes past me to enter the control room.

Reifa falls in next to Song Jie as he wrenches at the dead controls. Gein hasn't moved from his spot in the stairwell, hands clapped down tight over his ears. Song Jie points to a cubby by the control panel, gesturing for me to take off the door. Torn between the stairwell and its inefficient guard (Gein's not about to stop anyone from coming up here unless they're sympathetic criers) and knowing we need to get out of here, I don't follow his frantic pointing. My gut's all turned around, not wanting to trust Song Jie or any of these court calligraphers with my life. But Song Jie shot the man who was thinking about shooting me. Song Jie's whole body shakes as he pulls at the controls, blood splatters across his chest and face to match the ones on me.

It's that image—one of a man who has never killed before facing the atrociousness of what he's done—that makes me move. I stick the gun in my waistband and go to the control box, taking the long knife Reifa holds out—the same one I almost used on Song Jie—to leverage it open. It releases with a *screech*, the metal locking mechanism rusted to almost nothing. Song Jie elbows me out of the way, connecting wires and flipping switches inside until the whole room lights up. The floor seems to hum.

Not pausing to breathe, Song Jie goes back to the control panel, frantically pressing and pulling things, the multitude of lights blinking on and off again under his fingers, making him squint. Above us, rock seems to groan, and the hum in the room turns to what feels like an earthquake, knocking me to the ground. Light pierces the darkness outside the window, pure and blinding, like staring straight into the sun.

Song Jie grabs Reifa's arm, then darts for the door, dragging the old woman behind him. My hearing is going from high-pitched tone to a sort of hazy remembrance of what sound is supposed to be like; Song Jie's voice barely penetrating. ". . . I don't know how long before they'll get through the block I set up in the outer tunnel. Everyone who made it in is dead, but we don't have much time!"

He pauses to prod Gein with his foot—not hard, but enough to nudge him from his stupor, allowing me to pull the pilot up from the ground and lead him back down the stairs. Song Jie leads all of us to the cutout room where I saw the outlines of supplies. Gein stumbles along after us, staring blank-eyed at the tidy rows of boxes until Song Jie gives him a push toward them. He points to a pile of long, hard plastic boxes, sending Reifa and Song Jie each scrambling to extract one, then carrying them toward the heli. "Help us!" Song Jie calls back, only an outline of the words scratching through my ears. "We have to get out."

I pick up one of the long boxes, heavier than I would have guessed from its size. The beam of light above us widens as the roof slowly folds up. The sun highlights bodies on the ground: four City jerkins . . . and a set of Baohujia robes. It's Telan, face-down and motionless, a pool of red blood underneath him.

Opening the hangar door will allow us to lift off, but it will also give Reds a way in. I don't understand exactly what is going on, but it's obvious they knew to follow us here. We need to get off the ground now.

I glance up as the hangar door makes a world-cleaving, metal-on-stone grumble, the opening to the sky stuck at less than twenty feet wide. Reifa and Song Jie both pause, Song Jie's sweat-streaked face blank. He says something in Port Northian that punches the way only the very best of swear words can.

"Is it stuck?" I call.

He sets down his load, looking up into the sliver of blue sky. An almost escape, too narrow for us to slip through.

"Do you know how the hangar doors work?" I set the long box on the heli ramp, Reifa giving me a narrow look before picking it up herself to take inside. "Tell me what to do, Song Jie. I'll get the doors open if you just tell me how to get up there."

Song Jie takes a shaky breath, and then another, ducking out of the heli to look up again at the narrow strip of blue sky burning the darkness of the hangar into light. "We might have a chance if . . ." He looks back at me, barely pausing long enough to say, "Come with me!" before running toward the control room.

"I was part of the team that maintained this facility," he calls back to me when we hit the stairs. "The doors were camouflaged under dirt and scrub, but we haven't been able to get out here safely since the City started coming after the island. It's been eight years since any of this has been maintained—eight years of dirt, wind, and rain . . ."

He skids to a stop at the control panels, pressing buttons until a three-dimensional image appears in front of him, showing the doors partially opened. There's a red dot sending up a warning flare near the door's hinges. "Looks like we've got some kind of blockage. I don't know what could be so big the door wouldn't crush it, so there must be more than one obstruction."

"How do I get up there?" I ask.

Song Jie grabs something from under the desk, then bolts toward the stairs. "You only have one arm, and no idea how to fix anything."

"I have two arms. Didn't you not see me carrying boxes like a champion . . . box carrier?"

The lights flicker overhead as he skids to a stop and presses his hand against a silver stripe marking the wall at the top of the stairs. Just like the doors back at the island, a *click* I can feel through the stone floor releases a pocket door, the chunk of rock sliding back. It moves slow, Song Jie pacing back and forth in front of it, hand scrubbing through his dirty hair as he waits for it to give him enough room to pass. He turns back to me, holding up the thing he grabbed from the desk. "I've got a radio link that connects to the controls here—tell me if another light pops up once I've got the obstruction cleared. You'll have to input the command for it to open again."

"How long will you have to get down here before it crushes you?"

"Maybe five minutes?" He's already far enough away that I only catch the echoes of his voice.

"Song Jie!" I start after him, but stop after only a few steps. He's right that I wouldn't know what to do up there, so I go back to the hologram, examining the characters flickering at the bottom. They're almost the same as the ones I've been using my whole life, but there are odd twists here and there, characters that are squished together or slightly malformed from what I know, though from context I can generally understand. Thumbing through them, I find the manual override for the door, though it's grayed out because of the obstruction. The radio is pretty easy to find too, a little icon that is blinking yellow as if to say it's connected.

One of the character sets says something about external surveillance, so I press it, gratified when a video feed pops up on the screen mounted underneath the desk's heavy glass top.

There's a camera showing a sliver of the open door in the ceiling, a draft of air visibly ruffling rocks and dirt from its edge to fall into the cave below. At the very corner of the camera, there's a hint of movement. Fiddling until I get the cameras to change, I find an image of Song Jie outside on the roof staring down a tree trunk tipped at an awkward angle. He runs to a rise in the rock where the hinged edge of the door rests, pulling open a door to work on something inside.

The image of the partially open doors remains stationary, the single red light continuing to beat a warning. There's no sound from the video, but I can see the swear words erupting from Song Jie's lips, his face grainy and hard. Shuffling through all the different camera vantage points to see if I can be helpful, all I find is dirt, scrubby grass, and trees, not a single sign of hostile—

Wait. I shuffle back one camera set. Was it only grass waving in the breeze? The shadows twist in a way that seems out of sync with the plant life up there, but it's difficult to see because the sun is shining directly into the camera.

There it is again. Movement. A shadow larger than any dead dandelion stalk can cast. Then an outline, the sun's strength on the camera lens turning whoever it is into something spindly and alien.

Just as I'm about to click the radio, Song Jie's voice crackles through and the highlighted obstruction turns from red to green. "We're clear. Any other lights pop up?"

"Get out of there!" I hiss into the hologram, not even sure where the microphone is.

"What?"

The manual override icon turns green. Another shape slinks across the camera, then another. "Yuan's dirty bastard of a . . ." I hit the override to force the hangar doors open, then run for the stairwell, tinny *ping*s of gunfire crackling over the radio.

CHAPTER 17
Howl

MY SHOULDER AND CHEST ACHE AS I DART THROUGH
the open door disguised in a cleft of rock on the roof. Reifa's gun
feels like lead, pulling my good arm down as if it's going to
destroy the last piece of me that works. I haven't shot at anyone
in years. Not since I got to the City. My time before that was a
frenzy almost, where it seemed like the whole world was armed
and searching for me.

It wasn't. It sort of was.

All these years I've kept my finger off the trigger, even when
June's Seph-bitten family tried to hold us hostage, when Helix
came after us with a gun. When I thought Tai-ge was going to
shoot me or Sev or maybe even that stupid medic he brought
with us. Keeping my finger off the trigger was a safeguard. As if
discharging a weapon one more time would make my two years of
hiding from the things I did before slide off me like a coat, leaving
me with nothing in this world but a gun in one hand and hatred in
my heart.

The little girl and her doll. She wasn't the last I killed.

Song Jie's a crouched form on the far end of the rocky hillside, sheltering behind a rock as bullets *thud* into his cover. Based on the video feed, soldiers will be coming up from the lower side of the hill at the west end, right before it shears off into a rocky cliff.

When I get close enough to see the first Red, my finger on the trigger won't move for a moment. He's taking a second to reset, checking his cover and the soldiers behind him.

I don't want to go back to my old idea of the world, that there were only friends and enemies and nothing in between, because I know there are good people fighting for their lives from under the Mountain, scavenging Outside, even inside the City, all of them just trying to stay alive.

Good people who will still try to kill me if I'm the body standing between them and a safe life for their family. Good people who will hand over these helis and the weapons inside them to Dr. Yang, believing that safety is what he's offering instead of slavery.

The soldier takes aim at Song Jie.

My bullet hits the Red first.

The second Red falls just as quickly once I've accounted for the wind. The third ducks down, trying to figure out where the bullets came from. Song Jie darts toward me, the hangar's roof making a slow arc that will block the stairs in a minute. Another Red pulls himself up to join the one still alive on the grassy slope, but Song Jie's almost across, almost safe. When he gets to my spot by the door, Song Jie slides onto his knees, pulling out the gun he took from some soldier below, and begins firing wildly toward the rocks where the two soldiers are sheltered.

"Stop." I pull his arm down, the gun firing into the ground at Song Jie's feet as he jerks away from me, twisting to point the weapon again toward the Reds. *"Stop."* I can't hear myself speak, the sound from the explosion, the gunfire, all of it leaving my ears empty, and there's little chance Song Jie can hear me either, but he understands when I pull the gun away from him and push him back through the door to the stairs. His face seems to be nothing but veins and fury, as if everything bad in the world was sitting right outside and finally he can do something about it.

Like me, Before. Seeking to right the world one dead Red at a time.

It's only a momentary lapse. Song Jie swears at me one more time before running down the stairs to the holograms and video feeds. Tucking Song Jie's stolen gun next to Reifa's in my waist-band makes me feel part machine. I check the damage we did. Two dead men sprawled across the rocks, the other two still taking cover. Two killed by me, the others spared from Song Jie's wild shots. My breaths come in too deep and heavy as I follow Song Jie's sprint down the stairs. We get to the heli staircase just as Reifa goes to the controls to pull it up. She gives us a grudging nod before letting us in. Song Jie first, then me, blood-spattered and cold.

But alive. And on my way to making sure Sev is alive.

The acrid stink of propellant sticks to my hands, like memories I'd rather forget.

I did not want to kill those men.

I didn't kill them to save myself or out of revenge. I did it to save Song Jie. Sev would probably have said no one should've been shooting at all, but Sev doesn't know everything.

My mind goes back to when Reds took June and we knocked over their tent to get her back, Sev politely asking one of the Reds to sit still while she tied him up, but I blink the image away. She fought Luokai off when he was trying to tear me to pieces, stood between June and Tai-ge's medic right alongside me when I told him if he didn't stay away from her he'd be practicing nosedives off the back of the heli from ten thousand feet.

She hasn't had to deal with one of those split-second decisions between dying and killing someone else. I don't want her to ever have to.

I sit down and strap in, pulling the guns from my waistband to push them away where they won't be touching my skin. Almost glad that this time I can feel the weight of death, because maybe that means it isn't a part of me anymore.

The heli jerks into the air before I even realize the propellers are running. Tai-ge's heli *roared*, but this one is a snake, barely a hiss coming in through the windows. Gein jumps up from the controls even though we're in the air, the aircraft bobbing up and down in an unconvincing hover. He and Reifa grab four of the long, thin boxes I helped load onto the heli and take them into a side compartment just off the cockpit. Leaving Reifa in the compartment, Gein dashes empty-handed to the controls and takes us up so quickly, my head slams into the metal wall, pushing me hard against the seat, a sudden pressure in my ears.

Gein yells something from the pilot's chair, pointing frantically to the ground below, the heli jogging side to side as if it's about to collapse. I claw my way out of the seat to the cockpit window, peering down below us. Something seems to dislodge from the bottom of the heli, tiny specks falling lifelessly to the ground below.

One moment, the yawning hangar doors are below us, Reds dotting the hillsides all around. The next, there's fire billowing out from the hangar's open jaws. Rock and dirt and trees and who knows what else seem to collapse down into the hole we were just standing in, the whole Seph-bitten hillside turning from a military base to a cloud of ash and smoke.

It's the sound of the explosion unfolding that's the worst. The sound is so heavy it's almost silence.

I look away, my heart rapping hard against my chest as I crouch by the window. I've heard the stories about the weapons from Before. We don't have bombs like that anymore. Not the kinds that blow up whole hangars, whole *cities* like they did during the Influenza War.

But I don't have to look through the cloud of smoke to know. Everything below us, the hangar, the hill, the helis. The Reds Song Jie wanted to shoot. They're all gone.

CHAPTER 18
Sev

NO DAYLIGHT. NO NIGHT. NO SLEEP OR WAKING. Just endless rustlings and squeaks as medics walk through the room, pressure and pain when they inserted the feeding tube into my nose. More with the catheter and the other tubes that promise no one will have to do more than check the equipment spidering out from me to keep me clean. The air has been turned to stone. Every inch of me covered by the cold, suffocating weight that pins me to the bed. Every breath is only a sip of oxygen while my lungs dry up.

Alone. Except for the person with no mask and a beast inside them who slips into my room and sits at my bedside when no one else is here.

Time stops moving. The darkness rustles, full of whispers and specters. Only Mother notices I'm here. Or maybe it's the princess trapped under a spell of Sleep. It's hard to tell.

Sometimes it's just memories of her, her voice saying she's sorry, but she's speaking from the pages of a book. The book burns, pages charring to ash one word at a time. The princess's voice growls out from a throat left to rot for eight years, only to tell me she's going to die.

To go to the family.

I found my family. Where I came from. I found the cure. I know where to go. The papers are under our old floorboards back in the City, in the box where my sister and I used to hide our secrets.

But I can't move.

Then, after days, weeks, *years*, the princess stops her repetitive chimes and starts talking *to* me.

I know hallucinations come to people who are Asleep. They came to me the last time I went under, and they came calling in the years after I woke up. But here, trapped in the dark, it's hard to remember what is real, what is memory, and what is dream.

You know, Tai-ge didn't have much respect for you, the princess lectures. *He watched every step you took after the two of you stole the heli, waiting to catch you when you fell. It was never a question of whether you would. Never a thought to wonder if he was the one who'd stepped over the cliff.* Her voice seems to undulate back and forth, as if she's speaking to me through a long tube. Through time. It makes the little bit of me still here, the curled-up girl in the furthest corner of my mind, look up. *Howl trusts you to do your part. Your father was that way.*

"Father?" I ask. I hardly remember my father.

He would always look at the way I did things and start to laugh, as if I were from some other planet. I suppose I was. But then he'd say, "I'll try it. Maybe your way is better." Sometimes I'd watch him and follow. We tried to meet at the center.

Meet at the center. Fight on the same team. Though it didn't start out as a fight. "What happened to Howl?" I ask, as if she exists outside me, a ghost that can look at the world and report back. "I left him at Port North. He couldn't climb with me to get the cure from Gao Shun."

The cure wasn't there.

"I know. But we thought it was there. All of us did. Did Howl survive? Is he here? Is he dead?" And then the quieter thought: "Howl wouldn't have been hurt if it hadn't been for me. He wouldn't have been on the island at all."

Silence. But then her voice speaks, the lovely bell tones I remember before, not the paper-thin scratch of a woman almost dead or the harsh sobs of a mother in mourning. Her voice soothes the enflamed darkness of my mind. He *followed* you. *He's the one who climbed into the heli and the one who chose to step between you and that gore, knowing it might be the end of his life. You can't take his decisions and decide they belong to you any more than he can tell you what to think and feel. Both of you made your own choices, and those choices brought you here. Because you want to help June. Lihua. All the others Dr. Yang has hurt or will hurt in the future.*

"I killed you. I didn't want to, but I did."

Dr. Yang killed me, my little rose. He killed me the moment he put Sleep into my veins. It was never you.

"I'm afraid." The admission chokes inside me. I don't want to be trapped, to be Asleep. To know that Howl could be Asleep the way I am somewhere in this building and there's nothing I can do to help him.

I'm afraid I won't ever wake up. The medicine that was supposed to wake Mother up killed her instead. And even if I do wake up, what then? What if Tai-ge was right about me? I'm just a Fourth. What do I know about cures or escaping or any of that? I've had help every step of the way so far, and now I'm alone.

"What if I fail?" I whisper it in the back of my brain, the admission feeling almost like a failure itself. "What if it comes down to me facing Dr. Yang with a gun and I can't pull the trigger?"

Her voice seems to sigh, the sound a brush of cool air inside me. *We share faults between the two of us. Being able to kill is not always strength, Sevvy, but the reverse can also be a weakness. Allowing others a chance to right their wrongs, or even to explain themselves, is a quality I wish everyone possessed . . . but I still wonder what it is I should have done, knowing now how Dr. Yang planned to hurt you and the rest of the family. If I had decided to end him, I'd be alive. So would your father, your sister. It would have been my burden instead of yours.*

A hallucination. I know this is a hallucination. Does that mean something deep inside me blames Mother for where I'm lying now? It would be a lie to say I didn't wish Dr. Yang had been taken care of long before I was born. But I know that isn't fair. "You weren't a killer. You were a doctor. A savior."

I thought of myself that way, but it was my failing that killed your father. Your sister. So many others at Port North and Outside. She sighs. I know you're scared. I know you want to fix it all. But nobody can fix everything. You'll do what's right. You'll do more than you think you can. You'll have to be what I couldn't. Everything is going to be all right, because you have never once settled for less than that.

"Haven't I?" I settled for being Tai-ge's slightly embarrassing friend. For canning jars and limp cabbage dinners, a star burned into my hand when I'd done nothing to deserve it.

The specter in my head is silent for a long time. Then, finally, she says, *You never were one to give up. I'm here with you, Sevvy. I love you. This isn't the end unless you decide to let it be.*

Decide to let it be?

My inner self sits up, my curled spine going straight. I won't let this be the end. Not with so many people relying on me.

CHAPTER 19
June

MY EYES STAY OPEN AT NIGHT PARTLY TO BE SURE
the ocean doesn't gobble us down while I sleep, but mostly because
of Luokai. The only *real* sleep you get when SS is around is the
dying kind, and this bench is a good spot to keep watch, no matter how many times Luokai tells me it's warmer inside the boat's
canopy. I like to know where my enemies sleep. The water, just over
the side of the boat. Luokai inside, where the screech of a door will
give him away before he can get close.

Whenever Luokai isn't messing with the engine, he sits up on
the platform and breathes deep, letting the boat go this way and
that. At first it makes me watch him close, until he says, "If I keep
myself calm, they stay away."

They. *Compulsions.*

Luokai sees mine coming before I do, the horrible voice
screaming at me to jump over the side of the boat, to pull up the
floorboards, to yank at my own hair, not even leaving me a voice to
ask for help. He's always there when my mind comes back to me,

his arms restraining me still until I stop shaking. He's strong like
Howl. Soft like Sev.

Half *gore* like Dad.

Like me.

"Why do you worry so much about the water, June?" Luokai
asks from the engine controls. He's always saying something, like
he needs to remind me he's there, that I'm not alone.

"It's worrying that sends you into a compulsion." Luokai does
something to the controls, then climbs down into the room under
the canopy. "You have to relax. Think about good things and keep
yourself calm, because then SS has less to work with. When we
get to the river, it'll take us right to where I first met Jiang Sev.
A week or two of hiking from there and we'll be at the Mountain,
where Howl was headed. We're practically already there."

My ears perk at that. Didn't Sev first meet Luokai at Cai Ayi's
trading post?

Luokai is watching me, though, so I pull my feet up onto the
bench. Fold my arms. Close my eyes. Try to keep myself calm, like
he told me to. It starts with remembering the bubbles in Cai Ayi's
voice. Then I line up the kids Sev and I pulled out of the City in
my mind to wash their faces and check that their coats are zipped.
Their heads were shaved, and their insides were meant to be cut
out, but they're mine now, and so they're safe, because I know
what it's like not to have someone to take care of you.

As if you could take care of anyone now. The gore's breath huffs in
my ear. *You can't even take care of yourself anymore. Only thing you're good
for now is for Luokai to make sure he gets the cure.*

Another thought slips in behind this one, keeping quiet so my
gore can't hear. If we find the Post, I could leave Luokai behind.
One of the roughers would come with me to the Mountain to

find Howl. I could be safe again, far from SS and the monsters it makes of good people.

Luokai appears in the door, sending me to the railing with my hand clenched tight around the metal strip stashed inside my coat, but I let it go when I see he has a bowl in each hand. He settles next to me on the bench and hands me one of them, the smell of old rice soaked to make porridge welcome in my nose.

"I was hoping to ask you something." Luokai carefully places a bite in his mouth, chewing slowly and swallowing. "I understand you may not answer, and that's all right. I respect your silence. But if there is anything you *can* say, please do."

The bowl's rim feels like bone in my mouth. One sip, one mouthful. That's enough for now. I set the bowl beside me, wondering how long I can make the food last.

"It's my brother, Howl. I had to leave before he was even your age. He grew up alone." Luokai's eyebrows pucker the skin across his forehead like he's thinking very hard. "He's still angry at me for never coming back. For not finding him."

Luokai draws his fisted hand from his pocket, that communication thingy he likes to play with inside. Howl had one he used to hide from Sev, though I guess she found it in the end. "And there's another person. Sole." He opens his hand to show me the little metal disk. "I didn't want to leave her behind, but I did. I was so frightened of hurting them. . . ."

My shoulders hunch, the wind pressing in close. He left people behind to keep them safe? Dad's face seems to almost burn through the image of the gore who nests in my head. Dad couldn't let go, couldn't set me loose any more than I wanted to walk away from him. It was those things that almost killed me.

"I loved them," Luokai continues, and I sit forward, my brain finally all the way focused on what he's saying. "But now that I've been gone so long, I'm not sure they'll ever love *me* again." He smiles, that puckered-up sour fruit expression taking his calm face and making it into a real person's. "You know Howl better than I do. Is it in him to forgive?"

I let my eyes fall down to look at my hands, my fingers white with cold, even bundled up inside my sleeves. Forgive Luokai for leaving Howl with people who weren't his family, who treated him bad? The gore inside me starts to growl, but I hush him down.

"Not forgiving can be dangerous. When you hold on to anger, it feels like you're in charge, that you're keeping someone else from hurting you. But then that anger is trapped inside your mind with no release. It can turn into poison." Luokai rubs a hand across his face. "Not forgiving made me . . . hard. Made me refuse to help people when I should have." I can feel it when his eyes come back up, like little flies crawling across my skin. "There's some of that poison in you, I think. Maybe there's been too much to forgive in your life."

The gore's growls turn into bared teeth and claws. The wind holds her breath next to me.

"Forgiveness doesn't mean forgetting. It means letting go so bad things don't fester inside you. So other people's bad decisions don't spoil *you*. I'm still learning how to do it." He shrugs. "I want my brother and me to be family again. But I can't force someone else to give me another chance."

Sometimes there are no more chances. Sometimes the things you do are permanent. I touch my arms, long white scars streaking my skin like bird poop.

"What happened?" His voice is so quiet, like Tian as she pet my head and told me I'd done well when I'd return to camp with my arms full of dead men's things. Like the voice I gave Dad in my head after he couldn't speak, though since it's turned into . . .

The gore whimpers, gnawing on his own paws.

I kick my feet back and forth, take another bite of porridge and savor it in my mouth. Dad's voice became a gore inside me, showing me all the ways to survive, and then growling that I don't deserve it. I've been broken into too many pieces for anyone smart to want me anymore.

How do you forgive people who can't have a second chance because they're dead? Maybe that's the only time you *can*, because then you can be sure they won't hurt you anymore.

With a cure, maybe Luokai won't have to wait until he's dead to find forgiveness. Licking my lips, I look up and meet his eyes on purpose for the first time. They're brown and stupid and full of hope.

Hope that's inside me. The wind nestles in close to me, and I smile. A little.

CHAPTER 20
Tai-ge

SECURING THE FACTORY AND GATE COMES WITH only one terrible mishap. One of the younger soldiers found a friend sheltering inside one of the old worker dorms. It only took a moment for the Seph to get my soldier talking and then stab a knife in his chest before the soldier had even finished explaining what we were doing with the torches.

When Captain Bai found the soldier's body, the Seph was still kneeling over him, crying. Saying he didn't mean to over and over, pressing hands to his friend's chest as if he could somehow put the blood back inside. The fact that Captain Bai included these details when he reported makes me want to trust him. As if he's sending up a signal that he knows what I'm doing and it's right.

My stomach twinges with hunger as I walk with my soldiers, some of them joking and playing with one another as they go. Seeing them smile makes me realize how tight they were wound when I first got here. I wave them on, stopping to check the spot I hid my link. It's there waiting for me.

The deal with Mei is working already.

Leaning on the cement wall just outside the cafeteria door, I compose my message to Mother: Success. Factory should be operational within days of reinforcements arriving. Unfortunately, a small number of Sephs broke into the market square during the operation, fouled most of the food, and left Captain Bai infected. His expertise is needed. Extra rations and any amount of Mantis you can spare, needed to get us through. We've had radio failure as well. Probably a week before any of our other connections will be up.

Writing the words feels as if I've stuck a gun in my own mouth, my finger twitchy to shoot. Lying to my own mother. My General. The last hope for the City.

I've decided I can't let her see what I'm doing until it's a success. This is a risk *I'm* taking, so she can't be implicated.

Mother's response comes later than I anticipated. Not until I've already finished my first bowl of rice scraped from the pot and begun a discussion with Captain Bai about the best route to the Mantis labs. Expect a delivery after dark, Mother writes. The purple light is dim against the back of my hand, barely discernible even in the ill-lit cafeteria. We can spread ourselves no thinner after this. No more mistakes.

Mistakes. My jaw sets, teeth aching from grinding together.

"Is everything all right, sir?" Captain Bai asks. He still looks as if he's afraid our mission this morning was a dream and there are piles of dead comrades outside for him to drag away.

I stand up from the table, staring down at the flickering characters. It isn't in Mother's nature to accept that a subordinate—her own child especially—has come up with a better plan than hers. If we do succeed, if *everyone* can see it, not even Mother will be able to call it a mistake.

But if I succeed by disobeying her, that will mean I'm telling everyone that *she* made a mistake. How can I take the orders I was given and make it plain they hinted at what we've done instead?

Shaking my head, I dismiss the thoughts as premature. Before justifications can be drawn up, the initial groundwork needs to not disintegrate in a flaming mess. The fragile threads that link me to Lieutenant Hao aren't going to thicken and thrive unless food keeps coming and the promises I've made about Mantis are realized. I avoid Captain Bai's eyes when I respond to his question. "Everything is fine. We can start planning our approach on the First Quarter tomorrow when Lieutenant Hao is present."

"I look forward to it."

When I look up at the undercurrent of praise, Captain Bai locks eyes with me the way he's not supposed to. As I fill my bowl with a second helping of rice and vegetables and meat, a dangerous warmth fills me, because even if I'm not sure of everything, at least I know one person now believes in me.

Upstairs in my room, Mei sits against the wall with both hands pressed to her mask as if it will somehow keep her compulsions in. Her forehead knits when I hold out the bowl for her. Dinner isn't the only thing I brought from downstairs. I pull the length of cord I took from the supplies heaped outside the orphanage from my shoulder. "No word from your colleague downstairs? Should I expect a building full of dead soldiers in the morning?"

She stares straight ahead, her thick eyebrows crinkling. "You know it's just me."

I set the bowl next to her when she doesn't take it, then kneel next to her. "You want to eat first?"

She shakes her head.

"Is this where you want to be until the Mantis comes?"

Mei's eyes finally focus on me, her mask blocking all but the ice crystallizing in the air between us. "I hate you," she says. And puts her hands out to be tied.

* * *

I leave Mei in the room alone to take off her mask and eat, stalling the moment I have to go to bed until long after the sun has gone down. When I finally enter the room, Mei refuses to look at me from where she's tied to her bed, leaving me to lie down without so much as an insult. When I close my eyes, though, sleep seems to laugh at me, directing my attention to the Menghu only a few feet away, waiting for compulsions to take her.

Still, I close my eyes, hope with all my heart the knots will hold, and wait.

It isn't until hours later, my guard relaxed, that an agonized scream jolts me up from my fake slumber. Falling sideways off the bare mattress, I land on my knees, groping for my gun. By the time I have it up and pointed at nothing but darkness, my fuzzy eyes finally focus on Mei, her face cadaverous in the pale moonlight. She pulls against the ropes, her breaths rushing like steam out of the cannery vents before she lets out another desperate yelp.

"Please . . . ," she mutters once the cry is spent. "Please, there's something inside me."

Her voice croaks, her whole body twisting against the ropes, attempting to get a hand to her mouth. "Please . . ." She says it over and over again, each more pitiful than the last, until tears bleed down her cheeks. Her breathing is so fast I'm afraid she'll hyperventilate. Her head comes up slowly until she's looking at me, but her eyes are empty. "Please, Tai-ge . . ."

I turn away, the sound of my name almost worse than the screams. I'm ashamed to see her tied up and so frightened and . . . not *herself*, whoever that is. I'm the one who took her Mantis, who put her in this awful position.

When her breathing becomes more measured, I let myself look

at her again. She's still crying, her head bowed as low as the rope
will let her go.

"Mei?"

She doesn't move.

"Can I . . . get something for you?"

"I don't want anything from you, filthy Red."

"What about a sleeping bag or pillow?"

"Go back to your mother, Hong Tai-ge. It's where you and
every other Red belongs. Kowtowing to her shiny boots."

Mei is shaking, the raw stripe on her wrist now dripping blood
where she pulled against the rope. I turn back toward the wall,
eyes following the cracks in the plaster, hating the pity welling up
inside me. Her hopeless posture sparks memories I don't care to
remember. Sevvy used to go somewhere else—somewhere inside
her head—before she ran away from the City. She saw things no
one else could. I couldn't call attention to it or risk Mother or
Father sending her to the Sanatorium, and I never brought it up
because she never did. It seemed dangerous, a secret both of us
were keeping.

The words are out of my mouth before I think them through,
the very least of what I wish I'd said to Sevvy when I said nothing
at all. When I said worse than nothing. "I'm sorry this is happening to you. I know I don't understand exactly. But I'm sorry."

"How can you be sorry?" Her voice dies a little more with
every word. "You've *never* had to worry about SS. You've never
had to worry about *anything.*" The rancor turns me toward her
again, her eyes made of fire and hate. Arguments puff up inside
me, but I hold them back and let her speak. "You have never once
had your hands blistered over a fire when you did wrong or gone
to bed with welts and bruises after a day's hard work. You don't

know what it's like to finally escape only to end up here with a Red's rope around my neck yet again." She spits, the phlegmy string landing on my boot. "I'm not begging to you or your stars. Never again."

Her words sit like a hole in my stomach, an echo of something Sevvy told me about a girl she met in the Mountain. "Were you working for the City? Outside?"

She doesn't look up.

"Not all of us knew about the living conditions on the farms. I didn't even see a farm until I left during the invasion."

"If you didn't know, it's because you didn't want to. You ate the food as it came. Watched them build factory after factory, saw the helis carry materials from outside your Seph-cursed wall." Her head tilts, and the sight of her eyes glaring through a sheet of sweat-soaked hair, her face like an angry ghost, leaves me with goose bumps. "The whole Third Quarter should have been enough for you to understand why *you* didn't have to work. Just because there was no one there whispering in your ear what exactly the can of peaches in your hand cost doesn't mean we weren't trying to speak."

Anger unfurls inside me again, just like every time Sevvy tried to tell me that my life, my family, *everything* I know, is rotten to the core. There were good people here in the City. There *are* good Firsts, good Seconds. Scores of loyal people who wanted . . .

My head falls back onto my pillow. What did they want? What do *I* want? To be safe again. For the world to allow me to sit in the same room as my mother without the stiff angle of my salute as the yardstick by which she measures my love. It was war that did that. *Mei's* people invading, attacking us. Sev *leaving* and igniting the machine that ended with my home in ruins, the torch line sheltering a tiny heart of wellness in a body that is sick.

Anger is a comfortable refuge. With anger smoldering around me, it's easy to watch Mei's accusations burn to nothing, because she doesn't understand. She only sees things from outside our wall, where scavengers pick one another's bones until there's nothing left. Where there are no people, just monsters.

Monsters. The last memory I have of Sevvy looks like Mei does right now. As if no matter how hard she looks at me, she can't find anything of value. *I don't want you to speak for me, Tai-ge. I want to live in a place where I can speak for myself!*

I turn back to the wall. Clench my eyes shut. Listen to Mei's long, shuddering breaths as I wait for a sleep that won't come. After a long space of trying, I finally let myself sit up. Let my cold feet find the floor and carry me to the base of Mei's bed.

Sinking to the floorboards, I lean back against her mattress, the rusty springs squeaking.

"I told you to leave me alone," Mei growls.

"I know." I swallow, taking a long breath. "You're right that I don't understand. That I should, but I don't. It's my fault what's happening to you now, so, if you'll let me, I want to help. Until the Mantis comes." I look up at her. She's glaring down from her spot on the mattress. "So tell me. Everything you've ever wanted to say to someone like me. Say it all, if it will help."

Silence. The creak of the rope as she shifts. But she doesn't say no.

CHAPTER 21
Howl

I BUCKLE MYSELF INTO THE SEAT NEXT TO SONG Jie, the heli eerily quiet as it flies, almost as if we aren't in the air at all. "You all knew the helis were there this whole time—weapons enough to destroy the whole City. You could have blown up the entire staging area they were using to kidnap your people." All I can remember is Luokai saying something about Port North not being a warlike place. But is there really a group of people who would choose to sit back and watch rather than fight off the gores stealing children from their beds?

Reifa says something to Song Jie, but my interpreter's mouth is glued shut, the hard lines of his jaw dusted over with dirt. It sticks in muddy splashes where blood soaked his clothing. When he finally speaks, it's first to Reifa through gritted teeth, though he doesn't bother to translate for me. Then he says, "It was because of that hangar that the City bothered us at all. Without the hangar, we'd all have been safe."

His tone pulls Reifa closer, the two of them arguing in Port

Northian, Reifa's words swift and hard like the strike of a whip. Song Jie recoils.

"What did she say?"

"She said . . ." Song Jie swallows. "She said if not for these helis, I would have been born in the mountains with the rest of the slavers."

"They saw you as an outsider. But they trusted you to keep the hangar a secret?"

"I started long before the raids started. But yes, the Speakers trusted me. They saw me, not just my family tree. That's their job. Everyone else saw my father, how much he hated the island instead of what I had become. And then, when the bombs came . . . they only saw an enemy." His eyes sink to stare at his bloodstained hands.

My stomach lurches as the heli sweeps sideways. Based on the way Song Jie's hackles are raised, I don't think he's in the right state for prying. Instead, I let my mind race over the story he fed me about the Chairman's son. How they need to find the most likely places the Chairman's son would be.

The places with the highest population.

Song Jie scrubs furiously at the droplets of dried blood splattered across his hands and arms, all down his clothes. This heli, the plastic boxes I helped carry onto it . . . This isn't a mission to find a lost boy. This is a mission to kill everyone who has been killing them. At least, that's what it is for Song Jie.

When we've once again settled into smoother flying, I swallow the acid creeping into my mouth and try again with Song Jie. "You said you were part of a team that maintained the hangar. What were you trying to accomplish?"

He presses his forehead against the heli's thick window to look below us. "The island has known about the hangar since before the war. The techs and pilots weathered the first wave of SS bombs inside the hangar, then came to the island when they heard it was a safe place to shelter." Song Jie's voice is quiet, tense. He's still scratching at the bloodstains splashed across his front, unable to look at them and yet still trying to get them off.

Worried about one man's blood when his true mission must be much grander.

I let my eyes close for a moment, remembering the way he held his gun out like a badge of honor as the Red in the stairwell fell, dead. Was he really the first person Song Jie has ever killed?

The thought feels hollow in my chest, watching someone else wonder if the intimate and awful feeling of someone else's blood on your skin will ever go away. Wishing I could forget the first time it happened to me.

"Are you all right?" I ask quietly.

Song Jie looks up from scrubbing at his shirt, then forces his hands down to his sides. "I'm fine."

"Sure you are." I rearrange my aching shoulder, holding my arm close to my chest. Switch to the subject from before, wondering if that is easier for him than the blood. "The tech in the hangar was beyond what the City has access to. It's how you were able to rig those . . . *things* up on your towers to keep helis away." Beyond technology I saw at the Mountain, too, or if it was there, we lost the ability to make it work. The force of the bombs Gein dropped on the old hangar almost blew us right out of the sky.

"They scavenged everything they could from the hangar without crippling it." Song Jie nods. "The frequency weapons went up within a year of the City helis finding us." He makes a face in that pause, his jaw going hard again.

"And no one from the island ever even thought about using the helis once things with the City got unfriendly?"

"There were always Reds in the area, combing the forest acre by acre looking for it. Whoever walled you up in that city must have had records of the hangar, but no coordinates. We didn't have enough pilots to use all the aircraft, and taking one would have meant Reds taking the rest." He settles back into his seat. "But the Baohujia wouldn't give orders to blow the place up, in case we came up with a way to use them. I lived in those woods making sure the entrance stayed hidden for so long. . . ." He blinks something back, secrets I have no context to even begin guessing at. "The Baohujia brought me and the rest of the team I worked with to the island right before the invasion, to keep us safe."

A plume of smoke marks the sky behind us, though we've left the hangar long behind. "Song Jie, if you don't mind me asking . . ." The question I actually want to ask tastes like fire sparking in my mouth, but it's too bold. You can't ask a person if they're planning to kill thousands with bombs and expect a straight answer. If he thinks I'm going to try to stop him . . . There are too many people I stand to lose if I don't stay on this heli and somehow shape its warpath. "You said the Speakers trusted you. What is it they trusted you to do?"

"To find a way to end this. To stop the City from hurting us anymore." There's a sick kind of weight to the way Song Jie says "us," as if he has to emphasize that he is not from the City, even to me. "Whether it's by finding the boy they stole back from us or . . ." He trails off. But I know the rest of what he meant to say.

Funny. A few years ago, a bomb to the City Center would have sounded like just the right sort of answer to so many of my problems. The thought churns my stomach now, though. A few years ago, I didn't know any Firsts except those who'd defected. Not a single Second or Third, except as a shape at which I should aim true. I didn't know Jiang Gui-hua was a prisoner in a glass box, carving away her days one second at a time, trapped inside her own mind. I didn't know Sev. I didn't believe in hope. I believed in my gun.

The first day I spent in the City, a young man came to bring me dinner, thanking me for dealing with the scum Outsiders. My hand was on my weapon before I could think it through, but I didn't pull it out. I couldn't, not if I wanted to stay undercover, so I listened.

He was no less or more a man than I was. Scared. Worried. And then those horrible words Jiang Gui-hua said to me before she disappeared seemed to lodge in my brain. *Enemies look much more human when you see them up close.*

Reifa turns to look at us again, Port North's quick syllables pouring from her mouth too quick to catch. Song Jie's eyes narrow, and he looks down again. "She says we'll be in the mountains within a few hours. The Chairman has made it clear what is most important to him. If we take Sun Yi-lai back, then we can stop this." He gives a disaffected shrug. "If all those reports about him resurfacing are true."

Song Jie doesn't care one way or another. It's obvious, for him at least, that dragging me along was to get him coordinates for his bombs. Reifa might be silly enough to believe Sun Yi-lai will appear from millions of miles of forest at her call—but then I remember.

The Chairman did want his son. He *had* his son. Me. That's where the reports are coming from. I went to the City to play the part.

I was glad enough to exchange my silly story for the one Reifa gave me so long as it left me alive and headed toward Sev, but now everything seems so much more complex. What if Reifa's story is true and the Chairman didn't stop bombing once I showed up? Didn't stop demanding. Didn't stop *looking*. Did he know the whole time I was a stand-in?

It makes me wonder about the things Sev, Tai-ge, and I over-heard Dr. Yang say to the Chairman while we were hiding in his tent at Dazhai.

You should have known your power was gone the moment you saw the picture.

Is it possible Sun Yi-lai is alive? And if the Chairman knows I'm not his son, then why did he let me pretend I was?

"You never got to finish going over those maps with Gein. He needs coordinates for the places we're most likely to find the boy." Song Jie unbuckles his restraints and walks over the packs, extracting the papers Gein showed me earlier, the unmarked south where everyone I know is sheltering. My enemies. My friends. Family, as much as I can claim Sole after so many years of us taking care of each other. Sev's down there somewhere. It's only June back at the island who is safe from this heli's bombs. "You'd better show us City coordinates. Those and coordinates for any farms or outposts where he could possibly be held."

Reifa sits next to me, her eyes narrow. When she turns to Song Jie and says something, his face goes stony. "She says you don't believe me."

I put my hands up, keeping my face blank. "About what?"

He listens for a moment after translating my response, and Reifa's voice softens as she speaks. She puts a hand on mine, squeezing it. "She says it isn't just you who fears for the people you love. That she's here because the Chairman's son is hers."

"What is that supposed to mean?" I don't like the weight of her hand on mine, but keep myself from pulling it back. When she speaks, I hold her eyes, trying to keep from blinking. Telegraphing trust, the way I know she's trying to do to me.

"She says he was frightened. Brave." Song Jie's voice bottoms out, not a single drop of emotion to spare for Reifa. "Then someone stole him in the darkest part of night. We tracked him into the foothills, but whoever took him had a boat. Moved him up a river too quickly for us to follow. Toward your mountains." Reifa looks out the window, the light painting her dark braids silver. "He's out there somewhere. Away from her when they should be together."

Song Jie sighs. "She says she loved him."

"Are you saying . . . you're Sun Yi-lai's *mother*?" I pull my hand back, not able to keep the skepticism from my voice. The Chairman's wife is dead. Her picture was on his wall, watching me every moment I was there. I found him sitting with it more than once with tears on his cheeks.

"Weren't you listening, slaver?" Reifa sits forward with a huff once Song Jie has translated. "The boy is not her blood. He was hers because she chose to . . . to *love him*."

Suddenly, the way she's looking at me makes sense. She's trying to show me that she means it. That she cares about this kid, as if that will stop all the doubts I must have now that I've seen her bombs destroy a hillside. I have doubts aplenty, but not for the reasons she must think.

I look away from her, hating that she's trying to use me. Trying to pretend her purpose is full of love and warmth, not revenge and destruction. In that moment, my heart seems to beat too fast, as if it will break over the idea of this little boy. The Chairman's son. He was alone just like I was. Like Song Jie, who she can hardly look at. How much better could she have treated the next hostage entrusted to the island?

But, despite my doubts, I find myself wanting to believe for once that she's telling the truth. That there are good people in the world. Sev's mother tried to step in on my behalf. Told me she wanted me when no one else did. But Sev's mother was an aberration on this cold Earth. Reifa's eyes are dewy as she looks down at her hands, and I listen until my ears hurt, willing myself to hear through the translation to her real voice as she speaks.

Song Jie stands up. "She says she'd do anything to find her boy. To make him safe again." He walks toward the captain's chair, unable to sit still through what he must know to be lies.

"That's very . . . sweet."

Reifa gives a decisive nod as if she's the one who ended the conversation instead of Song Jie, then picks up one of the of plastic boxes they loaded onto the aircraft while Song Jie and I were getting the door open. A bomb.

She stows it in the side compartment, then ferries the rest into the little room until they're all ready to drop. I swallow, my throat dry as I look down at the map Song Jie gave me, wondering how I can possibly get to Sev while keeping Reifa, Gein, and Song Jie from killing everyone else. Is there a balance? Balances and acceptable human life cost are what make monsters of men.

Looking up from the papers, I run through the words once, twice, three times before finding the right ones, lies like berries in my mouth, tasting sweet and sour. "There's a little problem with landing close to the City."

Song Jie looks up from the console. "What do you mean?"

"You know there's a new contagious strain of SS, right?" I unbuckle myself from the seat, able to catch a glimpse of the side compartment as I bring the maps to rest next to Gein on the console. It's crammed with rows and rows of padded shelves, the plastic boxes we brought from the hangar only a fraction of what's in there. It sends chills up and down my spine, not even knowing what or how much I'm up against.

Making a fussy show of smoothing out all the folds and wrinkles in the map, I wait until Reifa comes to stand next to the pilot's chair, Gein swiveling toward me to listen as Song Jie translates. "The whole mountain area is choking on SS. City forces are in refugee camps outside the walls, others are looting and killing anything that moves. If you want to find the Chairman's son, you're going to have to trust me."

CHAPTER 22
June

IT TAKES A FEW DAYS' TRAVEL TO GET TO THE river that is supposed to take me and Luokai to the Post. At its mouth, the current tugs at our boat, trying to push us back out into the open ocean. The very idea—even looking into that flat, gray horizon—feels like old meat in my stomach. So. Many. Ways. To. Drown. The wind sits beside me, chilling my hands where they stick out from my cuffs, but I'm glad she's there.

Luokai does something to the engine to make us go faster, his eyes on the white-ridged waves curling around us. He must sense the fear in me, because he breaks the careful silence between us, as if noise is some kind of medicine for distress.

"Tell me how you ended up with my brother." He actually smiles, sort of. Luokai's face is too calm for a smile like Sev's, which was always full of warmth. Or Howl's, half dangerous, half joking. "Or maybe just who you are. I only know you're named June because Howl told me."

My wind twists toward his voice. I like that she seems to like him, even if she isn't always the best judge of people. She chose

Dad, after all. But that was before SS. I've got new family to take care of me now.

The gore chuckles. *Howl and Sev watched Luokai infect you and did nothing. You call that taking care of you?*

"I think you're a qilin in disguise." Luokai's voice comes again. The water is choppier here, and he's speaking so slowly and calmly. He must be able to see the way the waves make me grip the boat's railing, my knuckles white. "My mother used to tell me stories about them. Shy creatures so peaceful they refused to bruise grass by walking over it. You *have* to be lucky to have brought my brother back to me." The Speaker cocks his head, the gesture so Howl-like that I have to blink it away. "You aren't hiding horns, are you?"

I've heard of qilin before, and they didn't sound so peaceful. A story of teeth and claws that made Howl look at Sev to see if she was paying attention, and Sev blush and look up at the stars as if she wasn't. Howl must have heard about the beasts from his mom too—the same person, maybe even the same story, but he and his brother heard two different things. I scan the water, the river lapping up at the sides of the boat like a great tongue straining for a taste. I shrink lower on my bench, staring at my boots.

"If you're a qilin, then maybe we'll have enough good luck to—"

I look up as Luokai's voice squeezes tight in a watery gag, our boat jerking to the side as he does something to the engine. The water begins to push us sideways, the engine coughing into silence. Luokai stills, just like Parhat always did when SS whispered into his ear.

And that's when I realize that Luokai wasn't talking for *me*. He was talking to distract *himself* from a compulsion.

The gore inside me howls. *Nowhere to hide. No way to run. Water*

water WATER caging me in. For a fraction of a second I grope for the length of metal inside my coat, but then reason comes back into my brain, and I lurch toward the poles tethered to the side of the boat, fingers shaking as I untie one.

Luokai jerks out of his SS-induced stupor, slithering down into the covered portion of the boat. He slams into the door just as I shove against the other side and stick the pole through the handle to jam it shut.

The handle rattles, but the pole holds. A wave hits the side of the boat with a hollow *slop*, the water around us choppy, the current pushing us away from the river mouth. The next wave is larger, rocking the boat sideways.

My fingers don't want to let go of the pole keeping Luokai inside the room and me safe on the deck, but the next wave throws me to my knees, almost toppling the boat.

I go on my toes, straining for a look at the boat's controls. If I don't do something, the water will swallow us down. Maybe if I climb over the canopy, start up the engine the way I've seen Luokai do, then point us toward the river—

Only, there's a trapdoor up there that leads into the room Luokai's stuck in. He scratches at the door between me and him just like Parhat used to. *His knife dug into whatever it could reach.* The gore's voice is so loud. *X after x carved into trees, into the ground, into his arms, into you.*

Another wave begins to swell toward us, and my wind strokes through my hair, pushing me toward the canopy. My hands shake as I let go of the pole holding the door shut, sweat slipping across my palm. But I start climbing, pulling myself up onto the metal roof. The wave catches the boat just as I grab hold of the railing above, my fingers screaming as I cling to the metal bars, the boat pitching and swinging wild under my feet. My feet skid across the rusty roof, deep gray Underneath foaming around the boat hungrily as it watches me slide toward it.

Muscles screaming, I pull myself through the railing and hold tight until the worst of the rocking stops. My eyes skip over the trapdoor, propped open, a yellow light leaking from inside. There's a low *scritch-scratch* of fingernails on wood and heavy gasps for air that sneak up through the opening. He must still be trying to open the door.

Keeping my feet quiet, I creep over to the boat's wheel and buttons and dials. Biting my lip, I mimic what I've seen Luokai do, pressing the red button and turning a key while jamming a foot onto the lower pedal.

The boat jerks forward, choking to life.

Grabbing the wheel, I keep my foot on the pedal, trying to straighten our course. It goes slower than two snails, but the boat's nose obeys, turning back toward land. I grip the wheel with white knuckles, keeping us pointed into the river's wide mouth, my heart jolting loose every time the water tries to nip and twist us to the side.

But that's when the scratching down inside the canopy stops. My throat closes, memories of Parhat, Cas, Tian, of *Dad* creeping toward me with SS's ugly snarl. This time there's nowhere to run.

Luokai's footsteps trip toward the ladder. I hold myself perfectly still, my back pressed into the banister so hard I couldn't breathe even if I wanted to. The strip of metal I pulled from the ship's railing below digs into my side, the sharp edge jabbing my ribs through my shirt.

Luokai's head comes into view at the bottom of the ladder, his head jerking this way and that until he looks up.

His eyes find mine.

The gore inside me snarls, but I look away, my whole body

rigid as I pretend to be a piece of scrap metal, an extra rung on the ladder, a breath of wind.

The ladder squeaks as he climbs. One of my hands sneaks into my coat to touch the metal strip. Eyes are one of those things that can make you look threatening. Can remind SS you're there.

"Are you okay? Did I scare you?" Luokai's voice sounds pained, holding more feelings than I've seen from him this whole time on the boat.

The gore hasn't lain back down inside me, though, isn't letting me uncurl my fingers from around the metal strip. My wind pulls at me as I turn away from Luokai, gritting my teeth so hard it's like I'm biting myself. How many days have I been on this boat, eating Luokai's food, burrowed in the blankets he gave me, remembering how much he looks like Howl and talks like Sev? You can never trust a Seph, no matter how nice they are, no matter how sorry they look after doing something bad. You have to run and run and run until they can't find you. It's what Dad should have known all along. Even if it hurt worse than dying when he finally told me to go. It's what Luokai knew, why he let his family go.

But I'm not his family. I'm his hostage. His way to a cure.

Later, when the engine and the sun have gone to bed, I creep into the room where Luokai sleeps. The last few days stretch tight across my chest, the things he's done for me when he didn't have to. He's nice. I know it. And he means well, has kept me firm in this boat every time SS tried to send me into the water. But it's not enough, because it's not just Luokai inside his head.

I pull Luokai's pack out from under the bed and unzip it slowly enough that it doesn't make noise, then take the things I'll need to leave him behind.

CHAPTER 23
Tai-ge

MORNING COMES WITH TWO VICTORIES.

First: two crates of supplies in the square, dropped from the sky as if a pair of cranes brought them in the night. When I check the boxes, the Mantis bottles are on top. Enough to give to Lieutenant Hao for the Thirds he found to get the mask factory running.

Second: Soldiers have arrived at the base of the rice paddies below the City. A concentrated mass of black dots so far below us they look like ants, only with better formations. They'll be here before nightfall, which means Mei and I will be leaving in the confusion.

I haven't told Captain Bai that I'll be disappearing for while. Hope is a fragile thing, especially since it isn't just the captain's good opinion at stake. I have no doubts that if I stretch this man too far, it will end in Mother appearing here in the City, disappointment on her face.

When I sit him down in the cafeteria, I'm not sure what to say at first, running through the words in my mind over and over as if I can somehow change one or another to make myself sound more like Mother. Confident. In control. Having more facts but choosing to keep them to myself.

Instead I say, "I need to go away."

Captain Bai sits forward an inch, though his face doesn't change. "Sir?"

"Not for long, I hope. An issue has arisen that I need to address. Personally." I duck my head, attempting to meet his eyes the way he isn't supposed to meet mine, but for once he keeps his gaze focused on the table between us, brow furrowed.

"I'm confident you will be able to continue with our objectives," I continue. "You have more experience directing men than I do. Now we have some food and Mantis to bargain with for when Lieutenant Hao comes. The soldiers arriving should be bringing more resources as well. You should be all right until I get back."

Captain Bai cocks his head. "The General is very . . . generous."

The question underneath fills me with dread. "She—"

"Excuse me if I interrupt, sir." Captain Bai's cold eyes lift, finally connecting with mine. "But she wouldn't have sent supplies if I'd been the one asking."

My hands clasp together under the table, and it takes all the self-control I own to separate them, let them hang at my sides.

"I've seen quite a bit of forest Outside. I've seen the camps out there and the people inside them." Captain Bai glances toward the window, other buildings too close to see much of the City from here. "And I think this is the first time I've felt as if a commanding officer raised in the City may have seen some of it too."

My mouth hangs open, my tongue dry.

"I don't know what's going on with the General, Major Hong. Or with the Chairman, or with the camps, or with anyone else." He leans in, keeping his eyes locked to mine. "Only that something isn't right. But I believe that you won't let us die."

"I'm going after the cure." I savor the words in my mouth, trying them out. "We went to Kamar for it and were too late. I believe I know where it is."

He nods, as if that makes perfect sense. "I knew they wouldn't have sent us into Kamar for nothing. The invaders took it? And your little assistant is going to lead you to it?"

I open my mouth, not sure what to say. To contradict him when he's right? It's sort of gratifying to realize that Mei's just as bad at being a spy as I am at handling one. "How did you know?"

The captain's hand dips inside his coat and pulls out the knife he used to cut open the growth regulator bag. "I'm a fighter, Captain Hong. A soldier. A leader, when required. Not a man of politics. I don't have to see the whole picture to know there are things happening that don't make sense. That it's not only loose ends that are being left behind these days. If you know more than I do and know how to fix it . . ." He holds the knife out to me. "You be careful with that girl. She's not wearing her bones, but it's not difficult to see she'd like to add yours to them."

Mei's eyes didn't open before I left this morning, shadowed underneath though she managed to sleep after I talked to her. She didn't talk back much, but the sound of my voice seemed to help. Almost like she was pretending I was someone else. Someone she could trust to get her to sleep before another compulsion came. Last night it made me want to know more, to find out who a Menghu trusts. Or, rather, who Mei does. To understand more than her history working on a City farm, which led her to the Menghu. But, in morning's light, it's easier to forget that Mei has a history, likes and dislikes. Fears. Much easier to remember the way the point of her knife jammed against my chest through my coat.

Captain Bai places the knife on the table in front of me when I don't take it. "Protect yourself, Major. We'll have a Mantis lab secured by the time you get back. Maybe we'll be using it to make a cure instead."

I take the knife, the weight of it like a mantle spreading across my shoulders.

When I bring Mei a dose of Mantis, she grabs the pills from my fingers and swallows them dry, though I have a cup of water for her in my other hand.

"Untie me," she says once the pills are down. I kneel next to her, the knots resisting when I pull them apart.

Mei lets out a long sigh when her arms are free, pulling at her bootlaces, though for some reason I don't think the sigh has anything to do with tight shoes. Once one is off, her fingers massage her bare ankle, then pull off her sock, going after the arch and ball of her foot. She has dainty feet, her toenails painted light pink.

"Stop looking at my foot. It hurts," she snaps as she starts unlacing her second boot. "I'm assuming if 'Sevvy' is enough to make you abandon your post here, then you aren't planning just to check in with her. If you try to get her out, is she going to be happy going with you?"

Taken aback by her straightforwardness, it takes me a while to find words. "Is a few weeks of Mantis really enough for you to abandon *your* post and help get her out?" I finally ask.

"Just answer me." Mei pulls off the boot. "Would she trust you?"

"Yes." The lie makes my shoulders go stiff. It might not be a lie. I'd hope that in a secured Menghu facility, Sev would put aside our differences long enough to follow. I just can't make any promises about what would happen once she was Outside, breathing the air that wedged so much space between us in the first place.

"Good." Mei reaches for the cup of water. She downs it then drops it on the floor between us, wiggling her toes out in front of her. "That company of Reds you called in is getting here tonight, right? We'll leave as they come in."

I blink, but refrain from reminding her that I'm the one who is supposed to be in control. "That was what I was thinking."

"I'll meet you down there. You bring the supplies."

I sit back, watching as she massages her other foot, her eyes pinched closed. *Why isn't Mei more conflicted about getting Sevvy away from Dr. Yang?* It makes all of this seem much dirtier, as if I'm somehow now a part of Mei's plot instead of Mei being tied to mine.

Perhaps "dirty" is the wrong word. If Mei is interested in finding the cure—not leaving it in a Menghu-secured base—then what does that mean? I watch her wrinkle and unwrinkle her nose, rubbing her foot.

Of course, there's always the possibility Mei will try to kill me before we're even out of sight of the walls.

"Is that below you, finding your own pack and supplies?" Mei snaps. "Or am I going to have to sneak through all your stupid guards and pack your clean socks myself, *Major* Hong?" The return to my title after so pitifully using my name last night grates for some reason.

"Aren't you supposed to be *my* assistant?" I take the cup and stand, rolling the thin plastic between my hands. "I'll expect you and all my things down at the wall when we open the gates."

It's uncomfortable, watching her hands clench, and for a moment

I'm glad there's nothing within throwing distance. But then her wide mouth closes in a grimace. "Sephs and Reds, that's the worst joke I've ever heard."

Jokes are too hard. They leave everyone wondering what is true and what isn't. I decide not to try it again.

CHAPTER 24
Tai-ge

I WAIT AT THE TOP OF THE STAIRS ON THE WALL, looking down over the rounded peaks that line the horizon like jewels in a crown. A familiar view that leaves me with a pit at the base of my stomach, not sure when I'll see it again.

The soldiers who trudge up the switchbacks and through the gates are too quiet, their eyes jumping from the crackling torches to the empty buildings staring down at them from above. Shouldering my pack and looping the extra one for Mei over my shoulder, I walk through the gate.

"My assistant and I will be over by the Sanatorium inlets," I call to the soldiers standing guard on either side of the polished metal and stone. "So please don't do any reckless shooting in that direction."

"We don't have the bullets, not even for the *unreckless* kind of shooting, sir," one answers. The other keeps her eyes straight forward, the two of them accepting my explanation without thought.

I turn away from them, from the gates, from my home, and walk toward the first switchback, every step on the steep grade jarring. Mei is waiting for me just around the bend. She takes the pack I brought for her and starts down the hill without speaking, somehow able to balance her pack and keep from walk-running down the hill the way I've been doing.

When we first sight trees poking up from the roadside, Mei runs ahead a few steps, pulling something out of her pocket, and in a flash I know she's checking her link. The one I was supposed to steal before I *took care* of her.

Unease blasts open inside me. Is this a trap?

She only glances at the message written in light on the back of her hand before it's back in her pocket. But then, instead of continuing down the road, Mei hops the ditch cut into the ground and is out of sight down the mountainside before I can make it to the ditch's edge.

I pull the gun from my coat and stand at the edge of the crevasse, my heart pounding.

Her head appears over the lip at the edge of the road, brow furrowed in annoyance. "Come on, Tai-ge. Or is it too hard to think and walk at the same time?"

My name. Just by itself. Every time she uses it, it feels different somehow. It was almost a slip the first time, and then a plea. Now it feels as if she's stripping away all my titles, making me into something infinitely smaller. I do feel smaller Outside.

Following Mei down the mountainside is about as undignified as I've ever been. I'm only comforted by the fact that she is also doing a sad half-slide, half-scramble, grabbing scrubby pine branches for balance. When the ground levels out a bit, Mei weaves between rough-barked trunks, looking up and around as if whatever she's after might be perched up high in the branches of a hundred-year-old tree—but apparently not these, because she continues on, confidence in every step.

Even with my senses all on high alert, I don't see the man waiting for us until Mei is running toward him, practically hopping the last few steps to throw her arms around his neck. He catches her around the middle, bulky pack and all, lifting her off the ground and spinning her around once with a theatrical groan. "Mei, my little infected bug of a friend, look at you infiltrating the City and spying and still coming out in one piece!"

The gun's out of my coat again, pointed directly at him even with Mei a barrier between us. The man notices, but dismisses me, taking his time putting Mei down and then throwing an arm over her shoulders before he looks me up and down. His naked face is plastered over with a smile that prickles across me, very similar to my memories of seeing a gore up close for the first time.

"Didn't I teach you to disarm Reds before you take a stroll with them, Mei?" He glances over to her, short enough that their eyes are even, though he's twice as wide.

The hints of good humor I saw all over Mei's face before are all suddenly in full bloom, dimples creasing her cheeks like parentheses around her smile. "This is our guy, Kasim."

Their guy? I don't let the gun waver, holding it steady on the City seal embroidered into Kasim's jerkin, the fabric straining and creasing across his chest and arms the way it wouldn't if it had been made for him. His collar is absent of stars. "Who is this person?" I demand.

"She *just* said my name. Did you not hear . . . ?" Kasim looks from me to Mei with an exaggerated swing. "Did he not hear you? Or is he one of those people who doesn't listen very well when girls are talking?" He snaps his fingers, pointing his attention back to me. "Maybe all those bombs you dropped on your own people compromised your eardrums."

"Mantis for Sevvy, right, Mei?" I have to force my jaw to relax, the muscles threaded through my neck up to my temple aching. "How does he figure into our deal?"

"This is the only way getting to Jiang Sev works." Mei's smile almost hurts now because it seems to be full of sharp teeth. "You want to come, you play by our rules. Starting with giving Kasim your gun."

"How am I supposed to believe you're going to take me to her?" I hold the gun steady, wondering if my soldiers above would hear gunshots and come looking for me. Unlikely.

"Because I told you I would." Mei raises an eyebrow. "What's she worth to you, Tai-ge?"

What's Sevvy worth to me? It's not the girl herself I'm after. At least, that's what I keep telling myself. Sev made it perfectly clear she'd prefer never to see me again. The cure and the end of the war, however, *are* worth my life and everything else I've put on the line to be out here. Taking a long breath doesn't slow down my heart ticking the way I want it to. But I lower my weapon an inch, then let it fall by my side, a sick feeling blooming deep in my chest.

"You *do* have him tamed. Very nice work." Kasim's exaggerated smirk of approval makes me want to hit him. He lets go of Mei and walks toward me, favoring his right leg. His uniform pulls tight over some kind of brace underneath, but that doesn't stop him plucking the gun from my hand and zipping it into his pack.

Mei pulls open my jacket, takes the knife Captain Bai gave to me, and tucks it into her coat pocket. All I can think is that Captain Bai meant for it to be stuck in people like her, and shame wouldn't be enough to describe how he'd feel about a Menghu carrying it.

Kasim gestures up toward the road. "I was tailing the unit that just walked into the City. We should have a clear path down. It'll take us a bit to get to Dr. Yang's setup, and I was only supposed to be on a routine three-day patrol. We'll have to walk fast if we don't want Menghu to shoot us before we even get close." He turns back to me and winks. "Should be fun. Shall we?"

When we set our camp the first night, Kasim doesn't bother with a tent, pulling a hammock from his pack and stringing it high between two trees. He jokes with Mei, the two of them laughing together as he helps set hers just below it. It's very natural, as if all I've seen of Mei is a skeleton's view of who she is, but now that she has someone to talk to, she's turned back to flesh and blood. I guess my question about who she imagined talking to last night to make herself feel better has an answer. Maybe just one of many.

Mei has a life. Friends. I only saw her when she was being a spy and sleeping in an enemy's room. My thoughts scrunch over that, trying to look at it from more angles. She already seemed to know what was going on in the City, if not the particulars. Was happy to leave the moment the opportunity presented itself. Why did she go through the trouble of setting herself up in my room in the first place?

I pull my own hammock out, then look up at theirs swinging merrily above me. Do I set up underneath? In another tree entirely?

I've never tied a hammock in a tree before.

Kasim appears beside me, pulling the hammock out of my

hands. "Were you going to think it up into the tree, or do you just not like asking for help?"

"I'll show him how to do it. Tai-ge's probably scared of heights." Mei hops up and grabs hold of the slippery fabric, but I pull it back and walk toward the same trees where Kasim set up their two hammocks. She glances over at Kasim before following me, standing at the base of the tree as I start to climb.

"You sure you know how to do that?" she calls up. "Won't do us much good if a gore comes along and bites you right out of the tree."

Gnawing on my lip, I gauge the distance from the ground and pull myself up a few more feet, teetering sideways as I try to hold on to the branches and the hammock both at once. Pulling out the webbing meant to tether the hammock to the tree, I loop it around the trunk and start the knot. "So, what's all this about, Mei? A few hours ago, I was the person you hated most in the universe, and now I'm suddenly 'your guy'?"

When she doesn't answer, I look down from the webbing only to find her climbing up the tree opposite where the other side of her hammock is tethered. Once she's up high enough, she holds out her hands for the webbing that needs to go on that side. "Throw it over, Tai-ge."

"Tell me what's going on."

"I'm helping you set up a hammock." She snaps her fingers impatiently. "Throw. Webbing. Now."

I look down at Kasim, far enough away that I'm not sure he can hear us. "He's infected too, Mei."

Mei's hands drop, her mouth one hard line. "Excuse me? You think Menghu have extra germs when it comes to SS and you'll die just from sitting within breathing distance?" She snaps off the end of a branch and chucks it in my direction. I have to duck so it doesn't nick the bottom tubes of my mask. "You were born with that thing on, weren't you? The metal just grew right out of your face while you were still inside General Hong."

"I doesn't *matter* to me that either of you are infected." I toss the webbing to her, perhaps a little more gratified than I should be that she has to dart forward to catch it, making her branch shake. "If he's been patrolling out here by himself, he must have Mantis, right, Mei?"

She turns to set the webbing, then snaps her fingers again, waiting for me to toss the hammock's anchor line so she can link it to the webbing with a carabiner. Once it's set, she scurries down the tree, fast enough it almost looks like she's falling. When I get to the ground, she's already in Kasim's pack, extracting a fire-starter. Kasim's nowhere to be seen.

There are bottles inside the open pocket, siblings to the single one I brought for Mei. Kasim has enough medicine for both of them. "You agreed to take me to Sevvy with the understanding that I give you Mantis." I point to the Mantis bottles. "And you called Kasim here instead. Why didn't you have him shoot me?" I rub a hand across my hair when she doesn't look up. It's too long, spiking up and tangling as I try to pull my fingers through it. "If this is an attempted hostage situation . . ."

Kasim reappears from the trees, brushing his hands across his pants to dislodge bits of bark and dirt, a smile creasing dimples up his cheeks. "Who would pay ransom for *you*?"

Mei gives him a halfhearted push before turning back to me. "We're doing what I said we would. We're going to get Jiang Sev."

"Why?" I ask. Unfortunately, there's more truth to what Kasim says than I'd like to admit. Mother might be distressed at pictures of me with a knife to my throat, but I know exactly what she'd be willing to give up to get me back: nothing. Perhaps not even a tear.

Mei puts her hands up in mock surrender. "If you don't want to come, then walk yourself back up there." She points up the hill toward the paddies and the City above them, then turns away from me, kicking at the icy dirt to clear it of decaying bits of leaves and pine needles for a fire.

The two Menghu fall into a pattern that speaks of being long accustomed to each other. Kasim pulls out bowls, extracts water purifiers from my pack without asking, then sets off into the forest toward the Aihu River's roar. Mei's fire begins to spark, the flames casting an orange glow across her face as she assembles a cooking tripod.

I lower myself onto a fallen log, keeping an eye on Kasim until he disappears into the trees. Mei watches until he's out of sight, then looks at me. "I need your link, Tai-ge."

Sticking a hand into my pocket, I have to wonder if she can read minds, because I was thinking of what I should tell Mother. Maybe it's just another demonstration of me failing to keep my thoughts from scrolling right across my face. "Am I going to need it to call for help?"

Mei stirs the pot in slow circles, and when she looks up at me, her eyes are hard. "We can't afford Red attention, so I need you to give it to me. If Kasim knew you had it, he would have just taken it and *used it*. At least I'm asking nicely. Much as I'd like to drench you in blood and leave you for the gores, you won't be able to help us if you're dead. I'll keep you safe."

She holds my gaze without blinking, and after a moment I nod. It's a bloody mouthful of a promise, but I believe her. If there's a chance, no matter how slim, this could end with the cure in my pocket, I'm willing to go a little farther. So I throw the link down on a rock half submerged in old snow and crush it under my boot. For all that she's suggesting she won't use it to send messages to my mother, I'm not taking any chances.

CHAPTER 25
Tai-ge

WE HEAD SOUTH FOR A FEW DAYS, MOVING QUICKLY. My legs ache, blisters cropping up in the most inconvenient places possible, making every step feel like this is the worst mistake I could have made.

I hear Mei and Kasim whisper at night. Not enough to understand. About Mantis supplies and Menghu patrols and staying under them. Hanging back from the firelight after relieving myself in the trees, I catch Kasim with a link message glowing against his hand, Mei scoffing about how likely it would be that they'd ever see lab results.

"Wait. What lab results? What are they telling you?" I step into the firelight. Kasim's mouth shuts tight and slips the link into his pocket, but Mei keeps her eyes on me.

"Is it Sevvy? Is she . . . cooperating? Or are they . . ." I can't help but swallow the words down. Mother told me they were doing *something* to get her to help. "Please tell me. She's my friend."

"I have such a hard time swallowing that." Kasim's smile quirks. "Sev was too cool to hang out with someone whose collar is buttoned so tight." He shrugs. "I guess brainwashing goes deep in the City. Glad she got out to experience *real* people."

Mei snorts. "Didn't you hear who she was with on the island?"

Rolling his eyes, Kasim gives Mei's shoulder a push. "You don't know what you're talking about."

"You've met her?" I ask, forcing my fists to relax at my sides. "Do you think she's cool enough for your leader to torture her until she gives up whatever it is she's holding back about the cure?"

Mei puts a hand out to stop Kasim responding. "No one's torturing anyone, so far as we know. Dr. Yang isn't doing *anything* with Sev. That's why we're out here." She gestures at the forest around us. "He keeps promising a cure but isn't doing anything to get one. We're all stuck doing whatever he says, just hoping he'll come through."

I lick my lips, shivering in the cold. That sounds exactly like something Sevvy said would happen whether Dr. Yang had the cure or not. "That doesn't make sense. If he wants to finish this whole . . . bonding the City and Mountain together nonsense, he'll need the cure to persuade the Firsts and Seconds to go along with it. And what do you mean, Dr. Yang *not* torturing Sev is why we're out here?"

Kasim clears his throat. "Who has who trained here, Mei?" She shoots him a dirty look, but it's the end of the conversation.

Is it possible the two Menghu in these mountains who aren't aligned with Dr. Yang managed to find me and get me outside the City? Are there *more*? Sevvy told me Menghu believed it was her brain that could cure us, and Mei as good as confirmed it when we were still in the City. Which explains why Menghu came straight for us when I radioed for help back at the island. They dragged

Sev away without so much as a discussion about which prisoner should go where.

Mei asked me how close I was to her. She jumped at the idea of having help to break her out. If Mei believes the cure is locked away in Sev's brain and that Dr. Yang isn't trying very hard to get it, then perhaps there was never much to puzzle out about this trek through the woods in the first place.

What if Mei showing up in my room was always meant to end this way?

Kasim appeared long before he should have been able to, considering the short space between the time I decided to leave and the time we actually left. Maybe I presented Mei with a way to make it seem like it was my idea instead of taking me from my post by force. The realization sits like a stone in my stomach.

Mei turns to look at me as I head toward the tree holding my hammock, but I don't acknowledge her, relishing the feel of cold in my mouth and throat, the rough bark against my hands as I climb.

The cure was in that device. Why is Dr. Yang still telling everyone that Sevvy is the key?

The only option that comes to mind reinforces what I've thought this whole time: Sevvy must understand something about that device that no one else does, and, like Dr. Yang told my mother, she's not cooperating, leaving him with some unfulfilled promises and a sickness he engineered running rampant.

He must be desperate.

The thought makes a heady trill of success run through me. But only for a moment. It doesn't change where I'm sitting: swinging in a tree above two Menghu who intend to use me to get their hands on Sevvy. They'll take her, and with it the cure and every chance my mother has of saving what's left of the City.

Would Mei do that? The chatter between her and Kasim over the days we've been walking makes it sound like she *knows* Sevvy. Could she plan for her death while joking with Kasim and cackling over throwing snow in my hammock?

Mei stands up and goes to Kasim's pack, pulling out a bottle of Mantis, and suddenly all I can think of is the feeling of cement against my back when she slammed me into the factory wall, desperation in her eyes as she begged for her Mantis back. I've seen SS up close now, so maybe I can believe it. Percentages and risks. One girl's life, even if you happen to like her, traded for everyone else's sanity.

When Mei sits back down by the fire, I begin to plan. Whatever happens over the next few days, it isn't going to be Mei and Kasim who end up with Sevvy, the cure, or anything else.

CHAPTER 26
Howl

WE SET DOWN HALF A DAY'S WALK FROM THE
Mountain, far enough away Gein can't push any buttons that will
kill hundreds of people. Also far enough that if there's a high concentration of Sephs still hanging around the Mountain, they'd be
unlikely to see us set down. When Gein releases the door and Song
Jie pushes it out, a gust of icy air wafts into the heli's stale interior.

Pine needles and snow. Cold that freezes inside your nose.
Something in my chest relaxes now that I'm so close to home
again. Every moment by the ocean I felt as if one of my senses had
been stifled. Here the colors tell me how old a tree is, how far we
are from the Mountain. The branches cluster on the correct side
of the trunk, pointing which way is south. I can *see* again.

But with the familiar smells and colors comes a gritting of
teeth, as if there are eyes in the tree watching me. My home, where
the chemical tang of SS in my lungs is more familiar than the
scent of pine. Where gores are desperate, and people are gores—
the sound of wind rustling through the branches makes my skin
itch because it might not be wind at all.

Reifa was less than happy to hear about the Mountain, the Menghu invasion of the City, the refugee camps, the many places fictional Sun Yi-lai could be. Song Jie looks even more grim, as if his job went from plucking a dandelion out of the ground to gathering its seeds one by one where they've blown on the wind.

He shivers when I join him at the door, the two of us peering out into the frigid landscape. "You're sure these Mountain people will help us find where City camps are located? You've had contact with this Dr. Yang person who is in charge?"

"I was spying for them when the invasion forces went to your island. I got hurt just as news came in that SS was spreading. That's why I had to get back." I lean out, anxious to get moving, "They'll have all the information we need on where the Chairman might be." Lie.

Reifa slips in next to me, her eyes narrowed on the open door and the endless expanse of white beyond, listening to Song Jie's translation of what I've said. Sole might know where the Chairman is, I suppose, but it's doubtful. She's the only person who might know where Sev ended up who will also be willing to share that information, though. Also, the only person who can help figure out how to keep this death heli grounded.

Reifa taps my shoulder and holds out her hand as if she wants something. I look at Song Jie.

"She wants the guns. The one you took from her and the one you took from me."

"I dropped both when we were taking off." Lie. I dropped them very conveniently into a compartment at the back of the heli. "Let's go, Song Jie. You and me."

He blinks, and Reifa's scowl is sufficient enough to suspect she knows what I've said.

I point toward footprints marring the snow, though they're at least a week old. "Can you imagine?" I ask, keeping my spot in the doorway. "Hundreds . . . maybe thousands of people, all like your Speakers. Infected, but with no Baohujia to stop them when their brains go funny. Doesn't help that the surge in infections is probably making any soldiers out here even more jumpy than usual." I step down into the snow. "You know we can't take Reifa and Gein with us. Not if we want to live. They're too loud, and they move too slow. You'll have to persuade her."

Not a lie. I don't know what we'll find out there. If Sole is even still right in the head, or if we'll find her an empty husk with bite marks up and down her limbs.

Song Jie's huff of annoyance comes out in a cloud of condensation, a front, because he still won't meet my eyes. But he nods, scrubbing at his shirt again, though the brown stains have sunk in deep.

"It doesn't get easier." I say it quietly because it is a lie and it also isn't.

He meets my eyes, letting his hands fall to his sides. "No? You didn't hesitate."

"I didn't enjoy it. I killed those men to save your life."

"Oh, is that why?" He looks me up and down and can't meet my eyes again, a shudder rippling up his spine. "I know what you are. You can't hide it from me."

I look out into the trees, Song Jie's words crawling under my skin. I didn't kill him when I could have. I didn't kill any of them. I've been trying to do *right*.

Is Song Jie correct? Is that what I am? Born to scare the crap out of people?

It's what I was, and it stained me deep. But I can choose to be something new underneath. I'm not what he says. I'm not like *him* anymore, a vessel of revenge, expecting people to accept me because of my crimes and not despite them. I hope that's not a lie.

I keep hold of his arm as he tries to push past me. "Go through the storage on the heli. If there's equipment on this thing that's going to help us get through this alive, I want it in my pack."

Song Jie blinks, jaw clenching tight as Gein pushes by him into the snow to poke at it suspiciously with one finger. But then he looks out into the frozen woods, the chill turning his cheeks ruddy and his nose flaring as if can smell nothing but urine, gore scat, and a thousand shadows harder than his own. Fear of the unknown: a tool known to break even the bravest of men and women.

Not a lie.

We walk for hours, the stark outline of the Mountain like a monument to the dead against the sky. I take us by way of the river so we can refill our waterskins, but also so I can see what my home has become. It was always dangerous out here, but the prints, the trash, the blood splattered across the snow . . . It's hard to believe there's anyone left breathing. The air is the kind of cold that bites straight through you, an arctic chill before a storm blows in.

Song Jie doesn't notice me in his pack while he's attempting to fill his waterskin. Probably because the rock he was standing on shifted and dumped him onto the thick ice, cracks forming all around him. I don't find any special weapons or tools from the heli. My hands stall when I find the scored knife, the long one I almost killed him with, stashed at the bottom of his pack.

I zip it back inside, wondering when he exchanged it for the one he used to cut vegetables.

The two of us slide between trees, listening, watching, hiding our footprints as best we can, though there's almost no point in the mucked-up snow. Song Jie moves differently than a Menghu. Like he's being hunted rather than hunting. It's him who hears the crying first, though.

Yuan's double axes. I scrub at my ears, wondering how much damage those grenades did to my eardrums, disconcerted to see Song Jie go tense a whole second before I knew why. The sound is high, frightened. A child, or meant to sound like one. June—as she was when Sev and I first met her—flashes through my thoughts, her chicken-bone arms and legs barely enough to hold her up.

"What is that?" Song Jie's voice hisses as he fumbles with the top of his pack, groping inside, then peering through the opening when he doesn't find anything. Weapons don't do much good when they're inaccessible.

I walk toward the sound, Song Jie's following footsteps quiet enough to be acceptable. The sobs seem to needle straight through my heart, as if I'm absorbing them directly from the air.

When I first see the girl responsible for the sound, she just looks like a child in the snow. A confusing picture because there's a man sitting next to her, talking to her. But when I draw close enough to see tears dripping down her face, my eyes find the knife he's stabbing into the snow at her feet over and over as if it's a game to see how close he can come without nicking her.

We're supposed to be hiding. Not calling attention to ourselves. It's almost second nature to look away. File the image with all the other impossible situations I've had to walk by in my life, the girl's ribs sticking out like finger bones in a Menghu's bracelet.

I almost walked past June, so concerned for my own neck and Sev's that I didn't have room to think about hers, but this time I'm running before I even realize, shoving Song Jie to the ground when he tries to pull me back. The man with the knife doesn't look up, folding like grass in the wind when I hit him shoulder-first, hooking my leg behind his knee and flipping him over. His face hits the ground, but the loud *crack* that tells me something broke isn't enough to stop him squirming, bending at awkward angles to get free of my weight. A tremor of pain ripples through my shoulder as I grab hold of the knife in his hand and slam it into the ground.

The man's squirming intensifies, his elbow twisting under my arm. Pain tears through me as he pulls against my injured shoulder, and I have to let go. In less than a breath, he's on top of me, the man's low mutter—something about worms under the ice— like death in my ear. The girl cries out, and everything in me not focused on the man goes on high alert, wondering if she'll be the one to stab me, but no extra attack comes.

Song Jie's worn boots appear at the corner of my vision, the Islander wrenching the man off me by his collar. The two of us pin him to the ground, his fingers so tight around the knife I'm afraid they'll break as I pry them back one by one and then throw the weapon into the trees.

"What is wrong with you?" Song Jie growls, grappling to keep the man down. "We don't have time for this."

I step between the little girl and the knife, her eyes wide as she watches us hold the Seph down until his twitching subsides. "Thank you," the man finally wheezes, as if a switch of humanity inside him has suddenly been turned on. Song Jie lets go, allowing him to roll onto his back. His nose bleeds from each nostril. "We heard someone was down here who could help. Is that you?"

"Help with what, exactly?" I keep the little girl in view. She hasn't moved, though, teardrops frozen on her cheeks.

He doesn't try to sit up, each breath expanding his ribs all the way out and then contracting them in until I'm afraid I'll see his spine. "They said someone here was taking people in."

"The Mountain? They haven't been taking anyone for least a year now. No infected, for sure." I look back to the little girl, her hands still a hopeless snarl at her waist, then dig for some of the dried meat I brought from the heli in my pack. The skin over her wrists seems to be painted straight on bone, and her cheeks are so hollow I could swear her mother was a skeleton. "If you grip too hard, your hands will fuse together like that, you know? You can relax. I'm not going to hurt you." When she doesn't take the meat, I toss it to her, but she lets it fall to the ground, her eyes never leaving me. Clearly food isn't as important as watching for weapons.

"It's new since all the helis started buzzing north and SS started spreading. They said there's someone down there with food, even for infected. You aren't from there?" The man flinches away from me now, suddenly unsure. "What do you want?"

Sole told me over the link that she was trying to help. "You know where they're giving out food?"

The man gives a resigned sort of sigh. I didn't mean to sound threatening. "If you promise not to hurt us—"

"No." The little girl steps between me and the man. "What will you give us if we help you?"

Song Jie stands up, going into the trees to retrieve the knife. I let him go, raising an eyebrow at the little girl. "Seems like you could do with some extra hands to make sure you get to where you're going in one piece."

"He wasn't trying to hurt me!" It's almost a yell, turning Song

Jie back toward us, his eyes wide. The girl is defiant but still frightened. Ashamed that I tackled her father and she did nothing. That she was helpless to do anything. A feeling I know deep in my bones.

"He can't help it!" She's gaining volume. "And if you are going to treat us like slime, then just go away!"

Once I'm sure she's done, I sit back into a crouch, attempting a deferential expression. "I don't think you're slime. I think we're headed in the same direction, and I'm a little worried I'll get lost is all. I've got a bunch of these"—I pick up the dried meat from the ground where she left it—"and a few are flavors I don't like. So I guess we could share some of the gross ones, if that would be an acceptable payment."

Chest thrust out and feet square with her shoulders, the girl's eyes narrow. But then she looks at her father, taking in his bleak smile. "I'm not a child. Don't treat me like one."

Air feels heavy in my chest. I don't remember a time when there was enough room in this world for children. Not when SS turns fathers and mothers into strangers—into *enemies*—at will. Not with Reds and Menghu out here shooting down anyone wearing the wrong color.

Not with me standing right in front of her, her father's blood on my hands. I should have walked away from these two. But the thought makes me sick inside.

"I won't stop you if you want to go," I say. "But if we can help each other get to safety, then why not?"

Song Jie's face is a snarl of indecision when I stand, looking between me and the little girl. But I don't care.

I trust you. Sev said it, but that matters less than the fact that I can feel something *more* inside me than just wanting her trust. I didn't want to shoot those guys on the hangar roof. I don't want to bomb the City until it's nothing but ash. I didn't want to leave this little girl to her father's knife.

I'm not perfect. But everything I've done up until now has been like my feet are on shaky ground, not sure who I'm supposed to be anymore, just that I don't want to be the person I was.

And now the sun almost feels warm on my face. The snow looks bright and white, despite the footprints and mud and murder lurking just out of sight. It's not that I have to make the choice to change. I'm already different.

CHAPTER 27
Tai-ge

THE AIR TURNS UNBEARABLY COLD. MY MASK'S filters become so frosted over I'm afraid they'll clog up and suffocate me. By the time we stop for the night to make a fire, I'm practically in tears, missing the heating system in my room at the orphanage. I sit, warming my hands, and it isn't until my fingers are tingling with warmth that I realize something has changed.

Mei's sitting next to me, feeding branches into the fire, the two of us quiet. Kasim is gone.

"We're here, then?" I ask.

"Yes, we're here. You and Kasim are going in tomorrow."

I flex my fingers in front of the flames one more time before tearing myself away from the warmth to take out our cooking pot and tripod. Of course, the two heaviest things we're carrying ended up in *my* pack. As I pull out the collapsible tripod, my sleeve snags on the front pocket of my pack, dragging it open.

The bottle of Mantis I stole from the City sits inside the open pocket, cushioned by my half-full waterskin. I pocket the bottle of pills and the waterskin, then carry the pot and tripod over to the fire and set them up. Mei dumps a ration pack into the pot and adds some water, stirring it around impatiently, though it will be a while before the fire is hot enough to cook anything.

"Here." I hold out the Mantis and the waterskin, already looking up into the trees for a good spot to place my hammock. When she doesn't take it, I look back down, give the pills a shake. "Did you already take some?"

"No." She takes the bottle, turning it over in her hands. "Are you in charge of monitoring my medication now?"

"I was just trying to be nice."

"Why?"

"Because I'm a nice person." I shrug, throwing the waterskin back into my pack when she doesn't take it. I unroll my hammock, then go back to looking up in the trees for a likely spot to set the ropes, already shivering at the idea of sleeping suspended in the wind.

"Are you?" Mei asks, and when I look at her, her eyebrow is cocked. "I'm not sure I see it."

"Yeah, you're probably right." I think of the way seeing Mei with Kasim made me realize how little of her personality I'd seen before. "You haven't had a chance to see very much of me, though."

Mei snickers.

My eyes come back down. "What?"

"I just didn't realize you wanted me to see *more* of you." She puts her hands up, looking me up and down before pointing at my tightly laced boots. "Are we starting with ankles?"

"That's not what I . . ." But all I can see is that smile of hers. The same one from the first day I saw her outside the heli—too pointed for her to be the good little Second Mother would have

invited home for tea. "Right. Where should we put our hammocks?" The freezing cold isn't the only thing prickling through
me. I almost wish I could double up with one of the Menghu just
for shared warmth, but Kasim would probably suffocate me on
purpose, and Mei . . .

Mei is still snickering and would take it the wrong way. And
now I'm stuck with the idea of me and Mei tangled up in a hammock. I only just keep from rolling my eyes at myself, managing
to set my thoughts back on the focused path where they belong.
Mei is pretty, and if I were a normal person, maybe I'd think more
about it. But I'm not a normal person, whatever that means, and
neither is she.

"Don't worry, Major Hong." Mei stands up, her freckles lost
in the twilight. Bending down, she brushes against me to dig into
her pack. I look away, certain my cheeks are too red to blame it
on cold. "You might look nice enough on the outside, but I don't
need to see any more to know *exactly* what you are on the inside."

The heat bleeds from my cheeks fast enough when Mei pulls
out Captain Bai's knife. Next comes some kind of root, which
she begins to violently peel, the skins going into the fire under
our cooking pot. "Kasim'll be a while, so if you're going to come
up with something other than stuttering, now's the time to fight
back." She waits for a second, and I shrug, not sure if I'm supposed to make uncomfortable remarks about her now. Like an
argument, but with more leering? No thanks.

She rolls her eyes when nothing comes out of me but a fog
of frozen air. "He was supposed to report more than a week ago,
but we've got a story that should check out. And it's Guonian
tomorrow, so there's a good chance any patrols out here will be
distracted. Everyone will be wishing they were inside."

Guonian? Thoughts of warm fire and sticky cakes steam inside my head. Of my parents, my grandparents before they passed on, all of us tucked together at home as if nothing existed but us. A wave of homesickness washes over me at being out here in the snow with no one but Mei for company when I should be safe inside with the people I love most. The moon is dark overhead. I should have remembered.

"Kasim will let me know when to . . ." Mei looks up from skinning the root, her hands going still when she sees my face. "What's wrong?"

"Nothing."

"Never been away from home for holidays, Major?" She hefts the knife, brandishing it like the weapon it is. "Or were you wishing for a fancier meal?"

Her words are sneer-free, though, as if she's actually asking. "I'm fine," I respond, keeping my voice flat. Life and reality are what they are, and showing discontent only reflects poorly on the one with no self-control.

I think that might be a quote from one of Chairman Sun's pamphlets. The idea that it's a lying murderer's words that occur to me first makes me feel sick to my stomach. "When we're done here, I'd really appreciate having that knife back. Captain Bai loaned it to me."

Mei wipes it clean and stuffs it in her pocket. "I don't think he'll—" Her voice cuts off abruptly as she swivels toward the trees into which Kasim disappeared.

"What?" I ask. "Did you hear someth—"

"Shut up. We've got to move." She hisses, kicks dirt over the fire, and then, using her coat to protect her hand, she pulls the pot and the cooking tripod from over the still-flaring wood and hides them behind a rock. Taking my cue from her, I stomp at the flames until they're dead, a note of panic singing high inside me.

She grabs her pack, gesturing for me to take mine, so I throw my pack's straps over my shoulders and then pick up Kasim's, hugging his things to my chest as I follow her into the darkness. Wind whistles between tree trunks, icing my cheeks and forehead, but it isn't long before I see the glow of another fire in the trees.

We leave the packs behind a boulder—Mei runs an eye over Kasim's things as if by touching them I've somehow violated something sacred—then head toward the fire. Once we're closer, I make out three shapes huddled around the fire, a bird roasting over the flames.

Mei puts a hand out to stop me, her gloved palm against my ribs. I pull away, tucking my coat closer around me. "I thought we were staying away from Menghu patrols," I whisper.

"You think *they* are Menghu?" She raises an eyebrow as she looks back at me.

I squint into the darkness, and my eyes find a falcon-and-beaker insignia etched into the closest soldier's coat. They're Seconds. Like me.

CHAPTER 28
June

THE BOAT'S ENGINE WHINES AS WE POWER AGAINST the current, the river's shore dressed in six feet of ice on either side. The air feels frozen around me, like we're stuck tight in a chunk of solid ice.

After cold like this, snow will come.

When I first see the signs I'm looking for—the cairns at the side of the river that point people toward the Post—I know it's almost time. I run through my plan one more time, trying to look at it from other angles so I can find the ways it could be pulled to pieces. But then I can't think, because the boat is whining in the current, white rapids visible ahead.

"I thought we had a few more miles. . . ." Luokai goes silent— his replacement for curses. He drops the anchor and hops down to the deck, pulling one of the poles free from their lashings to push us away from an ice-crusted rock. The current shoves hard against us, grabbing for Luokai's pole, the water foaming around us like a sick gore's mouth.

He doesn't notice when I pull out the pack I've had under the bench. I'm sure he knew it was there, but even if he isn't as horrible as I'd first thought, he's still stupid, like most people. And now he's wrestling with the pole, attempting to right the boat instead of watching me.

I drag out the extra pair of pants I stole from Luokai's pack.

The most important thing if you fall into the water is to stay afloat. Dad's voice—the one I made up for him after he learned to use his hands to talk—creeps into my head. I remember that day clearer than I've ever remembered anything. *I'll show you how to tie a float.*

Using the long strip of metal I tore from the boat's railing, I fold the waistband of Luokai's pants over it once, then twice more, bending the metal in to hold the sharp folds in place. I only manage to get part of the knot done in the first pant leg before the words come back.

It's silly. Aunt Tian's voice this time. *She's not going to fall out. We have to go north before the farm's guards realize we were here, and if you delay the boat any longer—*

Dad pointed toward the shore, telling Aunt Tian to go away, but nicely. Because Dad was nice. Aunt Tian even smiled back before she left us standing there, ankle-deep in the river, the sandy bottom rough against the soles of my feet.

Then he held up a spare pair of pants.

The deck lurches under me, the boat's nose tipping sideways toward the rock, water splashing up over the railing like memories and fear. I finish tying the knot with a jerk, then put the open cuff of the other leg up to my mouth, blowing into it until the fabric balloons into a float.

Dad. We'd almost capsized on our way down south, and he couldn't stop thinking about it. That I'd fall in and drown. It was almost like a compulsion. We'd traveled on boats so many times before, and I hadn't drowned once. But this time he couldn't stop worrying, so he wanted to teach me what to do if I fell into the water.

SS takes your worry and does awful things with it.

The second my dad became a gore that day, I knew. But I wasn't fast enough to escape.

It isn't until I shrug out of my jacket and wrench my shoes from my feet that Luokai notices something has changed. I pull the second pole from its tether and jam it into the rocks, forcing the boat to veer toward the frozen shore. Looping the boots' ties together, I twist them around my coat and heave them toward the trees. The weight of my boots carries the bundle skittering over the ice, catching on a rock on the shore. Next, I throw the pack, but it doesn't quite make it onto the ice, the river sucking it greedily underneath. My stomach clenches tight.

Luokai uses his pole to push us back from the ice. "What are you doing?" he yells over the rumble of rushing water. "Help me! Bring the pole over here!"

Air bites through my sweater, twisting knots in my hair. My knees wobble, but I climb up on the bench and crouch, looking into the swirling water. The boat lurches, and I can feel Luokai panicking as he tries to divide his focus between me and keeping the boat back from the rocks.

The water slurps at the boat just below my feet.

That's where you were supposed to stay. It's the gore voice. It's what Dad turned into, even if he didn't ever want to. Even though I know he wouldn't say the stuff the gore says to me. Dad didn't want me to die, didn't want me to hurt. I know he loved me every second. How do you love someone back when they can't always remember they aren't a gore, and sometimes the gore is hungry?

You would have been safe underneath the water. If you jump now, you'd be safe just like I wanted you to be.

I pull the float around my neck so the waist will cushion my head, the two legs tight under my arms and around my chest, the one that's still open to add air twisted shut in my fist. Feetfirst, downstream. Even without the pack, the Post's trader caves are close, and I can start a fire. Go to the treehouses tomorrow. Cai Ayi'll have news. She has my kids. She might even know what happened to Sev and Howl.

Looking down at the water squeezes my lungs tight.

I can still feel my dad's hands on my shoulders, fingers bruising as they shove me down, water filling my lungs. *Jump.* The gore sneers. *We both know you were supposed to drown that day. If he'd really loved you, he would have been able to stop himself. If Sev and Howl really loved you, they would have found a way to take you with them.*

But then the words spark, not the gore anymore but SS catching onto my thoughts and setting them aflame.

JUMP, it says.

I don't want to anymore. My boots slide toward the edge, and even as I shake, I put one leg over the rail.

"June!"

JUMP. The boat gives a violent rock to one side just as my other leg drags after the first, the water swirling and crying for me to come in. *JUMP.* I clench my eyes shut, screaming for my body to stop, but then there's nothing but the silence of being airborne. Of falling. And then water surrounds me and drags me down, down, down.

CHAPTER 29
Sev

A DOOR OPENS, THE HINGES CREAKING WITH AGE. The sound sticks in my ears as if I could somehow catch hold of it, use it to reenter my body. Pull myself back on like a set of gloves so I can see who is breathing so quietly in my room.

Something drags across a hard floor. A chair, perhaps, legs screeching as they slide across the cement. The person settles next to me instead of by the far wall as they usually do. The creak of wooden joints adjusting, a sigh of relief at sitting down.

Shouldn't you be sending orders to Dazhai? Dr. Yang asked that day, the first time I noticed my strange visitor. And suddenly, I know exactly who it must be.

"I liked your mother very much, Jiang Sev." The same voice I've heard puncture the most secluded and secret places I hid in the City, whether I wanted it there or not. It was always going to be his voice.

Chairman Sun.

"We were good friends, even after we both married, had children." He pauses. "It was terrible the day she realized that the bombs falling from the sky were supposed to come from Kamar. She believed it along with everyone else, that her own family had reneged on our treaty, not even troubling themselves to extract her first. She was heartbroken. It broke *my* heart to watch her. That I couldn't tell her the truth."

He pauses. "She came when the last exchange died. Couldn't have been more than ten years old. I didn't really understand how difficult that must have been for her, how she cried at first. Not until I had to give Yi-lai to the island."

A treaty between our city and Port North. Leaders sent their children to be raised by their enemies. It kept bombs from falling on either place, until the City began bombing itself to keep its citizens in check and blamed it on Port North. Until Jiang Gui-hua, my mother, found a cure to SS, the cancer that kept people beholden to the Chairman and his Mantis stores.

The Chairman sighs, his breath itching when it brushes my cheek. He's not wearing a gas mask because he was cured long before Mother came along.

"Sending my boy away was like killing something inside of me." The Chairman sighs. "I was so angry. My wife got sick soon after Kamar took him, and without her little boy . . ." He trails off. "I knew that if I had children, one would go to the island, but I didn't truly understand what I was giving up until it was too late. My little Yi-lai was so happy and smart. . . . He was talking long before the other children his age, you know. Asked to wear stars before he even knew what they meant. The perfect patriot." Another pause. "Duty is much heavier than you could ever imagine."

My mind screams at me to sit up, to run from the man who commanded the kidnapping of so many. Who dropped bombs on his own people to force them to stay smashed beneath his thumb. Who hid

in his castle at the top of our City, hatching ways to pull the noose
tighter around us. The man who ordered SS injected in my veins and
sent my mother running to find a cure. My hands want to clench, to
rise up and grab hold of him. But they lie next to me, dead.

"When we found out Jiang Gui-hua was trying to save us from
SS, we tried to reason with her first. Threats came next. Your
sudden contraction of the disease—oh, that was an unfortunate
necessity. But then Gui-hua disappeared, and I knew she'd gone
back to the island. So it was only fair that my Yi-lai should come
home too. But when I demanded my son's return, Kamar wouldn't
give him to me. You see, Kamar hadn't spent their years building
walls or medicines or aircraft or guns. They built farms. Factories.
They trusted that diplomats would keep them safe. And without
their hostage, they didn't believe that we would leave them alone.

"So when Gui-hua came back, I put her up on the Arch," he
continues. "Told Kamar that if they didn't produce my son, I
would take every single one of their farms, every son I could lay
hands on, every daughter walking free. Still, they refused to let my
Yi-lai come home."

And he'd made good on those threats. Stealing every Port
Northian he could find, using them to make the City flourish. To
pick our pears, harvest our rice, and mine our metal. To provide
nightmares for our children and bodies to string up on our walls.
But he'd gotten Yi-lai back.

Sort of. He'd gotten Howl. Did he realize the difference?

"Dr. Yang was the one pulling the strings." The Chairman
sighs. "If only I'd realized . . . He was assigned to a farm outside
the City as a punishment after he tried to interfere with the Circle,
saying he knew a better way to do things. That must have been how
he got involved with the Mountain in the first place. How he got

Gui-hua to go there. He had the oddest ideas about who needed power and how to keep it. Didn't listen to instruction. But sending him away meant no one was watching him closely. In charge of all the Second medics in the southern garrison, with access to the City, access to Outside . . . He even asked for his First marks to be removed, to serve the City like the nuns, putting the good of the City before his own status. He came to me saying he'd found my son, that Kamar had told the truth about sending him back to us, only he'd been kidnapped by our true enemies at the Mountain. He extracted Yi-lai, brought him home . . . but I knew the moment I saw Howl that he wasn't my son."

He stops, silence lost in the drip of liquids and the slow rush of cold as the Chairman breathes on me. "I . . . wanted my son. I wanted *a* son," he whispers. "I watched him, made sure he couldn't hurt anyone or have any information that would undermine the City. I think I even loved him."

My heart hurts. He knew Howl was a spy, but let him stay? Because he was lonely?

"Having Howl there helped. But it made me all the more consumed with finding my real son." The Chairman stops, the sheet at my side twitching as if he's fiddling with the starchy fabric. "Dr. Yang is going to kill Howl when they find him, you know. He's crossed too many lines, made too many important people angry on both sides. It would be appropriate, no? To use a traitor to all sides in an attempt to bring everyone at war together?"

The quiet anger in my head shatters, the pieces burning all around me. Dr. Yang is going to *kill Howl*? Everything inside me writhes, begging my arms to move, my eyes to open. Howl has almost died too many times because of me. I can't . . . I *won't* let Dr. Yang hurt him.

But then I go back over the Chairman's words. *When* they find him. So, Howl isn't here? Mother sighs in relief in the back of my head.

"I'll be back to see you. I think you and I may be able to help each other."

Help each other how? *Why would I ever help you?* I want to scream. And though I know internal screams don't do much to hold people's attention, I'm infuriated when the chair scrapes the floor. The door squeaks. And then . . . silence.

He's left me with no way to answer back. I didn't believe there was a way for me to be less heard back when I lived in the City. I didn't realize how low you could sink.

CHAPTER 30
Howl

WE DON'T GET ANYWHERE NEAR THE MOUNTAIN'S eastern entrance before Menghu find us. The dirt on their clothes and faces is familiar, but the cocky arrogance that all my Menghu days carried seems to have siphoned away, leaving nothing but bare-toothed desperation.

"Howl?" one asks, his weapon only a finger away from being drawn. He looks around at the group. "Sole said to keep a lookout for you."

"She's still alive." A knot in my chest slips free. "Thank Yuan."

"I don't think Yuan had much to do with it." The other Menghu looks at me askance, adjusting her mask as if living in the City left me with a smell strong enough to filter through. Or perhaps she's heard of my reputation from before I left. "Who's this with you?"

"Friends." I stand with Song Jie, the man and his little girl a step behind us.

The fact that they aren't shooting first gives me enough hope to follow them to the disguised entrance, though I keep my eyes open. Our guides aren't Menghu I recognize, even if they know my face. All of them are armed, and at least one is an experienced knife fighter, based on the way he holds himself and his scars. What has Sole been doing down here?

We move through three levels of barricades, then into a hallway that's been cut down the middle so half is partitioned into tiny rooms. The air buzzes with electricity, and the hairs on my neck stand on end.

More people come to escort us, not all of them wearing Menghu green. Song Jie hovers close beside me, his eyes moving from the guns to take in the uniforms, the cement walls, and the little cubicle blocks. "What is this?" he asks.

"I don't know. They're all still alive, though, and that's promising." It means food. Water. Maybe even Mantis, like Sole was hoping for when she stayed here to help the people Dr. Yang left behind, the people taken down by the contagious strain of SS he created. A hope that thins when our guides leave their masks firmly in place. One of the Menghu who brought us in whisks a temporary door open into one of the little cubicles, heavy machinery staring out at us from inside like a promise of torture.

Levels machines. I look over at the man gripping his daughter's hand. After so many days under the sky, the ceiling feels low, the air stale as if it's been filtered over and over.

"Howl?" A jolt of adrenaline floods through me at the sound of my name combined with the figure rocketing in my direction from the far end of the hall, her face weighed down by a mask. "Is it really you?"

Song Jie darts behind me as I fall instinctively into a defensive stance, but when I catch sight of the girl's eyes—ice blue and staring without a single blink—I'm running toward her before I can think. Menghu start yelling behind me, hands grabbing at my clothes until Sole shouts them down.

Sole wraps her arms tight around me, a grunt of pain escaping my throat when her mask's filters bump my still-healing collarbone. "How did you get here?" When she pulls back to look at me, she holds eye contact, something I haven't seen from Sole in years. A tear pools at the corner of her eye, streaking down to gum up the edge of her mask. "Your messages were weird, and then you stopped *answering*, and I was so worried—"

"Well, here I am." I return the hug, the feel of someone I know and love like a balm for months of burns. Even my breaths come easier because Sole knows who I am. She knows where I came from.

She understands.

I let go of her, surprised when she meets my eyes again. "They took Sev. I need you to tell me where."

Sole's eyebrows scrunch as she looks over our bedraggled group, and Song Jie almost seems to shrink in response, as if an exit within running distance would be comforting. I know Sole doesn't mean anything by it, but it does look as if she's smelling something particularly pungent—which is probably fair, given how long it's been since we've bathed. "Let's get everyone through first. We have to test for infection. Contagion."

"I can't stay. Those last messages I sent you weren't the cure, right? They took Sev because she must have found the real one—"

Hand on my arm, Sole stops me. "The anti–Suspended Sleep serum? Those weren't the last messages you sent, were they?"

My thoughts flash back to Luokai, wondering what he's been saying under the disguise of my name. "It's a long story. But yes, they were." I glance toward Song Jie and the others, nodding for them to follow the Menghu into the cubicles. "But before I tell you any of it, I need your help. I've got a little bit of a situation on my hands."

"They have bombs that they want to use to get rid of everyone up in the mountains? And you led them *here*?" We pass an air lock to get to Sole's room, and she forces me to stand just outside her door while she fits me with a battered sling, claiming the light's better in the hall. When it's on properly, I let my arm rest and release a sigh of relief I hadn't realized was clenched inside me.

"The pilot and the woman in charge of their operation didn't know where Song Jie and I were headed. They won't be able to follow us here. Without coordinates for camps or the City, the most they could do is fly randomly and hope they find something to bomb, and I don't think there's fuel enough for that." I hope I'm right.

Sole sighs, the paper pasted to her doorway crackling as she leans against it. It's red, with handwritten characters that make up a Guonian poem: *Spring brings hope; the land becomes warm. The beginning of peace; the people become cheerful. Peace is coming.* "We can put the man you brought with you in quarantine even if his SS levels are normal. Then we can go out and collect the other two. Get rid of the weapons somehow."

I blink, immediately banishing the thoughts that occurred to me first: If *we* had control of the heli, bombs could be the exact kind of leverage we need to get Sev out. Dr. Yang couldn't refuse us once he's seen the explosions that thing could make of his army. But Sole's right. That kind of firepower would only complicate the situation.

"Did you know that Guonian is tomorrow? I can't see any sort of future." Sole looks up at me, her eyes wide. "At least you're here. We're inside, hiding from that old monster story like we're supposed to be."

I bite my lip, looking away from the decorations, because this wasn't supposed to be how I spent this night. There are real monsters waiting to pounce outside, and red paper on Sole's door isn't going to scare them away. "Tell me what you know about Sev. Why did they capture her, too? Dr. Yang took the device with the cure. He shouldn't have needed her anymore."

Sole opens the door to her room and sheds her shoes just inside, waiting until I follow suit and sink onto the sleeping pad pushed up against one wall. Her quarters are obviously converted storage space: rough gray cement walls, an elevated lab station with vials and chemicals, a sink, and an exam table that barely fits against the far wall. A beat-up wooden desk. A single blanket on her sleeping pad. It feels cramped and gray, like bad-tasting medicine.

"He needs her for the same reason he always has."

"The same . . . You mean the data on the device? Dr. Yang needs her to help decode—"

"There was no more than the notes you sent me. It was just the anti–Suspended Sleep serum, though I don't know how effective it is considering it killed Jiang Gui-hua when Jiang Sev gave it to her." Sole glances toward her lab table, test tubes set out, their contents waiting for her. "We've made some, though we haven't had the chance to test it."

"Didn't Jiang Gui-hua die because she'd been under for so long?"

Sole shrugs. "That's one possibility."

My mind rewinds what she's saying, trying to figure out what

she means. "The notes . . . Sev's not cooperating, then? She's supposed to be helping to develop the cure, but—"

"No, Howl. My guess is there wasn't anything on the device at
all. There have been no trials. No new tests. No cure."

No cure. The words don't seem to fit inside my head. "We all
knew if Dr. Yang got his hands on a cure, he wasn't going to just
give it out. Maybe he's got it in a syringe and is just waiting until
everyone is desperate enough—"

"I've got people reporting to me from inside the southern
garrison. That's where he's based right now." Sole unfolds her
legs, looking at her bare toes. "Dr. Yang put Sev to Sleep within
hours of bringing her back from the island."

The words fall like rocks in my stomach, my hands ball-
ing into fists so tight I can't let go. Ready to punch something.
"She's *Asleep*?"

"Our best guess is that he's collecting everyone he can who
has been cured. There are Firsts, apparently—the Chairman
included—who are all locked down in the garrison. Dr. Yang must
have gone back to comparing scans and hoping he'll be able to
spot something. That's what it has come to."

"That isn't going to work." My teeth grit together so hard I can
hardly say the words. "If it were a viable path, he would have taken
it years ago using Firsts in the City instead of having to manipulate
me and Sev into waking up Jiang Gui-hua. You know if that were a
possible avenue, then we would have had a cure years ago."

"I know he wasn't willing to cut into anything he couldn't
replace." Sole's eyes creep up and she's twitching again, her fingers
making knots of her white Yizhi coat. "We have to find a solution. Here." She gestures to the door, this underground bunker
she seems to have cobbled together out of nothing. "We've only

survived this long because we managed to secure a hall over to the deep storage facilities. Old stuff, but there's a reserve of Mantis. Ration packs. Water. Dr. Yang meant to come back for it, but my people are passing information that things are too dangerous here, so he's stayed away."

"If there's no cure, then . . ." *I see no future*, she said. Sole pulls off her mask, her face blank as she blinks through whatever thoughts are torturing her now. "It's just a matter of time before we're all dead." I wait until she looks at me to continue. "SS has spread too quickly. We won't be able to keep any kind of food production, security, anything up. Every time a soldier or a worker takes off their mask to eat, they're at risk of exposure. It'll be like the end of the Influenza War all over again."

But worse. With no way to escape. No safe havens, no walled City to keep out infection because SS can jump from person to person now. All it would take is one infection, one person who doesn't know what's hiding inside their lungs, to bring down a whole safe area. If there isn't enough Mantis to go around—and how could there be? With instances of infection rising exponentially every day—soon there won't be a world to save anymore.

"More people come here every day," Sole murmurs, her eyes crimping shut. "We're going to run out of supplies soon."

My skin feels tight. SS spread through the Mountain quickly, probably to most everyone who wasn't a part of the invasion force. Teachers, cooks, children still in school. Foragers, bureaucrats. Why would anyone stay in the maze of hallways upstairs rather than escape to open space where they can run?

Sole is still talking. "We've had some success gassing the hallways and using masks to pass through safely, so we've been able to get access to medicine and equipment from the labs, but it's getting more dangerous. When we can, we bring the people we knock out down here, and they're always happy to find Mantis pills next to them when they wake up." She smiles a little. "We've had to bar the doors, though, or we'd have a flood—way too many infected to treat. As it is, we're running out of Mantis fast. We're going to have to do something."

"You're gassing people and dragging them down here?" I squint at the gray ceiling. What can we do? If there was nothing to find at Port North, no cure stashed away somewhere for Sev to discover, then does that mean we're out of options? I close my eyes, my head hurting. "I should probably tell you it was Luokai who had the link. Um . . . Seth. We used to call him Seth when he was here."

Sole's brow furrows. "What?"

"My brother. He's the one who's been writing to you. So if my messages suddenly sounded like I fell desperately in love with you, now you know why." I try not to enjoy how her mouth hangs open, because even if Luokai turned into a transactional jerk, I know how long Sole's been pining after him. "Unless you were hoping I'd come home and my cradle is open to robbing?"

Sole's nose wrinkles, her mouth still open.

"Didn't think so." I smile, giving her shoulder a pat. "I have to go. I've been to the garrison with the Chairman—remember when I sent all those plans over for an attack? I don't know if General Root ever actually tried—"

"No." Sole's cheek twitches as she slips a hand into her pocket, her eyes glazed. "You . . . you can't go anywhere. We can't give up."

"I'm not giving up; I'm going after Sev."

She pulls out her link and stares at it against her palm, looking so closely I'm afraid she'll nose it right off her hand. "You don't really expect me to believe that, do you?"

"Why wouldn't you believe that I want to help Sev?"

"Howl . . ." Her lips press together hard, her eyes blinking too fast. "You've come a long way. When you first got back from the City, I couldn't believe how much you'd changed. But we both know what you do when things get sticky for you."

I stand up. *"What?"*

She startles back, her hand clenched around the link, flickers of light playing across the back of her hand. "You show up here in one piece . . . mostly, anyway." Her eyes touch my still-healing collarbone, marks from the stitches still scabby and red. "And Sev's right where we all worried she was going to end up: Dr. Yang's lab. All that talk about saving her before, running after her—"

"You think *I* did that?" It's plain from her face that she does. "Sole, I'm not the one who handed her over. I couldn't . . ." I don't know what to say. Sole is . . . technically right. She *would* have been right five years ago. But there's no *time* to convince her that things have changed.

She sighs. "I have a team set up to go in after Sev tomorrow. Kasim. Another Menghu you might not know named Mei. In any case, there's a Red company moving between us and the garrison from Dazhai. You wouldn't have gotten far even if you were telling the truth about wanting to go." She reaches up from where she's sitting on her sleeping pad to touch my arm. "You know I can't let you run away again, though, don't you, Howl?" Sole's dead skeleton impression of a voice again. "I'm not a research scientist, but there are Firsts who ended up here, people who will be able to at least try—" A tear streaks her cheek as she swallows down what she means to say. "We need the cure, and that means we need as much information as we can get. The Firsts here are guessing Dr. Yang is too worried he'll mess up to do anything. That's why he hasn't opened any of you up. But with them here to study you and Sev, we could stand a chance—"

"You know that isn't going to work!" I jerk my arm away from her, taking a step toward the door. "You're going to hand me over to some *Firsts*—?"

"Is that the only thing you can think of? Yourself?" She swallows, her fingers pulling at one another as if she can't sit still. "There are children out there, Howl. Fathers and mothers, families who are dying. Families who are *killing* one another. It's either try or give up, and it isn't in me to let all the people here die, even if our chances aren't wonderful." Sole's eyes are so sad. "I love you. You know that, Howl. I don't *want* to do this. But maybe it's a good thing. An opportunity to make up for . . . everything."

"So you just get to play nurse, while I have to *die* to make up for the things we *both* did?" Sole looks taken aback, but I just shake my head in disgust. "You got a second chance to change. Where's mine?"

I wrench the door open, rocketing into the hall, but they're waiting outside. Menghu, their ragged arms open and ready for me.

CHAPTER 31
June

THE SHOCK OF *COLD* TEARS THROUGH ME, WATER churning like a foaming mouth as it attempts to swallow me down, but my float keeps my head above water. I get one last look at Luokai as the water pulls me downstream, the pole in his hands jabbing toward me as if he can save me.

Dad's instructions ring like gunfire in my head, but they're in *my* voice now, the gore cringing in the back of my head after SS took his words and twisted me around them: *Keep your feet pointed downstream. Float, don't fight. Backside up so it doesn't catch on anything. Chin tilted down so you can see.* I angle for the shore, the current swishing me close to one of the slick boulders. I catch hold of it with my foot and end up pinned against the rock by the current, the stone surface so smooth it's only the icicles and frost that give me handholds to get up on top of it. Behind me I hear a gut-churning crack that makes me twice as glad to be off the boat, but I can't turn around to see if it's broken on a rock or overturned.

There's a series of boulders making the water calm, so ice forms a path that meets the river's edge. I leap from my rock's broad back to the next one closest to the shore and steady myself before placing my bare foot on the next. One more step, but this one is sneaky, the ice slicking out from under my foot, and I can feel the memory of water closing over my head even though it's only my feet that slide into the water before I manage to catch my fall.

My wind curls around my arms, slipping down to my fingers, holding my hand until I reach the shore. I breathe her in, safe with her so close. She doesn't make me feel warm, chilling me straight through, same as when she first appeared after Mom died. Or disappeared. *Whatever* happened to her. The wind stayed, as if this circle above isn't just for people with heartbeats and shoes and stomachs to fill, but that people Underneath leave a little behind if they don't want to go.

That's why my wind has always taken care of me. Pushed me in the right direction. Poked me before someone came, brought me the scent of gore or Wood Rat or Red or Menghu so I'd know to run when they came close. Found the right places to hide. And now her chill makes me remember: Keeping still will freeze me just as the water would have. So I grit my teeth, get up, and start running.

The gore grumbles inside me, but I don't care. I'm alive. I jumped into the water, and I'm breathing. I won, fair and square.

Finding my boots and coat isn't too hard because I'm good at remembering, but seeing the boat across the foaming water caught on its side between two rocks isn't something I *want* to remember. Luokai's pole stabs up from the water like a stick of incense lit for the dead. I cram my feet into my shoes and start walking even though they feel like blubber and jelly.

The closest of the caves that the Post traders stay in—the ones who bring bigger things up from the coast by boat—is maybe half an hour's walk if I go straight there. Dangerous, considering how many scavengers hide near the Post, but wet all over the way I am and without any supplies, I can't do too much hiding. Inside, there'll be dry wood, firestarter. Maybe even food.

My whole body is so far past shivers that it's numbly attempting to give up by the time I find the cave's mouth dribbling light out like oil into the snow. Sliding along the rock, I peek in at the two men sitting inside, their faces painted over in orange-and-red light from a fire, my eyes blurry with cold. It's already warmer standing outside the cave, and I stall for a moment, wondering if I can last until after they fall asleep. The sky's naked of clouds, the air made from nothing but ice, my clothes frozen against me. My wind sits next to me, quietly waiting. Two men who might kill me for my shoes, or the cold, which will kill me for no reason at all?

I step inside, my hands hurting down to the bone when I extend them toward the fire. The two men look up, one with a wooly hat and gas mask, his hand sneaking to the small of his back for a weapon. The second man has no mask, no coat, and a mouth that hangs open as if he means to eat by letting things fly directly in.

Luokai.

The masked man stands, gobbling my attention. He's large enough to be one of those frozen boulders in the river.

"June?" he rasps through the mask.

"You're *alive?*" Luokai says at the same time, rising from his place by the fire, still shivering and wet. He smiles, pulling his mouth all wide and funny. He's glad to see me.

And, I'll admit, I'm glad he's not a dead body, blue and swollen in the river.

The boulder man stands with his hands out where I can see

them as all the Post traders do, but it still takes me a moment to recognize him with half of his face covered. His eyes, once I'm looking, are familiar, though. Merry and surprised wrapped up in one. It's Loss, one of Cai Ayi's roughers.

"How did *you* get back here?" he asks, casually inserting himself between me and Luokai, blocking the Islander's attempt to come toward me. "You ran off with that City traitor and the Red, now you're a human ice cube . . . and you know this guy?" He lowers his voice and jerks his head to the side, toward Luokai. "Everything okay?"

Loss shrinks down a size when I nod that everything is okay, as if his hackles are falling. It feels like the right thing to say even if I'm not sure it's true. Luokai doesn't try to push past the rougher, returning to shiver by the fire instead, the apples of his cheeks ruddy with cold and his robes still dripping.

"I thought . . . ," Luokai starts. "I tried . . . " He glances at Loss, and I can see him choosing his words, using mountain ones instead of island ones. Suddenly, I realize that he's been using Port Northian on me the whole time, and I've understood. "I didn't realize what was happening until you were already in the water, June. I didn't get to you in time."

I look at my hands, fingers white and blue with cold, drips of water melting down from my sleeves. He thinks it was a compulsion that sent me into the water. I suppose it was, technically. Luokai knows enough not to say it out loud, but Loss, all buckled into his gas mask, must know about contagious SS by now and what our two naked faces mean.

"How did you get out of the water?" Luokai inches toward me again, keeping a careful eye on Loss. "How did you get *here*? How did you know—"

"Yeah, if you know this kid at all, you know you're talking to yourself, stranger." Loss cuts him off, not looking away from me. "Come on now, June. Get over here by the fire. You're like shaved ice in a fur coat."

I lower myself next to the flames, moving over when Loss settles in next to me to preserve an arm's reach between us. Loss hands me a bowl—some softened beans and rice mixed together to make a sort of mush. The smell by itself seems to growl in my stomach, all of me curving toward the food until I can get some into my mouth. But before I do, I point at Loss, gesturing for him to take out the weapon he has stashed in his waistband.

He laughs and pulls a knife out, setting it down at my feet. "You haven't changed. Except you look fed." Loss glances over at Luokai, who has now picked up another of the bowls. "I was restocking the cave and checking our markers down here, or I wouldn't have heard your friend shouting for help. Got down there just in time to pull him out of the water. Said he'd lost someone overboard, but I didn't know he meant *you*."

The worry inside me doesn't unknot the way I expect it to when I pull Loss's knife closer, out of his reach. My wind seems to hover close, prickling me all over the way she does when something's wrong. "My kids?" I ask.

Luokai's spine goes straight at the sound of my voice, his eyes widening. Loss tenses at the quick movement, but then when it goes no further, he turns back to the fire, staring into the coals. "*Your* kids, June? You're only a few years older than some of them. *Younger* than little Peishan."

I wait for him to look at me, but he doesn't. "They're fine. All of them are fine." He takes a drink from his waterskin. "You thirsty?"

I don't like the way he isn't looking at me. He gave me the knife, but he hasn't filled a bowl for himself. He just stirs the rice over and over.

"I'll take you up to the Post to see your little friends tomorrow." Loss says it so calm and low, as if he pulls people out of the river every day. "After we go pull your boat out—it's stuck pretty tight, so we should be fine to wait until morning to go after your things." He glances toward Luokai as if to ask if I want the Speaker involved.

I don't answer the unspoken question, though, my ears stuck on what he said out loud. The boat would be quite a find in these parts, especially left unguarded the way it is. Easy scavenging. Most people aren't stupid enough to leave something unguarded this far upstream.

Loss nods as if I've given him an answer, something wrinkling inside me at the offer made and accepted with no mention of pay. Luokai's still wet, but this fire is hours old. How long has Loss been here? If he was stocking the cave and fixing cairns, he couldn't have been in here making rice.

He's still not eating.

SS doesn't *make* you into a bad person. I loved my dad, even if Parhat, Cas, and Tian were worse than stepping in fresh scat. I was loyal, I stole for him, hid for him, fed him, kept him safe. I loved him, and he loved me even when he tried to kill me. I still love him and miss him, but I also hate that I feel that way, because he wasn't safe. Luokai's the same. I mean, I don't love him or anything, but all the nice things in the world wouldn't make him safe either.

Loss, though . . . I know every word he says, every gesture, belongs to him.

Being uninfected isn't a *reason* to trust someone. It just means Loss can choose the bad things instead of SS forcing him into them. I set my bowl down next to me, letting my stomach grumble, not sure how to stop Luokai as he takes bite after bite.

CHAPTER 32
Tai-ge

"DON'T SAY A WORD, TAI-GE," MEI WHISPERS AS WE stare at the flickering campfire and the soldiers sitting around it.

How is it possible that there would be Seconds here, not a two-minute walk from Dr. Yang's stronghold? Mother had no idea where Dr. Yang was camped. Finding out was one of her top priorities, and if she'd discovered him, she would have told me.

I think. Maybe she would have.

Maybe she did. I smashed my link to her.

Ignoring her command to stay back, I follow Mei toward the Seconds' smoky fire until we're just outside the ring of light, the Outside patrollers' voices clear once we're close. The soldier sitting closest to us, a man, is cleaning his gun. "I don't think it's worth it to send so many companies. Unless reclaiming the garrison is about the mines south of here . . ."

The garrison. The southern garrison? Dr. Yang took over a City base? I look back the way we came, wondering how far the bunker is. It was one of the biggest outposts outside the City, and if I remember correctly, it was one of the places Dr. Yang was posted before all this started.

And *I* was sent there less than a year ago for mandatory training.

It feels like a gift, as if the universe is handing this mission to me with a supportive pat on the shoulder. I'll know the layout when Kasim and Mei take me into the garrison, which will give me an advantage.

Mei's breath hisses through her teeth as she eases back a step. The soldiers continue talking, a woman adding her voice. "They'll be here in a day or so. Hopefully, the supplies the General promised will come with them. If not, things are looking sort of frightening back at Dazhai. Unless that mission to the City works out and we get new masks." The woman adjusts the straps of her own mask, some of the tubes unmistakably damaged.

Wait. Mother ordered them here? With more to come? And how do they know about my mission in the City?

Mei steps carefully around me, gesturing for me to follow. I resist when she pulls on my arm. "I want to listen!"

She answers by giving me a full-bodied shove, setting me off-balance and into a snow-crusted bush. Loud enough that all three heads turn in our direction.

Mei runs, prancing over roots and around underbrush as if she's nothing more than a ghost, her feet unattached to the ground. Two gunshots *thud* through the shadows to slam into the tree next to me. Silenced, but just as deadly. Did Mei pull me to get me to leave or was it to put the spotlight on me? Whichever, it's working to her advantage, because the group scatters in my direction, their footsteps heavy in the snow. Mei's heading away from the packs, but I sprint toward them instead, unzipping

Kasim's bag the moment I get there to extract the gun he took from me.

Seconds *cannot* find me out here. Far away from my post and with a Menghu.

It's hard to tell where they are. Feet thrash through the snow and dead underbrush, the three Reds calling to one another as they search. One pair of feet *thuds* closer and closer to where I'm hidden behind the rocks, the gun in my hand feeling like treason.

The footsteps pause on just the other side of the rocks, breath misting out into the air above me. I hold my lungs still, waiting. After a moment, the soldier walks away, muttering things about cold and old Yuan's dirty underwear.

I slide out from the rocks and slip between trees in the opposite direction, wondering how I'm supposed to find Mei. But then a yell spikes through the air, a throaty scream that leaves the hairs on my arms standing up.

Panic unfolds inside me as I follow the scream, grunts and cries of a fistfight filtering through the muting effect of the snow. I skid to a stop at a flurry of movement ahead. It's Mei, and she's made of nothing but pure energy and violence as she ends the fight, her boot connecting with the Second's temple, dropping the soldier straight to the dirty ice. Mei kicks her again in the head before turning toward me, the act of pointing Captain Bai's knife at my chest almost more forceful than kicking the patroller down was. She stops when she sees my face, though.

"There were three—" she begins.

A dampened shot impacts the air, and I barely have time to process the blood on Mei's side before she's on the ground. Lurching forward, I almost barrel straight into the other Seconds as they storm the clearing. Sliding to my knees, I hold very, very still. What do I do?

One Second checks the soldier Mei downed. The other walks over to Mei. He kicks her over so she's faceup, her eyes clenched shut.

I've always been a good shot. Enough that the snipers wanted me, though Mother and Father thought flying more suited to our family station. Enough to land a shot in a gore's eye from fifteen meters, even if the thing did collapse on Howl afterward. I breathe through my stance, set my knees at shoulder width. Extend my arms and line the sight up with my eye. But it's red stars I see instead of a target.

The one hulking over Mei opens his mouth. "You chose the wrong fire to kick over, little girl." His hands go to his belt buckle, pulling it undone. I don't grasp what's happening—not the slow way he looks Mei up and down, letting his undone belt hang free, and not the look of resignation on the other soldier's face or the way he looks away—until the soldier straddles Mei.

Understanding strikes me like an ax to the throat. Before his hands can touch her, my finger squeezes, and there's a bullet in his head.

Mei moves the same time I do, burying Captain Bai's knife in the soldier's throat, but he's already limp and falling forward onto her, his arms dead weights that trap her against the snow, his head a bloody mess.

The second soldier's weapon startles up at my shot, but not fast enough that he can dodge when my next bullet finds his shoulder, the one after puncturing his foot. Mei pushes the bloody Second off her, her eyes wide and teeth bared. Before I can move, she's on the second man, finishing what I did not with her knife.

Captain Bai's knife.

I let my weapon sag toward the ground as he falls, the soldier's last breaths streaming out of him in an icy cloud. The night around us is leaden and dull, the noise of branches and wind, of fire crackling and human voices extinguished.

After a breath of silence, I holster my firearm and walk over to Mei where she's scrunched on the ground next to the second soldier. I kneel beside her, and she flinches away, not looking at me. The first soldier Mei accosted—the one I saw her kick in the head—groans and shifts to the side, but I know enough about blackout injuries to know if the Second isn't opening her eyes yet, it's a bad sign.

"Back to camp." Mei's voice seems squeezed through something very small, both hands covering her side, her blood looking sticky and black in the shadows. "Kasim . . ."

"Let me look first. You've already lost blood. . . ." I take a shaky breath and pull back her coat, carefully peeling her shirt up from her skin. It all seems to be happening *to* me rather than by my own will.

Did I just kill my own comrade?

The wound is a black hole low on her abdomen. If the Second—I just killed a *Second*—had aimed another inch to the side, it would have missed her entirely. Wadding up her coat and holding it against the wound isn't going to help much, but it's all I know how to do. "Is Kasim a medic?"

Mei's eyes are glazed, but she shakes her head. "I think I'm okay."

"You have a bullet hole in your side."

"I'm *fine*." She hunches around the coat, holding it in place against the wound with both hands.

I stand up, everything inside me cold as I wait for her to uncurl from her pained crouch, my confidence in how *fine* Mei is waning every second she stays there on the ground. How fine could she be? Shot by that . . . *rapist*. When I offer Mei a hand up, she bats it away with a hiss and stands on her own, favoring her ribs.

"Does that . . . Is that something that happens often? Outside patrollers . . ." I can't say it. I couldn't even complete the thought in my head, shame at men I thought of as comrades suffocating me.

"I've seen the results. More than once. I wouldn't have let him—he *never* would have . . ."

Mei's almost as shaken as I am. Because no matter what she wants to believe, it *did* almost happen. If Mei hadn't taken that knife . . .

I can't believe that kind of response to a downed enemy. This *has* to be an aberration. One sick man who has been living Outside for too long. But then the other Second's face appears in my mind, turning away to let it happen.

The only thing for it is to tell Mother the moment I get back. Find out how common this sort of behavior is and train it out of our soldiers. Swallowing the plan of action down leaves me with acid in my throat, everything inside me is snarled together in a knot that even I can't untangle, because killing that soldier . . . watching Mei kill the others and then walking away from it with her as if it is the two of *us* who are comrades . . .

My jaw aches from clenching my teeth. I can't take back killing that Second, but I can't find anything other than shock inside me. Not an ounce of regret. What does that make me?

"I'm not . . ." Mei lists to the side and grabs hold of my arm to balance herself. "You knew Sun Howl, right?"

Knew? Howl's name in the past tense. I wish I didn't like the sound of that, wish I didn't care. "What about him?"

"He killed Menghu."

"When he was pretending to be the Chairman's son?" I wait for the justification. The comfort she's trying to give, though it grinds the betrayal I've just performed deeper instead.

"No." She finally looks at me, her steps dragging along behind us, leaving a clear trail to anyone who might follow. "He killed Menghu under his command. Soldiers who trusted him."

Not comfort, then. Condemnation? The black hole that opened up inside me the moment I first saw City uniforms seems to deepen, the darkness inside impenetrable.

"I only met him after he came back with Jiang Sev." Mei gasps as her foot slides, her hand pressing hard against her side. "He left the Mountain long before I got there, but my captain would talk about him. About what it meant to be a team that could rely on each other. Howl was on his own side, and sometimes it meant he came after the other Menghu too. He was a monster. If he's the only Menghu you knew before me . . . I just wanted to say that I'm not like him, even if we do wear the same colors."

The connections she's drawing between me and Howl cuts the muscles in my legs, making me want to collapse there in this spirit-starved forest. "Are you saying you think *I'm* like Howl?" I can hardly say the words, my throat closing around them. "Shooting my own soldier to help you makes me even more reprehensible than you thought before?"

Mei hardly seems to breathe as we walk. "I was trying to say I never expected a Red to shoot someone for me. Not someone who knew Howl first and learned to hate the rest of us because of him." She looks at me again, and there's no way to pick apart the emotions twisting her features, even if I did have the tools. "I might not have needed your help, Tai-ge, but I appreciate it. You know what it means to be on a team, even if we don't see things—*anything*—the same way. I guess it means that just because you're a Red doesn't mean you're a bad person. Just misled in every way."

I'd like to think any honorable soldier would have done the same as I did. I can see Howl in that soldier's outline, standing over Mei with his belt undone. *Our objectives align at the moment,* Sevvy said when she told me he was coming to Port North with us, shivering through her denial that he'd ever touched her. *He can help us.* She was frightened of just how well he could help us, and what would happen once he was done.

Mei's steps drag longer and longer until I wrap an arm under her shoulders, steadying her the rest of the way to where our camp was. She swears at me once or twice but lets me take some of her weight until we get to the ashes of our fire. I help her settle on the ground, then turn back for the packs.

What am I? Someone who kills? Yes. I've just done that.

A traitor to my own side? There are many who would look at what I just did and say yes.

A traitor to my own family? Mother would think so.

A traitor to Sevvy? That question again, the one I can't find a fair answer for. She made her choices, and I made mine. Mine were the right ones, of course. But it doesn't change the fact that the girl who has been my best friend for most of my life is sitting in a Menghu prison.

We were supposed to be more than friends. But she made it impossible. Or I did. She didn't even *want* it at the end because of . . . me, I think. I still don't understand what happened, and it bothers me, Sevvy dismissing me as if I were the cause of all the problems in the world. Because Howl taught her to believe that Reds *were* the problem, I guess.

Funny. I spent our entire friendship wishing I could fix *her* into something acceptable. Something to be proud of. But I'm the one who is wandering around Outside, lost.

The packs are just where we left them, the Seconds' fire a red glow in the distance. I return to the bodies. Captain Bai's knife stands straight up like an exclamation point where it's buried in the Second's chest. I pull the blade free and wipe it on the man's coat, his blood a sickly black in the moonlight. Second blood on a Second knife. The blood of a rapist.

Is this just another failure? As I stare down at the blade, I can't help but think that Captain Bai would have preferred his knife in this man's chest rather than accept what he was about to do.

Well, Captain Bai might have preferred it, but suddenly I don't know what he would have *done*. And that bothers me.

The soldier Mei knocked out, the one I thought might live, looks as though she tried to crawl back toward the fire and collapsed. Instead of checking for a pulse, I walk to the fire and stamp out the last hints my comrades were here.

Acceptable losses in exchange for the cure.

It doesn't feel that way at all. But I'm not sure what it feels like instead.

CHAPTER 33
Howl

THERE IS NO CURE.

The thought is bleak and true as the rough lines of cement under my hands, behind my back where it's pressed against the wall, my bare feet extended before me. Who takes a man's shoes? Sole does, because she knows me.

What does it mean that she knows me and still all she sees are lies?

I shrink down, my good hand knotted around my arm as I hold it close to my chest, willing the pain to stop. But it won't. It can't. Because it's inside me. The world is breaking down around us, hope a match that burned my fingers. When Sole looks at me, she sees someone too twisted to save. Worth more cut up for microscope slides.

I was different when I came back from the City, she said. But not different enough. *An opportunity to make up for . . . everything.* As if the only thing that could redeem me from my past is if I lay down and let her bring the scalpel.

I was defending my home when I still lived by my gun. My friends. My family.

But the truth of it is there, right underneath. *Myself. I was defending myself at the expense of anyone who came too near. Isn't that what I did to Song Jie? Sev is my family now. I want her to live. So I used Song Jie and his creepy heli to get here, then got him thrown in prison.*

I shift, trying not to think it, but it's there. It's real. Every step I've taken was for me. I tried to kill Song Jie with the knife. I thought about using those bombs on Dr. Yang. I want to run away now, to take the one last whisper of hope for survival away from Sole, and she doesn't expect anything more of me.

The cells are suitably gloomy to go along with the fact that the world is going to end. If this enclave under the Mountain is unsustainable, whatever it is Dr. Yang is attempting to accomplish—no matter how many lies he tells about the cure—will be unsustainable too. The Mountain, the City, everything in between—they're all going to flicker out like a quicklight that's been spent.

But *we* can survive. Me and Sev.

Is that ironic? I can never remember which is ironic and which is just people pretending to be smart by saying something is ironic when it isn't. Regardless, it's kind of funny: Jiang Sev and Sun Howl—the two sorry saps doomed from the moment Jiang Gui-hua sucked SS from our brains—*we're* the ones who could live. At least it would be funny if I weren't locked in a storage room converted into a cell, waiting for Sole and any research medics she has here to take chunks out of my brain one spoonful at a time.

I never was very good at waiting.

I trace the lines of the door with my fingers. The garrison's within a day's hike, but I don't know how many hours are left before Kasim and Mei break in to get Sev. I'll have to move faster than humanly possible to get to the garrison on time, and then somehow infiltrate the place without having done any recon. No backup. No *gun* even, unless Reifa hasn't found the ones stashed in the heli.

First things first: Get out of my cell.

I'll need some of that anti–Suspended Sleep serum, so the second thing will be to break into Sole's room. It wasn't locked when we went in before. And the way she talked about testing the formula makes me think it's there in her things.

Third, get out of the Mountain.

Fourth . . . The solution is so obvious and so wrong it hurts my head, like looking straight into a halogen light after being safe in the dark under the stars.

But there's no help for it. All these people are going to die anyway. The thought is lead in my chest, but I push off the feeling. When you live in a world of people hurting one another, you have to take care of your own self. Your own family. The ones who want you alive, anyway.

I kick the cell door, satisfied when it gives a metal *boom*. Storage rooms aren't meant to withstand violence, and Sole's little safe haven seems to be built on separating, quarantining, restraining rather than real imprisonment.

Using my feet, I drum at the door until the metal *thumps* echo up the hall and my bare feet begin to ache. Everyone down here is on Mantis, so Sole led me to believe. In this sea of people grateful they can finally rest, it isn't difficult to attract attention.

A guard's feet come tapping up the hall. "Everything okay in there?"

Frantic isn't so hard to fake. "I need help!"

I let the guard who so naïvely opened my cell door keep his mask but not his gun. He leads me toward the new arrivals quarantine, his whole frame shaking. He only tries to shout for help once before we start opening doors.

The first one we open makes my stomach jolt, the little girl and her father looking up from a plate of what looks like rehydrated vegetables and rice shared between them. "You guys okay?" I ask, keeping the guard's gun out of sight.

"We're just down here until they're sure he isn't contagious anymore," the girl supplies. "They have medicine to make his brain better."

I nod. "Good. Just . . . be good."

Sweat drips down the guard's temple as I back him out of the room and shut the door. Jangling the keys in my hand, I open two more cells before I find Song Jie. He jumps up from the sleeping mat the moment the door opens. "I *knew* we couldn't trust you. No First could ever—"

I shove the guard into the room, keeping the gun against his side. "What's your name?" I ask him quietly, ignoring Song Jie.

The guard's voice trembles. "Hanli."

"Nice to meet you, though I'm sorry about the circumstances. Clothes off, Hanli. And give me your mask. One sound out of you and I'll shoot."

The guard's eyes widen, silently pleading for mercy. I raise the gun and wait until he reaches up to unclasp the mask from his face, his hands shaking. He holds it up to his mouth and nose for a moment before pulling it away and extending it toward me. A tear slips down his cheek.

I can't look past the iron wall in my brain, the one that's going to allow me to get out of here in one piece. This kid was going to get sick anyway, eventually. The mask still feels like it's made from something slippery and rotten as I take it. "And the uniform," I instruct. "Come on, quick."

The guard begins undoing buttons, the Menghu uniform he doesn't quite fit into coming off one piece at a time.

"What are you—" Song Jie starts.

"Quiet." It's not hard to use the voice that made my whole company jump. It works even on poor Song Jie, his mouth clamping down in a grimace. "They put you down here, and now I'm here to get you out. Is that enough for you?" I gesture for him to stay back while I pull off my own clothing and exchange it for the guard's, down to his boots, which pinch my toes. Once I'm dressed and the guard is tied and gagged with strips of Song Jie's blanket, I go to the door.

Song Jie hesitates, crouched on the ground next to the guard.

I hold the mask out to him, raising my eyebrows when he doesn't reach for it. "You're mad I got you stuck down here . . . but you want to stay?"

A lump bobs in Song Jie's throat as he looks down at the mask. "They said I'm sick."

I put the mask in Song Jie's hand, then haul him from the room, pushing him down the hallway in front of me. "Just put that on. I'm going to take care of it."

"Take care of me being sick?"

"Trust me. I can make it better." Lies. I promised not to lie anymore.

But what else can I do? What else?

Song Jie doesn't need instruction on how to act like a prisoner as we walk out of quarantine. I keep my head up, wearing the uniform like authority, while he sags, keeping his eyes down. His breaths rasp faster and faster through the mask as we walk, and by the time we get back up to Sole's door, his face is red enough I'm afraid he'll faint.

Inside, Sole's sleeping mat is empty. I go to the desk crammed in at the end of the table, fingers shaking as I wrench open drawer after drawer, the lights from the exam table a dull glow by which to see.

"What are you doing?" Song Jie's voice is only half angry. The remainder is all fear.

"Making sure this excursion wasn't for nothing." Ten drawers, all unlocked, no vials like the one I stole from Dr. Yang to wake Jiang Gui-hua. Papers, chemicals with paper labels in protective containers, a half-eaten dumpling smashed into the binding of a book on medicinal compounds. If there aren't enough doctors or medicine to go around, I can see Sole trying to brush up on mixing medicine—no. That isn't what it is.

I look over the page with the dumpling wrinkled into the paper. It's a knockout agent. Sole did say they were using gas grenades to neutralize people upstairs. Based on the chemicals she's got stashed up here, she's the one making them.

When I open the bottom drawer, a bottle rolls loose inside. I pick it up, finding familiar green pills inside. Mantis.

My pack still sits on the floor by her pillow where I left it before. I shove the Mantis bottle inside, and when I check the rest of the contents, I find them untouched. Taking long, measured breaths, I set myself down on Sole's bed and look at the room from her perspective.

Sole knows I'll try to escape. If she believes a single word of what I said before about going after Sev, she'll know I'm going to come after the serum. Where would she have put it? What are the chances it's even *in* here?

"Can we please go now?" Song Jie stands next to the hinges of the door, watching it carefully. Admirable instincts, if all you know to do is hide. "What happened, anyway? I thought you said these people were your friends."

"Be quiet, Song Jie." My eyes catch on a ripple of movement, a paper on top of Sole's desk quivering in a thin stream of air. There's an air vent back there.

Sole used to have a box of things she hid. Not trophies, though that might have been what they were when she first took them. Reminders of the people she killed that she took out every now and then, as if she had to remind herself of the things she'd done. She hid it in an air vent back when she had a room in the Yizhi wing.

I stand and cross the floor, the close space making it difficult to get a hold on the desk to pull it away from the wall. "Song Jie, any time you feel like helping . . . ?"

Song Jie joins me, the two of us together managing to wrench the desk back from the wall with an ugly *screech* of metal on cement. My fingers find the vent cover's edges, easing it from the wall, then stick my arm into the opening. Inside, there's cloth. Twine. I pull the thing out to find a little faceless doll in my hand, just like the thousands produced in factories inside the City. I always thought they were a little creepy, but this one is a whole level worse, a brown stain marking its red dress and white apron, as if a doll Menghu shot this particular City comrade.

The doll's head is partially detached, loose threads poking out around her cloth chin. I pull the head back to find a plastic cap marked with characters I remember from Jiang Gui-hua's notes. Using my fingernails to pry it from the doll's torso, I'm rewarded with a vial full of clear liquid, the toy's stuffing knotted around the glass, the label on the cap clear. The serum.

"If you don't start talking, I'm going to—"

I tuck the doll into my pocket, waiting expectantly. "You're going to what, Song Jie?" I push the desk back into place, then wrench open the drawers I searched earlier, rifling through her books until I find the right compound again. "I said I'd get you out of here. And luckily, Sole's given us all the tools we need. Come help me."

CHAPTER 34
June

THE COALS GLOW DARKLY IN THE CAVE, MY STOMACH growling as I listen to Loss's deep breaths that sound like sleep. I'm unprepared for when Luokai pokes me in the back, his eyes alert. "I need to tell you something. . . ." He flinches as Loss stirs, rolling over.

"Are you two talking?" The rougher blinks blearily in my direction. "Get some shut-eye. Not many things that won't keep till morning."

I shrink down in the sleeping bag Loss let me borrow from the cave's supplies, his knife a heavy weight at my side. That's put-on sleepiness, sure thing. He's waiting for whatever he wasn't eating in the porridge to start working. Maybe it puts people to sleep?

"I . . ." Luokai's words slur. "The thing we were looking for went . . . like the mom."

Luokai was already eating when I got here. Could I have stopped this? What is he saying? What mom? We're looking for Sev, who had a mom.

"And . . ." Luokai blinks heavily, looking down at the little lights dancing across the backs of his hands like fireflies in summer.

"Sole hasn't spoken to me in days. But it's still . . . like I'm . . . my brother. This was his link first."

Definitely drugged. I roll a little closer, glancing carefully at Loss. Luokai doesn't seem to be hurt, just . . . sleepy. What does he mean by saying Sev's like her mom? Her mom isn't breathing anymore.

"He was supposed to have gotten to her by now. He was so sick when he left. . . ." Luokai takes another of those rib-cracking breaths of his, but it hisses out of him like a balloon leaking air. "If he'd gotten there all right . . . she would have said something." He's glaring at his hand now, swiping at the lights as if he doesn't remember how to make them go away.

Howl was sick. Sev's like her mom. . . .

Is he saying he thinks they're both *dead?*

The fire has brought the feeling back into my limbs, but every inch of me ices over, and no matter how far down into my sleeping bag I burrow, Luokai's there looking at me, and this . . . this *information* he's been keeping back from me . . .

Luokai slumps down to the floor, his hand going slack around the link. I ease forward, checking his heartbeat, his breathing. Hoping that the fact they are still there means something.

They can't be dead. I told them they couldn't die. Couldn't leave me with SS sucking at my ankles and clouding my brain.

But dead happens quick. I've seen it too many times not to know.

I shut my eyes, but then it's Sev in there. Bloodless. Cold. Lying in the dark of Underneath. They can't die because I'm not good enough. I can't take care of Lihua, Peishan, and the rest. I'm like Dad too now. Like Luokai. No one can trust me. Not without Sev and her cure.

The flames sink lower and lower as if they can feel my heart flickering out. Lying back with my eyes open, I count the seconds one at a time as if that will force time to stop, to go back until Luokai gives a great snore, a long rasping gurgle I've never heard from him before.

My insides try to swallow themselves down when Loss sits up. Looks Luokai and me over to make sure we're still. Stands. Picks up his pack and walks out.

Whatever happens to Sev or Howl or me or any of us, I can't leave Peishan and the others to whatever was in Loss's porridge. I wait until the rougher's clear of the entrance before following. The air is warmer than earlier, full of the promise of snow. No moon to give me light, but it only takes a second to find Loss's shadow creeping down the hill. Headed toward the river and the boat wreck.

Cai Ayi and her roughers scavenge when they can, and that's fine. That's their business. But luring Luokai up to the cave instead of pushing him into the river, then trying to drug the both of us . . . It's different. Desperate, if we're not the first people Loss has brought up here to rob. Loss's cheeks were dirty, red from cold, his mask chafing at his skin. Desperation might not even be the half of it.

I run back to the cave and check Luokai to make sure he's still breathing before taking his dry socks and the outer layer of his robe that he's tucked under his head like a pillow. Tuck the extra layer around me tight, zip my coat, warmed and dried by the fire, to my chin. Then I take Loss's knife, the one he set right at my feet when I asked, and stick it in my belt. Put up my hood. Sneak up the hill toward the Post.

It's a few hours' walk, the cold gnawing at me through my

winter clothes, the sun's first rays barely threatening to break
overhead by the time I get to the Post's trees.

Or, where they're supposed to be, because instead of trees and
platforms and old friends and almost family, there's nothing but
fire-torn skeleton trunks. Ash coats the snow, along with half-
burned planks that fell from up above. And there are footprints,
so many footprints, muddy and black in the old snow.

My wind rustles the leaves behind me, hanging back.

And then I see them, my eyes catching the blackened bit.
Bones. Sun and skies and cold and everything I love. My kids were
supposed to be here, and instead there are bones.

"June?" Loss must have walked double quiet and double slow
so I didn't hear. His breath hisses through his mask, the sound at
least thirty feet away. "Don't move yourself an inch, okay? I don't
want to hurt you."

Now my wind fails me? She who warns me when there are
Reds and Menghu and gores and Dad and water, and suddenly
I'm drowning and alone, so alone. I start running before Loss can
catch me, my hand on the long knife stuck in my belt.

"June *stop*. There are too many Sephs around here to survive
in this part of the woods." His feet pound the snow behind me,
everything inside me pounding along with them as I look for
somewhere to hide. The trees are ashy and broken, too burned to
hold my weight. "June, let me help you!"

My feet move still faster, scurrying over rocks and between
dead trees. Loss didn't follow me up here to chat, and he's stupid
if he thinks I'll listen to him play like he's nice now. He didn't lie
about the kids then try to put me to sleep because he wanted to
help me. Panic is a bubble inside me, about to pop, waiting for my
foot to catch on a rock or a root. Loss knows this area, knows the

trees, the ground. His legs are longer, faster. Even if I don't fall a single time, Loss can follow my footprints just as well as I could follow his.

"They burned it when you left." Loss's voice pinches as he calls after me. "Burned us all out. I think some of those kids might have gotten to the ground okay, but I don't know how they would have gotten past Red guns. I'm sorry about your friend and his boat, but a guy's got to survive out here." Loss swears, and I hear him trip behind me.

I veer uphill, toward where Sev and Tai-ge and me landed the heli . . . Was it really only a few weeks ago? I don't know. How long was I Asleep? And if the Post is gone, then what's left of the world I know? If I get away from Loss, where is there left to go?

What does he want with me?

The question spurs my feet all the faster. If I don't run, I'll find out, and then SS won't have a chance to suck me down to Underneath. Loss'll put me there faster than any compulsion could.

Uphill. To the rocks. The unburned trees. Up to the zip line Sev and I used to escape the Post when Loss and Cai Ayi were coming after us, Reds shooting up from the ground. They *burned* Cai Ayi. They burned the roughers. Peishan, Sev's friend-but-not-friend from the City.

"June, it's not a bad place I'm taking you!" My ears prick, but my feet don't slow as I scramble up the snowbanks. "They need hands on the farms."

Loss wants to chain me up with the City slaves? That's *worse* than Underneath. My heart pounds hard against my chest as I come to a spot I can't climb. I turn around, looking for him, his voice bouncing off the trees. All the hair up and down my arms stands up on end as he comes into view, tears making uncomfortable trails down my cheeks.

I'm trapped.

"They'll give you a bed. Maybe even Mantis—that's what they promised. You'll be safe. Safer than that guy you're with." He reaches out, moving slow. "I'm probably *saving* you from whatever he wanted—"

Lihua. I left *Lihua*, a little girl so much smaller than me. I ran straight to the top of the zip line with Sev and cut all the ropes that would have been everyone's emergency escape so they couldn't follow us.

I left everyone at the Post to burn.

Scooting out of reach just before Loss can grab me, I scramble through a snarl of dead bushes and roots, sending the branches back to snap in his face. My feet skid on the ice, the trees around me dressed in needles and bark instead of ash and char, so I'm past the burned part of the wood. The world seems to narrow, the Circle tightening until it's just me and the rougher's heavy breaths as he squeezes after me through the dense trees. But then the world yawns wide again because I find what I'm looking for: the Post's emergency exit. The zip-line cable.

I can feel the fizz of a compulsion at the back of my head, but not what it's going to tell me to do. All I know is it can't happen. Not if I want to live. I take a deep breath, like Luokai says. Focus on what's right in front of me. Try to blank out the thought of Loss sprinting through the snow after me.

Breathe. The wind is here with me. *Breathe or it will be your own lungs that kill you. Not Loss.*

The cable's a black slice against the sky. It leads me to a tree naked of leaves, a rope dangling down from one of the top branches. I don't need the ladder made from old boards nailed into its side to climb to a crux in the tree above the rope where the branches bend under my weight.

Loss stops at the base of the tree, his eyes squinting up into the shadows after me. "Don't make this worse than it has to be. It'll be a better life!"

There's a bag tied to this tree, up in its highest branches. I know it because I tied it here myself. Years ago, when one of the roughers first brought us to the Post. They found us, Dad's tongue cut out by Parhat's knife, bleeding as if everything inside him was about to come out.

I had to know there was a way out. Up in the trees it seems like there's no way to go but down. I think it was Loss himself who showed me the zip line. After I rode it down to test it, over and over until Cai Ayi laughed and told me to stop playing games, I left something here at the top, just in case sliding down the line wasn't enough. I'd learned that if people wanted to chase you—if they knew where you were the way Parhat had the day he cut out Dad's tongue—they'll follow you until the job is done. A zip line wasn't going to change that.

I needed a secret. So I tied one up in the tree.

Loss seems about to explode, his softened voice crumbling to thorns at the edges. "June. Please come down. We both know I can get up there just as well as you. I really don't want to hurt you, but I'll drag you the whole way by your hair if you make me."

I pull out his long knife, early morning sunlight glinting on the metal, and cut open the old canvas bag I tied up here.

"June? What are you . . ."

Holding it out where he can see it, I throw the blade directly at Loss's head.

He swears, sidestepping so the heavy knife lands blade-first in the snow at his feet. Then looks up at me, puzzled. "That was dumb." He bends to pick up the blade. "Why throw your only weapon—"

The back of his neck, exposed when he bends over, makes an easy target. The first stone from my bag hits him with a meaty *thunk*. He doesn't have time to recover before I throw the next and the next, the stones hitting his head and neck until he doesn't move anymore, slumped over the knife where it hit the ground.

I breathe deep, trying not to look at the blood that marks the snow where the rocks skittered away from Loss's body. The gore inside me gives an appreciative grumble, and for once, the wind is there too, patting my cheek and agreeing with the gore.

I didn't compulse. But that just means this bad thing is mine. No Tian telling me I had to, no Dad with his ribs showing. No SS twisting my head. I *chose* the rocks and the blood.

I am the bad thing that no one wanted. That no one could survive for. Not even Dad.

CHAPTER 35
Tai-ge

WHEN I GET BACK TO OUR DEAD FIRE WITH OUR packs, Kasim is there bending over Mei's curled form. He whispers something in her ear that makes her laugh, and then swear, because apparently laughing hurts.

He stands at my approach, holding his hand out for his pack. A thrill of fear prickles through me as he takes it without breaking eye contact. My gun, recovered from Kasim's things, feels cold against my skin where it's stuck into my waistband. Kasim isn't actively pointing any weapons at me, so Mei must have told him what happened. "You see any other patrollers?" I ask quietly.

"No." He sits down with his pack, unzipping the outer pocket. "It makes me worry."

"We need to get her to a medic." I kneel by Mei, eyeing the coat she still has clutched to her side, red marking the fabric.

Kasim shakes his head. "If we're not the only ones who know the doctor has Jiang Sev, then—"

"My mother does know Dr. Yang has Sevvy and that Sevvy has the cure," I interrupt. "But she didn't know where he was keeping her." Mother knew we couldn't fight him. Not with SS running rampant and Dr. Yang's finger on the Mantis supplies. That's why I was in the City.

Wasn't it?

I'm not sure all of a sudden. Brushing the thought away—like so many that have stuck in odd places over the years—is more difficult than usual. "What about Mei? She can't go in like we planned, and we can't leave her here."

Kasim sits back down and pulls a roll of bandaging from the open pack. "There's a place close by we can take Mei without blowing my cover here." He rubs his hands across his face before looking up at me. "We have bigger problems than Mei bleeding a little. Sev's Asleep."

"She can't be Asleep; she was already cured. . . ." Dread seeps through me. "You mean Asleep like . . . like what Dr. Yang did to Jiang Gui-hua?" Mother's words back at the camp feel like knives, every one. *Dr. Yang's had success waking patients when using the serum correctly. There's a proper procedure. A dosing schedule.* A dosing schedule we don't know. Only that if anyone tries to wake Sevvy up without it, she will die. Another card Dr. Yang holds with no way to peek.

Kasim pulls some bandaging out of his pack and kneels beside Mei. She averts her eyes for a second, but then her face hardens and she makes herself watch as he pulls the jacket back from her wound. "I've been stationed here for weeks, and it took Helix mouthing off tonight because of an SS outbreak in one of his units for me to realize they put her to Sleep." He grins at Mei. "Never thought old stick-up-his-butt Helix Lan would ever say a word against a leader, but he's angry. Asking if any of us know why Dr. Yang would have put her to Sleep instead of operating. Think Helix would go over to Sole?"

Mei shakes her head, her eyes widening. "I don't want Captain Lan anywhere near me."

"He's annoying"—Kasim makes a face, giving an offhand shrug as he mops up the blood streaking down Mei's side—"and maybe a little bloodthirsty, for my taste, but his support could change a lot, you know."

I only half listen as they argue about the captain, whoever he is, interrupting with my main concern. "The medicine Sevvy used to wake up Jiang Gui-hua killed her. Does your leader—Sole?—know how to wake up someone from Suspended Sleep safely?"

Kasim doesn't respond, wrinkling his nose as he sprays something into Mei's side. She flinches, a tear streaking down her cheek. It stays there, a wet line through her freckles, beading at the corner of her wide mouth, as if by ignoring it Mei can refuse to acknowledge she's crying.

"Don't know what that has to do with you, Major Hong." There's blood speckled across Kasim's fingers when he pulls them away from Mei's side. He glances down at them impassively, letting the blood stain.

"I know what you think Sevvy is. You're wrong." I unzip my pack, groping for my waterskin to help Kasim wash his hands, but my fingers close around something pointed and metal instead. My stars. I peer inside to find the waterskin, pulling it out carefully so it doesn't snag on the stars' metal points. I don't want to touch them anyway, not after killing the Second. And not after what he did to deserve being killed.

Kasim clears his throat. "Doesn't matter one way or another for you." He extends his hand for me, waiting for me to pour water over it. "Since Sev isn't in a position to care much who is wheeling her around, we don't really need you to persuade her to come quietly."

I let the water spray into his palm, washing away the red. "There's no way I'm just going to sit out here—"

"That isn't what we planned, Kasim," Mei cuts me off.

"But this guy's a risk we don't need to take now." Kasim pulls a gun from his coat. He points directly at my head, the muzzle of the noise suppressor less than six inches from my eye. "We'll just leave him with the other bodies. . . ."

I drop the waterskin, everything moving too slow: my hands flying up to jerk the gun's barrel up, a thermal blast of gas and powder burning across my face and hands as the weapon discharges. Droplets of water spray my boots and his, my waterskin hitting Mei's leg and slopping liquid across her ankles.

Kasim's boot hits me square in the chest even as I drop down—still trying to avoid the bullet that already shot over my head—and slams me into the cold ground, the heavy treads pressing patterns into my chest through my coat. His toe crushes the bottom tubes of my gas mask, threatening to pull it away from my face. I twist, trying to get a hand to the gun in my belt, but it's trapped under me.

Mei's face appears next to his over me.

"You Reds all look alike." It's hard to hear all of Kasim's words through the ringing in my ears after that shot. Even with a silencer, guns bite in more ways than one. I grab hold of his foot as he uses his toe to pull my mask up from my mouth and nose, letting it spring back against my cheek with a painful *snap* that leaves me exposed to unfiltered air. Kasim breathes deep, centering himself as I've done so many times at the range, my firearm steady on the target, ready to pull the trigger in the moment between exhaling and drawing a new breath. "The only difference between you and the patrollers out here is your soft hands."

He lets the breath out.

The sound of the gun, even muted, blasts my world open and shuts it all at once, my eyes closed because I don't want to watch myself die. But as the gun discharges, it's muddied by a grunt, and the pressure on my chest is suddenly gone.

Not sure if I'm in pieces or whole, I roll away from Kasim into a crouch, managing to pull the gun from my waistband, only to find Mei on the other side of it.

The contoured insides of my mask press painfully against my cheek where they're pulled askew, the smell of pine and snow like an icy glass of water over my head. It's been so long since I've smelled anything but plastic, every molecule of air in my nose scrubbed clean.

Does SS cling to clothing? To the outside of my mask? To Mei, who had that Second breathing in her face? Mother told me that people who were already infected could be exposed again to a contagious host and restart the contagion process in themselves.

Does any of it matter? Kasim is about to shoot me.

"Put that *down*," Mei hisses at me, placing herself firmly between me and Kasim, who is looking wildly between the two of us. He edges to the side, his hands still full of the gun, but not sure where to point it with Mei blocking his target.

Mei slumps down to my level, holding her hand out toward me, every inch of her steel, despite the bloody wound marking her side. "Give me your gun, Tai-ge."

I keep my hold on the gun for a second longer, my hands shaking. Failure seems to taste more potent without a mask between me and the world. But I lower the weapon, then pull my mask straight, the familiar sanitized flow of filtered air resuming with a rasp.

"Give it to me." She slides closer, wrenching the gun out of my hands, the handgrip scraping against my fingers, burned from shoving Kasim's gun away from me as he shot. It's a moment of hope when she points it toward Kasim.

Kasim keeps his gun pointed at the ground, curious enough to wait for an explanation. "You didn't tell me he managed to get his hands on a gun. You know you're not supposed to let yourself get attached to pets, Mei."

"Not attached. I've thought this through." She keeps the gun trained on him. "We both know I don't want to hurt you, but if this is what it takes for you to listen . . ." She looks him over. "You could still shoot a gun less a few fingers."

"You are so dramatic. I'm not even pointing . . ." Kasim rolls his eyes, putting both his hands up. "Fine. Tell me why we should leave this gore excrement alive."

"If you're going to be wheeling Sev out somehow, you're going to need someone to pretend to be a medic. Even if you put her in a body bag and pretend you're on cremation duty, it's going to take two people to carry her to the fires out back. I was never supposed to go in, and we can't risk it with Helix on duty. He knows I'm not supposed to be here."

"What if those Reds who shot you are in the area because of your little friend here, Mei?" Kasim's eyes narrow as I sit back from my crouch, spine so straight it feels fused in one vertical line. "If his side knows why Sev's important now, we can't afford to make any mistakes."

"He doesn't have any way to communicate; I made sure of that. And he *shot* two of the Reds, Kasim." Mei's teeth are bared over every word, as if defending my existence physically pains her as much as it does for me to hear it. "Just now, to help me."

"So, we know he shoots both his own kind and ours. I don't see why—"

"But you trust me, right, Kasim? He's on our side enough to make this mission work." Mei glances at me, then looks down at her own hands, her mouth pressed closed. "Nobody knows Tai-ge in there. If we put him in a white coat, his mask will make him look just like those Firsts Dr. Yang pulled in right after we went into Kamar."

Kasim's mouth goes hard. "So what if I do take Hong in there with me? What about you, Mei?"

Hong. As if I'm an object to be stowed and forgotten. From my mother's pocket to Kasim's. She'd be so proud.

"You're just going to hope no other Reds trip over you or our patrols don't notice your tracks all over the place?" Kasim continues. "Getting you and Sev to Sole is our first priority. Having to deal with Hong is going to muddy all this up." He doesn't even look at me as he says it.

Mei forces herself up onto her knees and then her feet, grimacing the whole way. The way she's holding her side makes me think of Sevvy's fractured ribs after the Aihu Bridge bomb. "I'll open the back door from outside like I was supposed to. And while you're in there, I'll see what I can do to draw Menghu toward those dead Reds. If that shakes up the hive, there will be fewer guards inside watching the halls. Everyone will be trying to figure out how close the Reds are, how many there are, and what they know. And you aren't going to cause any trouble, are you?" She looks at me.

I don't have time to respond, and don't know what I'd say in any case, before Kasim answers. "They aren't going to pull guards off the east side, where Sev is—"

"Wait, the *east* side?" I interrupt, my stomach dropping to my feet. "I think you need to tell me exactly what the plan is." The east side of this building is walled in by a morgue and a detainment unit. In other words, there are no easy exits unless you're a pile of ashes in a box.

"You know this place?" Kasim raises an eyebrow.

"Only what I've heard from reports." I keep my head down, hoping the dark disguises the lie. I know the floor plan. The most likely guard stations. The exits. Where the heli-field is. Whether or not there are aircraft coming in and out here is another question entirely.

"Jiang Sev's not in the cells," Kasim finally continues after a moment of quiet between us. "The detainment facility on the east side of the garrison has been quarantined because SS was spreading too fast inside. When I left a week ago, they were still working on how to fix the filtration system so it didn't poison the air everywhere else, though I can't see anyone wandering around without a mask at this point unless they're like us." He shares a look with Mei. "It's mostly political detainees in the detention block, and since they're all sick now, Dr. Yang and his First buddies are using them to observe the new strain of SS. Jiang Sev's on the southeast corner. In the real labs."

Labs. He must mean the annex on the southeast corner of the complex. It's set up for crop testing with sterile rooms. That's where the First's offices and living quarters were too. It makes sense that Dr. Yang would install himself there.

"We knew sneaking her out through the lab doors was a long shot when we came. But it's the only shot we can take." Mei looks down at me. "You're still set on getting her out, right? Even if Kasim here is a little friendly with the firearms? If Sev stays in there, she's dead."

If she goes with Mei and Kasim, she's dead too. She could be as good as dead already with Suspended Sleep in her system. I file that thought away, though. If there's no cure and Sevvy's out of the picture, then *all* of us might as well be dead. We could possibly manage to get mask production going, Mantis production too, but it won't ever meet our needs. The world will just get worse than it is now. Not just dangerous outside the torch line in the City and the camps. It'll be unlivable.

I can't accept that. So hope is what I'm choosing right now. Hope that the device had the cure and that Sevvy knows why, like her mother's directions to find family at Port North. I choose to hope that Firsts will be able to get her awake again, and that when she wakes up and sees me, Sevvy won't try to stab me in the eye.

That she'll come back to the City with me, not as a prisoner but as an equal. Because I don't believe she was completely wrong about everything anymore.

That Mother, when we come up with the cure, will be proud.

"If you stay here alone, you're dead, Tai-ge." Mei's voice brings me back to the forest, to the guns no longer pointed at me. Her tone says something else, though. It's not a threat so much as the beginnings of a plea. As if, maybe, it's not just wanting to use me that put her between me and Kasim's gun.

Maybe. But if I choose to believe the world isn't going to end, does that mean I have to think about how Menghu like Mei fit into that? She's the same as the Mountain forces in the City who were left behind. Not a part of the enemy we need to fight right now.

"Tai-ge?" Mei's voice sharpens. "Should I be regretting that Kasim's bullets aren't lodged in your heart?"

"No. I'm not going to back out now." I shake my head, still

trying to think things through. Wherever they are planning to take Sev after extracting her from the garrison must be close. Otherwise Kasim and Mei would be more worried about the bullet shards trapped under Mei's skin. I'll have to get the device and escape before they can take us to wherever that is.

Heli propellers hum overhead, lowering into the darkness in the garrison's direction, not the first I've heard in the days we've been out here. So they are keeping helis at the pad here.

"Good." Mei looks back at Kasim, lowering the gun. "And you're good with this?"

He gives a one-armed shrug. "Yeah, I guess. If he pulls any crap, it's on your head, though."

I take a shaky breath, not wanting to look away from Kasim and the gun he holds so casually. "I need you to tell me exactly what we're doing. Getting shot in the head because you drag me down the wrong corridor isn't the way I want to die."

Kasim's eyes are still narrow, but he lowers himself to the ground, arranging his braced leg carefully in front of him. "Dr. Yang's leaving for the next two days. We're going in with the evening guard change, just in case something delays him leaving."

"That's a start. But what about waking Sevvy?"

"We've got doses lined up already. Sole says there's a way to administer it that is safer than the way Jiang Gui-hua got it. We'll be able to get her awake again."

If we need to. The unspoken addendum chills me to my bones. But if there's a way to do it, then that means I can get my hands on it. Mother can help. She's got access to Dr. Yang and all the Firsts who escaped the City. If we need to steal the serum, then we will.

"All right. Let's plan this out."

As we go through our options one by one, I fashion myself an escape hatch. With an active heli-field providing a getaway and the floor plans like a beacon in my head, I can make this mission mine and give Kasim and Mei no way to follow. I'll get Sevvy out of here. We'll be safe. Free. Done with this war.

It isn't until after we're done planning and I'm huddled alone in my hammock that I let my hands anxiously check all the tubes on my mask, the filters, the clasps. As if my brain is frantically trying to fix something that can't be taken back. The air tasted so clear in those few moments my mask pulled away from my face, more than I've breathed of the real world between bites of food since I was on the island, trying to pull Sevvy to safety. Kasim and Mei have both been infected long enough that they're probably not contagious. The few breaths of air I took shouldn't matter.

"Shouldn't" is not going to save anyone from SS, though. It won't matter one way or another until it does. I'll know soon enough if those few exposed moments will change me.

What was Mei before she got sick? I wonder. An image of her face as she crouched between me and Kasim flashes through my head.

Give me the gun, Tai-ge, she said. And I did.

She keeps using my name, as if now we're friends. As if she has some right. I keep using hers because it's the only one she gave to me, the feel of it intimate on my lips.

I peer over the edge of my hammock to where she's strung below me. "Thank you for what you did."

Mei's eyes stay closed, but she turns on her side, the hammock swinging as she buries her head in the fabric, as much away from me as she can. I lie back and close my eyes, wishing I could breathe.

CHAPTER 36
Howl

THE MOMENT THE MOUNTAIN NOTICES WE'RE
gone is obvious. Radios begin chirping as Song Jie and I walk up
the hall. Soldiers who were at ease perk up, walking more purposefully as they listen to the radio chatter. Most people are in
their rooms, hiding away with the people they love to eat Guonian
dumplings made from old ration packs.

It isn't hard to lead Song Jie along as if we're both part of this
Menghu machine. I was one of them for long enough to know
how to fit in. I threw together some knockout bombs from the
chemicals in Sole's room, and now I hold them close, watching the
soldiers flood the hallways as we head for the long, barren stretch
that leads to the barricades. Song Jie walks a little too close next
to me, hand clenched inside his coat around one of the gas bombs.
They're not much different from what we used to do out on
patrols. I hope. They have to work. There's no other option.

The first barricade has two soldiers watching the halls, hands
on their guns. Fingering the grenade in my hand, I fall into step
directly next to Song Jie. "Take the closer one."

His shoulders tense, his fingers going to his mask, but he keeps walking. When we get to the barrier, one of the Menghu steps forward to stop us. "You can't leave now. There's a lockdown—"

Then he catches sight of my face.

Song Jie lurches forward, but that's all I see before dodging around the Menghu to kick the one behind him in the stomach. He folds over, one hand going to his radio, but I grab hold of his mask, wrenching him up by its straps and kicking out his knee. My fingers find the strap's clasp, undoing it and pulling it from the man's face. I press the mask to my own nose and mouth, then drop the gas grenade.

When I turn around, Song Jie is still grappling with the Menghu, but the soldier's mask is off, and with no protection against the gas it's only a few seconds before he drops to the floor with dead-weighted *thunk.*

Grabbing the radio as it chirps, I fiddle with the controls, finding the signal that links to the next two barriers between me and Outside. Inform them two soldiers will be coming through, then run.

Song Jie is jumpy as we walk past the next barricade, the Menghu manning them focused on their radios as they wave us through, waiting for some kind of tragedy, an outbreak of Sephs, an attack, or something worse to reveal itself over the radio. The barricade past that is empty, the place where the guards should have been, eerie and silent.

Perhaps SS got to them. Sephs. I try not to look as we pass, keeping hold of Song Jie's arm to pull him past the post.

"What now?" Song Jie rasps through his mask, his eyes catching on the empty chair turned over by the barricade's empty mouth. "Did you get anything from the people here, or was that just a colossal waste of time?"

I slip through the opening and pull him after me. "I got some coordinates, and I got you some medicine."

"Coordinates for what?"

I keep walking through the cave, the darkness leaking in through my nose and mouth as I drop the mask and start running. Kasim and some other Menghu are already trying to get Sev out tomorrow. I have to get there first. And if everyone else is going to die anyway and if Sole can't see any of me left to save . . .

I'll save myself.

My voice echoes in the cave, Song Jie's shadowy form like a spider crawling after me through the dark. "I know all you really want to do is kill people from the City, Song Jie. There's a company of Reds not far away, and if you bomb them, I can use the distraction to get you enough medicine to last a long time."

The lie feels like a sticky coating in my throat, Sev's face a light in the cave's dusty darkness.

"You want me to believe you now, after you just got me infected and thrown in a cell?" His voice goes flat.

I look over my shoulder, tossing him the bottle of Mantis I stole from Sole's room. He doesn't quiet catch it, stopping to fumble for it in the dark. "You don't have to believe me. You'll be able to see it for yourself. I've got no people left, Song Jie. The people here don't want me, and the City never did in the first place."

The only people I have left are Asleep. June on the island. Sev in the garrison. So close.

The darkness doesn't change when I emerge from the cave, evening stars blocked by a shell of clouds, the air suffocating in a haze of heavy snowflakes. No moon to cut through the night. Tomorrow's the first day of the new year. But tonight is the night the moon disappears from the sky and we're supposed to huddle inside with our families, waiting for monsters to pass.

Perhaps it's good that I'm not with the people I love. Tonight, I am the monster.

The heli sits there waiting for us like a promise in the snow. I have to duck under the tarp, the stairway lowering to greet us underneath. Reifa starts talking the second I put a foot to the stairs, her voice a quarrel of sparrows.

"She wants to know if you found out where the Chairman's son is going to be." Song Jie bumps my shoulder from behind me, translating.

"We both know that isn't what you're here for," I reply. "The Chairman's son is dead, and you're here to kill everyone who had a hand in it." I turn to look at Song Jie, still brushing the snow from his shoulders and coat, shivering as if his last drop of heat was already swallowed by the storm. He looks up slowly, finally sharing what I said.

Reifa's eyes fall, her face crumpling.

Is it possible she really did believe Sun Yi-lai was out here somewhere? Her expression cracks my sternum, grief a ghost that chills us all as she cries. Promises are hard when you want to find reasons to keep them, but it's no different from the hundreds of other promises I've made with words paper thin, no matter how beautiful they look from the outside.

There never was going to be a living boy at the end of this hunt.

There never was a cure. There never was a world that let people live because they were good, only a frozen wasteland that will kill you if you let it.

I turn away from the tears pouring down Reifa's wrinkled cheek and Gein's hand on her shoulder even as he shoots me a doughy approximation of a venomous look. It hurts to see that much hope, that much *wanting*, being crushed into nothing at all. I know the pain of watching your world be stripped of all its light.

Song Jie continues in Port North's nonsense words, pointing to the sky, the maps on Gein's screens, the buttons and lights. Reifa's back straightens, and she wipes the tears from her cheek as she looks *down* at Song Jie and his new mask. He looks more the part of a City Red than he ever did before with his metallic snout.

I've already told Song Jie about the Reds congregating near the southern garrison, a bunker meant to withstand bombs. How Dr. Yang is keeping the cure inside, and I need a distraction to get it out. The trail of soldiers will lead the heli back to Dazhai. What better distraction than a fight? Menghu and Reds alike will eat it up. Blame it on each other, feeding the fire dividing them.

I shed my wet coat and help myself to Gein's, where it's folded over the back of his chair. Go to Song Jie's pack and extract a pair of dry pants and socks. Promises of Mantis go far when dealing with someone newly infected. Instead of tucking it away with the rest of my amassed knowledge on how to get people to do what I want, the thought remains a dull ache behind my eyes.

By the time I'm changed, the propellers are rotating in their creepily silent fashion and the aircraft is jolting into the sky.

I retreat from the main cockpit and edge into the weapon cache, my heart thumping hard. *This is the fastest way to get to Sev. The only way to get there before Kasim and Mei do.* Inside, I focus on the shelves where Song Jie said I'd find a parachute. Once it's out, I check the cords and pull the way he told me to, the long tubes I know to be bombs pulsing behind me like warning lights. *This is the only way to get to Sev on time.*

Since there's no cure, the lives that will be lost are the same ones that will be taken over by SS within weeks, months, maybe years if they're lucky. Would the soldiers on the ground think it a fair compromise? My life and Sev's for theirs?

I promised Song Jie we'd meet back up twelve miles to the south, that with enough medicine to keep him well, we could go to the City, to Dazhai, to every farm in these Mountains if he wants. By the time they've waited long enough to know I'm not coming, Song Jie will have spread SS to Reifa and Gein, and then that will be the end of the black Islander heli wreaking vengeance on the people who have wronged them. SS will be their king. Same as the Reds they're going to bomb tonight. Same as the rest of the world.

Even so, I can't stop myself turning to look at those long boxes. So small. So *boring* looking, as if it isn't soldier's lives piled up in front of me, waiting to be burned.

Deep breath. Another, until my ribs threaten to pop, Gein's roomy jacket drowning me. I pick up Song Jie's pack and turn it over, dumping the bags of rice, dried meat, and fruit so they skitter across the floor at my feet. Once it's empty, I press a button alongside the first bomb, the couplings disengaging so I can wrestle it free. I shove it into my pack, then go down the brackets, stuffing bomb after bomb into the empty mouth of the pack, cramming them in until the fabric strains. Only eight fit.

Even if I could fit them all, it wouldn't be enough. My heart feels so cold inside me as I look up and down the wall, not knowing which of the things in this little room are weapons and which aren't. I might not have even taken the worst of it.

"What are you doing?" Song Jie's head pops in just as I tie the pack's top down, the sides comically stretched.

"I found the parachute." I pull the chute's straps over my shoulders, buckle them in place, then pull the bag of bombs over my front, holding it close like a bellyache. "Show me again how to open it?"

He takes me to the heli's side door. "No time. We're coming up on the base you told me about."

My feet tap impatiently against the metal floor waiting for Song Jie to open the door. How do the bombs know to explode? Mines you have to step on or walk through a tripwire. Chemical bombs from City helis sometimes hit the ground, sometimes explode above a target, pouring SS over Menghu heads in a shower of sick. But with these . . . is there a fuse? Is it impact that sets them off? Or is it somehow the distance they are from the ground, and I'll be a human firework show for the Menghu and Reds to enjoy?

With the moon a dead thing in the sky, perhaps we all need the extra light.

Song Jie stands next to me as the door slides open, a hand on my shoulder as if we are comrades, though neither of us believes it. He thinks his journey is just beginning, full of anger and blood and righting the wrongs done to him. Mine's watery and left over, full of regret.

"How long do you think it will take you to bomb the camps and get to our rendezvous?" I ask. There's a steely glint in his eye, despite the tongue-lashing he just took from Reifa. I can feel it welling up inside him, the prospect of revenge. That he'll somehow be able to prove to Reifa and Gein he's an Islander same as them.

But I can't find it in me to be angry or disgusted with him. There's no room even for pity inside me. Song Jie isn't my enemy, because I am nothing. I'm not from the City or Mountain. Not a Wood Rat, and not a Seph. I'm something else that never did quite fit.

"Probably an hour," Song Jie replies. "We'll wait another forty-eight for you to show up before we come looking."

"That should be plenty of time." There are lights in the distance, the garrison waiting under our silent propellers. It won't be hard to get in. The Menghu could have gotten in any time they wanted before. They just wouldn't have gotten back out. Not with the kind of numbers it would have taken to push the stronghold over.

Me and Sev alone, though? That is manageable.

The serum weighs in my pocket. Sev's only been Asleep for weeks at best, not the eight years that left this serum with no choice but to kill her mother. We'll escape.

We'll be *free*.

I wish the word didn't taste so bloody where I hold it under my tongue. Wish I didn't wonder if Sev will only see the cost and walk away.

I am strong. I command myself to believe it, an echo of what Sev said to me once when we were sitting outside in the dark. Right before I kissed her the first time and Sole told her to run from the monster inside me, the one that's all she can see now. Sev was the only person who saw strength when she looked at me instead of brutality.

I won't give up, and that isn't wrong. It's not perfect, but I can't cram myself into someone else's box of right and wrong.

But the real reason, the one that hides underneath, is that I know what I am, no matter how much I wanted to believe that I've changed. I'm the one capable of sending a heli with bombs to camps crammed with soldiers. I'm the one who saw an entire tent full of supplies, and when Song Jie came in, the thing I chose to pick up was a knife.

I'm the one who drew Sev along behind me to the Mountain on promises and dreams. It was me who knew she was going to die, and I didn't say anything.

If I can't save myself, at least I can save her.

With that thought, I jump.

CHAPTER 37
June

THE SUN IS UP AND SO ARE THE PEOPLE EATING from the Post's burned remains by the time I gather myself enough to climb down from the tree. I can't see them, but I can hear their scraggled breaths, feel their hot eyes on my shoulders and neck as I walk by Loss's body. Small flurries of snow fall all around me to dust over the dirty ice on the ground.

Everyone in the area must have known about Loss using the cave, so going back there would be dumb. The thought of Luokai still lying there drugged sinks like a rock in my stomach, nothing between him and scavengers who will take everything down to his shoelaces. The gore growls the thought away.

I can't take Luokai with me. It was like with Dad. I didn't want to leave him with no sure way to get food even after everything that happened, but I've got to focus on keeping my own guts inside me. I don't want to be dead.

Maybe Luokai was really like Loss anyway. Like Tian and Cas. He infected me. He followed me. Took care of me, but only because he had to. He wanted the cure, and I was the way he was going to get it.

All the people who matter are dead. Dad. Mom. Now Cai Ayi and the rest of the Post. My throat closes over the next ones on the list: Lihua, Peishan.

Howl.

Sev.

My whole new family. The thought grits in my teeth as I run. It was the three of us against everyone else, and three stones against a whole bag just isn't enough.

I stumble toward the river, not sure where I'm supposed to go now. Step one: Find shelter. Step two: food. I've got to live through this so I can . . .

So I can what?

I stop, looking up into snow as it falls from the clouds, the image of Loss in my head a bloody mess. Sometimes it's between you and someone else . . . *and no one really wants to be the one that stops breathing.* The gore's voice huffs to finish the sentence the way Tian used to before sending me out for supplies.

Just use your elbows if they get close. Those Sephs'd kill us if they knew we were here. They'd take our tent, our food, our pots and pans. Might even eat that old Pa of yours if they's hungry enough. She used to get down on the ground, try to look level into my eyes, but I'd always keep them to myself. Looking straight into anyone's eyes makes them think they know you. Lets them see things they shouldn't, so they can use the secrets inside you like strings on a puppet, moving your arms and legs even if you don't want to go. *If it gets bad, use the knife. They won't expect it from you. You're so little, with the face like a spring flower. Somehow people forget that little folk get just as hungry as the big ones.*

I sink down, my arms clasped around my knees as I try to keep my breaths steady, keep myself moored here on this side of the circle where I belong. Snowflakes thunder down from the sky like an avalanche, ready to bury me alive. I wasn't supposed to stay dead forever. I wasn't supposed to sink Underneath with SS still inside me. Sev and Howl had the cure. They were going to bring it to me. Fix me. Be with me forever.

But they are gone, and I am here. There's not a single breath of wind in all this snow.

That wind isn't your mom taking care of you, June. It's just wind. The thoughts press hard on me until I can't think, can't feel anything but the gore inside me tearing me to ribbons.

That day in the river, Dad showing me how to tie a float, I still remember the way his eyes glazed over. I started away before he even came at me, knowing it was time to run.

It's just that he was much faster. And I left him, dead under that dirty Menghu's gun. Dead like Loss, even though they're supposed to be different. How are they different? How are they different from the world chasing after me because I'm the last one left to kill?

Not even the gore has anything to say to that.

The white around me swirls and twirls until I can't even see the frozen falls I know lie ahead, the rocks, the river or anything else, just snow all around me. And then there's a *crack*.

Ice? I didn't think I was *that* close to the river. The night was so cold last night, and now with snow heaping on top of everything—

The world tips out from under me as the ice I didn't know I was standing on breaks. One last gasp of air is all I've got before the water closes over my head, swallowing me like it's been trying to do for all these years. The cold is like a whip against every inch of my skin, my lungs demanding a breath of surprise.

Should I even try to fight anymore? Maybe this is where I've always belonged. Underneath the water.

But then I remember that *I'm* alive, I'm alive, I'm *alive*, and I don't want to be a thing lurking Underneath. Water presses hard against every inch of me, clawing through my hair and pressing at my lips, trying to force them apart. I kick my feet, tear at my bootlaces through the frantic, watery haze of blur and blue and dark and raw cold. I manage to pull them off just as a familiar shouting starts, the voice so much louder than my gore: *KICK*, it says, taking hold of my arms and legs. *KICK AIR SWIM.*

But the water presses down, down, down, in on my ears and eyes, almost like a pair of hands holding me under. Like Dad's hands, his brain so afraid I was going to drown that SS couldn't remember if that's what he wanted or what he was trying to stop. I kicked and hit, bit his hands as he held me down, water foaming all around me, the rocks tearing long cuts into my arms as I thrashed.

Ice seems to freeze me over as I kick hard against the current, toward the hole of light I made in the ice above. It's so close, so close. *KICK KICK AIR.*

Lungs burning, eyes burning, every bit of me *burning* even though I'm so, so cold. My fingers find the edge of the hole, and I pull myself up toward it. But the ice cracks, the sharp pieces pressing into the joints of my fingers until it crumbles to nothing, the river current dragging me down once again.

My last breath of air gushes out in a frozen wasteland of

bubbles, and the darkness reaches out to pull me down. I can almost see Dad down there waiting for me. It makes me feel warm. Down here, there's no food to worry about, no sleep to lose, no gores speaking poison in my mind, just the end. So I let the water take me.

CHAPTER 38
Tai-ge

IT SNOWS ALL DAY AS WE PREPARE THE SECOND bodies for our plan to get in the garrison. Mei watches me as we pull the frozen soldiers apart, her lips pressed together in a long line. I leave the one who attacked her in the snow facedown and frozen, his belt still undone.

When it's time to move, Kasim and I don't try to hide, walking straight toward the garrison's north door. There aren't any guards visible at the entrance, but I notice two in the trees overhead just before we pass them, the feel of guns pointed at me itching across my back. It's tempered only by imagining their looks of confusion when they see what we're dragging behind us: one of the bodies, bundled up in a hammock.

My hammock, of course. Good thing I'm not planning to use it again.

A soldier comes out when we're about fifteen yards away from the door, her gun pointed at Kasim's head. "Identify!" she rasps through her mask.

"Wu Kasim," Kasim answers, dropping the hammock's cords

to put both hands in the air. "And our guest from Dazhai." He nods to me.

The soldier doesn't answer, whispering into her radio for a moment before looking back at Kasim. "You weren't supposed to leave the barracks after reporting last night. Your second debriefing is supposed to start—"

"Soon, yes." He walks right up to her, leaving me to drag the dead man. "I ran into some Sephs while I was doing the long patrol. He"—Kasim points to me—"is part of the team working on the cure. He requested an actively contagious victim for the labs. I knew where to find some from my patrol, so . . ."

The guard shifts her gaze to me for a moment, her distaste growing as her eyes stop on the jagged hole where my stars are supposed to be. "You can tell when Sephs are actively contagious?"

"I . . ." I glance back at the body. "Of course I can. Can't you see the . . . vein strata?"

"Just let us in. He's not good at speaking like a normal person." Kasim shares a grimace with the guard.

She looks out into the forest past me then, as if she can feel Mei there watching, ready to lead any guards we can tease out of this place to where we found the Seconds last night.

"That's not the most interesting part, though. We found Sephs, but not the kind we were expecting." Kasim pulls the tarp open to show the Second's muddied City jerkin. "Reds. Not more than a mile from here. He wasn't the only one."

The guard holds her position, a twitch pinching at her eye. "Probably fugitives from the City or—"

"No. There's a company of them, and they're headed in this direction."

I nod to back it up. "The City sent out a call for help over the radios not too long ago. I wonder if it was some kind of cover to distract us while—"

The Menghu's gun swivels to point at me. She gestures to someone behind her. Several Menghu, red tigers snarling from their collars, file out of the bunker entrance. "Check him."

They look the man over, searching for weapons and I don't know what else. But he really is dead, and Mei emptied his pockets before we came, so there isn't much to find.

"What was your name?" the woman finally asks, looking at me.

"I'm Director Chen." I meet her eyes squarely, hoping it helps. According to Kasim, there *is* a Director Chen here, a traitor who agreed to help with whatever it is Dr. Yang is doing. He left with Dr. Yang on the heli this morning. I hold my breath, waiting for her to laugh and shoot me in the head. If she's met the real director, my fancy mask isn't going to be enough of a disguise.

She looks me up and down, the name registering. Then she waves us in, leaving Kasim and me to pick up the cords to drag the body. "Could we have a bag for this body, please?" I let out a sigh of relief, trying to pretend my request is a normal one. Maybe for Director Chen it would be. "And a gurney, perhaps? This victim is an especially interesting case." I rack my brain for more First-speech, the things I tuned out at state dinners. "And his unique cerebral . . . configuration may be of help in our—"

"We're taking him to the labs," Kasim interrupts, not looking at me. "There's something odd about the way SS has been spreading. We need to keep the body from contaminating anyone else. Bag might help."

The woman's eyes widen. She rasps something about hurrying into her radio.

* * *

Once the man cocooned in my hammock is zipped away on a gurney, the Menghu who let us in accompanies us as we walk deeper into the bunker. When we near the checkpoint that will take us into the restricted lab section, I run back over my memories of this place, the polished cement floors. The chalky walls. The pinched quality to the air, made even worse by my gas mask. When we get to the labs, it's exactly as I remember it: The First area is closed off by a set of open double doors, two guards standing outside them. Past the checkpoint there are two main hallways. One for labs, which ends in the refrigerated room through which Kasim *thinks* we're going to escape. The other side has rooms and a lab for the First family in charge of the garrison. It lets out by the helifield and is where I'm going to take Sev once I ditch Kasim.

The guard escorting us moves to speak to the Menghu posted at the door, but stops when all of them salute someone coming up the hall behind us. I turn to see a young man, perhaps a few years older than I am, walking stiff as a rifleman in a parade. The guards, including our escort, stand at attention until he nods for them to relax.

"Kasim?" The newcomer's hair is slicked down, his cheekbones high, a look of distaste permanently fused across his mouth. The tiger at his collar is black instead of red like those of the other Menghu around us, and suddenly I feel as if I've failed somehow because I don't know what that means. "I thought you were confined to the barracks until we get the rest of the details about the extra days you spent Outside."

Ah. Superior officer of some kind.

"We found Reds in the woods, Captain Lan. . . ." Kasim shrugs, but his shoulders straighten and he clears his throat. A superior officer with a temper, then. The one they were talking about last night, mouthing off about Dr. Yang not having a cure yet. "And there's something funny about the way they are infected. This body was priority, but I was coming to you next."

Captain Lan transfers his gaze to me. "There haven't been reports of Reds anywhere near here."

I keep my back straight, my head higher than the captain's. If I know anything, it's how to deal with military. "Kasim is correct about both Seconds close by and the odd nature to their infection." Calm. Formal. Prickly, as if I expect commands to be obeyed before I even voice them. "I've already radioed Dr. Yang, and if there aren't extra security protocols in place by the time he gets here, there will be consequences."

"Excuse the interruption, sir, but have you been listening to the radio reports?" The guard who led us here looks up from her radio, gaze focusing on Captain Lan. Kasim called his commanding officer something else outside, he and Mei both rolling their eyes. Helix, was it? "They just found two more dead Reds and evidence of others passing through."

Captain Lan's brow creases. He pulls an earpiece from his pocket and fits it into his ear. "Then get moving, Lieutenant Huang. I'll be in the control room in . . ." He looks over the body, zipped in the bag. "What is this?"

"We managed to get a . . . specimen." My brain is full of my comrade's demise, my bullets in his arm and leg, Captain Bai's knife across his throat. But I hold Captain Lan's gaze, banishing the image. "I've been working with the notes Dr. Yang provided at Dazhai when I heard about these particular Seph . . . behavior patterns. I was concerned. I'll have to ask you to lead me to a clean lab immediately or kindly get out of my way. This might provide a breakthrough on the cure."

For all that I sound like a child lying about stealing honey cakes from the kitchen, my mask is a filter, distorting the words so they sound like sharpened scalpels. It works better than I expected, Captain Lan's eyes opening wide. "This is something that will help? You said you radioed Dr. Yang?"

I nod. "He's on his way back now."

Something in the captain's eye sparks. "If it truly means the possibility of a breakthrough . . ." He looks to the guards. "Open the doors." Then he points at Kasim. "You get back to the barracks where you're supposed to be. Your reports have been noted and acted on, it seems, without even consulting me. I'll debrief you when I'm done here."

Kasim doesn't move. "You're going to leave the control rooms when we might be under attack, Helix?"

"*Captain Lan*," the officer rasps through his mask, his eyes narrow. "Get back where you belong."

Kasim looks from the captain to me, but gives a confident nod as if that's exactly what he wants to do. He walks back the way we came, my heart jumping to the beat of his stride. Kasim wasn't supposed to leave me alone. All the better.

Captain Lan—Helix—goes through the doors first, gesturing for the guards to help with the gurney. "We'll get the body to one of the labs first. Progress with the cure has been going so much more slowly than we were promised."

My mind is running too fast as I try to think on my feet, something at which I have little practice, because plans and sticking to them works so much better.

The device and whatever Dr. Yang has gotten out of it will be important, but I can't drag a body to his office. And I need the gurney and body bag to get Sevvy out of here. "As I mentioned,

I need specific notes in order to begin. Take this body to the lab where Jiang Sev is and . . . keep his temperature down." That's what they do with bodies being used for study, right? Refrigerate them? I can't quite wish I'd spent more time in the Sanatorium, but for this one moment, I do wish I'd paid just a fraction more attention. "I'll get the information I need from Dr. Yang's office and begin in a few moments."

Helix slows, appraising me. It's hard to read his expression behind the plastic curls of his mask, but the pause only lasts a moment before he leads me down the left-hand passage, directing the guards with the gurney down the other.

"Which notes did you need to look at specifically?" he asks. "You must have been briefed on the situation with Jiang Sev."

"Are you questioning what I need?" The words cover the way my stomach drops, not sure what it is he could be talking about. "You're an expert on brain tissue and medical . . . science? You like to keep tabs on your superiors' work?"

Helix's eyes narrow, but his voice becomes less authoritative. "I was under the impression that the work Dr. Yang had done on the cure wasn't working. The device we got from the island was empty, and it finally fell to opening up Jiang Sev along with any other cured specimens we could get our hands on."

That's consistent with what Kasim and Mei seem to believe. I attempt an unconcerned shrug, mining deep for the right level of condescension. "There could be more to the device than Dr. Yang realizes. He was only a low-level First. Not even admitted to the Sanatorium. We've only begun to collaborate on these things, so I haven't had enough time to educate him."

Helix nods slowly, his jaw tense, as if someone with City stars educating an Outsider isn't to be borne, but he refrains from arguing with me. Yuan's ax. This isn't going well. When Helix opens the door to an office, all I can see are tidy piles of papers, some smeared over with ink and calculations of some kind. No sign of the device, worthless or not. "Captain Lan, would you mind . . ." I bend down to pick a paper that's fallen to the floor and find a gun barrel in my face.

Ah. Captain Lan is a jumpy fellow. I can't blame him.

I stare at the gun, the barrel less than an inch from my forehead, Helix's finger on the trigger. Apparently, he doesn't trust someone from the City to be doing anything other than trying to kill him.

Which, if not exactly true, is close enough.

Putting my hands up slowly, the paper I picked up in one of them, I wait, my insides all squeezing so tight I cannot breathe. Helix holds for a second, but then lowers the gun with a casual air, gesturing with it for me to stand. As if guns and what they do don't bother him much anymore.

Going to the desk, my mind whirs, but nothing new appears to supplement my lack of plan, only repeating over and over that I have to get rid of Helix, find the device or any notes in this room about it—

A knock sounds against the door and I act before I can think. In the split second Helix's chin turns toward the door, I pull the gun from inside my coat and slam it into the side of his head. His gun comes up, but my fingers are tangled in his mask, pulling it sideways with one hand while hitting him again with the gun. Still he comes at me, an angry roar caught in his mouth, and I barely manage to smash the gun directly into his temple. The Menghu captain's eyes roll back in his head, and he sags, limp against the desk.

CHAPTER 39
Sev

FIRM MATTRESS PRICKING INTO MY SPINE. COLD fluid flowing in through my IV, spidering up my arm and into my body. Everything is the same in this dark forever I live in, the one Dr. Yang will keep me in until I give up.

But when I hear a pained grunt, then the violent *slam* of a heavy weight hitting my door, I know something has changed. The door's hinges squeak, and quiet feet slide into the room, something heavy dragging after them. A body? More than one. And then the soft *whir* of a gurney's wheels.

All the hairs across my body stand on end as the person leaves the gurney and walks over to my bed, the imaginary feel of eyes looking me up and down making every inch of me strain to move.

"Sev?" It's Howl's voice. *Howl*. A hand touches my shoulder, then smooths up to my chin. Mother's voice inside my head cheers, even as she's crying because what can Howl do other than get caught?

Dr. Yang is going to kill him.

"I have serum to wake you up. Sole made it."

Sole's alive? And making medicine, so that means . . . But then the tube in my arm jerks to the side as Howl screws something into it.

Panic. He knows the serum killed Mother. I know she was Asleep for much longer than I have been, but still, what if the serum kills me, too? I don't know *why* it killed her, just that Dr. Yang seems to think there's a way to avoid that problem now, and I don't know what it is.

He takes a deep breath in, and his hand touches my arm, running up to my shoulder. The mattress under me shifts as he pulls himself up next to me, the cushion pressing down so my body lists to the side. "We have about ten minutes until the guard patrolling this section of the garrison passes. I'll take you on a gurney so people will think you're a body. I've got a door jacked open, then I'll give you the medicine right before we sneak out. That way, if it does anything weird to you while it's taking effect . . ."

Like *kill me*? He moves, his side brushing mine. *Howl.* The one person I had to see again. Who, after everything, I *knew* would come if he was alive. But I can't bypass the white-hot, burning fear that, if he gives me the serum, I'll only get to see him for a few minutes before I'm dead.

Another deep breath, the buttons of Howl's coat pressing into my ribs. "Today's Guonian. Did you know that? I thought it was going to be another one alone." He shifts as if he can't stop moving, and when his arm presses against mine, I realize he's *shaking*. "Do you remember the story I told you about the star who married a qilin herder? It was that first night we were Outside—there was a gore howling, and you were afraid." I remember that night, him pressed against my side, laughing at his own story as if the world was a game and he was the one telling me the rules. "I'm the one who needs a story now." He breathes deep, twisting again on the sleeping pad next to me. "But you can't tell me one."

Dread pricks inside my stomach, wondering where the cocky, calm version of him went. Howl clears his throat. "I'll try. You have to be scared, trapped in there the way you are. Stories are what we're made of, you and me. They're the only thing left that isn't broken.

"I never finished the one about Hou Yi, the archer." He laughs a little. "The one I told June as she . . ." As she fell Asleep, but I'm glad he doesn't say it out loud. "The archer in that story was really a man. I just thought June would like it better if it was about a girl like her. After Hou Yi shot down the suns, the gods rewarded him for saving Earth. They made him a king and gave him a pill that, if he ate half of it, would give him eternal life—a life up in heaven's court in the sky. He got married to the girl he loved—her name was Chang-e—and they were happy."

Pause. *Happy.* I can feel him tasting the word. As if the world is a place with something in it other than war and guns and blood and SS. Where things are simple enough for a boy and a girl to decide they like each other and have that be the end of it. Or the beginning.

Howl's words even out a little as he continues. "Chang-e and the archer decided they wanted to stay on Earth for as long as they could before going to live in the sky. Every day together was a dream, with everything anyone could ever want, but all they wanted was each other." Longing strings through his voice.

"But," he continues, "after years and years together, the

archer forgot about the suns he'd shot down. He forgot the people he took care of at the foot of his castle. He even forgot his beloved wife. All he could see were the gold coins piling up in his treasure rooms and the beautiful gems his servants wove into his hair."

He *forgot*? My insides seem to go cold, wondering why Howl is telling me this particular story.

"'Am I not beautiful enough for you?' Chang-e asked her husband, but he was too busy counting his coins to hear her," Howl continues. "The archer king had heard of the riches in the sky where the immortals lived and decided he wanted to take it all. He called his swordsmen, his archers, his riders. Set a day on which he would take the pill of immortality he was supposed to share with his wife and use it to find the way into heaven, lead his soldiers where they should not have been able to go, and take the riches of the gods. Chang-e, the girl he'd loved so much for so long . . . She couldn't see the man she loved anymore." His voice grinds down to a strained whisper, the words far apart.

Silence. For too long.

Howl's finger runs again down my arm, so dangerously close to the tube feeding directly into my vein, the serum waiting to go in. *Ten minutes until the guard patrolling this section of the garrison passes*, he said. How much of that time has passed?

His story continues in that awful whisper, as if every word pains him: "When Chang-e heard what her husband meant to do, she went into his rooms in the dead of night to steal the pill. It glowed like a light in her hand as she snuck out, and the guards outside his room called out an alarm to wake him. And the archer king—her best friend, the man she loved for so many years of her life—chased her down the hall, his bow in one hand, an arrow in the other."

Every inch of me wants to move, because I can hear the end coming, and the tube connected to my arm feels as if it's on fire. *What are you trying to tell me?* I want to scream, but the words are trapped in my dead, dead mouth.

"Chang-e ran until she came to a window, and though there was a cliff below, with nothing to gain but death, Chang-e shoved the whole pill into her mouth, and the light went inside her, every inch of her glowing. Then she jumped."

She *jumped*? Chang-e married the man she loved, lived with him her whole life, and then, when he decided he hated her, she *jumped out a window*?

"I love you, Sev." Howl's voice tingles through me. "If you don't hear anything else, please try to hear that. I came here for you. Sole was going to kill me, and you too, because it might be the only way. She says there's no cure. That the whole world is going to die. And instead of letting her try, I came here."

There is a cure! There's no way to tell him. If he puts the serum into my arm, no one will ever know. My silence has killed the whole world.

"I never told you about Helix and the others. You asked me before why they were all so scared of me. Why they hated me so much," Howl says. "You said it didn't matter, but it does. I said I'd never lie to you again."

Mei told me. I know what people said about Howl. There were rumors he got people killed on his own team on purpose, but there was never any proof. I don't believe it, because that's not who Howl is, no matter how people have decided to paint him.

"Helix . . . *everyone* . . . thought I let people who trusted me die. That I sent anyone who picked a fight, disagreed with me, to their death." Howl is still for a moment. "It's all true."

My heart, already so, so silent, stops.

"I mean, it might as well be." Howl's voice breaks. "I didn't *kill* anyone. Not on purpose. But I wonder now if I did something without even knowing it. If, back then, I was dead enough to any kind of feeling that I saw the world wrong. That there were ways to keep everyone safe and I couldn't see them. I have hurt a lot of people, Sev." His voice is fracturing into little shards and he curls next to me on the bed, shaking, shaking, shaking. "I almost let Dr. Yang kill you. Led you right into his web when I knew he wanted to suck you dry, that he'd take you as an offering instead of me. It's the only way forward I saw, because I couldn't see anything more important than myself."

You didn't send me to my death. You wanted us to switch, for me to be the cure, but the moment you saw I was a real person, you couldn't do it.

"And when I found out you were back here, I . . . did it again. I led people here who want revenge, who want to kill anyone with City stars. All to get to you. What does that make me, Sev?"

You wanted to kill everyone with City stars not too long ago! The fact that you're even asking these questions matters. The world isn't made of right and wrong, because that would be so much easier. I want to yell it, want to force him to look at me, to lift up his shoulders where I can feel them sagging. *I've never seen you hurt people just because you could. You've always tried to do what was right.*

"And here I am hoping you'll run away from everyone else, leave everyone else to *die* because there's no hope. But that's what you are to me: hope."

That he's sitting here now, saying these things before I'm awake as if he couldn't get them out otherwise . . . It makes me love him even more. He's trying to do the right thing when I'm not sure right things exist.

Tai-ge

I manage to catch Helix before he falls to the ground, the knock sounding again at the door. Dragging him to the desk, I pull Dr. Yang's chair back and shove Helix in the empty space, fitting myself in beside him just as the door opens.

"Director Chen?" a voice asks. Helix's eyelids clench, his forehead creasing with pain. I hold absolutely still, my weight against him to keep him from flopping sideways.

Footsteps come into the room, and there's a swish of papers riffling against one another. But then the footsteps walk back out, and the door shuts. I let Helix spill out from under the desk, pulling his bootlaces free even as he groans, his hand traveling toward his head. I wrench his wrists behind his back and tie them, then turn him facedown on the floor to tie his feet. Once that is done, I go to the table, trying to choose a paper that doesn't look important. But in the end, Helix begins to make noise, so I grab one at random, crumple it up, and stuff it into the Menghu's mouth.

With no other leads to go on, I try the desk drawers, the cabinets, even run my hands along the walls for hidden compartments, but there's no device. Denial, fear, *failure* a burning inside me, I grab all the loose papers I can, each one covered in sciency gibberish I don't understand, and cram them into my coat pockets.

Sparing one last look for Helix where he's shoved under the desk, I run toward Sevvy.

CHAPTER 40
Sev

"THERE'S SOMETHING *WRONG* WITH ME, SEV," Howl whispers. "I thought it was just that I've spent my whole life trying to keep from drowning, but not even Sole thinks I'm worth anything alive anymore." The admonition takes the last breath out of him. "I came here hoping to be with you. Hoping we could escape, that I could make you happy. But when you wake up, I'll be the same as I've always been. Me plus whatever it is that's wrong in my brain that made me such a good Menghu."

His arms fold around me, his voice against my neck. "Only a few weeks ago, you thought I was going to chase you to your death." His voice whittles down to nothing, a whisper I almost can't hear. "You jumped, just like Chang-e."

You didn't want gold and jewels. You wanted to live. It's not the same thing. I want to say it. I command my mouth to move, but it doesn't. I want him to kiss me. No, I want to wake up so I can kiss him and tell him he's wrong. The plastic edge of the syringe digs into my arm. What will Howl do if I die from that serum, with him the one who put it in me?

"Things are going to get worse," Howl whispers. "With no cure and not enough Mantis out there, I'll have to be . . . whatever it is I am. Could you live with someone like me, who will defend you? Who will want you to defend me too?" He turns so his breath dusts across my nose, warm enough I can feel him close. "Is it wrong to defend yourself if it means someone else might die?"

It's the same question I've asked myself over and over, wondering how that day in the tower at Port North—Tai-ge dragging me up the stairs, taking the device from my shaking fingers—would have gone differently if I'd only had a gun. *I don't know all the answers!* I want to yell. *I don't know what is right and what is wrong.*

"I'm scared that when you wake up, you'll jump again. That you'll fall the way Chang-e did, and then—"

SLAM. The door's rusty hinges scream, and the metal echo splinters inside my ears. Howl is off the bed, and all I can hear is the vicious sound of flesh hitting flesh, the grunts and muffled swearing of a fight.

A breeze from the hall beads across my skin. The bed jerks to the side, and my foot falls over the edge. There's a squeal of rubber on cement: shoes on the floor.

And then a horrible, deadly silence.

But then Howl speaks. "What the hell are you doing here?"

"What are *you* doing here?" Loathing. Self-righteous. Indignant.

My gut clenches. *Tai-ge?*

"If you think for a second I'm going to let you lay a hand on—" Tai-ge's voice makes my insides crawl, as if he still thinks I'm a little doll he wants to sit on his bed.

"Last I checked, it was you she was trying to run away from, Tai-ge. You're the one who called in the Menghu who made her

Sleep." Howl's footsteps creak closer to the bed. "Put down the gun. We both know you don't have the balls to shoot me."

Gun? Every inch of me screams to get up.

"I didn't realize balls and trigger fingers were linked for Menghu. I know at least one who'd be happy to shoot you. You'll have to tell her she doesn't have the right body parts to pull it off." Footsteps retreat to the opposite corner of the room. When Tai-ge speaks again, his voice is strained. "I didn't know Dr. Yang was tuned into my link. I called for Reds. My mother promised Sevvy would be safe. Which is more than the promise of a *murderer.*"

Howl's voice is right over me as if he's all that's between me and Tai-ge. "Your mother promised Sev would be safe? What makes you think coming here is going to end up differently than what happened at Port North? The Reds are doing exactly what Dr. Yang says."

"Not Mother." Tai-ge clears his throat. "And I came alone this time."

Howl's hands on the bed next to me press hard into the mattress. "You know a Menghu who'd be glad to shoot me . . . ?"

"They got me in the door, but I'm not going to let them have Sevvy. They just want to cut her up."

"The ones Sole sent. Does she know you're with them?"

"I don't know." There's some shuffling, Tai-ge's voice inching closer. "There are helis here, and I'm going to fly her out. What was your plan exactly?"

Howl's weight leaves the mattress. "I've got the serum to wake her up." The tube in my arm shifts, and all the sickness inside me wells up, waiting. Mother cries. "Why don't we ask her who she'd rather go with."

"No, wait!" The bed jerks to the side, and the tube in my arm goes slack. All I can hear is fabric tearing, skin and bones and muscle hitting the floor.

Does Tai-ge know the medicine will kill me? Or is he just trying to get rid of Howl? I hope for the former so hard it makes the insides of my head warp, sucking in as if I'm holding my breath. Could Tai-ge fix something for once instead of screwing it up?

If Howl will listen.

Which it sounds like he is not. The bed lurches under me again, Howl letting out a muffled grunt that turns into a gasp from Tai-ge and then his voice, strained from the floor. "Get *off*. It killed Jiang Gui-hua because—"

"She was old." Howl's voice draws close again, and his arms fold under me, moving me to the side of the bed. "She was Asleep for eight years, and they didn't know how to take care of her."

No. He sets me on a hard, flat surface, the cushioning thin enough I can feel the metal bars beneath it. A gurney. *No.* The tubes twitch again, pulling against the tape on my arm as Howl picks up the syringe. *NO.*

Tai-ge coughs, his voice strained and coming from the floor. "There's a specific way it needs to be given. In doses." The words stretch tight from the floor as the tube in my arm flexes. "Please, Howl. She was my best friend. If you kill her now, that'll be the end of our hope to cure SS."

The tube in my arm relaxes a hair.

Howl's voice is rough. "There is no cure."

A blare of sound shatters the air, my ears screaming. Everything inside me wills my hands to move, to cover my ears, to get my body away from the awful shrieking. An alarm.

The gurney jerks underneath me, my body lurching to the side and my brain lurching with it because I don't know who is moving me or where we're going. Out in the hall, the sirens blare even louder.

Suddenly, the gurney gives a violent spasm under me, and then I'm somehow on the floor in a mass of pain, my arm and side pressed to the cold, hard cement, my IV pulling at my skin. The floor rumbles underneath me, a noise even louder than the sirens pounding through my head. Was that a *bomb*?

"What was *that*?" Tai-ge yells over the sirens.

Howl is coughing, but his hands find me, checking my arms and legs and ribs for breaks. His voice is tight. "I . . . stole some bombs from someone, and I probably should have realized they'd notice. They were supposed to be headed for the camps. Help me get the gurney right." His arms inch under me and lift me from the cold floor, my shoulder and hip aching from where they hit. But it's hard to concentrate on that. Bombers. That Howl led here.

"What do you mean, they were *supposed* to go to the camps?" Tai-ge demands.

Howl's heartbeat is a deep drumbeat against my ear, racing too fast, his breaths too shallow. "Get away from me. Away from Sev. You're all dead anyway without a cure." He adjusts his hold on me, one arm shuddering under my weight.

"Mei was right about you." The black in Tai-ge's voice sends cold shivers up and down my body. "You'd kill *anyone* if it meant—"

"You can tell me you've never hurt anyone before, Tai-ge? Intentionally? *Unintentionally?*" Howl's moving, his voice rock hard, but I can hear the cracks.

Boots sound against cement, and my head lolls to the side as Howl starts walking. Hair slides across my face, itching on my forehead and tangling in my eyelashes as shouts echo closer, until suddenly a door shuts and everything is a little quieter. I think back to what I remember of the hall outside my door, my last look at the world before Dr. Yang put me under. We must be in one of the other labs.

A radio crackles just outside the door. Howl crouches next to me, his muted swear a breath of hot air in my ear.

"Do you know your way around the garrison?" Tai-ge asks, and I feel Howl nod, his whole body moving with it. His arm supporting my legs is shaking now, my weight too much for him. *His shoulder,* I remember. *The gore bit his shoulder.* "There are probably soldiers down both halls on this side of the bunker. If we get out through Dr. Yang's living quarters, there's a helipad outside—"

My head lurches back. "Take her," Howl says urgently. *"Take her."*

Every inch of me rebels as Tai-ge grabs hold of me, the buttons of his uniform pressing into my ribs through the thin hospital gown. Shouts start in earnest, and I hear my name among the words. We have to get out of here *now,* and I can't so much as take a step.

A door slams up the hall. Then another, a little closer. They're checking all the rooms.

Howl's voice, a few feet away: "If we could just get back to the gurney . . . There's a way onto the helipad, you said? After that, you march right back to whatever soggy rice terrace you crawled out of, understand?"

"You can't take her. There was a cure at Port North."

Another door slams. This one closer. "No, there wasn't."

"There was. I took it. Then the Menghu took it from me." Tai-ge's arms hug me closer. "My best guess is that she knows something—that it's hidden or coded in a way that only Sev will understand."

Slam. They're coming closer.

"Why would Dr. Yang put her to Sleep, then? Sole told me the device was empty." The doubt in Howl's voice feels tangible, angry, and disgusted all in one. I want to reach out and touch him, make him look me in the eye and give him hope. There is a cure. And I know where it is. *I know where it is!*

Tai-ge's voice shakes as the shouts come nearer. "My mother said it wasn't empty. And I'm guessing Sleep was the only way Dr. Yang could think of to coax the information out of her. If you know Sev at all, you know how scared she was of going back to Sleep. . . ."

Howl swears. Then again, his voice breaking.

"I'm only here because so many people are dying, Howl. People in the City, people in the camps. The things I was asked to do to my own people . . ." Tai-ge's voice cuts off as the alarms go silent, leaving nothing but ringing in my ears. For a moment I think my hearing has been compromised because Howl isn't answering, everyone stuck in time as if the world has stopped.

"You believe in that City of yours," he finally says. "That they want to help."

"I believe in myself. I disobeyed all my orders because I couldn't leave Sevvy. . . ." Tai-ge stops, the old nickname sickly sweet in my ears. "I know she'll know where it is. Her mother didn't send her to Port North for nothing. And Dr. Yang isn't keeping her here Asleep for nothing, either."

Slam. Three doors away.

"You know the right way to use the serum?" Howl whispers.

"I'll find it," Tai-ge says. "I promise you. I want her awake as much as you do."

"And you're not going to take her back to the City? Not to Dr. Yang or your mother or anyone else? You want to do this her way?"

There's a long pause. "I'll make sure she's safe."

"That isn't good enough."

"I'll . . . figure something out. I won't take her back to my mother. I promise."

Lies. It *must* be lies. Tai-ge doesn't know how to operate without his mother's stamp of approval. Doesn't know how to listen to anyone who can't obtain one.

When Howl finally speaks, there's something different in his voice, both too quiet and too loud. "Give her to me for a second."

Tai-ge steps forward, and there's a moment of vertigo with arms under me and over me, and I don't know which belong to who. But then Howl's voice is in my ear, my cheek warm against his chest. "If there's even a tiny chance that Tai-ge's right, I can't . . ." He kisses my cheek. "I love you, Sev."

Then he hands me back to Tai-ge, and I'm cold. "Take care of yourself. Do what I would do," Howl says, sounding too far away. "Actually, don't. You always take care of everyone else, and that's what makes you good."

Another *slam*. Two doors.

"When she wakes up, you'd better listen to her. If anyone is going to stop the fighting—"

"I know, Howl." Tai-ge's breath is jagged. "I promise."

"I'm taking your gun. The distraction won't last long even with it, though. Run fast."

Tai-ge flinches to the side, and there's a silence inside me. My mother's voice is crying again, as if she knows something I do not. But then the door is open, and Howl's gone. Shots fire and boots slam into cement, shouts and confusion. He's gone, and I'm cold, so cold.

Running boots down the hall, the soldiers outside all following Howl. One last echo of a shot.

Tai-ge's chest is still for a moment as we listen. There's nothing to hear but silence.

CHAPTER 41
Sev

EVERYTHING INSIDE ME IS STILL—HEART, LUNGS, and everything else, as if something more than SS has taken hold. My brain replays what I heard over and over: Howl running out of the room. Shouts. Gunshots. Silence. Again: Howl running. Shouts. Gunshots.

Silence.

Tai-ge walks slowly, my legs and arms flopping with every step because I still can't move. I'm not sure I'd be able to even if my body weren't trying to die. Tai-ge sets me on the gurney and zips something up over my face: a body bag that's sticky under me, smelling of death as if I'm not its first occupant. It settles on my nose and cheeks, the air inside too hot within seconds. The gurney moves under me, one wheel squeaking.

Then there's the harsh *crack* of close-up gunfire. The gurney jerks to a stop. Shouting, swearing, bargaining. The zipper covering my face rips open. Air in my lungs, but it's dead, like Howl might be. A blanket falls over me, the tightly woven fibers rough against my cheek. Tai-ge's voice moves farther and farther away.

The gurney moves. Arms pick me up and put me on a familiar pad. Fiddle with the IV until something cold floods into my veins.

My body, exactly where it was only an hour ago, eternally at rest. Once again, the only thing moving is the quiet *plink, plink, plink* of fluid dripping.

When the Chairman comes to visit a few days later, his voice is dry and shriveled. A hopeless wheeze of a chuckle that might actually be tears. "I can't save him." His chair squeaks as he leans to one side or another. "Can't save Howl."

The momentary spike of interest goes away as fast as it came. I've already heard Dr. Yang crow over how Howl was wounded and now he's safely locked up where he can do no more harm.

Go away, I think. *I don't need to hear your useless mourning. If you cared anything for Howl, he wouldn't be in a cell. If you cared anything for anyone but yourself, we'd all have been cured a long time ago.*

"I am a broken man, Jiang Sev." The Chairman clears his throat. "Dr. Yang has taken everything from me. I knew Menghu were going to break the City walls down all those weeks ago. Take our Mantis stores. They were already inside the City, already spreading SS. He told me they were coming. That he could save me, save my son."

My interest pricks again.

"My *real* son," he amends. "He brought me a picture of my boy, grown. With his eyes closed, lying in a box. . . ."

The picture.

The *picture.* When Tai-ge, Howl, and I overheard the Chairman and Dr. Yang talking at Dazhai camp, Dr. Yang said it was a picture keeping the Chairman in check.

Letting the Menghu in to storm his own people. Giving them

food and the farms. All of it has been about his son? Thousands displaced, infected, killed, enslaved. This whole war has been about one boy?

Voice choking, the Chairman grips the side of my bed, his fingers trembling against the sheets next to my arm. His voice is husky and raw. "Dr. Yang brought me the picture and vial of medicine—said I'd be able to wake little Yi-lai up, save him from your mother's fate—if only I did what he told me to do. And now I give you that same option. Help me. You can save yourself from your mother's fate if you do what I tell you to do." Something clinks against the side of the bed, glass on metal.

Help him *what?* I'm lying here mostly dead with nothing to offer. I know where the cure is, but he doesn't know that. What game is he playing?

The Chairman takes a deep breath, the sickly air brushing over me turning to a hot stream as if he's leaning forward to look at my face. "Is it ironic to be giving this to you now? What I would have given to have this serum six months ago. To wake your mother up, to take back the cure trapped inside her head. You're like her, you know. I know you'll help me."

The anger seething deep inside me seems to cool a degree, Mother's face as it was before I fell Asleep at eight appearing in my mind. The Chairman isn't the only person who has been willing to wage war over a single life that was important to him. Mother wouldn't give up the cure because of me. I wouldn't give the cure to Dr. Yang mainly because of June and Lihua. But they're just the faces I know, two of thousands in the same position: needing the cure but with nothing to offer in exchange.

The chair squeaks again, and the damp brush of unfiltered breath is replaced by stale air. The hospital gown flips up at my side, and he pushes something cold against my bare skin, then presses something over it. Medical tape. The tubes at my elbow twitch as an awful coldness seeps into my arm. Panic wells inside me at the medicine in my veins that I know will kill me.

"There's a dosing schedule. I've just given you the first measure. A medic will come for you soon to administer the rest. Now, listen carefully because this is an exchange. If you don't hold up your part, I will find you and kill you and everyone else you love."

My skin chills at how calmly he says it, as if he's talking about the weather.

"Two Outsiders tried to break you out of here a few days ago. Howl was with them and the General's son. One Outsider was caught by Dr. Yang's men, the other by soldiers loyal to me. Dr. Yang doesn't know of his betrayal, and the Menghu has agreed to take you and my medic back to the Mountain in exchange for our silence."

The Chairman settles back into his chair with a creak and popping of knees. "There's some group holding out at the Mountain, though who knows how long they'll last."

A group holding out at the Mountain? *Sole?*

His chair squeaks, his voice close to my ear. "The Mountain is where Dr. Yang was strongest, the only place he'd have the technology to preserve my son. You are going to go, you are going to find him, and you are going to bring him to me. I've taped a link to your side. The moment you find him, send me a picture. We'll plan from there."

My arm stings as the medicine enters my veins drip by drip.

"And I'm sorry, but you can't go after Howl. I've heard what they say about the two of you from General Hong."

From General Hong? What would she know about me or Howl, either

*one of us? Mei and Helix or Kasim would know a thing or two, but
General Hong?*

But then I remember Tai-ge's arms around me, and if my teeth
could have ground together, they would have.

"I know you'll want to get him out. Dr. Yang knows it too,
and he'll try to use it against you once you're gone. But you can't
come back unless you've got my son." The Chairman pauses,
thickness entering his voice again. "You're the only hope I have in
this world. The only hope little Yi-lai has. If you could have had
even a moment with your mother, I know you would have taken
it. Please, give me this." His voice is too quiet, crumbling at the
edges as if he can't quite believe that he is asking for my help.
That he has to ask for anything at all. "With my son secure, I can
tell the Seconds to fight Dr. Yang. I'll let you be a part of the
First Circle, let you change the quarter system or hand the cure
to every sorry Third in this whole mountain range. I'm ready to
let things change, so long as I get my son back. You send me the
picture proving you've found him, and I'll get the both of you to
safety. If you don't find him . . . if you don't contact me within
two days of leaving, you know the consequences. I'll start with the
Mountain holdouts. We'll clean the whole place out."

The door's hinges screech, and he's gone, leaving me alone with
the darkness inside my head, a circle of cold metal pressed hard
into my ribs under the medical tape. Feeling as though I'm surrounded, but I don't know by what.

CHAPTER 42
Tai-ge

WHEN I WAKE UP, I'M ALONE.

It's shadowy and dark inside this place, the ceiling close in a way that feels familiar. There's a low murmur of voices outside, footsteps walking by. It's as if I've been transplanted back into another era of my life, but I can't identify when. What happened to the Menghu who found me in the labs? To Howl? To Sevvy, lying so limp in the Menghu's arms as they dragged her away from me?

I sit up in one jolt, muscles sore. My hands brush the rough fabric that makes up my sheets, and I try to remember from where I know this bed, this tent. It isn't that hard to place it. I just don't want it to be true.

I'm at Dazhai.

My stomach twists. Was everything I lived over the last month a product of my overstimulated brain? Was it all only a nightmare? I practically fall from the cot in my anxiety, bumbling into the box pushed up next to it as some kind of nightstand, knocking something to the ground with a rattle. I lunge for the tent flap—I have to see if the world rewound back to my time sitting alone in my tent at Dazhai, waiting for my mother to acknowledge my existence—but I don't make it that far. My eyes find the thing I knocked onto the floor before I can even take two steps.

I bend down to pick up the little paper cup lying on its side, two green pills spilled onto the ground next to it, now coated in dirt.

Mantis.

It's hard to let myself breathe even as I notice the smell of mud. Of garlic and ginger. Musty linens and sweat. The world has been so sterile for so long, strained of everything so I could hardly taste that I was alive. I clench my eyes shut and reach up to touch my face. It almost feels as if it belongs to a stranger, naked of the plastic tubes that kept me safe for so long.

Everything that happened at the City—working with Captain Bai, Mei sleeping in my room, Sevvy's cold, dead skin—it's not part of a nightmare. *This* is the nightmare.

I put a hand to my throat, contaminated air choking as it goes down. Just as contaminated as what's inside me, because I'm the one who's different now.

Mother doesn't wait three weeks to call me in. This time she doesn't start with reassurances.

"What is *wrong* with you?" Her jaw clenches, twitching her mask up and down as I stand in front of her collapsible desk like a felon pleading for mercy. That's the only register of emotion, though. She leans forward with a pen to enter some information, as if she weren't the one who called me here and I was interrupting. "Dr. Yang was practically giddy when he handed you over, *Asleep*, and now the Chairman has forced me to pull out everyone within ten miles of the garrison. Not to mention these . . . these *bombings.*" She finally looks up at me, her eyes disappointed. "That was our chance to get the cure, and you just destroyed it."

It's hard not to keep my breaths shallow even though SS is already inside of me. Hard not to see the way she's looking at my naked face. The day Menghu invaded the City, I pretended I'd caught the disease to get to Sev where she was being kept in the Hole, a prison. Mother and Father had both looked stricken the moment I first pretended to compulse. Stricken, then angry, then very, very quiet, as if they were quite sure SS victims no longer could comprehend basic language. They'd never believed Sev could understand anything they said.

It was Mother who sent me to the Hole, then. To a cell far underground where I couldn't embarrass her. I'd known that was what would happen, and suddenly it bothers me. That I expected to be banished for breathing the wrong air.

"I knew the cure was there." I say it quietly. "I had an in. It was a risk, but—"

"You were a distraction, Tai-ge! You were supposed to stay up in the City sending reports about City forces getting the Mantis supply under control. You were supposed to keep Menghu attention on *you* while I addressed the real problem at the southern garrison." She closes her eyes, attempting to smooth the wrinkles from her forehead with the palms of her hands. "I *knew* we'd have to go after that device and your little *traitor* friend the moment you briefed me on the situation. The mission was under way, Tai-ge! You set off all the alarms right before we meant to go in. That bombing could have been the perfect distraction! The universe was bending for us, Tai-ge, and you made it break!"

I stand, transferring weight from one foot to the other. It

seems obvious now. Obvious that Mother didn't expect me to succeed or do much of anything at all. My assignment to the City wasn't a show of trust, a means for me to make up for the wrongs I've done. It was to get me out of the way, same as sending me to the Hole. I touch my naked cheek, my skin cold.

Mother sent me on a humanitarian mission, so she called it. Armed with poison gas instead of Mantis and food. The thoughts inside me feel like the worst failure of all, but I can't stop them from breaking holes through my every thought. Mother was going to have me kill hundreds of people. As a diversion.

There's an odd feeling brewing in my chest. A sort of heat laced through with acid.

"Dr. Yang gave me your 'assistant.' The one who managed to persuade you to leave your post and took you to the garrison. They found her outside the lab doors, waiting to take whatever it was she wanted you to break out of that place." Mother stands from her desk. "If there's anything you can give me to help her interrogation, now's the time to say it."

My hands are cold, my spine hot, and all the spaces between are a war between the two making me feel ill. Dr. Yang handed Mei over? I don't think I've ever heard of a punishment quite so awful—being given to the enemy. I raise my chin an inch, but I still know not to meet Mother's eyes. "She's infected. Unhappy with Dr. Yang. She and . . ." I lick my lips, Kasim's name trapped inside my mouth. Do I want to give him away?

Lieutenant Hao back in the City had a sort of treaty with the Menghu who were abandoned in the City. Captain Bai doesn't like the way things are being handled.

The Seconds in the camps are scared.

I'm scared. I don't see how Mother means to continue forward.

Not without capitulating or substantial loss. If there's no future for Reds, then there's no future for me. There's no future for me here anyway. Not from the moment I disobeyed Mother's orders.

Because that's what I was doing. What I've been doing this whole time. Disobeying orders.

"She's unhappy with Dr. Yang and . . . *what?*" Mother's voice crackles with impatience.

I swallow. I've never been a part of interrogations, but I've seen the results. "Mei—the Menghu—she might be willing to talk without any extra *motivation.*"

Mother's brows fall. "We both know you have a problem with making the wrong kinds of friends, but if you are trying to protect a *Menghu*—"

"No!" I'm glad Mother is concentrating on the reports instead of my face. Glad for the shame I'm supposed to be feeling right now, which lets me keep my eyes lowered. I don't feel shame. I don't feel anything but *anger.*

That's what it is. This awfulness swirling in my chest, consuming me from the inside. Anger that gives way to something frightening and new inside me.

Mother isn't going to listen to me. She isn't going to let me out of her sight, maybe not ever again. But even if my hands are tied to Mothers', my life wrapped up in our dead City, that doesn't mean I have to give up.

I keep my eyes down as I talk. "Dr. Yang's hold on the people from the Mountain might not be as strong as we thought. Dr. Yang came to power during the invasion, and there are many Menghu, my 'assistant' included, who don't trust him. He isn't giving them the cure the way he promised to. She wanted to take it to some other group that's holed up near the southern garrison."

Mother's eyebrows rise, and she sits back in her chair. I can feel her looking at me, as if she's poised over me with a scalpel and magnifying glass, deconstructing each layer one by one.

"She trusts me . . . at least a little." The image of men falling to the ground, their blood spattering down over Mei fills my head. "We aren't friends by any stretch. But if you let me talk to her, she might be willing to give you information. It could be a way to undermine Dr. Yang."

"That's a useful start." Mother taps a finger against her mouth, eyes thoughtful. "Perhaps I'll send her back with you to the City." She bends back over the reports, gesturing toward the door with an annoyed flick of her hand. "With an advisor who actually knows what he is doing to make sure you don't destroy anything else."

"Wait." My lungs stall at the annoyance wrinkling Mother's forehead when I ignore her dismissal. "One other thing . . . I saw something out there. One of our soldiers tried to rape a wounded Menghu while another soldier stood by and did nothing." I lick my lips, waiting for some kind of reaction. Anything. "That might something to bear in mind before sending any more soldiers out. Perhaps a retraining of some kind, or stricter punishments—"

"Tai-ge." She glances up at me, and even I can see the disgust. "Perhaps you should at least pretend to know which side you are on before you continue that sentence. At least half of Menghu forces are female. It isn't a form of aggression I care for, but if it makes Menghu even a fraction more timid or lopsided in the way they deploy their soldiers . . ."

"Half of *our* forces are female. And even if they weren't, are you saying you sanction . . ."

One look from her is enough to slice my argument off at the hilt. "Just go, Tai-ge. I had hopes for you, but it's obvious to me now you'll never amount to much of a leader. Keep your head down and try not to embarrass me."

My mouth won't quite close, my tongue flailing lifelessly over arguments, incredulity, despair. . . . Mother's looking back at the papers in front of her, eyebrows furrowed, as if I puffed out of existence the moment she looked away. I let my head drop in a deep nod before I back out of the tent.

Every step feels too heavy as I walk away, unable to even process what she said. That I'm a failure and that she wants nothing to do with me. There's something very badly wrong with me. Something broken. Because *I don't care.*

It's the failure of not speaking, of what I've allowed myself to look past until now, that makes the vomit begin to rise in my throat. I've failed at making the City what it is supposed to be: a safe haven. I've failed Sevvy and the whole world of people I didn't realize were there, just waiting to be noticed.

But at least I can *see* my own failures. What is this *thing* war has made of my Mother?

Unless Mother hasn't become anything at all. What if she's been this way all along, and I just never noticed until now?

The two metal stars are once again in their place at my collar. They prick through the fabric into my neck when I pull them free, as if they know what I am now. I don't deserve them, and they aren't worthy of me.

I won't let the little bits of metal point my way anymore. I am not them. I will make myself into something new. Someone Captain Bai and Lieutenant Hao in the City will recognize when I set down in the market.

Maybe even someone Sevvy would be interested in knowing again, if that's possible.

Mother is right that I'll never amount to anything among the Seconds. I *am* a failure.

It's that thought that gives me the most hope of all.

Later, when I gain admittance to the prison unaccompanied, Mei's eyes go wide as they slip over my unmasked face. She sits up from where she was lying on the ground in her cell, crossing her feet and leaning back against the wall as she looks me up and down. "SS finally came for you?" She picks at her fingernails, turning away from me. "Fitting, I guess. Now you know what it's like."

The lock is rusted and old, and I haven't broken a lock since I got Sevvy out of the City during the invasion. But any door will open if you have the right tools.

Mei jerks up from the ground as I begin to pick the lock, her brows knit together. "What is this, Tai-ge?"

The lock clicks, and the door swings open. I hold out a link. "I want everyone to not die, including you. Will you help me?"

The world has become a string of impossiblities. The City full of infected. Outsiders prevailing, my mother a monster. And me, the General's son, working with a Menghu.

Mei's eyes narrow, but then that smile of hers, the one that first pricked at my sensibilities all those weeks ago at Dazhai, takes her wide mouth. She holds out her hand, and I place the link in it.

CHAPTER 43
Sev

"DON'T MOVE, OKAY?" IT'S A MAN'S VOICE, MURMURING through the corroded filter of a mask. His hands on my arm pause, and then there's a soft laugh. Someone came in twice between the Chairman first injecting me with the serum and now to give me additional doses, but this is the first time he's spoken. "It's funny because you *can't* move. Pity you can't laugh, either, Sev. I know how much you like my jokes."

The ice in my veins turns to fire as he inserts something into the catheter, the sensation flaming up through my arm, down my spine, blazing across my brain, then flickering in an ashy smolder to my fingertips. I can't gasp, can't twitch away from the pain or punch the man in the nose.

My left hand twitches, my fingers moving centimeter by painful centimeter. It startles me enough to make me stop, wondering how I did it. How to do it again. When I twitch my finger a second time, it's a triumph, but not enough. Not enough to hit the medic as he adjusts my head, then pulls off the itchy tape securing the tube inside my nose in one burning swipe. The tube gives a jerk as he begins to extract it, every inch it moves as he pulls it out seeming to leave a burning line of acid in its wake, like a slug leaving a trail of mucus as it burrows out through my nose.

"This shouldn't hurt," the medic muses, the progress stalling for a moment, as if he's looking me over. "But then, I've never had to have someone pull a tube out of my nose. It'll be better than the other one coming out. And *much* better than those scratches on your back." He gives a little giggle. "You were so upset when I figured they were from your stars and not from the gore. Much less cool." He keeps pulling on the tubes, talking to himself as if he can't quite help it. "Faux gore wounds. You know, that could be a good way to make friends around here, if those creepy Outsider soldiers would just think it through. Trip, scratch yourself up, blame it on a gore, and suddenly you're a hero."

Faux gore wounds?

There's only one person I know capable of being so insensitive and ridiculous all at once. Not to mention there are only a few people who know why I have cuts all up and down my back: Tai-ge, who is most definitely not here. Howl, who is locked up. June, who is still at Port North. That leaves Xuan, the annoying medic who also happened to save Howl's life after the gore bit him.

Xuan isn't supposed to be here. My throat seems to want to expel the tube faster than he can pull, all of my muscles clenched and ready to vomit. His fingers pause as the end of the feeding tube pulls free, leaking something wet and warm down my cheek. I silently vow to stick a hose up Xuan's nose and then jerk it out again the moment my hands can move, to show him exactly how much it doesn't hurt.

"I can see you're already regaining control. . . ." He touches my fingers and then presses them into my palm, though I don't know what he's looking for. "Yes. I can't give you the last dose for another fifteen minutes, so don't get upset if you can't do more than flop. That's actually a good thing, because right now it would be best for you to look dead." A light cloth settles over my face. Then arms lift me up from the table and plop me on a gurney, stopping to rearrange my feet so they're straight and my arms so they're crossed over my chest.

The gurney jerks underneath me, then begins to roll. My neck muscles tense and then release, tense . . . and then my eyelids crack open. A combination of the assault of light and movement makes nausea bloom in my stomach, forcing me to clench my eyes shut again. Inching my head over to the side, I try again, and this time, even filtered through the cloth, the light still hurts, but it is bearable.

"Here's the plan," Xuan's voice rasps as the gurney stills under me, the light flashing to darkness for a split second as he walks by. "The Chairman told me I can have a free pass out of this place if I can get you out too."

Xuan *was* out. What is he doing here?

"I have to assume you know more about the Mountain and whoever it is we're supposed to meet outside. I need you to really try with your dead impression since we're leaving via the burn pile where they take the bodies."

I'm supposed to go in a pile of corpses? None of this plan sounds like it could work, most especially the part where I end up with my hair on fire.

A smaller voice inside me says something even more painfully pathetic, ducking under anything that could be called rational. *Dr. Yang has Howl. The Chairman said he is going to kill him.*

If there's some ridiculously small chance of Xuan sliding me out through the burn door, what's the harm in adding one extra body? I force my fingers to curl into a fist, then open them again.

"See," Xuan whispers, touching the back of my hand through the cloth. "That's exactly what we don't want. Think *dead girl.* After the last four weeks, it can't be that hard."

Four weeks? It felt like three lifetimes glued together. I stretch my fingers, then flop my arm over the side of the gurney, trying to pull off the sheet draped over my body.

"I'm so sorry! Yuan's ten illegitimate children!" Xuan coughs through his mask's filters, and suddenly turns the gurney to the right, jerking my limp body to one side. His words aren't angled toward me anymore, as if there's someone else here. "I must have tripped. Thank you for helping me stabilize this thing, I think the wheel's broken. They needed this one in lab two, and I'm afraid the Firsts will cut my rations if I'm late again, so if you'll excuse me . . ."

We turn another corner, and then the gurney speeds up, Xuan's shoes slapping hard against a cement floor. We turn again and then stop, the sound of a door closing blocking out the echoes from the hall. The sheet pulls completely off my body, Xuan's breaths coming fast. "Think you're funny? You want us both to *die?*" he demands. "I'm trying to *help* you."

I open my hand again, attempting to flop it across my stomach, up to where his hands must be on the gurney, but don't quite make it. My tongue feels like an entire limp fish shoved into my mouth, every breath whistling around it. But I force it to move. My lips, my teeth. "Why?" I try to ask.

Xuan swears again, then walks around the gurney. My hand limply searching, I find his wrist as he picks up the tube snaking into my vein. Adds another jolt of medicine, but this one isn't frozen or burning—it feels like sunlight, warming me over.

I open my eyes. The light is dim, and Xuan is a mess of rubber tubing lurking over me, an oversize mosquito about to suck me dry. "Why?" I ask again, my tongue still feeling oversize despite the final dose of serum, but he understands me this time. "Why are you even here?"

"Your slurring is pretty cute." He looks away, toward the door, I think, and then back to me. "Remember when your friend Howl-not-the-Chairman's-son got all gore-bitten and we set up a deal where I snuck into a very dangerous Second camp to get him medicine and you were going to tell Hong Tai-ge I was dead and to stop looking for me?" He takes a long breath, replenishing his lungs. "Long story short: I got caught."

I did ask him to get medicine for Howl after the gore mauled him. I wasn't sure he was going to *do* it, though.

Xuan sighs. "Had to pretend I was separated from invasion forces. And now I need a body to get me out of here away from Chairmans and Seconds and Outsiders and everyone else. *You* are that body, so you are going to stop moving *now*."

"If bodies go out so easily, why didn't you just submit your own?" My mouth. It's *working*. My throat feels crinkled and dry, every word painful.

He doesn't shake off my hand clasped around his wrist, looking down at it. "Because I can see that you're important. And having important friends means you live. There was no way I was going to get into Kamar after all those helis blew over it. And even if they're all holed up underground, I'm guessing Second marks are as good as a death sentence on the island now." He looks down to the two hash mark scars between his forefinger and thumb.

I nod slowly, relishing the movement. Luokai told me as much himself.

"And then I heard about your little debut back here as a POW. That Dr. Yang went after you in particular. So I came back and whispered to all the right guards until the Chairman heard he had a Second on his side." Xuan straightens his collar, touching the tubes of his gas mask as if to reassure himself it's still there. "A very skilled one, if I do say so myself."

Blinking, I try to keep my eyes open, everything going fuzzy for a moment. I let go of his wrist, and he holds a hand out to me, as if he wants to help me sit up. I stare for a moment, then attempt to move my hand to meet his.

It's clumsy. It makes me feel motion sick. But it works. My vision blackens at the edges, my head practically floating off my shoulders as I sit up. There's an uncharacteristic knot in Xuan's brow, barely peeking out between strands of shaggy hair. And a strap snaking under his lab coat at his shoulder. A gun holster.

"The Chairman promised most of the army that going to Kamar would bring back a cure. Then those other soldiers from Outside said it was you and Howl we needed to fix SS. They brought you back, grabbed Howl when he came in after you. And yet both of you are still here in one piece. No cutting, no execution yet, and also no cure. I'm not the only one who has noticed. You have something they want."

"I know where the cure is, just like I told you before. You didn't believe me. You're going for fairy tales now, Xuan?"

"It's only a matter of time before I get SS, Sev. If there's a fairy tale with a grain of truth?" He looks down. "There's already . . . There are people out in the forest now. . . ."

"Your girlfriend. The one with E. coli who ran away when she got SS. You're hoping she survived."

He adjusts his mask filters, nodding slowly.

"I need Howl."

"Yeah, that's not going to happen. He's got an ax hanging around his throat, even if Dr. Yang hasn't set a date yet. Which . . ." Xuan gives an awkward shrug. "I didn't really like the guy, but it seems sort of sad after I taped him up so well. He's in the infected holding cells, and there's no way we're getting in there."

I press my lips together, press until I realize I'm biting down on them, that there's a taste of copper in my mouth. The infected holding cells.

I could let the Chairman and a cocky medic make all my decisions for me, but I won't. I'm done letting anyone else tell me what to do based on what they want. I'm done being a stone in someone else's fingers.

"They have to get rid of the dead on both sides, don't they?" I ask quietly.

"Yes, but that side is a high-security—"

I grab the sheet from the floor, then swing my feet back up onto the gurney and lie down, relishing every time my muscles do what I tell them to. There's still a lag when I want to move, a lisp with every word, but I'm a person again. Not a corpse that hasn't forgotten how to breathe.

Pulling the sheet over me like a blanket, I look up at him. "That's where we're going. The infected side of the cells, then out through the morgue." I flip the sheet up over my head. "Howl can pretend to be dead too."

"I don't have access to that side, Sev. Come to think of it, I don't even have access on *this* side. The only reason I've been able to walk through here is because the Chairman—"

"Stand up straight. Look like you know what you're doing. Flip your access badge over so it's harder to see." I close my eyes, the fabric heavy against my eyelashes. Howl got us into the First ring of tents back in the camp where the key was. What was it he said to get us through? That we had new information on SS? "I have a way to get in."

Xuan doesn't say anything, his fingers drumming against the gurney's metal frame.

Pulling the sheet from my face, I look up at Xuan, smiling as prettily as I can manage. "If you take me anywhere else, I'll show this whole place what SS looks like when it gets really bad. Outside-style. They'll shoot you too, probably. I'll burn your ticket out of here quicker than you can run."

My smile widens when the gurney starts to move, and I pull the sheet back up to cover my face. "We'll need to find a mask."

CHAPTER 44
Sev

"WHAT IS GOING ON? WHERE DID THIS COME FROM?" a nasal female voice rasps through a gas mask's filters. "There's a strict protocol. . . ."

"I'm sorry, I just got transferred here from the northern camp, but this is the contaminated side, right? Where they're studying SS?"

"Is that a dead inmate from the other side of the cell block? Why is it wearing a mask? We're very low on resources, and this should have been reissued to an active-duty soldier the moment . . . he? She?" A hand plucks at the sheet as if the speaker wants to peer in at me, the mask plastered to my face, clutching my every shallow breath. It tastes as if whoever had it before me did not care to brush their teeth. "You need to go through the labs at the end of the north wing and make sure they know this mask is functional."

"She's not an inmate, and she isn't dead, either." Xuan's voice is so stilted it makes me wonder if this woman is a First. Not much else would bleed all the color from the medic's sense of humor. "We need to take her through to this lab right away. She's infected."

"Infected? So that *is* a malfunctioning mask, then?" The woman's voice. "Let me look."

"Don't touch her. This girl didn't break any protocols, hasn't been Outside for more than a month, and as far as I can tell, her mask is functional. I'm worried . . ." He lowers his voice, his shadow leaning over me to talk to the woman. I groan internally at the awful manufactured quality of Xuan's acting, as if he's part of some propaganda play. "I'm worried it got *through* her mask somehow. Something changed so SS became contagious. If it's changing again, we need to know *now*."

"It got *through* her mask?" another voice breaks in. One of the guards. Menghu, probably. The Menghu have seen what SS looks like up close, and not in a lab with restraints like a First. "You just brought her through here without notifying anyone? Through the *base*?"

Feet pound across the floor even as the first speaker—the woman—snorts in disbelief. "There's no need to *run*, you stupid Outsider; the likelihood that SS somehow mutated to become small enough—"

A door slams, and then a loud bell begins to drum overhead. The shrill sound pricks at my eardrums, almost as much as the idea of Menghu standing over me when I'm not supposed to move, but I keep still.

"This is ridiculous. The mask must have malfunctioned." Her fingers touch the skin around my mask. "Uneducated savages with no—"

The words end in a violent, bone-splintering crunch, and my eyes fly open in time to catch an eyeful of dark hair and

single red stars on either side of the woman's collar as she collapses. I was right about her being a First. More interested in
peering at us through her microscope than running to save herself and everyone else Xuan and I could have infected, because
she doesn't believe she could be wrong. Xuan stands over her,
the handle of a gun still raised as if she might need another
good hit.

She doesn't.

I stay on the gurney, the Menghu trapped on the other side of
the glass wall staring at us as Xuan grabs her identification cards
and wheels me toward the reinforced door between us and the
cells. The Menghu don't try to come back inside the quarantine
area, as if they're unsure whether or not they should try to stop
Xuan from breaking *into* the prison.

I don't know if they even *can* stop us with the alarm blaring
something about contagion and lockdown. The City had two years
of telling people not all SS victims responded to Mantis. Menghu
lived with it, barred people from their Mountain because of it,
came up against people who'd long lost any sense of control over
themselves wandering out in the forest all the time. Pair that with
airborne contagion, and the chance, even the slightest one, that gas
masks won't be able to keep it out . . . I wouldn't have opened the
door either, if my blood was clear.

The heavy door barring the prison opens with a *thunk* as Xuan
waves the woman's identification over the telescreen next to the
door. As soon as we're through, I hop off the gurney. Doors slam
shut all the way down the dim corridor even as we run, weighted
metal *thunks* of locking mechanisms punctuating the sound of the
alarm blaring down from the speaker system. My legs quiver as I
try to run, my days on my back and Sleep in my veins still dogging

my steps. Feet dragging slower, I have to stop, coughs racking me to the core until my vision starts to go white.

"If this is the same layout as the other side, the lab should be that way." Xuan pulls me up from my hunch and tucks my arm over his shoulder before pointing straight down the hall. "The cells should be in blocks through here. He turns me to the left, my legs shaking under my weight and my ears ringing with the alarm until we get to the first glassed-in cell.

A woman stands inside the cell. Her head is shaved, scabs climbing up from her cheeks to cover half her skull. She thumps her head on the glass barrier, her eyes following us as she hits her head again, again, each time a bone-splintering *crack*. We keep walking. Past a man lying facedown on the cement next to his cot. A young teenager scratching at his arms. An old woman who stares wide-eyed as we pass her cell, pressing herself against the glass when we come close and following us, her hands outstretched until she comes to the end of her cell.

Horror floods my chest. This is like a new Sanatorium. A quarantine where the doctors perform their experiments. I stumble to a stop in front of the last cell in the row, which is empty. I bang a fist against the glass and turn back to the room. "Howl, where are you?" Louder. *"Howl?"*

"Sev!" Howl's voice cracks through me, spinning me around. There's a narrow passageway to the left that blends in with the gray, gray, gray of this place. There's cement and a wall and glass and then *Howl*. Inside.

I crash into the glass wall, looking for a door, a keypad, any kind of opening. Xuan has the woman's identification card. "Xuan, get over here *now*!"

"Sev?" Howl's voice sounds panicked, but I can't focus on

him, searching for the way to get him out. "What are you doing
here?" He looks down at my hospital gown, anger a tick in his jaw.
"Tai-ge didn't get you out? He sold you straight back—"

"No. He got caught." I don't look up, eyes latching onto a
metal box on the floor. Is that how this thing opens? *"Xuan?"*

"Sev." Howl crouches on the other side of the glass, only
inches away. We're almost there. "Tell me there really is a cure."

"There *is* a cure," I assure him. "How do they open the door?
Where do they give you food? How did they get you in?"

Howl seems to wilt, leaning forward to slump on the glass. "It
doesn't matter. If you've got a cure, then . . . that's it, I guess."

"Howl, how do I get *in*?"

He swallows, his eyes so, so tired. "This is an observation deck.
The only way in is through the floor. Sev. Look at me."

My stomach sinks. There's no way in from this level?

"Why won't you look at me? Please, Sev?" I make myself look
up, taking him in. He hugs his arm to his chest, and there's a red
shiny scar peeking out from his collar, still scabbed over in places.
When I get to his face, his eyes, everything inside me goes blank.

He's staring at me, almost like a last wish. One last moment
before he jumps. "You're going out through the morgue?" he
asks quietly.

I nod.

"It's not going to take the Menghu long to figure that out, if
they haven't already. Whatever you did to get rid of the soldiers
isn't going to last long enough to get me out of here."

Tears spill out of my eyes and down my cheeks. Because
I know.

"Run. Get out while you can."

I put a hand up to match his on the glass, staring at his palm, fine lines of scars crisscrossing the skin. "Your story. The one you were telling me when I was Asleep. Before Tai-ge got there. You didn't finish."

He licks his lips, his eyes holding steady on mine. "Go, Sev."

"Sev!" Xuan's voice echoes up the halls. "Yuan's ax, where *are you?*"

"Just finish the story. You like happy endings so much, so what's Chang-e's happy ending?"

Howl leans forward, his forehead pressing against the glass, just opposite mine. "Um . . . Chang-e eats the double dose of immortality and jumps out the window. And, instead of falling, she flies. Her husband tries to shoot her down with his arrows, but she flies right up to the moon."

I blink. "Wait. She ends up on the moon? Immortal. Alone."

Howl tries to laugh. "It's just a story, Sev—"

I slam my hand against the glass, startling him back. "Why do all your stories end up with everyone *alone?*" My hand hits the glass again, tears burning down my cheeks. "I know you make half of them up. Can't you just try for once to make it happy? Right now. Please?"

Howl drops his gaze. "You heard everything I said. What people say about me in the Mountain . . ." His lips press together, hard.

"Howl, I already knew about those things. Mei told me back in the heli."

"Then why are you *here?*" He puts his hand to the window. "It's time to jump. You *have to jump.*"

Anger balloons inside me. "You are not an archer or a lost star or a monster or a Menghu or anything else, Howl! All of us have made sacrifices, all of us have hurt people, and there's nothing wrong with you! It's the *world* that is wrong." My heart aches. "Please help me get you out, Howl. I don't want to live on the moon, I don't want to be a star on the opposite side of the sky, and I am sure as Yuan's bloody ax not going to leave you—"

"Sev, there's no time. You *have* to jump."

"*I don't want to jump.* You came in here to save me, Howl, not to shoot me down." I try to get through all the things I wanted to say before, when I was paralyzed and he was baring all his fears. "I know you've had a rough time of staying alive, Howl. Keeping *me* alive. Leave it behind you. Forgive yourself. We're all doing the best we can with what we have."

He shakes his head. "You don't understand."

"I understand *just fine!*"

Xuan careens around the corner, skidding to a stop in front of Howl's cell. He waves the card frantically over the metal box at the floor, across the seamless glass, up to the corners. Nothing moves. There isn't a door. He grabs my arm without missing a beat. "Nice to see you, Howl. We wanted to help, but now we've got to go."

"Let go of me!" I twist away, but Xuan grabs me, and I'm too weak to escape as he drags me toward the next row of cells. Howl pushes up against the window, his hand still pressed against the glass, and then we're around the corner, through a door.

Xuan dumps me on the floor. Before I can dart back out, he grabs my arm and looks me full in the eyes. "We can't get him out."

My whole brain is on fire, useless, stuck in that moment, Howl on the other side of the glass, so close. "*Let go of me!*" I try to elbow Xuan in the stomach and hit his arm instead. "We can't leave him!"

"You're going to get us both killed, and I'm not okay with that outcome." Xuan catches me around the ribs, hefting me over his shoulder, where my fists can only pound on his back.

"I *hate* you and your self-centered—"

"Shut up. You can join the club later, when there aren't Menghu actively attempting to shoot me. And it's not just us who will die. Everyone will, because whatever it is that you've got in your head will stay there."

The cure. In my head. No, under the floorboards of my old house, just waiting to fix the world. I stop hitting him, my body going limp. Xuan turns abruptly down another passage, his shoulder digging into my ribs to send bile rushing to my throat. A shout sounds behind us just as we get to another doorway, Xuan frantically waving the card until it swishes open and he deposits me on the other side.

It slams closed. Inches of metal between me and Howl.

Grabbing my arm again, Xuan pulls me through lines of heavy shelves, my body moving too slow. Shelf after shelf holds long metal boxes, the aisle set with two tables and instruments arranged neatly to the side.

A cadaver lab.

We only make it a few feet before the door crashes open behind us. I duck between two rows of refrigerated boxes, Xuan folding in behind me as the room erupts with the sounds from the cell block. Feet file in quietly through the door. Only two sets, I think. Why would there only be two soldiers?

Xuan points down the rows toward the back wall. I let him go first, then tiptoe after him, trying to blink away the afterimage of Howl on the other side of the glass. Trapped in a prison, in an observation cage, the exact situation he ran from when he first left the Mountain. What he's been running from all along. Ready to lie, hurt, or kill in order to survive. That's why he took me to the Mountain. Why we know each other at all. It was supposed to be me inside the cell, taking his place.

But now? All he did was tell me to go.

At the back of the lab, there's a thick metal door with a key access and some kind of extra reinforcement. Just as Xuan steps up to the door, a Menghu slides out from between the aisles.

"They're over here!" she yells.

I swallow hard, mind racing. I don't have a gun. I have a hospital gown, a stupid medic, and . . .

A shot tears through the air. I flinch, waiting for the pain to start. . . .

But then the Menghu falls forward, blood pooling beneath her. There's a gun in Xuan's hands and a shell casing the floor at our feet. How did I forget he had a gun?

A second Menghu steps out. Maskless. Short and wide, gun pointed at the ground. It's Kasim.

He smiles, giving me a little wave as he ducks back behind the boxes when Xuan raises his gun again. "Hey! Good to see you, Sev!" Then gunfire explodes and Xuan jerks backward, slamming into the door.

Kasim pulls out from behind the boxes. He winks at me, then shoots Xuan again.

CHAPTER 45
Sev

I FIGHT WHEN KASIM PULLS ME AWAY FROM XUAN. Fight when he throws his coat over my head and picks me up. Fight when he squeezes my arms straitjacket tight at my sides and carries me like a princess from one of my old fairy stories. But in this story, he's carrying me *toward* death instead of saving me from it.

I hear the door open, cool air on my bare feet. Light. He's taking me outside? I scream, twisting, kicking . . . yet nothing makes him pause. Gravel crunches under Kasim's boots, then changes to the firm tap of heels on cement. Something slams into my head, as if he didn't quite manage to pull me clear of a doorway.

Finally, he sets me down on the ground, and I'm already rolling away, determined to meet this upright and with my eyes open. My hands come down on something soft. A uniform.

It's occupied. Sort of.

I'm in the midst of a pile of bodies.

"Done trying to escape?" Kasim asks.

I stand up slowly and back away from the corpse I just touched. Kasim waits, his hands folded across his chest.

"Run," he says. "You've probably got about two minutes to find the guy who's supposed to get you out of here. If it takes longer than that, Dr. Yang's guys'll find you."

"Why did you . . ." I know I should be running. But the dead are all around me, and Xuan's blood is still warm on my chest as it seeps through the hospital gown.

"Sole needs you. I was with Tai-ge when Howl screwed up our rescue operation a few days ago, and now *this* Red bastard"—he looks back, Xuan's limp arm visible through the door—"almost managed to screw it up again. At least he saved me shooting Huifen to keep my cover. There aren't very many infected guards in this place, and no one else would come in, so it'll be easy to pretend you got away while I was trying to revive her. Maybe she'll even live." He points to the trees. "Get out of here."

"Xuan woke me up. He got me out. He was supposed to *help*—"

"He's not *dead*. And it was a miracle you made it this far. Whatever his plan was, if bringing you through that cell block was part of it, the end goal wasn't to get you out."

"He's a good medic, and he helped me. I made him go through the cell block because of Howl."

Kasim flinches. "There was never much chance at getting Howl." The two of them used to be close, but based on the way he looks down, there isn't room for old friendships during war. "Now go."

"Please, Kasim." My eyes burn at the cold dismissal, at the threat of guards and Sleep and Yuan knows what else will happen if I don't walk away right now. But if Xuan isn't dead, I can't leave him here, even if he is annoying. My tears blur Kasim as he picks his way through the bodies on the way back to the door. So many victims. Waxy. Empty. Dead. "Xuan was trying to help."

Kasim limps to face me, anger tearing at his expression. "Haven't enough people died? Your head is the only thing that can stop it. Get out of here!" When I don't move, he starts toward me in a chaotic burst of speed. "If I have to give up my cover here and drag you myself, I will."

I skip back a step, and he stops, his face sagging with emotion. I search for the smile I remember from the Mountain, for something that reminds me of the young man who is supposed to be Howl's best friend. It's hard to see anything but blood. There are cracks in his expression, something vulnerable underneath that just looks broken.

"Fine." He whispers it. "I can't make you any promises, but I'll do what I can to get the medic out. Now start running." He points up to a craggy peak towering over the trees above us, so sharp not even snow will cling to it. "Remember what I told you when I first took you Outside on patrol?"

"Get up high?"

"Find a tree a safe distance away and wait. Sole's guy will find you." He turns back the way we came, a brace on the leg he broke during that patrol.

"What about Howl?" I call after him, my voice hoarse. "You're his friend."

Kasim glances back over his shoulder. "I wish they'd shot him straight out. It would've been easier on him. Dr. Yang's only kept him alive this long because of the cure. And because of you." He yanks the door open and disappears inside.

CHAPTER 46
June

DROWNING IS EXPECTED. SOME PART OF ME KNEW I would end this way. But I honestly don't know what to expect when I wake up after I die. Blurry eyes, sore muscles. That makes sense, I guess. It's the fire I'm wondering about, and the prickly feel of a blanket, heavy and a little bit damp.

A figure comes into view, dropping something into the fire in a shower of sparks, poking at the flames with the broken end of a long pole. *Dad?*

He squats next to me. "Are you awake, June?"

Not Dad. His voice has been gone since Parhat cut his tongue out. No, this voice I know: It's Luokai.

"I saw your hands just before you went under and just barely managed to grab you. Cracked the ice with the punt." He sets the broken pole across his knees. "Skies and gores, what were you doing walking out into a storm like that? It turns places you know into places you don't."

I know that. But when you're afraid enough to run, you don't always remember the things you should. Blinking feels too frightening, as if closing my eyes will push me back to where all the dead people live. I swallow, and it chokes every inch.

We're in a cave. A different one than before, but it's another of Cai Ayi's, the doorway shielded with supplies spilling out from compartments at the back. Luokai must have found it while he was carrying me.

Luokai settles next to me. When he finally speaks, it's quiet. "You're still frightened."

My eyes close by themselves, and I hardly manage to peel them back open.

"I promised my brother you would live. You're Howl's family, which makes you mine, too. The world has lost too many little girls, and today we foiled it. Together."

I stare up at him, my mind catching on every word but not sure how to proceed. One word. "Sev."

He stares at me, frozen for a moment. "You're talking to me."

"Sev's gone." I pull the blanket over my face.

But Luokai peels it back. "We can figure it out. Sole says she's already made progress on the antidote."

An antidote? To *death*? His calm is something I'd like to smash. Not only is everyone dead, but this Seph just saved my life. I don't like owing people.

Luokai's long blink dissolves into something horrified as he stares at me, more of an expression on his face than I've seen on him since we met. "She's not . . . Skies above, June. Jiang Sev isn't *dead*. She's Asleep. Like her mother was. There's an antidote, and it's complicated. They have to figure out the right dosage, and it's dangerous, but there's a chance they can wake her up. Sole didn't say any more." A little bit of a smile curls at the corner of his mouth. "Well. Until just now. She hadn't sent anything in a few days, but this morning she sent me a message to go die."

I'm too cold to feel anything at all other than *Sev's alive, Sev's alive, Sev's alive.*

"Don't you understand what that means?" Luokai leans forward. "*Howl must have made it.* The only other person who knew I had the link was Howl. If Sole knows I'm *not* Howl, then Howl must have told her I was the one on the other end, so he must be alive."

Sole. The girl he left with Howl, the one he wants back in his family.

He smiles a little more. "They're alive, June. Howl and Sev are alive. We're not that far from them. There are supplies here." He gestures to the cave. "If we go together, we can make it. We can get Mantis. We can *live* again. If you take me with you, then I can help with . . . everything. Compulsions. I know how to get into the Mountain."

Words don't usually come easy for me, but . . . "You *infected* me."

Luokai's swallows. "I need you, June. Without help I'll never make it back."

My chest feels tight. "You hurt me. You *broke* my *head.*"

Luokai's eyes well up with tears. "I'm sorry. I know an apology won't fix it. But I was sorry as it happened and I'm sorry now."

I feel the wind again, tousling my hair. Dad was always sorry too, but it didn't stop him from hurting me.

"What I did was wrong, and I've been trying to make up for it every moment since. My whole life has been full of doing things the wrong way. With my brother. With Sole. And now you." He looks down, his lower lip trembling. "I want SS to be gone. This cycle of hurting needs to stop. It wasn't just you I hurt that night.

I wanted more from life than a cold room and people to restrain me back when compulsions come. I don't want to exist in a state of waiting anymore." He holds up the link. "The girl on the other end of this thing is all I ever wanted from this life. I was too afraid of . . ." He takes a ragged breath. "Too afraid of what I became. As if SS made me into a new creature. Something that shouldn't mix with humans or animals, too warped to belong anywhere here on this Earth."

Like Dad. Like me now.

Luokai shakes his head. "But I never was that creature or any kind of creature at all. It's the choices that have made me . . . less." He sighs. "I shouldn't have forced Howl and Sev to leave you. I shouldn't have infected you. But the part of us that is sick doesn't diminish us. I don't deserve to be alone, and neither do you." He looks out toward the cave's mouth, toward the snowstorm, the ice, the woods that will swallow us up. "Together we might be able to survive. I need you, June," he repeats. "But even more than that, I *want* you with me."

I cough, my lungs contracting hard inside me, thinking over my years running through the trees with Dad. Away from him. Who would I have become without him? His soft way of signing to me, his gentle hands, the way he hugged me and kept me close when his mind was clear. And that last night, when he told me to go because he couldn't let himself hurt me anymore.

I hated him and loved him. Back then, I knew if I wanted to keep breathing that Dad wasn't going to be any help. After that day at the river, I could see in his eyes that he knew it too.

But then Howl and Sev walked into our camp, and Dad set me free.

He loved me. It squeezes out of me, tears like fire on my

cheeks. No matter how hard I tried to put him inside the gore skin, the gore *voice* that tells me everything wrong with me and the world, that wasn't him. He loved me, and I loved him. And him giving me away was his last desperate gift.

The gore inside me sighs, and it's as if a weight on my chest has been lifted. If Dad loved me, if he wanted to keep me so badly but still let me go, then maybe even with SS, I'm not just a little lost girl.

Luokai's voice jerks my attention from my thoughts. "It was so close, you falling through that ice. I don't know what I would have done if you had, June. Not just because of what Howl would think or the cure or because of compulsions. Because you deserve to live."

His eyes are closed, that stillness that takes him when he's trying to calm his brain, like a sheet over his head. Pushing compulsions away as I've only seen Luokai do. Parhat, Tian, Cas. Even Dad. They never saw them coming well enough to try. Luokai's fingers *tap-tap-tap* against his knee, his arms shaking. "The hole. It was so dark. And you were down inside it."

His spine snaps straight. And then he stands. Turns toward the cave opening. Goes out into the snow. I pull myself up, folding the blanket around me as I follow him outside. Icy water soaks through my socks as I trail after him until we reach the river— right where the ice cracked under my feet.

I start running before my brain catches up, the gore yelling in my head and my wind at my back pushing me faster. *You could let him go, but what would it help?* they say. *It would just be more death. But if you help, even with all he's done, you can stop the cycle.*

Isn't that what he called it? The cycle of hurting.

I'm quick, the wind and the gore both beside me as I crash into

Luokai's back and wrap my arms tight around his legs to keep him from walking.

Luokai screams something in Port Northian, words I don't understand, as he claws at my arms, then drags me along with him, heading toward a black spot in the ice. The hole.

I trip him. Throw the blanket over his head and sit on his back, stuffing his face down into the snow so all he can do is writhe.

Luokai saved my life, so I owe him. He also kind of took it away, so maybe I don't.

But neither one's the reason I stay with him until he goes still, his hands gathering up to his chest as the shivering cold takes him.

I slide off him and offer him a hand up. He wipes a streak of blood from his nose, his eyes following the red without surprise. We limp back to the cave together, Luokai wraps the blanket back around me, and it's the first time I've thought that maybe some people are worth giving a second chance—not just for them, but for me.

Later, once we're warm again, Luokai watches as I begin packing up things from the cave. The food, waterskins, and other supplies that will keep us alive. "You're going?" he asks.

I zip the pack shut. "*We* are."

CHAPTER 47
Sev

THE DEAD LYING IN THE OPEN COMPOUND SEEM to watch me as I run into the trees. Are they all dead because I wouldn't give Dr. Yang the cure? Dead because there aren't enough masks or enough Mantis to go around? Dead because I ran, like the Menghu lying in her own blood back inside the morgue? I've never killed anyone before. Not with my own hands, anyway. Wouldn't . . . *couldn't*, even when it mattered. And now they all watch me, asking if what I'm doing was really worth their lives.

My hands aren't clean. Maybe they never were, every person who has been killed because of me a drop of red on my palm. Is the cure worth it? Exchanging all of these lives for the hope that more lives might be saved in the future? How can I even measure something like that?

Then Mother's voice comes back to me: *They made their decisions. You make yours.*

Running is hard, all the adrenaline from waking up and seeing Howl spent, leaving me an empty husk. The trees are large enough that the fluffy coating of new snow on the ground is patchy, and

I can pick my way through without leaving too many footprints. My bare feet ache, then burn, then go numb as I creep along. One hand touches the tape on my stomach. I'd almost forgotten the Chairman stuck a link there, but I'm too tired to remove it.

I reach a tree with low enough branches and climb. When I'm halfway up, a man shambles under the cover of my tree, his black eyes glinting as he looks up at me in the falling darkness. Prickles dust across my skin as he smooths a hand across his naked face, the shadows making him look more monster than human. I hold extra still, wondering if he's the man on the other side of Kasim's link or if he just heard me limping along and felt hungry. He isn't wearing Menghu green or a City jerkin and looks worn around the edges, as if every bit of him has been sanded down.

"You can walk, I take it?" he finally says.

"I'm sort of hoping you can't climb," I whisper back, under my breath. He smiles, showing me a mouthful of broken teeth.

"I can," he answers. "But if I have to chase you down from that tree, it'll make getting back to Sole a little more difficult." My stomach calms for only a second at the name of my friend. Howl said she tried to kill him. That she wants to kill me. And Kasim made it pretty obvious why he broke me out. For my head.

The man scrubs a hand through his hair, looking down for a moment. "I already moved the medic, but he isn't going to last long out here. Neither will you, holding still. You're shivering so badly that Dr. Yang's soldiers can probably feel it from their barracks."

My shaking has taken control of my arms and legs, spasming in my abdomen. Sole is reasonable. If I tell her about the cure, then she'll help me get to it.

I hope.

I take the climb down slow, wincing when my numb feet hit the ground. The man looks me over once, then gestures for me to follow him. We walk parallel to Dr. Yang's base until we come to a man lying prone under a tree. I stumble down next to him, his shoulder marked dark red. "Xuan?"

Xuan's eyes peel open, a breath twitching his Second jerkin up and down. His mouth opens, and I'm ready to laugh at anything he says, anything to tell me he's all right. Instead, the man grabs Xuan's arm, jerking him up from the ground, provoking a flood of salty language that makes Xuan sound like a very angry robot as it comes streaming through his mask.

"Clothes are in my pack in there." The man catches my eye and points to the twisted tree trunk. "Make it quick. Patrols are already out here looking for you."

Hands numb, I draw a pack out from the hollow and pull out a pair of canvas pants, a shirt. Socks and boots. A warm green coat with a tiger's snarl at the collar. My stomach twists as I duck behind the tree and put them on. Once I'm changed, the man has Xuan on his feet, the medic's arm linked over his shoulder. He starts off, his pace too long for Xuan, so he's almost dragging him. "Keep your mask. It'll protect you if they use gas. We're going to have to run."

I don't recognize the forest as the guide leads us. Hardly notice passing time, only that my feet get colder and colder, and I begin to worry about frostbite. Xuan doesn't speak to me or the man, holding his side as still as he can, hand balled up against the wounds in his shoulder.

We walk all night, through hills and trees. We walk until the sun bursts into the sky, but the slight warmth isn't enough. I find myself wishing for more suns in the sky today, which makes me think of the story of the archer who shot down the suns, which makes me think about Howl and June—and then I have to stop thinking or I'll explode.

When we finally come to a cave's mouth, my brain is completely dull, hardly registering as the ground swallows us down. The light flashing when the guide places his palm against the rock is a little more familiar, though when the telescreen begins to glow, it's only a barb of light that imprints against my eyes and then disappears. No questions of who we are, ID chip verification, quarantine, or confiscation of weapons. No muck-encrusted showers. Just a black hole and a stranger leading me down it.

Inside the tunnel, a light fixture ignites, revealing a passage clogged with Menghu. The bones clasped about their wrists and necks seem to call to me, cackling with each movement they make.

"She's the one Sole wants," my guide says. He points to Xuan. "Take him to the quarantine."

"No, he stays with me." I clear my throat, trying to blink away the blurriness in my eyes. Xuan hardly looks between the two of us. For once, he's out of words.

Inside, I lean against the little cubicle into which Xuan disappears to get his SS levels checked. The Menghu standing at attention stare as I unbuckle my mask, pull it from my face, and take a grateful breath. The moment it's off, I regret it, the guards' eyes eating at the birthmark under my chin. It's just like the one Mother had, as good as an identification card: I am their cure, if only they can tear me open and drink my insides.

Our guide from Outside has to go into a cubicle as well. When both he and Xuan reemerge from the SS tests with a clean bill of health, we proceed past an air-locked door, the fittings new. On the other side, our guide points to Xuan's mask. "Air's safe in here. Let's have those."

I hand mine over to one of the guards trailing after us, trying not to watch Xuan's hands flex at his sides, not quite ready to give up the barrier between him and SS.

"Why aren't you taking *your* mask off?" Xuan asks the same Menghu. The man doesn't answer, one Menghu grabbing hold of Xuan by the shoulders and bending him over so another can undo his mask's clasps. When they let go of Xuan, his face looks so much smaller without a mask. His eyes follow the two guards until they disappear around the corner.

Our guide takes us in the opposite direction, past more people than I could have imagined living down here underground with an SS bomb waiting to explode just overhead. Men, women, children, most of whom do not seem to be wearing any sort of uniform. The halls seem to stretch forever in long lines in every direction, though we don't get to find out how long forever really is because we turn down a side hall into what looks like a sick bay.

Sole kneels on the floor by a bed just inside, a young man lying pale against the bedsheets. She's holding his hand, the patient's fingers threaded through hers, white-knuckled as he grasps at her. "Only a few more minutes," she murmurs. "A few more minutes and you won't be able to feel it."

"I hurt, Sole." Tears steam down the patient's cheeks, his hands dwarfing Sole's. "When the gun fired . . ."

I can't force myself to move from the doorway, watching her whisper to the man until his eyes drift shut. Our guide clears his throat. Sole's shoulders jolt in surprise, and she takes her time unthreading her fingers from the patient's, smoothing his hair back from his forehead before turning toward us. Even then she doesn't quite meet my eyes or the Menghu's, her attention pulled to the blood on Xuan's shoulder.

"Where do you want her?" our guide whispers, as if he's afraid a full voice would startle her.

"I think we need to get this one into bed." Sole nods to Xuan. "What's your name?"

Xuan swallows painfully as he tells her, somehow unable to keep himself from adding, "The bed thing is low-hanging fruit, but I think I lost my personality on the way here. Pretend I said something funny."

Our guide backs out through the door, then reappears with another medic to lead Xuan away. I put a hand on Xuan's arm before he can go. "Are you going to be okay?" I ask quietly.

Xuan gives me a shadow of a smile. "So sympathetic. Tell you what, if you ever get shot, I'll ask you stupid questions too." He turns to the medic waiting to lead him away. "If we figure out this whole cure thing, I expect a double dose for getting Jiang Sev here." The medic rolls his eyes and leads Xuan out of the room.

Sole is staring at me, blinking too irregularly, but when she does it takes too long. I kneel down so I'm at her level by the edge of the young man's bed. "I need your help, Sole."

"Why don't you go get some food?" She looks past me to the broken-toothed man who brought me in. He narrows his eyes, his fingers twitching as he looks me over again, but then nods and leaves the sick bay. Standing, Sole's hands tremble a little as she checks the young man's IV and vitals one more time before going to the door. "Let's walk. You can tell me how Mei ended up captured when she and Kasim went in to break you out. Or maybe where Howl is. I hoped he'd be with you." Her voice darkens, but I'm not sure what she's insinuating. That Howl ran off again, maybe?

"Mei?" I lick my lips. "Was she the Menghu who was helping Kasim? And Howl didn't run away, if that's what you mean. Didn't Kasim tell you what happened? Howl tried to distract the soldiers after us so I could get away." But then I remember. Kasim wasn't there with Howl and Tai-ge. And when he carried me out of the garrison, he just said Howl had screwed up his rescue attempt. "Howl's still there in a cell. That's one of the things I need your help with."

Sole's steps slow a degree, and she blinks, one, two, three times. I'd forgotten about her twitches and stares, as if she's stuck in a loop of reactions and can't quite get out. But they seem muted, more under control than before. "What do you mean, you need my help?"

I bite my lip, still not sure how to say any of what happened. The resigned look in Howl's eyes. The way he told me to go. "I need to get him out of there. And then to get to the City."

"The City? Why? Everything except the City Center and a few core blocks have been completely taken over by infected. And what isn't infected is being controlled by General Hong."

My jaw clenches. "How do you know all that?"

Sole sighs. "I may be only a field medic, but I knew if we were going to stay safe down here, I'd have to be able to keep an eye on what's happening."

I laugh a little, because I'd honestly expected to find nothing but Sole trying to force-feed people Mantis as they tried to bite her fingers off down here. "You've helped so many people." We pass a family, two little kids running back and forth in what looks like a semiviolent game of tag. "I never could have imagined this place. It's . . . safe."

Sole stops at another air-locked door, accepting a mask from the guards and putting it on before taking me through into a stretch of hallway laced with plastic on all sides and another air-locked door at the end. "I've had lots of help." She nods to the guards who give her a stiff salute as they let us through the air lock to the other side. "Not everyone likes what Dr. Yang is doing, and so they came here." She looks back at me, tracing the line of my skull with her eyes. "Now that you're here, maybe there's hope that it'll last longer than our Mantis stores."

I shudder. "I didn't come here so you could cut me open, Sole."

Something in her expression hardens, a decision calcifying there in her eyes. I can't blame her for it, but I don't like it. She squares her shoulders as best she can. "We can talk about this in a minute. You need to see some people first. They've been looking for you."

"Who . . . ?" But then I shake my head. "I don't have time to see any people. If you can get me to the City, then we'll be able to—"

"No. You need to come see."

A thread of surprise begins to unravel the calm sewn so tightly across my face. Sole isn't the same as when I left her, even if there are blinks and twitches and her fingers clenching oddly at her side. She interrupted me. She's *leading* me. She doesn't care that I said no.

I suppose war changes people in more than one way. Sole being in charge down here doesn't seem like a bad thing. That was our plan, Howl's and mine. Back when we had a heli, a hastily drawn truce between us, and hope that there was more than a ten percent chance of success. We were going to bring the cure back to Sole, because she'd give it to everyone.

Seems like this Sole would stick in the needle without asking first.

We walk down the dim hallway then up some stairs and come

out in a brightly lit corridor, all the doors flung open with voices chattering between them. A child runs out in front of us, stopping to wave at Sole before ducking into one of the rooms. Sole waves back, leading me to the last door. Inside, there are two beds crammed up against opposite walls, barely enough room to slide sideways between them. Peishan, my old roommate from the orphanage, sits on one bed, two of the kids I left at the Post fighting for a spot on her lap. Lihua is lying on the other bed squinting at the pages of a book, mouthing the syllables as she reads.

Lihua sees us first, throwing the book down to run at me. "Jiang Sev!" She slams into me so hard my ribs ache as she wraps her arms tight around my middle. I kneel, joy and relief and confusion all flooding my brain. How are Lihua and Peishan here, and where are the rest of the Sanatorium kids I left at the Post?

"You're safe!" I pull her back to look at her, then hug her close again, her still-short hair prickling through my shirt. "I was so worried about you and the others. . . ."

She pulls away against my arms, wrinkling her nose. "You smell funny."

"I haven't washed behind my ears in a few weeks."

Lihua's mouth drops open. "That's gross, Jiang Sev."

"Sev?" Peishan stands, her voice almost a croak. I stand, wondering what she's decided about me now. She said a lot of things between me finding her in the Sanatorium and leaving her with the kids at the Post. She told me that I was a killer, a bomber, a traitor. That I'd earned every inch of my star brand. For her, all of the nights we stayed up talking about Tai-ge or the factory or the nuns weren't worth remembering anymore.

Peishan lurches toward me, and I flinch back, wondering if she'd hit me in front of the kids, but instead she throws her arms around my shoulders. Wet leaks through my shirt where her cheek is pressed against me, tears burning into my skin. "They came. The Reds. I thought they must have gotten you and Tai-ge and June. . . ."

"We got out okay. We are all . . ." But I can't say "safe," because June's Asleep somewhere and Tai-ge never was safe in the first place.

"Wait." She pulls back, concentrating on wiping her cheeks rather than looking at me. "You knew the Reds were coming? And you *left us there?*"

Sole looks at me, the disappointment in her eyes clearly saying that she believes this was all Howl's doing. I bristle at the thought, but keep my voice to myself. Because Peishan is sort of right.

I did leave them.

CHAPTER 48
Sev

MY STOMACH SINKS AS PEISHAN GLOWERS AT ME, a new layer of betrayal adding to the ones she already believes are mine. Everything went wrong for Peishan about the same time I disappeared. She got sent to the Sanatorium only days before I escaped the City, had a death date affixed to her name. I may have gotten her out before they could kill her, but I carried contagious SS and a Menghu invasion with me. She's seen death, and I was the one who brought it all.

I push back the angry retorts that spring to my mouth. About saving her from Red sharpshooters and First medic students. From the City that would have left her to be shot in the street when the Menghu came, and if the Menghu hadn't killed her, SS probably would have by now. That I spent the last four weeks stuck inside my own head so she and the others could have access to the cure. But I can't, not with Lihua and the other kids listening.

Instead, I change the subject. "What happened? How are you *here*?"

"Cai Ayi brought us. The Reds set fire to the trees, but she got

us down. Wasn't happy when she found out about contagious SS."
Peishan shrugs. "We heard about a safe haven taking survivors and
came this way."

I turn to Sole. "You're taking people in? Even infected? This
isn't just Menghu who aren't happy about having to share their
roast duck with Chairman Sun?"

"The closest thing we have to ducks is chickens, and we can't
eat them. We need their eggs." Sole's face cracks in what I think
is supposed to be a smile, but it looks sort of like a grinning skull
attempting to amuse a baby. "We have some Mantis. And now we
have . . . you."

My jaw tightens at that, but I press on. "Are the others here?
Cai Ayi and the rest of the kids?"

"Cai Ayi is." Peishan's quiet voice is an accusation. Lihua
stares up at me with wide eyes.

I nod. And then I nod again, as if somehow one shaky
acknowledgment that these four might be all that is left of the
kids Tai-ge, June, and I saved from the invasion wasn't enough.
I stand, suddenly not able to stand being in the room, consequences not just of my actions but of the world and how far it's
fallen too heavy to bear. "I'm glad you're safe. I . . . I need to
talk with Sole now."

"Where are you going?" Lihua's eyes go wide, and she looks
nervously toward Peishan. "You're not going away again, are you?"

"I'm . . . not . . . ." There isn't a good answer because I don't
want to leave her again, but getting Howl out of his cell and
getting the cure means I can't stay here for long. Maybe not
even hours.

Sole steps forward, putting a hand on my shoulder. "I'll help
Sev find you all in the cafeteria at dinner."

Dinner in a cafeteria. So normal and yet so different from anything that's happened in the last few months. I hug Lihua one last time. "I'll sit by you."

Lihua smiles and pushes away from me. "Only if you take a bath."

"I'll see what I can do."

Outside the room, Sole leads me quickly down the hall, touching each doorway as we pass. "That little girl needs you," she says.

"Alive or with my head split open?" My breaths start catching in my throat as I try to keep up with her, my muscles and lungs and even bones feeling as if they're disconnected and soft. "There's a cure, Sole."

Sole stops dead in the hall, facing me down. "Spending time with Howl has made you less honest. We both know you didn't find anything at Port North. Can't you see how dire the situation is? We need to *do* something." Sole's hand finds my arm, her fingernails biting into my skin.

"Yes. You have to help me get to the City. Where my mother hid the cure."

She shakes her head. "It's you or them. Those kids, your friends, all of the people down here are going to die if I don't figure out how to help them. I don't want to force you into anything. . . . I tried to force Howl, and that didn't work. . . ." Her back hits the wall, and she sinks to the floor, dragging me with her. Her eyelids start to flutter, every breath beginning to gasp. "They're all . . . they're all counting on me." She looks at me. "*Me*, Sev. I can't be trusted to be in charge of anything. How did this happen?"

I look up and down the hall, trying to pull my wrist free, but her grip is like a manacle, iron tight. "You're taking care of people, Sole. It's safe here. You found food and Mantis, and you're actually *sharing*—"

Sole lets her head *thunk* back against the cement that cuts me off. "We're *trapped* down here. And people keep coming, and everyone is looking to me for answers." A laugh bubbles out of her, cold and hard, and suddenly I'm worried she's going to take a bite out of my arm. "Look at me, Sev! I can't do this. Don't they know that I'm a *killer*?"

"If you were a killer, then you'd be the only one down here, Sole." I extract my arm, rubbing at the marks her fingers made. "Last I checked, killers don't keep an open cafeteria, even if you don't let anyone eat the chickens."

She pulls something from her pocket, clasping hard so an orange light flashes across the back of her hand. A link. "Now even *he* thinks he'll be able to come here. That somehow everything is going to be all right."

"Sole, I'm not following anything you're saying." I crouch next to her, not sure how to help. Sole has never struck me as the most stable person, but why is she breaking in front of *me?*

Maybe she doesn't have anyone to break in front of. Howl's gone. The two of them didn't have anyone else.

"I told him to stop talking to me, but he keeps writing and writing and writing, not even pretending to be Howl anymore, asking me questions about . . . everything, about the Mountain and the food I eat and whether I have a partner or a roommate and whether I'm *happy!*" She throws the link on the ground, sending it skittering across the cement. My brain twists, attempting to figure out what she's talking about, until I remember the island. Howl and me in the cell at Port North, bent over Howl's link to send

Sole Mother's notes. The link that disappeared after we slept in Howl's brother's room.

Sole did have one other person who was taken away along with her family: Luokai. Luokai took the link when he heard it was connected to Sole because the two of them used to be a thing.

Luokai has June. I carefully pick up the link from the floor, hoping the way Sole threw it didn't do any damage. Luokai will know whether June is awake. Whether she's alive.

Sole's still talking, her hands twisted up in her hair. "Now he's asking about Howl and the Chairman's son. . . ."

I look up from the link, only seconds from squeezing it, tearing through it message by message for news of June, but I pause. Luokai's asking after Sun Yi-lai?

"That's who those bombers wanted too. The ones Howl brought here."

Bombers? Howl did say . . . I gasp in surprise as something vibrates against my skin just under my ribs, like a bug caught in my clothes. It's the link, taped to my side. I pull the strip of tape free with a painful yank, then squeeze it in my fist to find a message waiting for me. *I told you to contact me within two days. You are out of time.*

I look at Sole, her hair still in knots around her fingers. "Is Sun Yi-lai here?"

"How would I know that?" She peers at me through her hair.

"The cure is in the City under the floorboards of my old house. I have a plan to get it that will go much more smoothly if we can find him." A horrible, undeveloped plan that comes out even more fragmented and ridiculous than it sounded in my head. "The Chairman thinks his son is here, and if he's right and we get our hands on him, then we might be able to leverage a heli flight into the City. Maybe more help than that, even."

Sole shakes her head. "How could any of us trust *Chairman Sun*? Even if that man hadn't spent the last decade trying to kill off everyone Outside, how would you even talk to him?" She puts her head in her hands. "And you need to drop all of this gore scat about the cure. If it existed, especially if it was magically under the floorboards of your house, don't you think Dr. Yang would have found it?"

"I know it's there." I look down at the link, typing out a quick message to the Chairman. *Just arrived. Negotiating help.*

It buzzes almost immediately. *You have two weeks to produce my son.*

Howl? I send back.

Sole is looking sideways at the link, her forehead crinkled, and I'm not sure if she knows it's different from the one she threw on the ground. It buzzes again before I can pocket it. *They've announced Howl's sentence,* the message reads. *Execution, as we both knew it would be. Yang is trying to draw you out.*

I put a hand out to steady myself against the wall, my knees suddenly made from water, my spine from broken ice.

"What did he say?" Sole asks, craning her neck to get a look at the message, her eyebrows coming down when she sees it's not from Luokai. "Who are you talking to?"

When? I type before answering, taking my time with the characters as I try to think. "We have to figure out where Sun Yi-lai could have been kept if he was here. He must be Asleep the way Mother was, so he'd be somewhere Dr. Yang could have stashed life support. Food and water automatically feeding into him . . ."

"Are you telling me that the Chairman knows you're here? *That* is the Chairman? Talking to you?" She jumps up from the floor, her eyelid twitching. "You're just as bad as Howl. You're going to get us all killed."

"He didn't give me a choice, Sole. And he already knew you were down here." I hold up the link, the feeling of needing to do *something* like static electricity dancing through all my muscles. "We can use this to our advantage. Where would Dr. Yang have been able to keep Sun Yi-lai?"

Sole shakes her head, agitated and walking the width of the hall, back and forth over and over again. "It doesn't matter much now. If anything broke or jammed or ran out, he'd be dead. Dr. Yang's been gone for more than two months."

Ice settles in my stomach. We'll have to hope that isn't the case, because somehow I don't think the Chairman will accept expired goods. "We can start looking once I've gone back to the garrison. Kasim's still undercover there, right?"

"You can't go to the garrison."

"They're going to kill Howl."

"Sev." Sole stops her frantic pacing in one movement, as if I skipped a few seconds of time so one moment she was walking and the next her fingers are once again around my wrist, her blue, blue eyes too close to my face. "The cure is not just sitting in a box somewhere, and there is no way for us to break Howl out." She leans forward so all I can see are her blue eyes. "Are you listening to me? *You are the only hope we have to make the cure, Sev.* Howl doesn't deserve our help anyway." She chokes on the words, letting go of me to cover her mouth.

"What in *Yuan's bloody name* is that supposed to mean?"

"You know." A tear wells at the corner of her eye, then streaks down her cheek like a needle against her flesh. "Howl only cares about himself. We can't risk the limited resources we have on . . . someone like that. We can't risk losing you."

I stand up so fast she reels back, her hands clenching into

fists. "He gave himself up to get me out. He was going to let Tai-ge take me and sit in Dr. Yang's cells all by himself, just because he thought it might give you and everyone else trying to survive out here a chance. Where does that fit into your story about Howl?"

Sole bites her lip, silence hanging heavy between us.

"If *anyone* deserves our help, it's Howl." I can't let it go— Howl's story, the way his voice cracked as he told it. "He trusts you. He *loves* you. And you told him the only thing he was good for was brain matter. That he was too broken to save. When he got to me, he just gave up because he doesn't believe he's worth the air he breathes anymore."

Sole's eyes fall, her hands knotting together. "I've known him a lot longer than you, Sev."

What she's saying sets a new wave of fury loose inside me. "I've known him a lot more recently than you. Look at yourself, Sole." I grab her hands, pushing them up so they're right in front of her face. "Are you still a killer? Or are you saving people *every day?*"

The link buzzes, so I let her hands drop, my fingers clasping hard around the gadget, desperate for anything that will help. The message isn't that. All it says is, *Two weeks. After that, we'll come for all of you down there.*

Two weeks. Does that mean Howl has two weeks as well? Somehow I doubt it. My chest feels hollow, electric, caged, and wronged. Howl's going to die, and the Chairman isn't going to give me any help fixing it. Leaning back against the wall, I pocket the link, my arms feeling too long and my mind moving too slow. Sole is still staring at me, her mouth full of condemnation she can't bring herself to spit out.

I'll have to find my own way into the garrison. But I can't find the Chairman's son by myself. "Help me, Sole," I whisper. "Give me a chance to prove what I'm saying about the cure is true. If I'm wrong"—I gesture vaguely at my head—"you can have at it."

She squints at me, her hands still in fists. But she nods.

CHAPTER 49
Howl

"I DON'T UNDERSTAND." HELIX STANDS WITH HIS forehead pressed to the cell's glass wall, his eyes glazed from alcohol. Odd because when I knew him, Helix wasn't one to drink anything that could compromise his judgment. Impaired vision could be the difference between surviving or not when you live by the bullets in your gun.

My eyes blur as I try to concentrate on Helix's outline. Energy seems to be eating me from the inside at what I've done. I've closed the last door. The one between me and escape.

I made Sev jump.

Helix's hand slaps against the glass, a loud *crack* that makes me shudder. "You know what Dr. Yang is doing, don't you? Why he wouldn't take the cure from Jiang Sev? Why he isn't cutting you open now?" Helix slaps the glass again, his head going with it so he recoils with a pained snarl.

"Everything he's ever told you was a lie." My voice croaks, stripped of any veneer. Raw, real, and honest. It feels good. "If there was a cure inside me, why didn't he cut it out a year ago?

Five years ago?" I stand slowly, walking over to the glass until Helix is just there on the other side. "There aren't very many choices, and all of them are about power. If you think Dr. Yang has the answers, then you follow. If you think he just needs one more ingredient, one more weapon, one more hostage, and it will mean being free, you obey."

Helix's glazed eyes water as he stares at me, his mask pressed awkwardly against the glass.

"Dr. Yang is never going to set you free, Helix. There aren't enough ties between him and the Menghu. You and the other captains are doing what he wants until he gives you the cure. Why would he give it to you?" I look over the smudged glass, eyes finally focusing on Helix's battered gas mask. "This situation we're in now, with SS spreading, with fighting worse than it has ever been? It's your fault for still believing Dr. Yang when he has let you down over and over again." I shake my head and turn away from him. "Sev says there is a cure. It's not in my head or hers. Dr. Yang definitely doesn't have it. How long are you going to keep running for a man who doesn't care if you live or die?"

Helix slams the window with his open hand again, rebounding away, glassy-eyed. "How did you manage to blow up the whole eastern side of the garrison? That's tech we need, Howl. You used to be a Menghu. Loyal. On our side." He chokes on the words as if he doesn't believe them. Helix never was much of a liar.

This isn't my fight anymore. My stone has been placed on the weiqi board, and there's no moving it now. It's the things that I can't fix, can't change that feel like regrets now. Sev was so quiet, so *angry*. As if I'd taken back all my apologies and laughed in her face. Does Sev want anything to do with me now that she's seen what I'm made from, past and present?

Does taking those bombs to save Reds or giving myself up make up for any of it? Or am I condemned because stealing those bombs just provoked Song Jie and Reifa to follow me here instead?

I don't know if taking lives and giving them is something you can balance like weights on a scale. I don't know if there are answers at all. Only that I did what I came to do. Sev is out. The world will continue. I just won't be in it.

"You are nothing," Helix snarls. "Less than nothing. So selfish you want to take us all with you when you die. Just the way you always were." He gets up close to the glass. "You *are* going to die, and I don't care how it happens. Scalpel. Bullet. Whatever. I just want to watch."

I look back over my shoulder, waiting until he meets my gaze. "I do have one thing that might help you. If you see a heli that doesn't belong to the City—a black one?" Helix's eyes focus on me for a second, and I wait a second before continuing to make sure he's listening. "Whatever orders Dr. Yang gives you, find a way to bring it down. You think the blast here was bad? It's going to come for you and every other person alive in these mountains. Drop it out of the sky, or there won't be a war anymore because there will be no one left to fight it."

They're not my people, but they're still people. I can see myself in Song Jie. Thinking if he can just show Reifa what he's capable of, she'll change her mind about him. I regret Reifa's sadness, her mourning for a son she'll never see again.

I don't want them to die, but I don't want hundreds, maybe thousands, to die here in the mountains, killed for no other reason but revenge.

Gein was kind of a gore hole, so whatever.

I lie back on my cot and close my eyes. Shut out the too-bright light, Helix's voice as he continues to yell through the smudged glass. This is what the world has always been. It's blood and death and tears and wishing things were different. I guess that's why Sev needed me. Not just to talk her into letting go of the past so she could look forward. She sees the world as if it's a gore that's going to turn into a butterfly if only she talks to it long enough. I'm the one who twists it to the ground while she casts her spell, because gores don't dream of butterflies. They dream of meat and blood.

The cot feels plasticky and uncomfortable, a sad place to let my body rest when I've spent so long pretending I could run forever. But, for the first time, it's my choice. I'm choosing my own end. Not Dr. Yang. Not the Chairman or that Seph-cursed gore that tried to bite me in two. I chose this.

I close my eyes and wait.

CHAPTER 50
Sev

LIHUA PLOPS DOWN NEXT TO ME AT THE TABLE, her eyes wide on Sole, who is sitting across from us. When Sole smiles, the little girl buries her face in my side.

Sole's eyes fall to her hands clutched around her bowl, the conversation we had yesterday heavy over us. I can almost hear what she must be thinking. *If I've left behind the bad things I've done, then why is this little girl frightened of me?*

I wish I could tell her it's because of her expression, not because of some killer aura hovering over her. But then I notice the link peeking through her fingers. Maybe she's not thinking of Lihua or me at all.

She said Luokai thought it would be safe to hide here. With her. Does that mean he's coming? And if he's coming, does that mean . . . the thought of golden curls, of June's scratched-glass eyes. I can't imagine her staying with Luokai. Not after everything that has happened. But I hold on to the idea of her, alive and on her way.

"So, we have two weeks," Sole murmurs, poking at the

gray-and-brown mush that is supposed to be dinner. She lowers her face to her plate, inspecting the grains of rice that have mixed with her vegetables. "Given our supply situation, I'd say two weeks is the longest I could give you before we need to start being more aggressive about the cure. If the boy *is* still alive and here somehow, the setup would have to be self-governing as much as possible. If there's a machine performing vital functions, feeding him, giving him medicine, keeping him clean . . . that would take power."

"Isn't there a way to see where power is being used? Or if Sun Yi-lai is here, wouldn't Dr. Yang have to have easy access so he could take care of him? So we should probably check . . . I don't know, Dr. Yang's office? The Yizhi wing?"

A girl sitting down looks up at the mention of power. Sole doesn't notice, her chin tipping up as she looks at the ceiling. "Most of the power through the Mountain is down. We managed to link into the main solar panels from down here, but it cut things off upstairs." She goes back to stabbing at her meal with her chopsticks. "It's more likely we're looking for a . . ." She glances at Lihua. "Not a live person."

"I can't think Dr. Yang would just let Sun Yi-lai *die*. If he left him here, wouldn't he have thought through that problem? Like, with a generator or something."

"With enough supplies hooked up on timers so he's fed and hydrated?" Sole shrugs. "That seems very unlikely."

"But possible? Dr. Yang couldn't have risked leading anyone to him by accident, so whatever setup he had would have had to be mostly automated."

"We won't know until we find him, I guess." Sole's only saying it because she doesn't want to argue. Though she can't seem to stop herself from tacking on a caveat. "*If* we do."

I push my bowl away. The girl who has been eavesdropping on our conversation slides closer. "Are you guys wondering about the power grid? It would pick up an individual generator. They geared it to pick up any power flares so people couldn't slip in and then squat in places with lower traffic, like down in the storage rooms." She ducks her head when Sole's frozen stare finds her. "I mean, not unless they wanted to sit in the dark all the time. The grid's up in the Heart."

The Heart. Up above the sectioned-off hallways, up past the Core with its windows to Outside. Above the greenhouses, to the very top of this place. Through how many levels of people who are infected, too scared or too confused to escape? "Could you take me up there?" I ask the girl.

The girl is already shaking her head, eyes wide. "I couldn't go up there. I just . . ." She swallows. "I was just barely learning about it, anyway. I was in my last year of school with Jiaoyang." The teaching collective that took care of kids.

Sole waves her away. "You should probably eat, Gala. They need more hands over in the hospital rooms, and I know you've been helping a lot in there."

Gala ducks her head again, blushing. "Yes, ma'am," she says, then slides away.

Lihua looks up from where she's nuzzled against me. "I'll go with you, Jiang Sev. There's lots of stuff up there, I hear. Peishan was talking to one of the guards, and he said that's where everyone used to live, so there were windows and stuff."

Sole takes a too-big bite of rice. "What we need is more medical supplies, and the Yizhi wing has been completely cleaned out. You can't ask people to risk their lives up there with no definite benefits."

My cheeks heat up at her cool tone. "You mean like maybe saving a kid's life, no matter that he'd be a valuable asset."

Sole shakes her head, slow and steady. "Unless you could think of a way to get something we need—"

"What about Dr. Yang's office? He had to have *some* things up there. . . ."

"He had a whole lab." Sole taps her lips thoughtfully with her chopsticks, but she goes back to eating. "It's probably coded shut, so there's a good chance his supplies are undisturbed. It's likely there are devices and materials inside that could be valuable . . . but if you're suggesting a joint mission—checking the power grid and bringing back supplies at the same time— we'd have to send medics up with you to identify what to take, and I'm afraid we can't spare even one, Sev. We need our medics down here."

"I can think of one you might be able to spare." I hate myself even as I say it.

It doesn't take long to find the medic I have in mind, because he's confined to a hospital bed. Xuan smooths his blankets, sitting with his back against his pillow. "You want me to help you go play with the infected people upstairs?" He looks at me. "I don't know if you've noticed, but I've been *shot*. A couple of times."

"We need your genius medic brain, Xuan. I don't know flesh-eating bacteria samples from painkillers." I lean closer. "Remember how you got me out of the bunker because of the cure? This is how we get it."

"I've done my part." Xuan pulls his blankets up to his chin. "It's my turn to lie in bed and pet furry animals."

"The only animals we have down here are chickens. . . ."

Sole's brow creases. "They haven't let *chickens* in, have they?"

"Sole says she could spare a few Menghu to get us up there to check the power grid." I explain about the Chairman and the deadline to find his son, and our plan to get anything of value from Dr. Yang's office while we're up there. "I'm not going to pretend this is a really good idea. The Heart is up really far."

"Where most of the infected seem to be." Sole glances up from Xuan's charts, biting her lip. "This man shouldn't be out of bed, Sev."

"See?" Xuan points at Sole. "She's a good medic, says exactly what I want her to."

I lean in close so Xuan has no choice but to look me in the eyes, my finger an inch from his nose. "If you don't come through for me here, I'm going to go find the guy who shot you and—"

He puts his hands up. "Calm down! You are so *violent*. I didn't say there was no circumstance under which I could be *induced* to help. What's one more poorly planned excursion with you that will most likely end in worms eating my eyeballs? I just want to make sure that if I'm being assigned to a suicide dive that there's a cookie at the end."

"*With* Jiang Sev?" Sole's eyes zero in on me. "She's not going."

"Yes I am, Sole." I lean forward in my chair, not wanting to meet that mechanical gaze.

"You have no tactical training, and if this mission is going to succeed without casualties that we *cannot afford*, I can't send more than one person who's going to need hand-holding the whole way up," Sole says sharply. "Not to mention if we don't find the cure the way you say we will, *you* will be our only path forward." Brisk and brutal. As always. "You honestly thought I'd risk your head upstairs when we need it so badly down here?"

I touch the back of my head, wondering where the first incision will be. "I'm going, Sole."

"Think what we would lose if you get killed, Sev. Sometimes being a hero means staying behind."

Xuan raises his hand again and clears his throat, adjusting his shoulder theatrically when we both look at him. "If I might interfere before the two of you begin knifing each other." He points to Sole. "You've been taking infected in from Outside. Did a girl come in? Uh . . . a woman? She's twenty-six. Gorgeous. Answers to Fan Luyuan. First marks." He touches his own thumb and forefinger, rubbing at scars that mark him a Second. My heart stills a second, his pain sticky like glue. "I might find myself significantly more motivated if you've got any information on her whereabouts."

Sole sighs, rubbing her temples. "We do have some Firsts who have come in. She's the kind of First who does experiments or the kind who knows only how to eat?"

"She's a medic. Taught up on the Steppe in the City until . . ." He pauses. Until we evacuated to Dazhai. "Her specialty was infectious diseases. The things that girl could do with a test tube . . ." Xuan trails off, his heart not really in it.

"I'll ask down in the quarantines. She's infected?"

Xuan nods slowly, his eyes still stuck on Sole, who is now fiddling with the bedsheets, one hand sneaking into her pocket where she stowed the link.

Infected. Missing. I wonder whether she finally wrote back to Luokai.

"If you find out she's here, will you let me know?" Xuan asks.

"That's all you want?" Sole's head bobs forward as if it's about to fall off.

"I would also like a continuation of the fabulous service here. Including a chicken or two to pet." He grins. Or he tries.

"Right." Tapping the telescreen next to the bed despite the long scratches marring the surface, Sole points to Xuan's shoulder. "Your medical reports indicate your wounds are clean of fragments and that you should heal quickly, so long as you stay still." Sole blinks a little too hard. "If you're going to go up there, then I'll give a list of materials you need. You'll have to check if the things you find are viable, which means we'll need you coherent."

Xuan sighs. "So this chipmunk's dose of painkillers you've got me on is going to go away."

Sole nods. "You'll be going through with a full protective detail and—"

"Some packhorses to carry all the crap we find and walking machine guns to shoot the bad guys." He scratches at his neck, grimacing when spatters of dried blood come away under his fingernails. They haven't cleaned him up beyond the wound.

Sole glances at the reports again before letting them fade from the screen. "Do you feel capable of executing this plan? There will be stairs. Running."

"What, I have choices now?" Xuan looks at me with a shadow of a smile. "You're the worst, you know that?"

I smile back, tears unfolding inside me, and its only force of will that keeps them hidden. "Yes. I know." Sole waits until I look back up to gesture for me to follow her.

Sometimes being a hero means staying behind. As I trail after Sole, I wonder what she has given up to save people. Running into danger isn't Sole's life anymore. Now she has to ask others to do the dirty work. If she dies, this place loses its fair-minded leader. If I die, what would we lose?

Howl. No one would try to save him. Sole knows where the cure is now, though. I don't know that I ever had much more to contribute.

She stops me just outside Xuan's door. "You know you have to think further ahead than if we miraculously find the Chairman's son."

"Yes. I get it. You need me to be alive even if you do know where the cure is and—"

"No, Sev." Sole's teeth dig into her bottom lip. "The Chairman knows we're here, and he knows we're after the cure. He might say all he wants is his son, but that man has been ordering kidnappings, beatings, and killings since before either of us were born, to keep his seat on top. Dr. Yang wants to take his place. The Red General does too." When her eyes meet mine again, a chill runs through me. "I know you think getting the cure will magically fix everything, but really it would just point every powerful person in these mountains toward us. They're snakes, all of them, and they'll bite the moment they feel threatened."

I look down. Yes. I know what she's saying is true.

Sole grabs my shoulder, her fingers pressing hard. "How do you see this ending, Sev?"

Closing my eyes doesn't make the truth of it go away: that if we're going to stop the fighting, we're going to have to stop the people who have been making us fight all along. When I open my eyes, Sole's gaze is hard.

"If we kill them, then how am I better than they are?" I ask quietly.

"If we don't, then how many more people will die because you don't want to get your hands dirty? If you have the means to stop the killing but don't, then is it them killing or is it all of us doing it together?" she asks.

"This from you? When you refused to be a Menghu anymore because you'd done enough killing?"

It's Sole's turn to look down. "I'm responsible for all the people sheltering here." She waves toward the room with Xuan inside, the hall beyond where medics and patients mill back and forth. "When it was just me, I could make the decision not to fight and call it my own penance. But my choices now shape the lives of hundreds of people who trust me to keep them safe. If I choose not to defend them, they'll die. All of them. If you refuse to look at all the holes in your plan to stop a war that's been going on since before any of us can remember . . ." Sole shakes her head. "Then you're sacrificing lives so you can feel morally superior."

I nod, my lips pressed so hard together, I'm afraid my teeth will cut through. How many people died because I refused to tell Dr. Yang where the cure was? Aren't my hands already dirty? It's what mother said in my head . . . or really what I was saying to myself inside the prison that Suspended Sleep made of my mind. So I nod again. "We can talk about this after we have Sun Yi-lai."

CHAPTER 51
Sev

IT'S HARD TO TELL WHAT TIME IT IS UNDERGROUND, but Sole told me the excursion to the Heart is supposed to leave in the early morning. I make my way to Xuan's room to wait, the hallways dimly lit, as if they can't find the energy to ward off the dark. It's only been a day or more since we got here and already the artificial daylight turns my skin to gooseflesh, the stale air from the vents catching in my lungs. *How did they isolate their vents from upstairs?* I wonder. *From Outside, where SS is in the very air, it seems. A filtration system, like the masks?*

Xuan is up and waiting for me, and neither of us speak as I help him out of bed and down the hall until we're to the air-lock doors. Five people wait for us, one of whom I was not expecting: Peishan.

I pull her away from the others. "What are you doing here? Sole said they weren't sending inexperienced people up there."

"They told us they needed people who know how to sneak, and I figured after sneaking here from the Post, I qualified." Peishan blinks at me, the now familiar sourness that has replaced my friend's open smile somehow exaggerated by the way she looks toward the door. She shifts her weight from foot to foot and runs fingers through her short hair, making it stand up in spikes around her gas mask's straps. "Did they ask you to come too?" A little hope cuts the vinegar in her expression, as if having a friend on this excursion could make up for a lot of what's come between us.

"I'm . . . I'm not supposed to go." It's a pathetic finish.

The last semblance of goodwill that reappeared when Peishan and I found each other evaporates from her face. Not to rancor and blame as it did when I first saw her in the City, or to annoyance and rejection from when we were at the Post. This time her shoulders sag. "Oh."

My eyes prickle, and I touch her arm. "I *want* to go, but Sole says—"

Peishan pulls back. "It's okay. They said it could save lives. That it needs to be done. That we've eaten enough food, and it's time to give back a little." She glances toward the heavy metal door where a Menghu is handing out knockout grenades and checking masks. She adjusts her mask, the straps tight enough that the plastic digs into her cheekbones. I look down when she walks over to take her share of grenades.

"I guess I'll see you when I get back." She turns toward the door.

Xuan steps up next to me, putting a hand on my arm. "You're a jerk."

"You *know* I want to go, Xuan."

"I also know the cure isn't in your head, and risking you isn't a problem. You told Sole where the cure is?"

Nodding feels clunky, because I can see where he's headed. I know what the right thing to do is. But all the people upstairs . . .

"So if you die, she can find it just as easy as you can. You want to come on this mission, then come. Sole isn't here to stop you." He adjusts his shoulder. "Though if I were you, I wouldn't. It would be too hard to stand in my shadow. Heroes are born, and you whine too much to make the cut."

"*I* whine too much . . . ?"

The door hisses open, a Menghu slipping through ahead of us to check the second door. Xuan looks steadily forward, his cheek twitching under his mask. Peishan holds her grenades close, like eggs gathered from a chicken coop.

The others—a Menghu with a tiger screaming from her collar, and two people I assume to be Outsiders based on their hollow cheeks and patched-together wardrobe—lean forward, watching the first Menghu check past the door. There's a rack next to the entrance lined with weapons, grenades, masks. It's a sadly spare display, like the orphanage banquets at Guonian, all of us huddled inside and scaring one another in the darkness of the first night with no moon. When Peishan and I were too young for factory shifts, we'd giggle and hide with pots and pans to scare the monster when it passed over. I remember an empty stomach, but that we were happy.

Peishan looks just that small now, eclipsed by the reinforced metal door. The only thing between her and the hundreds of people infected with SS on the other side.

When I was scared, facing down monsters and hallucinations as I left the City the first time, it was Howl who stood right next to me, my personal guide through the levels of hell. He was brave and told me I could be too, so I believed it.

Don't do what I would do, Howl said.

I don't have to do what Howl says.

I grab Xuan's arm before he can fall in line with the others about to step through the door and give him a sharp nod. He smiles and returns the gesture.

"Yuan's stillborn triplets!" he swears. My hand on his arm is soft, but he curls around it as if I punched him right in the bullet holes, dropping to the floor with a melodramatic flair.

The Menghu and Outsiders turn, alarm like needles in their eyes. Peishan darts toward us, but one of the Outsiders moves quicker than she can, pulling her back. Watches him writhe on the ground, all the oxygen seeming to leave the room as they all wait to see if Xuan is compulsing—if the mission is going to fail before they even leave the air lock.

With all of them focused on Xuan, I slip over to the rack of supplies behind them, pull on a mask, and grab two of the knock-out grenades. The door is cracked open, so I go through to the other side, where the Menghu who opened it for us waits. There's a short hallway and a second reinforced door that leads to the contaminated parts of the Mountain. The last barrier between us and whatever is waiting upstairs.

"Ready to go?" The Menghu looks past me to the others gathered around Xuan by the weapon racks. "What's going on?"

"I guess the medic is still recovering from something." My hands want to shake, but I hold them still. "Hope he doesn't collapse while we're up there."

"That's a good thing to hope."

He taps his fingers impatiently as Xuan lets Peishan help him up from the floor, his horrible acting back on display. "Wow. It seemed quite serious for a moment there, but I guess it was just gas."

Peishan pats his arm awkwardly, the other Menghu and two

Outsiders filing in hesitantly behind her as she leads him through the door.

"This floor should be clear, so we'll have some time to . . . get used to things." The Menghu with me looks us all over. "Seven of us?"

The other Menghu looks up. "I thought—"

"I was late," I cut in, refusing to look at Peishan as her eyes narrow over the robotized voice issuing through my mask. The Menghu who started to argue nods, dismissing me once again. She doesn't look at Peishan, either, as if the two of us are the first who will be torn down, and the loss isn't one she'll worry about.

The second door in the air lock swings open, showing a black hole on the other side. Sole said the power was out, so we break quicklights to cut the dark. I have to blink twice to make the shadows stop crawling onto the floor and across my boots before I can force myself to walk through.

The male Menghu leads us, whispering instructions over his shoulder. "Save your grenades for groups, not individuals who we can run from or walk past. Most people up here aren't exactly lucid, or they would have left. That doesn't mean they are compulsing, though."

"Compulsions aren't always violent, either," I say, trying to remind myself as well.

"This strain seems to make Sephs more difficult." One of the Outsiders this time. Scars crisscross the backs of his hands like City hash marks, so far below the City's estimation that they'd left him outside to count them himself. "Or perhaps it's just that everyone is more afraid."

Peishan pauses at my side, Xuan at the other. "Why did you come through?" she whispers.

"Because I didn't want you to have to face this alone." I gulp the words, wishing I could say them with conviction. She looks away, her brow twisting her face into something hard.

Before she can tell me to go away, Xuan gives me a push that sends me after the others. "Gushiness later. Let's get this done, ladies."

The lower storage corridors give way to stairs, and then to gray hallways lined with telescreens I remember from when I was here. I stay close to the four people assigned to get us to the Heart and Dr. Yang's office, red light leaving their faces drawn and corpse-like.

The moment we pass into nonpatrolled territory feels like stepping through a City gate from one quarter to another. My light finds trash and broken electronics littering the hallway. We have to step around a telescreen partly torn from the wall, its shattered face grinning at us from the floor.

"We'll go past the track, then up the south stairs," our lead Menghu whispers, the instructions passed from mouth to mouth until they find me. Goose bumps needle my skin at the thought of going through the large underground track with its glass ceiling, anyone above able to see our lights traipsing across.

When we get there, it's worse, the quicklights fading just as a frantic scrabbling noise comes from our left. Xuan falls in next to me, Peishan just behind, my new quicklight igniting before the others can get theirs out.

The red light shakes as I hold it aloft, the two Menghu pointing their guns toward the sound. A shape steps clearly into the light, feathers and claws glinting in the red. A scrawny rooster, his comb dangling down over his beak.

We move on, up so many sets of stairs I lose count. Shuffling and scraping seems to follow us, starting and stopping as we do, breaking into a run on one occasion, though no matter how high I hold my light, it doesn't catch anything in the darkness.

"Is it usually this unpopulated?" Peishan whispers to the two Menghu, but neither of them answer. Broken glass crunches under our boots.

I don't recognize much until we come to a glass wall, the space on the other side stabbed through with harsh natural light. The brightness of it hurts my eyes as I take in the horror version of the Core, where I ate my meals the few days I lived here. It was also where the Menghu danced for Establishment celebrations. Now the wooden counter where they served meals is blackened to ash, and the glass lining the walls up to the Heart seems to be cracked through, crystalline shards littering the floor.

Inside the Core, there are people lying in the beams of light. Some with bones sticking out at odd angles, their clothes torn and bloody. Some with ribs that move up and down with life. Others walk back and forth on silent feet, their hands dragging across the scored glass walls.

We stay back from the windows, the Menghu in charge point-ing us up a back stairway. I jolt to a stop when a face pops up in the window next to me, a girl with long dark hair and wide eyes. Her eyes bore into me, her fingers pressing hard into the glass.

Xuan's next to me, his voice low. "Keep walking, Fourth."

Fourth? It's enough to shake me loose from the girl's eerie stare. No one's called me that since . . . well, the last time I saw Xuan. Peishan pushes forward a step to walk alongside me, our arms brushing as if she can't stand to feel alone, even if she has to cozy up to me. The closeness doesn't relax the tight knot twisting my insides, but serves as an anchor. I wish I could reach out and grab her hand like we did when we were little, keeping each other safe from nuns and compulsing orphans, mean Red teachers and grumpy soldiers. But I don't.

As we walk, I duck under a bouquet of wires spilling like intestines from the wall where the telescreen has been torn free. The paint on the walls is scored deep, debris coating the floor so every step is a careful negotiation to avoid shattered glass and bent metal rims from lighting fixtures. I've only been to the Heart a few times. All I remember was lots of glass, lots of stairs, and lots of people looking at me askance because I wasn't supposed to be there.

"We've got followers. Move quick," the lead Menghu instructs. We come to a turn in the corridor, and the second Menghu lags behind, waiting until all of us are safely past to pull one of his grenades free. He throws it, running after us before I even hear the *ping* of metal on cement and the flower of sound that follows.

We come to a room with a domed ceiling and arched doors dotting the circular walls. Between them, there used to be shelves and shelves of books. My feet drag as I look around at what used to be a library, the last remnant of my mother and what she brought to this place: Knowledge. Beauty. Stories.

It's all gone now. The books. Even most of the shelves are missing, broken into slivers on the floor, a few nailed across one of the hallways as if to form a barricade.

This is where Howl brought me, his face soft as he watched me drink in the sight. Howl, who told me that, here in the Mountain, the misbehaving princess put to Sleep woke up at the end of the story. That she lived happily ever after.

I was so full of hope and longing then. So, so stupid.

But I can feel it still in me as I look across to the hallway that leads to Dr. Yang's office door. There won't be any people rotting away forever in my story. No lovers imprisoned on opposite ends of the sky. No one jumping out of a window to escape the man she loves.

"Sev?" Peishan's hand tugs at my arm.

I let her pull me forward, ignoring Xuan's eye roll, which seems mostly a cover for the way he's holding his arm stiff at his side, his stride off-balance. He's in pain, sweat streaming down his neck.

Howl believes he's dead. *Jump,* he said.

Jump.

I won't. Howl's a part of my story I refuse to give up.

CHAPTER 52
Sev

OUR GROUP SPLITS IN TWO: PEISHAN, XUAN, ONE Outsider, and the lead Menghu staying with me to head toward Dr. Yang's office and the medicine we hope is there. The other three break off toward the Heart's control center to check for blips on the power grid. It isn't long before footsteps echo up the hall after us and one of the Outsiders uses a grenade to stop whoever's following. Then another when we hear voices ahead. Another when a sort of howling comes ricocheting up the whitewashed hallway, sinking into the torn-up carpet.

By the time we get to Dr. Yang's office, we only have five grenades left among us, a deficit that gouges holes in my middle as I try to comprehend walking back the way we came. The office door itself is metal, flanked by telescreens that are all broken but one. The Menghu pulls something from her pack, linking some wires into the unbroken telescreen that link to a handheld one from below. "This is a bit of luck. If it still works, I can give it some power, then . . ."

But nothing happens, not with the screen, not with the hall or the ceiling, and certainly not with the door. It stays exactly where it's meant to: between us and Dr. Yang's things.

Swearing, the Menghu looks over to the Outsider. "You've got the other thing?"

"If we use it, we won't be able to close the door." The Outsider pulls his pack from his shoulder, unbuckling the top. "And it'll be loud, so we'll draw attention."

"There might be a way to close off the door. Depends on what kind of extra security he had in there." The Menghu transfers her focus to me and Peishan. She's not wearing a bone bracelet, which lets me look at her in the eyes without flinching, even if it doesn't mean she doesn't *have* bones. When I was here before, I saw bracelets, necklaces, even an anklet—Menghu wearing their list of kills with pride. "We'll just have to do this quick."

Perhaps with Sole in charge, that kind of pride isn't appreciated.

"You two are in charge of keeping anyone drawn by the noise away from us. Keep as many grenades back as possible, since we have to get back out of here somehow." There's a strained quality to the Menghu's voice as she checks Peishan's grenades, a sort of unraveling that collapses in my lungs. She's not sure we *are* going to get out.

Peishan stands steady, looking one way down the hall with her three grenades cradled against her. I keep the last two close, squaring myself as I stare down the hall in the other direction, Xuan standing between us.

"Make sure you catch any bullets coming this way for me," Xuan whispers as the Menghu and the Outsider set what looks like an electrical saw to the door's recessed hinges. "I've done my quota in that department."

"They gave you quotas up in the Red Quarter? It would be nice to know I could quit after two bullets." I flinch as the saw whines to life. They put the blade against the metal hinges, and the whine turns into a metal scream.

The sounds seems to drill straight down into the floor, and I can imagine all the people we saw below in the Core looking up at the disturbance. Fear trills down my arms and legs as a young woman comes lurching around the corner, a wooden two-by-four clutched in her hands. She stops at the far end of the hall, distant enough I can't make out her expression, just the casual way she leans on her board, as if it's a walking stick. Others file in behind her. Not rushing us or slamming into the walls or crawling through and licking each other's toes. Just looking.

"Who are you?" the girl yells over the noise, her voice husky as smoke.

The Menghu looks up from where they've cut through the first hinge, pulling back while the Outsider sets the saw to the second. "Save your grenades unless they attack," she says, low enough I hope those gathered to watch can't hear. "Try to distract them instead."

"We're from below," I call back to the woman. The saw begins screaming again, the sound grating down my spine.

"The people who come up here to gas us and take our food?" The woman takes a step forward, hefting the two-by-four.

"You can come with us when we go back down. It's safe."

The woman smirks at me as she shuffles closer. "You're going to let *us* in? Sephs?"

Nerves needle through me as the distance between us closes from twenty feet to ten. One of the men behind her begins to shake, his eyes darting between the wooden board and me. It happens in a second, the board suddenly in his hands, a yell in his mouth.

The grenade slips in my palm, but before I can throw it, the girl wrenches him back by his long tunic, one of the others grabbing the two-by-four away from him. But his compulsion sets off what looks like a chain reaction, others in the group startling back, running, screaming, one slamming himself up against the wall.

The saw's screams stop again long enough to change over to the door's locking mechanism by the handle, but there isn't going to be enough time. More of the Mountain's stalwart residents have crept up the hall on Peishan's side, the sight of the first compulsion sending ripples through all the assembled crowd.

"Stay back!" I say it in the calmest voice I can muster, terror bubbling through every word. "I don't want to—"

But I blink, and the world changes. The girl who first spoke runs at me with hands outstretched, broken nails swiping toward my neck. I raise my arm to throw my grenade, but a hand catches me from behind, hauling me off my feet. My feet scissor back and forth on the floor, trying to find some kind of leverage, but whoever's got hold of me is too strong, hauling me up, then throwing me to the ground.

Carpet burns against my skin as someone jerks me backward, dragging me inside a room a few degrees warmer than the hall. A sheet of wire-threaded glass slices between me and the girl who had the two-by-four, her hands outstretched to grab me.

She presses a hand to the glass, her fingernails scratching against it as she pushes into the obstruction. Another body slams into her from the side, jerking her away from the frosted surface, others streaking by, shouts and more gunshots muted through the barrier.

"That'll keep them out." The Menghu stands up from Dr. Yang's desk. "Dr. Yang was particularly paranoid about access to his office, I guess. Enough to have a fail-safe bulletproof door installed just like General Root did. Maybe they didn't trust us even then."

Xuan sits huddled in on himself just inside the doorway, his hand to his wounded shoulder as he takes deep, measured breaths. Peishan is just next to him, her whole frame shaking. The fingers digging into my ribs let go, allowing me to slump to the ground, and the Outsider steps over me. "You've got more fight in you than I expected." He grunts, rubbing his ribs where I elbowed him.

I stumble to Xuan's side, looking between him and Peishan. "Are you okay?"

His eyebrows go up in what would probably be an annoying smile if I could see the bottom half of his face through the mask. "The fact that I am still conscious is only because of my astounding levels of pain tolerance." Peishan doesn't answer, her face pale. I put a hand on her back, rubbing softly as if that somehow could help when there are still yells sinking through the frosted glass from the hallway.

"Come on, we don't have a ton of time here." The Menghu gestures impatiently at us. "I don't know how long that glass is going to hold." She points to me and Xuan. "You two, get in here. We need to move fast."

The Outsider reaches out to steady himself on the doorway as he walks past the Menghu, and she slides in next to him. A shock goes through me at the way they fit together. I'd thought the two Outsiders and the two Menghu had been sticking to their own kind, but the way these two look over one another, checking for blood, I recognize partners. Friends.

An odd feeling comes over me, trying to reconcile these two with Helix shouting into the night with his gun drawn, looking to put a bullet in June because she was a Wood Rat. The rules have changed since I left the Mountain. Or maybe Helix just likes shooting people, and not everyone under this rock is prejudiced.

I sort of feel stupid for not having thought of that.

"You watch the barrier." The Menghu points at Peishan.

Peishan stands slowly, her eyes on the glass behind me, her face pale.

"Why don't you go help them." I step between her and the glass, trying to smile. She looks so frightened. "I'll stay here."

She shudders and ducks her head as she follows the others into Dr. Yang's lab. Arms prickling, I turn to see what she was looking at.

The girl who first spoke to me is standing only inches away on the other side of the glass, her eyes locked on me. She's recovered her two-by-four, and the wood is bloody, red dribbling onto her brown coveralls when she leans on it.

I fall back a step, only one knockout grenade slippery with sweat in my fist, the other lost during the tussle in the hall. The girl cocks her head to the side, her voice, muffled by the barrier, so normal it hurts. "Why are you here?"

I button my lips, not sure why it matters to her why we are here. Just that no one seems very happy about it.

"Nei-ge was all telescreens and desks. What's in there that's so important—"

A shriek that penetrates the glass cuts her off. Her head jerks to the side, eyes widening at something I can't see. She drops into a ready stance, two-by-four at the ready, but then slowly relaxes. Deep breaths rack her chest, and she closes her eyes for a moment, leaning heavily on her weapon. She takes a moment to settle herself before turning back to me. "Whatever it is, if you want to get out of there alive, you're going to have to give us something."

"What do you want?" My voice barely squeezes free of my throat.

"Food. Medicine. Something." She pulls at her blood-spattered coveralls. "You keep the air locks up, let some people into your safe haven even while forcing others back. There are no set rules, no process to follow to get in. You abandon most of us to this place, then come back to collect anything valuable. When is someone going to come up here to collect *us*?"

A voice booms out from behind me: "We don't have anything to give you." The Outsider emerges from the lab, setting a pack crammed with bottles next to me on the floor.

The girl sucks on her lip, a slow, studied effort. "Then we don't have any reason to leave you alive." Her lip curls. "You think we haven't figured out your gas-and-run strategy? We let you come up here to see what was so valuable that you had to bring portable generators with you to make sure you could access it."

Portable generators? With the power out, wouldn't bringing things like that up here have drawn anyone with half a brain right to us? I can't look away from her, my heart beating hard against my rib cage like a wild bird being kept as a pet. There are so many questions I should have asked before we came up here, but I wasn't supposed to come. So I didn't.

"If there's nothing for us to take, then we'll just kill you." The girl looks me up and down thoughtfully. "Take your generators. You can't have more than a few more knockout grenades, and we aren't going to crowd up all polite and let you blank us out all at once. You want to live, then you have to give us *something.*" Her voice cracks, but her eyes don't waver.

I know that desperate feeling. "What's your name?"

"Aya."

A shiver runs through me. "Aya was my sister's name."

She blinks. "So?"

My sister was sick too. Or the City made her think she was. I'm not sure now. All I know is they killed her before she could grow into a proper adult. They took her life, just the way *this* Aya's life has been taken. Not even a stone on Dr. Yang's weiqi board. More like a speck of dust he brushed away and hasn't thought of since. "The other three who were with us—they went to the Heart. Are they safe?" I ask.

Aya shrugs. "I don't know."

Yuan's *blades.* I don't want people to die, and I don't want to walk away from this with nothing. "We're getting materials to make medicine, and our friends were after some information from the power system. Let us through, Aya. There's room for more people below. If you come with us past the air locks, there's food down there, Mantis—"

Hands grab hold of my coat from behind, the Outsider jerking me back a step. "Shut up. This isn't a negotiation."

"Let go of me." It's the calmest, coldest my voice can go. "Sole let you in. What makes you think the people up here won't be welcome?"

"Because there's only one of me, and I'm not infected." He slides between me and Aya and pushes me back from the glass, sending me stumbling toward the door into the lab. "Life isn't balanced out to be perfectly fair. Right now that means there isn't room for everyone." He jabs a finger toward the lab, instructing me to go help.

"No." Aya's eyes burn on me as her hand goes into her coat. It comes out again holding a gun. "Don't go help the others. I want to talk to you."

"Don't waste your bullets on this glass." The Outsider waves Aya away without really looking at her. He focuses on me, eyes hard. "You go back there, where you can't do any more damage."

"Damage?" It comes out of me in a hiss. The dismissive wave sets my insides burning with acidic anger, the way he pushed me, as if even though we're all supposed to be working together to save each other, the fact that he's taller than me means he's in charge. "Don't touch me again."

"Little girl wants to be in charge?" He takes a step toward me, but I refuse to back away even as he towers over me.

Tap-tap-tap on the glass. I don't look away from my staring contest with the Outsider until the girl's voice filters through. "Cover your eyes if you want to keep them."

The rest happens so fast—there's a *thunk* against the glass, then another and another, a spiderweb of cracks curling out from one spot right at the center of the glass. She's shooting the same spot over and over, and I barely manage to jump back before a bullet comes singing through, glass exploding after it like the tail on a comet.

Another girl slides to a stop in front of the glass next to Aya, something metal and spidery in her hand that they feed through the hole the barrage of bullets made, but then the Outsider is on me, grappling for my arms, fear punching through me. "The grenade!" he yells, the sound ringing too loud for the consonants and vowels to line up correctly. An electrical *pulse* fuzzes through my ears, shattering what's left of my hearing and the rest of the glass, the shards falling like droplets of water from a cliff. My fingers fumble over the grenade, trying to find the pin, my fingers sweating and sliding across the warm metal.

"Give it to me. . . ." The Outsider grabs the grenade and knocks me sideways to the floor.

Another gunshot.

Red buds up from the Outsider's chest, and everything seems to move too slow and too fast at once as he drops to his knees. The grenade falls from his limp fingers, but I can't hear it hit the floor. I can't hear anything at all.

CHAPTER 53
Sev

GLASS SHARDS CRUNCH AS I SLIDE DOWN NEXT TO the Outsider. His eyes are open, blinking, but he isn't looking at me.

"Move away from him." Aya's voice is muted in my ears. "The rest of you . . . !" she yells toward the lab. Peishan and the Menghu stand horror-struck in the doorway. "Slide your weapons out first, then come out with your hands up. You—gather up everything they were trying to pack out of here." She's talking to someone else. More of the people from the hall?

I can't concentrate, can't make myself even look, staring down at the Oursider. His eyes blink once more, a long gasp sucking into his mask filters. And next to him, lying so quietly on the floor where he dropped it: the grenade.

My hands are on it before I can think, the pin coming out easily between my fingers. I throw it toward the two girls standing framed by the ruin of broken glass as if they own the world and all of us.

The other girl runs out into the hall, covering her face, but cold-faced Aya hardly flinches as the grenade comes to rest at her toes, knockout gas foaming around her ankles. Then suddenly she's on top of the Outsider, wrenching the gas mask from his dead face, pressing the filters hard against her nose with one hand. Her gun is in the other hand, switching between me and the Menghu as she inches out from the lab.

"My crew will kill you the moment you stick your noses outside this room if I don't come out first to tell them you're okay," she hisses through the mask. "They know enough to stay out of the gas."

The Menghu's eyes leave Aya for only a split second, long enough to take in the Outsider—her friend—lying in an ocean of blood. Peishan hangs just inside the doorway, her hand tight over her mouth.

"Tell me quick." Aya's voice shakes as she turns to me. "You said you could get us below. How?"

"Did she?" Xuan says as he comes to kneel next to me, his hands checking over the Outsider. But there's no reason. Both of us know he's already dead. He looks at me. "Maybe try asking for something like . . . all of our lives staying intact before promising the world to these people."

"You're going to look just like him if you don't start telling me something I'll like," Aya interjects.

"They won't let you in downstairs unless you're with us." The lie tastes bitter on my lips, bringing Howl's face to my mind. I should have tried making a deal with this girl before saying anything else. Howl's the one who taught me to outline parameters, to bargain, to mistrust. He's the one who taught me that you can still love in a broken world, that sometimes actions aren't what they seem. That sometimes killing is desperation, the way mother said it in my head. *If I had killed Dr. Yang first . . .*

"Get us to our friends in the Heart first. There's something in there we need."

Aya nods. "Fine." She points to Peishan and the Menghu. "Hands up until we've checked you for weapons. Huishan?" she calls. The gas is dispersing down the hallway, and shapes appear in the mist, sleeves and shirts up over their noses to ward off the last wisps of gas. A girl sticks her head inside the ruined glass, waiting for orders.

"Take two over and scout out the Heart. See if you can secure our way." The girl nods and ducks back out, tapping two others hanging back in the hall. Aya gestures the others, five frazzled and bloodied teenagers who look about my age, into the room. "Check them. Grab their packs." Without watching to make sure they obey, she turns back to Xuan where's he's still crouched by the dead Outsider. "You're a medic, I'm guessing?"

Xuan purses his lips, flinching when one of Aya's crew members starts patting him down. "I'm never sure if people ask that because they want my help or because they want to get rid of me. Put me down as a maybe?"

"He is." I keep my hands high until the person twitching at my clothes backs away. I stand, pulling Xuan up once he's been checked and am instantly sorry when he gives a pained grunt, a hand going to his bandaged chest. "If you have wounded, we'll help any way we can. But it'll have to be on the way." Peishan shrinks away from me, the Menghu at her side glaring at the blood marking my clothes.

A dead man's blood soaked into my knees, his body a cooling lump on the ground. It breaks through for a second, the horror, but I push it away. I hate that I've seen enough bodies now that

I can bar it from my mind. Hate that even if it's monstrous, it's what I have to do right now.

This Menghu probably has seen more death than I have. But this man meant something to her. "What was his name?" I ask.

She jerks away from the man patting her down and heads to the door without answering, looking everywhere and yet at none of us. "They've got our stuff. Let's get over to the control room and then out of here."

Aya nods, running out in front of her into the dark hallway, the other members of her crew forming a vague circle around us, waiting for us to follow. I grab Peishan's hand and follow Aya into the hall, measuring my steps to allow Xuan to keep pace. Aya stops when we come to a broken shape on the floor, one arm lying at an unnatural angle under a cloud of dark hair. The Menghu stops too, her nose flaring.

"She got hurt in the fuss. Pick her up," Aya rasps.

"Wait, I have to see if she can be moved. . . ." Xuan drops to his knees next to the body.

"We don't have time." And then Aya's running again.

I bend down to leverage the girl onto her back, but the Menghu elbows me aside. "Not enough muscle on you to make it very far," she mutters, gesturing for Peishan to pick the girl up by her boots as she loops her own arms under the girl's armpits.

I shrug it off, hand a quicklight to Peishan from my pocket, and take the girl's feet anyway. It's an awkward way to walk, the light bobbing madly, shadows seeming to bite down on us every step. She feels light, hollow-boned, like a bird. But I can't think about it. Can't think. The other crew members seem to sink back into the darkness, though I can feel them there behind us.

When we finally catch up to Aya, she's lodged behind one of two huge metal doors that seem to have been pried off their hinges, then set cockeyed halfway across the corridor. The room beyond looms large enough that it swallows Peishan's light. "This is where they were supposed to be?" I whisper.

As if in answer, something in the room rustles. And then there's a horrible dry snicker of laughter, like dead leaves swirling in the wind. The hair on the back of my neck stands on end, my arms trapped under the unconscious girl's weight.

"Ari? Em?" Aya's voice is a sliver, the sound pricking at my skin. "Huishan?"

Something unbalances inside the depths of the room, like something heavy crashing to the floor, the broken pieces skittering in all directions. Aya raises her gun, eyes wild because there's nothing to see. "Light!" she hisses. "I need the City-cursed *light*."

The red glow shakes erratically as Peishan holds up the quicklight toward the black of the Heart. Suddenly, I see her, the only light in this terrible darkness, like a flare for anyone with a weapon—

"Peishan!" The yell comes out before I can hold it back. "Get rid of it!"

She winds up, throwing the little bar of light toward the sound. The quicklight hits the floor just as I see an elongated outline of black that seems too large to be human. It's coming right toward me.

The wounded girl's weight pins me to the ground, and the thing is on me before I can take a single step, that schism of time that happens when one moment you're safe and the next you're about to die, with no memory of how you got from one place to another. Hands scrabble through my hair, then scratch down my face to the soft skin at my collarbone. My arms are pinned by one of the wounded girl's legs, my hands straining uselessly to slap the thing away. There's a sharp prick of teeth against my skin, and my attacker's hands rove down to press my shoulders hard against the ground, knees digging into my rib cage.

I don't want to die in the dark. It's one bubble of a thought as the prick of teeth sharpens to a bite. Flailing, I get one arm free, my fingernails scraping down a stubbled cheek, desperate to stop the pain. *Please, not in the dark.*

There's a bright flash of light and sound, and the man on top of me goes limp, his head heavy against my neck.

"Sev!" Hands pull the weight off me, Peishan's voice in my face. "Sev, are you okay?"

"I'm—" It chokes out of me, but there doesn't seem to be any more to say. My hand, shaking, goes up to touch my neck, sticky and cold.

A light flares in my face. Xuan's face joins Peishan's as he bends over me, his hands gentle as he touches my neck. "This is all he got?" he asks quietly. "Does anything else hurt?"

I can't breathe, not yet. I sit up, skittering back from the body lying on the ground next to me. Just a man. A very sick man, my blood in his teeth. But I manage to muster a nod.

Xuan wipes the hand he touched me with on his coat. "We'll clean it out when we're in a safer place. But from now on you need to be more responsible. No more letting boys kiss your neck. Especially if they're so obviously bad at it."

Peishan's nose wrinkles, and she only watches long enough to see my lungs are still working before turning away. "Where are our people? And yours?" She shrinks back from Aya, who stands alone just inside the Heart.

She points, Peishan raising the light enough to gloss over the shattered remains of telescreens, metal, plastic, and glass piled around something dark in the middle of the room.

"They're dead."

CHAPTER 54
Sev

"WE NEED TO GET OUT OF HERE. NOW." AYA HOLDS
the gun steady at her side. "Whatever you needed out of here, it's
not worth my life. That guy didn't kill the rest of my team and
yours by himself."

Peishan shies back as Aya passes her, barely lit by the fallen
quicklight. She doesn't look at me or the dead or any of us, her
eyes tired, as if her body wants to close her eyes so she doesn't
have to see anymore.

My stomach churns, eyes not wanting to focus on the pile of
bodies making a centerpiece in the destruction of the room. I can't
stop myself seeing a curled fist, a braid with half the strands spilling free, though. "It *is* your life on the line. Mine too. And everyone's. If we don't find something on the grid, Chairman Sun's
going to send soldiers in to clean us all out."

"*Chairman Sun?*" the Menghu hisses.

Xuan kneels next to the girl we carried in, checking her pulse,
then bending down to check her breathing, a bleak look in his eyes.

"What do you need, then? It's now or never." Aya's lack of

expression makes my heart pound even harder, her fingers fiddling across the safety of her gun.

"We need to find something powered by an independent generator on the electrical grid. Sole said we might be able to see it from up here."

Aya skips over a river of broken glass, stopping in front of a downed telescreen. She shoves her gun into her waistband, then gestures impatiently toward me. "Help me!"

I run to her side, helping to lift the shattered screen down to find a cube that's a little taller than me stashed behind. It's made from some kind of see-through plastic, the inside riddled with what looks like corridors, rooms, wide spaces, and a circle drilled about a third of the way through from the top. At the bottom of the drilled hole I can see a miniature reproduction of the triangle kitchen opening and the amphitheater where I first ate lunch with Howl, thinking my life was about to change for the better. It's the Core, only much, much smaller.

Aya swears, rattling something plugged into the side, a twin to the mini generator the Menghu tried to use to activate Dr. Yang's door, brought up by the two members of our team lying dead in the middle of the Heart. "I used to work in the Heart. That's why my crew did so well up here. We knew it backward and forward." When the cube is properly plugged in, the lights at the very bottom corner of the cube strengthen a hair, but the top goes dark—the only electricity running marking the safe haven in the basement. That leaves only a few isolated spots burning like stars in the night. Aya balances the cube, looking at me. "As you can see, most of the Mountain is out. How much power are you looking for?"

"I'm not sure." The dark seems to push in on me, questions about where the man who attacked me came from, where the rest of his friends are, and how long before they get back making my words come out in a stutter. I can feel Peishan cowering behind me, Xuan at my elbow. "Something like . . . like the City Center, Xuan. My mother in her box."

Xuan's face quirks. "So, a generator big enough to power life support. Um, basic hospital functions. Food, water that's somehow self-sustaining."

"Where? Generally, I mean." She pulls at the cube, and pieces come away, expanding so we can see inside the Mountain room by room, the little flames of light scattered across the top.

"Somewhere no one would think to look."

A shot fires into the room, and the Menghu shrinks in her spot by the door, hands groping for weapons she was made to leave behind in Dr. Yang's office. She darts forward, grabbing a long section of hard plastic, hefting it in front of her like a sword. Peishan remains a statue on the other side of the lintel.

"Hidden. Like down in the storage levels?" Aya concentrates on the plastic cube, hardly looking up as a second shot comes in from the hall.

I flatten myself against the wall. "Maybe? Would it be easier to hide something upstairs where no one would notice extra power being funneled out?"

"Maybe. But look at that." Aya points to a pitch-dark section down at the base of the cube, opposite where Sole's safe haven glows with power. "Who's down there? That's records, probably. Or maybe plate metal or wood storage. No outside doors are nearby. No food or water or supplies to glean."

Xuan pulls Peishan away from the wall, leading her to hide just inside the doorway. "Faster, please!" he hisses, shouts clouding the air.

I pull the cubes out to expand, taking note of the designation etched into the plastic. BW12—SECTOR THIRTEEN. It's down deep, the way Sole's safe haven is. She'll know how to get there. Another bullet sings through the opening, lodging in the electrical grid representation, little sparks flaring all around the melting plastic.

"Is there another way out of here?" I gasp.

"Nope. Let's get moving." Aya darts toward the girl on the floor and hoists her up by the shoulders. I take her feet, then follow as Aya leads me to the open doorway. There's nothing but darkness outside, but noise enough to fund an entire war. "We're pinned down here."

"You think?" the Menghu snarls back at her, brandishing the plastic strip.

"Yeah, get into the hallway wiring. Hit it the second you can." Aya's voice stays calm.

"What are you talking about?" My voice rises an octave, fear pinching it tight.

Which is when the lights in the hall flick on. My eyes scream in protest, barely able to process the blobby dark blurs against the painful white stab of light. One falls to the ground under Aya's gun as he blinks at the sudden light, the other two taking off down the hall when they see they're outnumbered. More shots pepper my ears, leaving them with nothing but a high-pitched whine. Aya drags me straight into what sounds like an assault, Peishan running to help me with the girl's weight, not stopping until three girls come into view ahead, their ears covered with protective gear.

They signal to Aya to turn the corner. We run, the girl's dead weight dragging more every second until we get to a hallway where the sound has died down. The three girls who covered our exit herd Xuan and the Menghu behind us, checking over their shoulders as they holster their weapons. "Why are we doing this, Aya?" one mouths, the sound stopped at my eardrums. "We've already attracted way too much attention—"

"Gather your things, ladies." Aya's voice thumps against me, muffled as she hands her injured friend over to the Menghu. "We're headed downstairs."

The girl we've been carrying doesn't wake up. The next time Xuan forces us to stop so he can check her, he spends a long time listening before finally sagging back. Aya waits for a moment, as if she believes Xuan will tell her it's going to be all right, but when he's silent, she just nods and steps back from what's left of her friend. We leave her in an empty corridor, Aya and her compatriots hiding her body inside a closet and covering her so thoroughly it makes me wonder what they're hiding her from.

Then I force myself to stop wondering because it's too easy to come up with reasons, and it doesn't make running any easier.

Because Aya and her friends will have to go through quarantine, we have to go Outside to the main entrance to the safe haven. Only, with all the dodging and hiding it takes to get to one of the Outside doors, by the time we to a door that leads to the outdoors, light has fled the sky, and hungry gores sing from the trees.

We settle into the corridor near the Outside door and block off the passage that leads upstairs, though after everything today, no matter how many old desks and doors we use to barricade the hallway, I can't imagine closing my eyes ever again. Gore cries aren't much comfort either, filtering through the heavy door even after Aya pulls it shut and locks it down. Memories of Howl in a frame of jagged yellow teeth . . .

Howl. Kasim said Dr. Yang only kept him alive because of me. The Chairman said the doctor would use him to draw me out. I close my eyes, breathing in deep and letting the air flow out of me until I'm empty inside.

I'm going to get him out.

Aya's eyes remain expressionless as she settles on the ground across from me, crossing her ankles and leaning back against the wall. The three girls left of her crew sit around her in a too-quiet huddle, clumsily cleaning their guns. The Menghu watches them from the end of the hall near the barricade, her eyes narrowed on Aya like a cat watching its prey.

Peishan stays near the Menghu, cowering in her shadow as if it gives her something to do other than talk to me. She did the same when we first left the City, spreading her arms out to protect the little ones we pulled out of the Sanatorium from me, from June and Tai-ge, from anyone who came close, because it was easier than facing the enormity of the City burning under her.

She won't look at me. As if everything is, once again, my fault. I suppose it's true. I'm the one who got her sent up here. We found the little blip of power where it didn't belong down in the Mountain's intestines. With my luck, it will probably be a storage room light some overworked record filer forgot to turn off. All this for nothing.

I swallow the thoughts down where I can't see them, my hands clenched as I sit down by Xuan. "How's your shoulder?" I murmur.

"Probably gangrenous. That's catching, you know, so if you won't carry me the rest of the way, I'll rub it all over you."

"You are the worst medic ever. Gangrene isn't contagious—even I know that." I lean back and put a hand to my aching head, my ears still ringing. "And if it *were*, wouldn't carrying you get it all over me?"

"I'm too tired to make sense. I need sleep." Xuan nods to Aya and the other girls. "And they need watching."

"Yeah. I'll switch off with Peishan and . . . the Menghu. Do *you* know her name?"

"She's the other one I kind of want to watch all night." He puts his hand up, stopping me before I can tell him to be quiet. "Not in a creepy way. In an *I don't like getting stabbed while I sleep* sort of way."

I look over at the Menghu, her legs curled up so her knees brush her chin, her hand pressing her gas mask hard against her face. A buckle broke at the back during one of our altercations today, forcing her to do everything one-handed or risk SS sneaking in.

"Hey, Sev?"

I drag my attention back to Xuan.

"There is a very real possibility I won't be able to get up in the morning. Adrenaline does a lot for people when their lives are on the line, but it only goes so far. So I just want you to tell me something before I close my eyes. You know, for, like, motivation to get them open again."

"I'm not wasting any pity on you, Xuan."

"I just want to know that this has an end."

I look down, wrinkling my nose. That's what Sole said too. *How do you see this ending, Sev?*

"That story you told me and Sole about the cure being in the City. That's true, right?" The strain of hope in Xuan's voice sets my jaw. "This whole . . ." He tries to gesture to the group, to Peishan huddled alone, the Menghu's predatory gaze, Aya and her crew . . . but more than that. To the Mountain. To everything we all gave up to be here. If there is anything left to give up. The whole world has already cracked open and is gobbling us up, one by one. Like the Outsider upstairs. There—stupidly, annoyingly, aggressively there—one second. Now gone. "This was for a reason, right?"

"Yes. It was for a good reason." I reach out and squeeze his hand. "Thank you for believing me."

He smiles, sinking down to the floor, making a pillow out of one arm, the other leaden on his chest over his bandages. "You're the only thing left to bet on. What choice do I have?"

I wake to a ghostly buzz in my pocket. The link.

Peishan looks up when I sit up from the floor. She agreed without arguing when I asked her to take the second watch. Didn't even ask what she was supposed to watch for. Even now, she prefers silence to wondering why I'm awake.

Turning my back to her, I squeeze the link to see the message. *Execution postponed.*

Postponed? I didn't even know when it was supposed to be. Postponed until when? Howl's face burns in my head, the Chairman's insufficient information stoking the flame.

It continues: *If you know anything about the heli bombing our camps, please share.*

A heli? Howl's confession about bombers rises in my mind, but it sounds like the Chairman knows that much.

Yang's already moving southern garrison forces to the City by heli. Soon the General and I will follow.

My insides churn. Dr. Yang is headed back to the City? What if he figured out Mother's message all on his own? Or decided to go through our old house again just to see what he can find?

The link buzzes again. *Yang is using the rogue heli threat as a reason to band everyone together. They bombed the garrison while you were there and have since grounded most of the helis at the airfield at Dazhai. The execution is in four days, under the Arch. After that, I might not have enough sway to get a heli out to you. I'd rather leave everything in ruins than allow my soldiers to die under Yang. Find my son. Four days.*

Four days. *Four days.* That's a lot less than two weeks.

Four days until Dr. Yang kills Howl. Under the Arch, just like my mother. Like my father. My sister didn't make it that far. Four days until Dr. Yang, General Hong, and the Chairman are all going to be in one spot.

How do you see this ending, Sev?

Outside, a lonely howl breaks the night's silence, escalating into a series of excited yips. Other voices join the first, turning it into a hair-raising chorus, gunshots joining the cacophony. And then a scream.

I clamp my hands hard over my ears, trying to drown out the hunted creature's death.

Something shifts in the hallway behind me, the movement catching at the corner of my eye. It's Peishan getting to her feet, coming toward me too quickly for it to be just for a chat. "She's gone," she rasps through her mask, pointing toward the barrier. "I wasn't watching, and now she's not there anymore."

I sit up all the way, fear bubbling up inside me without even knowing who she's talking about, just that something's wrong. Xuan's next to me, his chest moving up and down with the long breaths of sleep. Aya with her girls from the Heart are all here, the one who is supposed to be keeping watch snoring so loud it echoes off the ceiling.

But when I slide over next to Peishan, it's not hard to see. In the spot just around the bend in the hall, where the Menghu is supposed to be sleeping, there's a startling emptiness.

I grope through Peishan's pack until I find the cool glass and metal of a quicklight and break it, the red light washing clear down to the end of the hall and the door we barricaded. It's untouched. But when I come back around the bend to where Aya and the others are sleeping to check the Outside door, the Menghu is standing over Aya, a knife in one hand.

My muscles all freeze, the gores beginning to howl again Outside. The creatures outside just want to eat, sleep, perpetuate their species, but the ones inside have learned how to hate.

My body won't move, brain refusing to make sense of what's happening right in front of me—the knife, Aya in her stolen mask, the Menghu—not until Peishan beats me to it, sliding between the Menghu and the girls from upstairs.

"What do you think you are doing?" Peishan whispers, her hands up as if she's being held at gunpoint.

"She killed my friend for no reason." The Menghu hefts the knife, her balance off because one hand is glued to her mask, keeping it in place. "Get out of my way or I'll get rid of you first, City girl."

Aya stirs at their feet, her eyes opening. She elbows the girl next to her, and suddenly they're all awake, oozing violence as the Menghu brandishes her knife. Her arms look too thin, limp almost, as if the blade is the only strong part left of her.

"We don't need you," the Menghu growls, backing away from Peishan and the girls who rise behind her. "Not any of you. You'll eat our food, take our medicine. We didn't even need to go up past the air lock because we were *fine*. . . ."

I stand when Aya's gun comes out, putting myself between her and the Menghu alongside Peishan. "There's no need for that. You are all from the Mountain except Peishan. You're all from the *same side*."

"That was before she got sick." The Menghu snarls, jabbing the knife to point at Aya. "Before she *killed*—"

Aya starts to push past Peishan, but Peishan grabs her arm, putting a hand over her grip on the gun.

"Do you mean before Dr. Yang let SS spread through the Mountain without telling anyone? Before he *abandoned* Aya and everyone else up there?" I turn back-to-back with Peishan, grateful when she stays firm behind me, shoring me up the way I'm trying to help her.

It's surreal, defending Aya who I saw murder a member of my own team. "What would it help?" I ask, my voice cracking because I honestly don't know. "What would it help to kill me or Peishan or Aya or *anyone* here?" Xuan lets out a snore from where he's huddled against the wall, oblivious. "It would just add to the dead."

"It would be a life for a life. His life for hers. She took his life, his mask, before he'd even gone cold. . . ." The Menghu's hand presses hard against her mask's filters, muffling her words. "I need that mask more than she does. She's already sick. Why should I listen to you anyway, cozy with that Red medic? He didn't even *try* to help when—"

"Xuan risked his life to come here," I croak. "If we can't walk peacefully into the safe haven when *nothing* is blocking us, then what do we have to look forward to? This is how the war started between the Mountain and the City. Refusing to help each other, assuming the other side would take everything . . . Wait." I pull the buckle on my own mask, tearing it from my face, relishing the first taste of stale air in my mouth. Making sure my hair covers my birthmark so this girl doesn't recognize me and make things even worse. "Here. Take my mask. Just please don't hurt anyone, either of you."

The Menghu's eyes go wide, her knife hand shaking as she looks over my naked face, eyes trailing down to the mask in my hand, extended toward her.

"It's a time for friends. For trust. For giving. For sacrifice and forgetting. If any of us want to get through this . . ." I link my arm through Peishan's, her whole body trembling against me, but she stands firm. "None of you mean *anything* to Peishan, and yet here she is standing between you. She probably could have gotten out of this mission. Could have stayed safe downstairs, but she's risking her life to help people she doesn't even know."

Peishan pulls her arm away from me. "No, *you* came because you didn't have to, Sev. Is that the point you wanted to make? That you're so fabulous to risk yourself instead of playing the *I'm important and don't have to do dirty work* card? *I* just want everyone to calm down."

"Let me go back to sleep, all of you, or tomorrow you'll be less a medic." Xuan's voice runs ragged through his mask filters. He waits for a second before rolling over, his back to us. "None of us are good or bad. None of us want to die. There's no instant karma that lets good people survive and bad ones die. We're all just *here*. It's random and unfair, so let's leave it at that and get some rest. Sev, if they don't listen to reason, just let them kill each other. We'll just leave their bodies here, and they can see if it makes them feel better."

His weary tone falls flat between us, the tension bubbling down as we all look at him, the packs of medicine we brought from above piled around him like pillows. Peishan doesn't move an inch behind me, her hands still firm on Aya's gun. "I don't want anyone else to die," she whispers. "Not you"—she meets the Menghu's eyes—"or any of you." She can't quite look back to acknowledge Aya or the two girls flanking her on either side. "I've seen you do impossible, brave things. You are people I want to know. I hope there's still a chance that's possible."

The Menghu blinks too slow, taking in Peishan's trembling lip, the way she fights back tears even as she firmly keeps Aya's gun pointed at the floor.

The Menghu lowers her knife. Reaches out and takes my mask. Closing her eyes, she holds her breath and lets her own mask sag away from her face. Placing mine over her nose and mouth, she turns away, walking to her spot by the barricade, out of sight.

I swivel to face Aya. "You didn't have to kill that man upstairs. You didn't have to threaten us."

"He would have killed me. The rest of my team *did* die, all because you all came up here."

"If you had tried talking to us instead of attacking us—"

"You gassed us. None of you wanted to talk. Would we be here with you, headed downstairs, if I hadn't stood up to you?" She leans forward a hair, her teeth bared. "None of us would be fighting at all if they had let us all go downstairs in the first place."

"Just stop!" There are tears trailing down Peishan's cheeks now.

I hold myself very, very still for a moment before I step back. Aya rolls her eyes, but she puts her gun away. It's true what she says, only there isn't enough Mantis or food for everyone. If there were enough, the City and Mountain never would have started fighting in the first place. Or maybe they would have, and it would just be about different things. About the places we live, the food we eat, or the language we speak. It seems like there's enough reason to push the Chairman from his throne because he didn't just want to live, he wanted everyone else's lives too. Is that what power is, squeezing others until they rise up and bite, only to take your power for themselves?

Is that what we are? When there was safety only a few hours away, food, water, a bed to sleep in, still the Menghu drew her knife. Aya didn't apologize, didn't back down, didn't curl up and wait for forgiveness.

And I understand why.

Maybe this is all we have to look forward to. Even if I find the cure, Sole makes it, and we give it to everyone . . . maybe they'll keep their uniforms and their scars and their grudges and find new reasons to kill each other.

In fact, if we don't give them good people to follow, I know they will.

I settle next to Xuan while the girls from upstairs huddle close to one another across from us as if they can't bear to sleep alone. One of them stays up to keep watch. To my surprise, Peishan slides to the floor next to me.

"You're brave," I whisper.

She swallows. "I'm still mad at you."

I nod, too tired to argue.

Peishan looks at the floor, her hands still shaking. "How did the world turn into this? Death and knives and guns and . . ." She takes a shuddering breath. "I feel like one moment we were alive and happy, even if it wasn't easy. You and me, the other orphans. We had lives. And then in one day, it became . . . *this*. Unlivable. The worst."

All I have is another nod. Everything *is* the worst. If I can't even help two people who grew up in the same community stop and listen to each other, how can I even begin to help the people *Outside*? The ones who have been shooting at each other with no remorse since the day they learned how to fire a gun.

Peishan leans forward to touch my arm. "I'm still mad, but I'm glad you came up here with me. I think . . . I miss being your friend." She looks up at me, her brow furrowed. "Would you sit up with me to keep watch? Everything that happened today . . . those girls . . ." She gives Aya and her friends a leery look. "I'm scared." It comes out in an ashamed whisper.

"Of course I will, Peishan." I know the shame of fear. It's like an aftertaste to the horrible things you couldn't stop. The Menghu and Aya *stopped* fighting because of Peishan. Because she's human, and she showed them. But still, the shame remains.

Howl. His name tastes like hope this time. *Sole. They changed.* Because they started seeing humans instead of enemies.

How do we show everyone with guns out there that most of us—minus the ones manipulating people like stones on a board— just want to live?

One thing I do know, though. Fear is the tool of the powerful. Fear is easier than hope, easier to share, easier to grab hold of. Unless I can find a way to give people hope stronger than fear, then it's like Sole hinted. There will be no end to this war.

I know what I have to do. It feels like tar inside me, like the blood still staining my clothes and caked on my skin. But the people who use fear can't continue. Not if we want these things to stop. For all that death is unwinding in my chest, having Peishan there next to me feels like hope, too. We sit up the rest of the night, back-to-back, watching. Together.

CHAPTER 55
Sev

WHEN WE GET DOWN BELOW, SOLE IS WAITING FOR me, her face like death under her mask as she walks straight past Aya and her friends going into quarantine.

"I don't have time for you to be angry, Sole." I keep one arm linked under Xuan's shoulder, Peishan on his other side, whispering for him to keep walking. "I've got a lead and no time. And Xuan might die just out of spite if I don't get him some pain-killers. You can check the supplies we brought. Xuan says they'll be useful."

The deathly glimmer to Sole's eyes doesn't disappear, but she calls for people to take our packs and pulls out a stretcher for Xuan herself to wheel him into an SS testing booth. I follow close behind her, pausing only long enough to be sure everyone else from our party goes through. The Menghu on duty keep their hands on their guns every moment. Aya and the Menghu take booths as far away from each other as possible, Peishan looking helplessly between them as she takes one in the middle.

I stay by Xuan's side while Sole moves him into the large tube, scanners humming as they wait to scan him. Once he's inside, Sole keeps her eyes flicking across the screen as it analyzes his brain. "You going on this mission was incredibly irresponsible, Sev."

"Actually, it wasn't at all. You've got all the information you need to make a cure."

Sole's eyes narrow, her voice so tight it could strangle. "You might be pinning all your hopes on finding a box under your old floorboards, but the rest of us can't take that chance. If you die, our last chance of surviving will be gone, and all of us will *die*." She turns from the machine, her face aggressively close to mine, her skeleton fingers digging into my shoulders. "We made a deal. You have the rest of your allotted two weeks, but not if it puts you at risk. Do you understand me?"

I push her hands off me. "I thought you weren't going to force me into anything, Sole."

Sole takes a step back. "Only because I know I don't have to." She turns to the screen, watching as the scan lights up green.

"We're out of time. They're going to kill Howl up in the City in four days." I close my eyes, clenching them shut. "Wait, what time is it? Maybe it's three now."

Sole looks up from maneuvering the bed out of the tube. "Who told you? I gave strict orders that no one share that piece of information with you."

"Three days?" I ask.

She narrows her eyes. Nods.

I pull the stretcher over and help transfer Xuan back onto it. He feels so much heavier and so much less annoying now that he's asleep. "The Chairman told me, Sole," I say. "You were going to leave me in the dark?"

"Of course I wasn't going to tell you. Dr. Yang is broadcasting about Howl on every radio frequency because he knows you'll come running."

"You know about the bombings, then. Some heli that's gone rogue? They moved everyone up into the City."

"I knew there were going to be bombings. Howl's the one who brought that thing here." Sole looks disgusted. "It's some leftover from Before that Port Northians got hold of."

"He brought them here so he could help me. To get the cure."

Sole bites her lip. "It's not what I would have done."

My face hardens. "Stop pretending you're morally superior to him. You would have done anything to get me out of that bunker. You just didn't have a bomber to work with."

Sole flinches, but I don't have time to care about her feelings anymore.

When we get to Xuan's room, I help move him onto the bed. He groans with pain, his eyes flicking open. He groans again when he sees me and scrunches them shut. "Go away," he slurs. "You're the *worst*."

I stifle a smile and step back from his bed, waiting until Sole looks at me. "I'm not going to let you lock me in a room while they execute Howl. This just makes things easier. Howl and the cure are in the same place, and I'm going after them."

Sole's brow furrows, and she busies herself reconnecting Xuan's IV. "After all this, you're still folding Howl into this ridiculous fairy tale you're telling yourself. Get the cure, everyone stops fighting, your head stays in one piece, and you get to live happily ever after with the love of your life?" She fixes me with an ugly stare, her hands knotted around the IV, and I'm glad Xuan seems to have fallen back asleep, because I wouldn't want him to hurt even more than he already does. "Dr. Yang wants you to go to the City. He wants your head in his lab, and he's going to get it if you go." She shakes her head, turning toward the door.

I grab her arm, pulling her to face me, and I'm surprised to find tears in her eyes. "I'm going to save him, Sole." She won't look at me, but I get close, forcing her to meet my gaze. "Howl has done horrible things, but so have you. So have I. And we are *all* worthy of a second chance to make things right. I've thought about what you said before, and I'm . . . ready to talk through our options." Because what does the end look like? Unless leadership changes, the world will stay the same. My next words come out slowly because I don't like them. But they're the best I have. "Think about it: Dr. Yang, the Chairman, the General—they'll all be there at the execution."

Sole's eyes narrow. But then she nods slowly. "Yes. They will."

We both know there's only one way to end this war. Out loud, I can't even make myself say it. But there's no room to argue, no room to think things through again. I only have four days to plan a cure extraction, a rescue mission, and . . .

And a three-headed assassination. "Now tell me: How do I get to BW12—sector thirteen?"

CHAPTER 56
Sev

"HAS IT ALL BEEN LIKE THIS?" PEISHAN'S VOICE echoes down the empty hallway, our light creating a bubble of red in the dark.

I hold my light up a little higher, red catching on nondescript doors, each with a plaque detailing its contents. We had to come through an air lock to get here, but Sole said the whole of sector thirteen was likely to be empty. There might have been personnel down here when SS started spreading, but it's dark, and there's no food or water, and nothing of value to keep anyone here, unless they have compulsions to file things.

That Peishan volunteered to come with me feels like a warm outline to the darkness. I'm trying to pretend it didn't have anything to do with the fact that we found Lihua covered in some kind of soot, and that getting her washed up was going to be a more difficult battle than walking down empty hallways.

"I know I was brought up to believe anyone living Outside had something wrong with them, but after the weeks I've been out here . . ." Peishan jogs across the hall to check the identifying marker on the wall: BW10. We're close. Peishan heaves a sigh before continuing. "I'm beginning to wonder if they were right."

"Cai Ayi wasn't bad, was she?"

"She's down in quarantine. Nearly killed herself getting us here."

"And the roughers? June?" Even saying June's name hurts. Where is she? I wonder. Is she awake? Did Luokai even have access to the resources he'd need to take care of her after the invasion?

"June was nice," Peishan agrees, her light bobbing as she jogs up the corridor. "But the others . . . I don't know. It's hard to know what people are really like when they're always worried about dying."

"I'm sorry we yanked you out of the City without explaining what was going on." I hold up my light this time to check the wall, punching our coordinates in a link that connects me to the Menghu watching the air lock we came through. If we don't send anything through for fifteen minutes solid, they'll come after us.

"Whatever happened to Tai-ge?" she asks. "How many nights did we sit up talking about him? That boy would have broken his own arm to make you happy."

The question hits me right in the stomach. I close my eyes, flickers of nausea winking in and out clear to my throat. Of course she's going to ask about Tai-ge. We used to stay up late talking about him. About how it was hopeless but how much I wished . . . wishes that were hollow and shallow and senseless. I didn't understand who he was or who I was either. I lick my lips, trying to find an answer that won't require hours of explanation. "He did once. Break his arm, I mean. After the explosion at the Aihu Bridge." She laughs a little at this response, but waits for more. More I don't want to give. "He might have been willing to break an arm for me, but he would have broken every bone in his body for his mother. And she doesn't like me much."

"Would have?" Peishan looks back at me. "Are you saying Tai-ge's . . ." She frowns, not wanting to speak the word out loud.

"No, he's not dead. I don't think. He might be now, I guess." She frowns over the casual way I say it.

"Are you . . . okay?"

"I will be. Once we find BW12. And the Chairman's real son." I haven't told Peishan about Howl. His was one of the murders she laid at my feet when I first found her in the Sanatorium. The reality of who Howl is and what's happening to him now seems like too much to explain. But the inadequacy of how I explain away Tai-ge makes me want to laugh and cry at the same time. "Things just didn't work out."

We enter a new hall, an unblemished coating of dust covering the floor and BW12 on the wall in blocky letters. A curl of anxiety tightens inside me as we stop and look at the doors. There aren't any lights to show a generator humming down here. No footprints to mark visitors. Dr. Yang's been gone two months. What if that light on the grid was a malfunction? Or worse, a fluke: a generator that kicked on to keep a gigantic fish freezer from defrosting or something.

Three more days. It's like a City-wide announcement, ringing between my ears. *Three more days until they kill Howl.*

It's an offshoot hallway, two doorways on one side, three on the other, one making a dead end. Windows cut into each door, labels underneath each that I can't even understand. One says INSURANCE CLAIMS with a span of five years from Before under it, the next with the same label, only a later span of years. When I shine my light through the windows, all I see is filing cabinets.

I try the door. It doesn't budge. "Help me, would you?"

Peishan's eyebrows go up. "Help you . . . ?"

I take a running start, slamming my shoulder into the door. It shudders under the impact but remains solidly shut, leaving me with a dull pain down my arm to add to all the aches and pains from our excursion upstairs yesterday. Peishan tries next, then kicks it with her full weight, and the door slams open.

A billow of dust clouds out at the violence, but my mask filters it out. Peishan follows as I lead the way into the room, perfectly square and divided by three rows of filing cabinets.

My hands begin twitching as if I'll be able to find the Chairman's Yuan-cursed son if I just keep moving. Or maybe if I wish hard enough the filing cabinets will melt and lighting will strike and suddenly Sun Yi-lai will rise up through the floor in a glass coffin like my mother's. I go out to check the hallway again, making sure I didn't read it wrong. The numbers are there in black and white. "Is there any way I'm remembering the number wrong?" I ask.

"What happens if we don't find him?" Peishan walks back inside the room, running her light along the walls for anything we missed. There's nothing to miss, though. Four walls and filing cabinets.

"Um, the Chairman will try to kill everyone down here." I blink at Peishan's alarmed expression. "He probably won't be able to. There's a reason the City never came head-on at the Mountain, but it would make it a lot harder to get food in here. I was just hoping that if I found his son, he'd help me get to the City. That's where the cure is."

"And if we don't find the cure, then you die. Right?" Peishan's biting her lip when I look at her. "That's why Sole was so anxious to get you here. Why she marched you straight to my room, so you'd see Lihua and agree to let her experiment on you."

"That's the long and short of it." I let out a long breath, the air catching in my mask the way worry is curdling in my stomach. Heaving myself onto one of the filing cabinets, I brush dust away in a big arc around me, the fuzzy feel of it sending squirms of disgust down my spine. No Sun Yi-lai means no leverage to get help from the Chairman. No way to reach the City at all within the three-day deadline.

No way to save Howl.

An explosion of movement catches me off guard, sending me careening off the metal cabinets to escape, visions of monsters made from dust and darkness or a toothless old SS victim happy to have found meat after so many years of living off paper and ink. It's Peishan, though. She backs up and slams her shoulder into the cabinets on the far wall again, her eyes glassy.

My whole body goes cold. "Peishan?" I whisper as her hand slides off the cabinet, scraping blood from her palm, but she just goes back to pushing. "Peishan, are you okay?" She can't have SS. She had her mask on every second we were outside the air lock—

She grunts, the metal screeching against the floor. "How about you *help me*."

The filing cabinet she's pushing didn't slide out into the aisle between cabinets. It pushed *into* the one next to it, fitting inside. I run to her side and put my hands next to hers, the two of us pushing together. When the cabinet folds another inch, she gives a cry of triumph, the metal cabinets folding up inside one another to leave a blank space of wall.

Not blank. There's a metal door flush with the wall.

"How did you know to do that?" I ask, staring up at the wall, not sure what to feel. Excitement, dread. Awe.

"The first one was already folded back a little." She presses a hand to the metal door, and it swings back easily. The lock must have shorted out when the power went down, I guess. Peishan licks her lips and looks back at me. "Think there are more filing cabinets behind there?"

Hope unfolds inside me, tentative because I know the slightest bit of doubt will turn it to ash. But when I hold my light up into the room, the red leaks through the darkness to touch . . .

A box of glass.

The link to the Menghu guards buzzes at my side, a message spelling across my hand. *Everything okay?*

I type back quick, my hands shaking. *I think we're going to need some help. Come fast.*

Because inside the glass box, there's a boy.

CHAPTER 57
Sev

SOLE GOES TO WORK WITHOUT QUESTION THE
moment Menghu wheel Sun Yi-lai and his box into one of the few
empty spaces in the allotted hospital space: Xuan's room. His vitals
are written across the side in blocky characters that blink angrily
when Sole instructs the Menghu to disconnect him. He looks like
a doll the way my mother did, propped up and waiting for someone
to take him down to play. Only, his skin hasn't turned to paper, his
muscles firm instead of wasted to nothing.

He's alive. *Healthy*, as much as a boy who has been locked in
a box for who knows how long can be. I shove Xuan over a few
inches to sit on his bed, unable to stop staring as Sole works on
him, snapping at her team of medics to do things this way and
that, the boy's eyes closed. Not a boy. He's older than me. Howl's
age, or a little older.

He's asleep the way I was. A weiqi stone so dangerous, Dr.
Yang hid him away from the board.

He looks like Howl, a little.

He looks like a piece in *my* game of weiqi. One I'm not sure where to move next. Though the thought immediately sends spirals of shame from my head to my toes. People aren't pieces to be played.

Sole looks up as a Menghu comes in, the girl walking straight to her to whisper something in her ear. Fingers tangled in a mess of tubing over Sun Yi-lai's chest, Sole barely glances at me before going back to what she was doing. "They need you at the outer barricade."

"Are you kidding? I'm not leaving until you tell me you can wake him up." My hand goes to my pocket where I stowed the link. I have the Chairman's son. *Alive.* He'll want him back as soon as possible, which means a heli sent out in this direction, which means—

"A girl named June. You know her, right?" Sole kneels next to the box, her fingers pinching at the boy's skin. "She's coming up to the inner doors right now with . . . with Seth. Luokai. Whatever he calls himself now."

I freeze. *"What?"*

"They're both here. Keep them away from me, okay?" Her eye twitches, and suddenly I wonder if she's not kneeling to get closer to Sun Yi-lai and the mess of tubes keeping him alive. She's hiding.

"You okay, my little *niangao*?" Xuan prods my arm. "Isn't June that girl—"

"The one you helped turn into an orphan. Yes. You call me that again and I'll shoot your other side."

I slide off the bed and run up to the surface level and through the two inner barricades to meet June, tears like fire in my eyes. June. Alive. June *safe.*

June here.

I was supposed to make the world a better place for June. Find the cure, bring it back to her. But the idea that I can is the worst kind of bravado, even if I didn't know it when I made her those promises back at Port North. I'll have to tell her that Howl is going under the Arch. That we have a way to the cure, but it'll turn all guns on us. That I'm supposed to assassinate three well-guarded people but don't know how—and that it might not help anything anyway. I was okay at weiqi, able to keep from disgracing myself, but this game seems to break all the rules I thought—

I stop just inside the barrier, hands raking through my hair. The Menghu guarding the inner barricade drops a hand casually to his weapon, watching me from the side of his eye.

Stones. June. The two together seem to close a circuit in my brain.

I know what the Chairman wants: his son.

I know what Dr. Yang wants: me. He wouldn't be shouting all over the radios about having a gun to Howl's head if this weren't a play to get me to come to him.

I know where the cure is: under the floorboards in my old house.

I know where Howl will be. Under the Arch. Surrounded by Firsts and Seconds evacuated from Dazhai. Menghu flown in from the southern garrison. And whatever comes in between, the people who only follow because they need food and Mantis.

A picture of June's weiqi game back when she, Tai-ge, and I were sitting under the heli, planning how to steal a map encryption key that would lead us to Port North. *Too many people playing. All in each other's way,* she said. *We can do whatever we want.*

When June's snarled curls, her scratched jade eyes, appear on the other side of the barricade, I can't help but run, throwing my arms around her. To my surprise, her arms clutch at my back, holding me close, her face crushed into my chest.

We fall to the ground, laughing, crying, and everything in between, no words enough to encompass what being alive and together again feels like.

Later, as we sit in quarantine sharing bowls of soup, I can hardly look at June's companion. Luokai is a horrible reminder and a motivation rolled into one, because I'd forgotten how much he looks like Howl. A battered, shaved version who has forgotten how to smile.

"Sole?" he asks quietly. "Is she here?"

I press my lips together. "If she wants to talk to you, she'll come down."

A humorless smile quirks at the side of his mouth, and he gives me a restrained bow from where he's seated.

June's so quiet, so still I can feel her heart beating against my skin like a little mouse held in the palm of my hand. "Howl?" she asks.

Luokai looks up again from his soup, setting his spoon carefully into his bowl.

My stomach clenches, my lungs contracting. "June, I need your help."

She listens as she always does. Howl under the Arch. A black heli, Luokai's eyes narrowing at its mention. Menghu and Reds together in the same space. People infected with SS trapped inside City walls, the Chairman waiting for word of his son.

"I'm going to tell him we found Sun Yi-lai and that we have conditions upon returning him." I stand as Peishan and Lihua rocket through the door, masks tight over their noses, crashing

into June and bowling her over. Luokai blinks at the ruckus, inching back as if to give June some room, but it's with the shadow of
a smile. Once they've quieted down, I continue. "If Dr. Yang is
following traditions around the Arch, there will be a big denunciation before they . . ." I look at Lihua, pressing my lips together.
"Could we finish this reunion at dinner?"

Peishan, who perked up at the mention of the Arch, nods,
herding Lihua back out of the room, though she complains the
whole way. "I made a walking stick, June!" she yells over her
shoulder as Peishan hands her off to Menghu outside. "One of
the Menghu helped me carve it, and he says it's like magic and will
keep bad guys away and . . ."

June's smile is so big it hurts, and I don't want to quash it
down, but we don't have time to be happy just yet.

"If Dr. Yang is going to execute Howl the way they used to under
the Arch, it'll be a big gathering with speeches and yelling and throwing things, anyone who is important there to watch. It's not enough to
just get Howl or the cure. We need people to *listen* to us. They'll all be
there, together, scared, and unless we can persuade them to follow us
instead of breaking into little groups, it'll turn into anarchy."

June nods, her forehead wrinkled. "So many people in the City
at once."

"Yes, that's what I was thinking. Lots of confusion about
who goes where. Lots of helis flying in right now to evacuate the
camps, and all the people on them hate one another. I don't want
the Chairman to get his hands on his son before we get something
out of him, so we can't have him send a heli for us." I pinch at my
fingers, sucking on my bottom lip. "Kasim—one of the Menghu
who was working at the garrison—maybe he could get us onto a
heli going to the City."

June's face scrunches as she thinks, an expression so familiar that I don't know how I'd forgotten it. I can't believe she's here. As if she's a ghost, a memory, a hallucination. Even as I watch, she brushes a snarl from her face, and her hand freezes in her hair, her whole body going tight. Her other hand jerks to the side, knocking her porridge to the ground.

"June? June!" I kneel down, pulling her hand out of her hair as she tries to yank it out. Peishan holds her down on the other side. June's lungs are moving too fast, breaths blowing in and out of her like a stormy gale. I don't let go until her shoulders relax.

I try to help her up, try to hold her, but she brushes me off, glancing at Luokai. He gives her a small smile and closes her eyes, calming the breaths racking her chest until they smooth into something deep and calm.

"Are you okay?" I ask, the idea of compulsions lurking inside my friend when she's spent so many years running from them burning like acid inside me. "Oh, June, I'm so sorry." How did I not notice that the soldiers down here didn't give her Mantis?

She inhales again, her shoulders upright. "Send the picture. You said the Chairman wanted a picture."

The way she sits so straight . . . It reminds me of Luokai and his compulsions. Of accepting them. Living through them. Letting them pass, not a storm inside you so much as one overhead, not worth paying attention to as it rails against the roof.

June reaches out to touch my hand, her eyes soft. Her hand on my arm feels like strength, as if for the first time since we've met, I feel like she's solidly here. Not on her toes, ready to run.

"Tell me what he says once he's seen his son and find out about Kasim's heli." June pulls Luokai's bowl in front of her and takes a bite. He smiles and allows it. "Then we plan."

* * *

I try to hold on to the image of June's strength, her *control*, as I speak to the woman in charge of quarantines, asking her to give June and Luokai Mantis. But it disappears as I head up the stairs. We've used most of today hunting for Sun Yi-lai, which makes it only two days and a few hours until they put an ax to Howl's throat.

When I get to Xuan's room, it's clustered full of medics with Sun Yi-lai's body inert at their center, like bees serving their queen. The Chairman's son merits a bed now, only a normal number of tubes feeding into him rather than the horror-show glass box that seems to be yanked right out of a scary movie from Before. His eyes are still closed, though. It feels like the first stage of panic, churning inside my chest. Did Sole start giving him the anti–Suspended Sleep serum yet?

The medics part for me, letting me pull out the link and hover it over his face, the purple light brushing his angled features, to take a picture. I round Xuan's bed, tucking his blankets around his sleeping form before jumping up next to him to send the photo, and with it, my message to the Chairman: *If you want him, there are some things I'm going to need first.*

Xuan's eyes flicker open at my weight next to him on the bed, and he groans, turning onto his side. "Go away."

"You don't like being tucked in?" I watch to make sure the message went through, holding the link tight in my fist, willing the Chairman to answer immediately. Preferably offering the world and then some to get his son back. He did as much for Dr. Yang. "Where's Sole?"

Xuan opens his eyes all the way, looking over his shoulder to glower at me. "You are the one vertical with your eyes open.

Think through the logic of asking me of all people that question. And while you're realizing how silly you are, would you please tell all of these ridiculous excuses for medics to *get out of here?*" He pulls the blanket up over his head, muffling the rest of his words. "There's a thing called bedside manner!"

I pull the blanket back down. "Why isn't Sun Yi-lai awake yet?"

"Medicine is complicated, Sev. He was Asleep longer, he's bigger than you, his contamination was different. We came up with a dosing schedule most likely to succeed based on what I know about the anti–Suspended Sleep serum." He grabs the blanket back from me and flips it up to cover his floppy hair. "Now go get me a custard bun."

"Not likely." I slide off the edge of his bed and head out the door, stopping one of the medics to ask her to get Xuan his custard bun before heading toward Sole's room.

Worry and curiosity war inside me as I remember the way she crouched behind Sun Yi-lai's box, telling me to go find June at the barricade. I suppose I shouldn't be surprised by Sole since I don't actually know her that well, but it just seems like she's so in control of herself now. Focused. She was upset about finding Luokai on the other end of the link, sure, but for some reason I thought she'd give him a reserved bow and then go back to sticking people with needles if she ever came across him again, not hide under the covers. When I get to her door, I hesitate with my hand on the knob. Then take a step back and knock. "Sole?"

Nothing.

"Sole, I'm coming in!" I push the door open to find Sole sitting cross-legged on her sleeping pallet, a girl across from her, back to me. "Oh, sorry, I didn't mean to interrupt—"

The girl turns around, a familiar round face, wide mouth and dark brown hair sending bolts of surprise through my chest. *"Mei?"*

She smiles, brushing shaggy bangs from her eyes. "I was glad to hear you didn't die."

"What . . . how . . . ?" I swallow, jerking my attention to Sole. "What is she doing here, Sole? Mei was with Helix when I got caught at Port North." My voice rises, the horror of those hours sitting in the belly of a heli, knowing I was dead like molten lead burning through my veins. "She can't be here. She'll tell *everyone*—"

"She's been with me ever since Dr. Yang put you under. She and Kasim aren't the only Menghu who realized he wasn't going to be handing out anything but orders that weren't necessarily in their best interest after he didn't use you to make a cure." Sole's face has moved from skull-like and brittle to some kind of iron. "Mei was one of the Menghu who tried to break you out of the garrison, but she got caught." She gestures for me to sit down, but I don't, my hand clenched on the doorknob, not sure if I should run or fight. "And she says she can help with our plan to get the cure and . . . save Howl."

Our plan. I refrain from rolling my eyes. Wasn't it only yesterday that Sole was calling it a fairy tale?

Mei's jaw clenches, her eyes widening a fraction. "We're doing what, now? Cure, yes. Save creepy murderers, no."

"He is not creepy or a murderer, thank you very much." The Chairman's link buzzes in my pocket, and I take it out, shading my hand to see the message drawn in light across the back of my hand. *Proof that he's alive first. After that we can talk.*

"Sev." I look up to find Mei's wide mouth twisted into a smile. Her wrists are bare of bones, her hair a familiar mess of mud and twigs. "We've got a window of opportunity here with the execution going on. Sole says you have some leverage on the Chairman. I've got some people who will help on General Hong's side. We could sneak in, arrange for the guards at the execution to be people on our side—"

"A window to do what, exactly? What's your end goal, Mei?" Is Mei already feeding Sole my plan, centering it around herself and putting Menghu back in control instead of where our focus should be: on saving Howl and changing out bloodthirsty leaders for people who can see that SS is what we need to fight, not each other? Needles shiver down my arms and up my neck as I remember the last words she said to me in the heli before she signed me over to Dr. Yang: *I hope you die better than this.*

"There's a high-ranking Red who is sympathetic to working with people like us. You in particular, Sev." Sole looks up at me, her eyebrows quirked. "I believe you have a relationship with Hong Tai-ge. Is that correct?"

CHAPTER 58
Sev

"YOU WANT TO STICK *TAI-GE* IN AS LEADER OF the Reds. And you think he can get Menghu behind him too?" I don't have the words to convey just how awful her plan is. *"No."*

There isn't enough forgiveness in the world for Hong Tai-ge. Not from me. That boy is Red to the core, the hero of his own story with no ears to hear anyone else's view, and it almost killed me. He may have persuaded Howl not to inject the anti–Suspended Sleep serum into my veins, but only Yuan knows where he meant to carry me after that.

"The Reds are divided against one another. And there are so many of us who don't want anything to do with Dr. Yang." Mei glances up toward the levels above us, all the people left there to molder until the doctor could come up with a cure. "Even Helix has been complaining about him not delivering on promises. He's said from the moment I met him that all he wants is a safe place to live. A place to raise a family."

My skin stabs through with goose bumps, memories of his spider hands on my back crawling across my skin. I can't imagine him with a partner. Children. He's hard, every inch of him made of metal, bullets, and a thirst for blood.

Mei continues, "If we have a real cure, this could be a perfect chance to . . ." She shrugs, and I hate the words that come out of her mouth, because they're mine. "A chance to start something new. Tai-ge was right about you. He said you must know something about the cure—"

"No." I go to the door. "Luokai's in quarantine, Sole. I think he wants to talk to you."

Sole bites her lip, teeth digging in hard, and I'm suddenly sorry for trying to use that as my exit line and can't make myself go out.

Mei cocks her head, brushing those jagged bangs out of her eyes. "Tai-ge abandoned his post, trying to get you out."

"Yeah, because he knew I had the cure. Think he would have given any to you once he got it out of me? That the Reds or anyone else . . ." The words spark in my mouth, and I can't even bring myself to continue.

"He let me out." Mei's voice is quiet. She pulls up her shirt, revealing a dirty bandage taped to her side. Her cheeks flush a bit, and sickness twists inside me at the sight. "I got these right outside the bunker and might have gotten a lot more if not for him. He shot two Reds. For me. A Menghu. He lied to his mother, ran away from the City. And since he's gone back to his post, he's been trying to find a way to push his mother out entirely."

"He's been saying that?" I step closer to her. "Because I have a lifetime of experience with the things *Tai-ge says*."

Her wide lips press together, freckles standing out against her nose. "For someone who seems to believe so much in a documented killer, you sure don't have much faith in people changing."

"Howl isn't a documented killer. He did what he had to do just like everyone else. You've even made *him* believe he's irredeemable. Isn't that enough without discounting him as a human being, too?"

We stare at each other, tension bleeding from the air. Mei leans back and folds her arms after a moment, her muscles taut as if she thinks I might attack her and she needs to be ready. "What do you want to do, then? Grab the cure and your butcher boyfriend and then what? Dr. Yang will just come after us."

"Tai-ge's hands are *not* clean. And neither are yours." I stand up, stuffing the link back in my pocket, anger like a fizz that coats the inside of my mouth "Sole, I need your link to Kasim. We're going after the cure tomorrow."

Sole nods. "You know it's the full moon tomorrow, right? The end of New Year?"

My stomach twists. At the end of two weeks of celebrations, the City would put on a fireworks show, daring enemy helis to come nearer because we weren't afraid of the monsters in the sky. That's the day Dr. Yang chose to kill Howl? A holiday, so he could make it into a party?

Bile rises in my throat. "I'm going, Sole. I've still got some planning to do, but keep this one far away from everything."

Mei starts to get up, her hands balled into fists. "Who do you think you are? You're just a grunt worker who grew up bowing and scraping to the other people around you. The cure is a good start, but it's not going to fix the world. There are real options going forward here. Why do *you* have the right to say you won't take those options when it's our lives in danger too?"

"There's a better way. Go straight to the troops. Get rid of *all* their leaders." Even as I say it, the words writhe in my mouth. "Cut off the snakes' heads, then give their followers a direction to go."

Sole's eyes go wide. We hadn't said it quite like that yet. That we're going to kill three people. Every word feels as if it's made from bullet metal and broken bones, but it's what I'm going to do. *Don't do what I would do,* Howl said. Maybe it's *not* what he would do, but a step more extreme. Of course, this war is a step more extreme than it was when he was hiding from gores and making Reds his targets.

Mei arches an eyebrow. "*You* are going to kill Dr. Yang?"

Black feels inky inside me. "Can you think of another way?"

CHAPTER 59
Sev

WHEN SUN YI-LAI WAKES, IT'S WITH A SNEEZE.
June, tucked in next to me as we finalize all our plans over the link
with Kasim, stifles her own sneeze in response, as if the suggestion
was too much for her.

The Chairman's son is sitting within minutes, up on his feet
not long after I've sent his image awake and blinking to his father.
His mouth opens, his voice a jarring mess of words and syllables I can't link together that sound foreign and familiar at the
same time.

"He's asking for his mother." June's voice is small. "But like
an Islander."

He's speaking Port Northian?

The link buzzes, and I hold it up to my face, my nose scrunching so tears won't come. This boy has been in a box for so long he
doesn't even know his own mother is dead. That she probably has
been since before he was even in the box. The message is a barrage
of instructions from the Chairman: where to take his son, where
to wait for the heli.

I send him a message back, detailing the list of things June and I came up with together, then look back up at this boy, who has been at the center of so many years of war.

He smiles at me. Guileless, young-looking though he's probably older than me. There's nothing but hope in those eyes. "I don't know where your mother is." I hate the way it sounds as June translates. "We want to help you. But before we can do that, we need your help."

June's translation feels pained. "He says all he wants is his mother. He's happy to help in any way he can."

The Chairman's wife has been dead for years. Not much we can do in that area. Doing my best to smile, I lean forward. "How are you feeling?"

He gestures to his head. "Glad to see and hear something other than whatever it was I had to listen to in here."

"Brain stimulation programs?" I ask.

June shrugs, then her head cocks when he speaks again. "It was a long, long wait in the dark," she translates.

Dr. Yang tried to keep him sane, then. Gave him something to look at and listen to. Took better care of him than he ever did my mother, if Sun Yi-lai's health is anything to go by: He has muscles to hold him up, where Mother's had long wasted away. I didn't have a muscle stimulation setup to keep me strong when I was at the garrison. I guess Mother and I weren't royalty, untouchable. The Chairman's own blood. But I push that thought away. "When I first woke up, I could hardly believe the world had kept turning. Everything was different." It had been, the first time. My mother and father were both gone, and everyone I knew shunned me. A Red branded my hand and sent me to live with nuns who didn't seem to care much if I lived or died—a poor exchange for parents who loved me.

Sun Yi-lai sighs, speaking. "He doesn't even know what about the world is different," June supplies. "Only that he's grown. He wants to believe his family is still out there. His mother . . ." She brushes a wisp of hair behind her ear, glancing at the bed, where Xuan is snoring, a shiver shuddering through her.

She hasn't run away from Xuan like last time. Or even mentioned his connection to her mother's disappearance. But I can see it there, lurking beneath the surface.

When her eyes come back to me, she continues, "Reifa. That's her name."

"His mother's name?" I try to hold back my surprise, because I happen to know his mother's name was *not* Reifa. Unless the Chairman's wife isn't who he is talking about. "Was she from the island?"

When June queries and then nods to answer, I can't help but wonder what I've missed and whether or not it will be important enough to tip this already harebrained mission over sideways. This boy is like me and Howl combined. Used and orphaned, hidden away. One of Dr. Yang's pieces lined up in his tidy rows. "I'm going to do everything I can to find out if Reifa—your mother?— is still alive, Sun Yi-lai. But I'm afraid that we'll need to do some things first. I'm going to need you to listen very carefully."

Kasim manages to delay a heli for us to meet, one of two waiting to take off. He hurries us into the port, hissing for me to keep my head down and not to talk to *anyone.*

As I'm pulling June and Sun Yi-lai into their seats, attempting to shield their faces from the other Menghu nervously chatting among themselves in the heli's transport hold, I notice Kasim pushing the door to the other heli closed.

He runs to our aircraft as the propellers roar to life, climbs in to check in with the pilot up front, then closes the outer door. It's hard to think as we take off, nervousness brimming inside me as the heli's frame begins to shake, June's hand in my white-knuckled grip. None of us speak. Yi-lai is pale under his mask, and June's characteristic silence suddenly seems less out of place. Everyone on this heli is worried.

I reach out and take Yi-lai's hand, June keeping hold of my other one as the heli lifts off the ground, the three of us linked together until we find smoother flying. Even then, though, the Chairman's son holds on to me, as if the connection between us is valuable. Precious.

When we get to the City near dusk, I can't help but gape down at the battered outlines I thought I would recognize. "What happened down there?" I whisper to Kasim, sitting on the other side of Sun Yi-lai. My borrowed coat feels too large and too small at once, the high collar with the Menghu's screaming tiger pinching at my neck. The river is cloudy and gray below us, snaking through the rows and rows of buildings, many reduced to ash. The market is covered with helis, and all the booths and buildings that used to crowd the square have been destroyed.

Kasim doesn't answer, keeping his eyes on the pilot sitting ahead of us, a picture of patient relaxation, but I can see his fingers tapping against his arm. June's eyes stay open every moment, her face encased in a gas mask, hair under a fur-lined hood that leaves only her green eyes visible.

Sun Yi-lai's eyes are clenched shut. One of his hand presses his gas mask hard against his nose and mouth as if it's a relief to have his skin covered. After who knows how long inside a box, it must be difficult to have been so exposed these past days. I grip his hand in mine, remembering how much worse heli drops were when I was less used to the feeling. "We're almost there," I whisper. "Your father is down there."

He shrugs, murmuring something I don't understand. "He doesn't have a father," June supplies. "Not that he remembers."

I try to loosen my fingers a degree or two, but he's gripping me back hard enough to bruise my fingers. "That's why we're not handing him over, exactly."

We cruise over the top of the square and circle back over the wall. The City's black gates and the tiered rice paddies contouring the side of the hillsides below are a dim, indistinguishable mess in the twilight. The moon is a full circle that glares down on us, washing us all over in corpse light. I keep my eyes focused on the ground, rejecting the moon, rejecting Howl's story of escape and of living alone forever . . . "They're taking us down to the bottom of the Third Quarter, by the gate," I murmur to Kasim. "Is that—"

"With all the respect in the world," Kasim leans toward me, his lips hardly moving, "if you don't shut it before someone hears you, I'm going to throw you out that window, and you can tell me all about it when I get down there."

"You know the plan. Yi-lai will stay with Kasim until—"

Kasim's hand comes down on my knee and gives it a squeeze, even as he flashes me a toothy smile. "Shut. It."

I push his hand away. Trusting him almost hurts after seeing Xuan's blood splattered across his face. Maybe it should count for something that he managed to get Xuan out. Maybe that really was the only way to do it without getting caught. But every time I look at Kasim, it's as if I can hear the gun discharging over and over, my ears ringing.

Our plan is simple. All of us will leave the heli and head toward
the barracks where they're housing evacuated Menghu. June and
I will break off and sneak into the First Quarter to get the cure,
while Kasim fakes getting sick from the torches that are, apparently, all that keep infected from rushing in on the refugees. Sun
Yi-lai will help him toward the medic center, then double back
to the helis. Once we have the cure, June will take it down to
where Yi-lai is waiting for her, and they'll sneak outside the gates
until we're ready to take off. I'd have left him back with Sole,
but we need his face to lure the Chairman onto our heli when we
we escape.

Kasim and I are going after Howl. And the leaders who have
been starving us, kidnapping us, and killing us for the last decade:
Dr. Yang; General Hong; The Chairman, though he doesn't know
it yet. His loyal soldiers will get us in, help us get Howl, then
help all of us, including the Chairman, to escape after we've dis-
patched Dr. Yang and the General. We'll have a few minutes with
the assembled forces to say that we have a cure and a better way
forward that doesn't involve shooting people. Then the Chairman
will come with us down to the heli, bringing a pilot with him and
escaping with his son.

He actually seemed grateful for the plan. A way out, he called
it, a way for him to finally be free of his responsibilities and focus
on what's really important.

The likelihood that he's playing us is about 120 percent, of
course. Which is why, once the heli has safely landed, we'll kill the
Chairman and any of his soldiers who resist. If things go badly at
the City Center and we fail to appear down by the heli with the
Chairman and Howl within an hour, June will sneak Yi-lai and the
cure down the switchbacks to the forest below and run for Sole.

Even if nothing goes to plan tonight, the cure will get to where it needs to go, and Sun Yi-lai will have a chance at a life not confined inside a box.

I absently rub my traitor mark. It'll be better than what I grew up with. Better than the horror show Howl survived.

Killing all of them—the words still feel like swallowing a blade—is only a beginning to the end of fighting. Things could go very badly tonight, and getting rid of the leaders might make things *worse*. But Mei was right when she said people are scared. People don't trust the leaders anymore. The Port Northian heli that's been dropping bombs for the last few days doesn't help. Maybe if there are people waiting for the right moment, people who will listen to me and Kasim, they will stall chaos long enough to give everyone who's been fighting a new light to follow.

Light. My fingers brush the window frame, and I have to squint against the blaze of torches and spotlights lighting up the City. Isn't the doctor worried that the Port Northian heli will follow these light like a beacon? Unease twists inside me.

It's hard to see into the dark of the City beyond the chemical torches, but I can imagine the people we left behind looking up at the roar of our propellers, drawn to the heat and noise of their people returning, unable to resist like moths toward flame.

I press the gun into my side, trying to find strength in its sharp angles. If we win tonight, then we'll be able to help them. I'm not leaving the victims of SS below us to Dr. Yang for a moment longer. Not to the Mountain that so callously shoved Luokai from their midst, or to the City who manufactured SS and fed it to its own citizens. The people down there in the dark are my people, the ones cast aside without a thought the way I was. The way my mother, my sister, and my father were. If anyone deserves justice from our leaders tonight, it's the moths who have already had their wings burned away.

I wish I knew how to tell them. How to ask for their help tonight.

The heli drops, blasting over the buildings in a thunder of propellers. "What are the chances that black heli didn't see all of us congregating here?" Kasim asks as we lurch to the ground, the pilot not so skilled as Tai-ge was, apparently.

The worry in my gut twists again, because if I can see that Dr. Yang has marked a great big target around the City for the heli to find, then everyone can. Which means something is at play here we haven't accounted for. I unclip my safety harness and help Sun Yi-lai to do the same. He doesn't move to help me, merely nodding his thanks and standing up to follow once June and Kasim are up. His hand finds my shoulder as if he needs a guide the way a small child would, and I put a hand on top of his and look back, giving him a reassuring pat.

We file out with the rest of the Menghu, the soldiers ahead of us walking with a light-footed grace that tells me they're no more comfortable inside City walls than I am. The wide road ahead is lined with torches that seem to breathe out instead of burn. Shapes move in the purple light on the other side of the torches, following our progress at a safe distance.

When we draw nearer to the market, the smell of char hits my nose like a wave of nausea before I can pull my mask tight against my face. It has been more than two months since the invasion, but some of the buildings still seem to be smoking, brick and cement all that's left of the factories flanking the square. The wall separating the City Center and the market square from the First Quarter hosts a line of newly dead bodies strung up like lanterns at a festival, their clothing frosted white in the cold. More Port Northians? I'd think the threat of bombs would be enough to scare the people hiding here.

June huddles in close to me as we walk, her arm linked through mine as if she wants to anchor me against the onslaught of bad memories: The dirty looks I would get in the street. The cold indifference of the nuns. My mother, the princess in the coffin.

At the edges of the square, the torches bend in closer, the chemical outline of the smoke traced hot against the air. My gas mask sanitizes whatever it is they're burning, but Kasim's nose wrinkles, and he covers his nose and mouth with his sleeve.

The library sits up the hill, a blasted remnant of marble, tile, and jade, the black walls bowed in defeat. I can almost hear the flap of pages on the icy wind, the books so long imprisoned inside its walls now flying free.

A swell of people push past us into one of the side alleys, so we go around, walking alongside the main road a block down. Buildings to either side of the alley twinkle with lights, shadows dancing across the windows. A banner hangs from a balcony above us, a Menghu tiger inked into the faded fabric. In its mouth is a stylized City star, blood leaking down both sides of the tiger's mouth. Sun Yi-lai's brow furrows as he looks up at it, his feet slowing. June grabs his arm and pulls him past it.

"Are all the Menghu here in the City?" I whisper to Kasim. "I know they evacuated most of Dazhai to come back here. How can anyone expect Reds and Menghu to exist in the same space?"

Kasim's eyes catch on the banner as we walk under it, a wry smile curling the sides of his unmasked mouth. "I don't know." He looks up again at the buildings. "Wherever the City-folk are, at least Dr. Yang was smart enough to put them far enough away Menghu can't see them."

The alleyway doesn't run straight, bringing us closer and closer to the line of torches. The closer we come, the slower Kasim seems to breathe, until every breath rasps in his throat. He grabs my arm, walking us faster. "This is as good an opportunity as any," he whispers. We only make it within twenty feet of the torches before Kasim falls to his knees, though I'm not sure if his distress is manufactured or real. Sun Yi-lai stops, crouching next to the bulky Menghu. Others from the steady stream of Menghu break from the torrent to loosen his collar and drag him back from the chemical stink.

If anyone notices June and me slipping between torches into the shadows beyond, they don't try to follow.

CHAPTER 60
Sev

I HATE THE FEEL OF THE GUN AGAINST MY SIDE under my coat, the metal pressing into my side as June stops just off the main road. She stills, scanning the area—and gives an annoyed frown when I almost stumble over my own feet behind her.

A hinge creaks in the darkness just behind us. I look back, but June is off into the street, my hand held tight in hers, pulling me into a fast walk that slams my boots loudly into the cobblestones. She shoots me a glare but doesn't slow our pace.

We pass over the lower bridge from the Third to the Second Quarter, picking through debris as we go. Food wrappers that seem to have come from one of the factories. A mess of shattered glass littering the bridge, Bricks, bits of fabric and clothing. A chunk of hair, lying in the middle of the street like a dead rat.

None of that compares to the flutters of movement following us from the high windows in surrounding buildings, the whisper of laughter that slicks through my hair as we squeeze into an alleyway between two Red family compounds. The roof tiles overhead seem to be ragged, broken in some places. As June and I emerge from the alleyway, we spy movement ahead, a man's silhouette black against the darkening sky above us.

We run.

Past Tai-ge's old neighborhood, where a barricade of furniture and razor wire now blocks several streets. The gap in the barricade where a guard should have been standing looks barren and bereft. Lonely, now that whoever was meant to watch it has left.

Where are all the people? Even if SS sent people scurrying for cover, it was only Firsts and lucky Seconds who were airlifted out before the Menghu invasion. That leaves thousands of Seconds and Thirds, all of whom seem to be made from shadows. They couldn't have gotten past the chemical torches without masks, so they must be out here somewhere.

I point June along the streets, following when she abruptly diverts from the path I meant to take, steering us in another direction until whatever threat she sensed is gone. I feel blind, as if threats I should be able to see are breathing down on us every moment and my eyes are somehow glued shut.

Just as we catch sight of the gate leading to the First Quarter, June spins back, slamming me into an alley wall.

Bricks dig into my spine through my borrowed coat. June's slight form presses against me, so still it seems she's even stopped her heart. Everything seems too quiet, every inch of me quivering, because the only thing worse than running or ducking bullets is waiting for the shots to start.

A young man slips into view, the torn remnants of a factory uniform wrapped tightly around him. He walks straight toward us, his eyes wide, as if he's forgotten how to blink. "We're supposed to be headed for the People's Gate into the City Center. Come on."

June tenses, her hand slipping inside my coat to touch the gun. I put a steadying hand on top of hers.

The young man watches us with a sideways tilt to his head, one hand tapping a rhythm onto his arm. "Didn't you see the signals? An hour after dark."

Fear trills through me, leaving my skin pebbled from my neck down. "Right. We're coming."

He nods, still not blinking. Then shambles on.

What is going on?

June tugs my sleeve, the two of us slipping through the gate to the First Quarter together, the moon's icy glow guiding our way. Every moment we're exposed in the open street makes my heart pound, and I tense for an attacker that I'm sure is waiting ahead, just out of sight. But no one comes.

Why is no one coming? And what are they doing instead?

We take Renewal Road up the Steppe, walking through the old neighborhood I remember in ghostly outlines as if I'd only seen it in a dream. Now the street seems to have cracked, the tiles stolen from the roofs of the old First homes, the gates sitting crooked on their hinges and obscenities scrawled on their stone walls.

When we finally turn onto my old street, I see it as I did the last time I was here: The house empty as a body after death. Father on his knees in the courtyard, snow curling around him in a gray-tinged shroud. Mother, gone.

After ducking under a bent lamp and almost tripping over a downed line of paper lanterns, we finally come to the house that used to be mine. It's hard to look at it, to face the crooked lines of my childhood that all lead back to this place. Sick with Sleep in my old room, Mother's crying voice, my sister Aya by my side,

Father arguing with the doctors. The scene is swollen in my mind like a tick left to feed. Engorged with the blood of my memories.

Wrenching my shoulders straight, I force myself to look my past straight on. To take in the house beyond the front gate, door painted red, a pair of cranes carved on either side of the frame.

It's just a house.

June slips a hand into mine, looking up and down the street as if she wants to pull me one way or another but isn't sure which direction is right. "This is it?" she asks quietly.

"It's not quite what I remember," I whisper. The gate to the outer part of the compound hangs limply on its hinges. I walk up the steps, fingers running along the geometric lines that frame the entrance. A gold-and-red card is pasted to the door for New Year. BLESSINGS, it says, positioned upside down to welcome any stray blessings into the house. It's peeling and faded, from last year.

Opening the door, I brace myself, waiting to feel Aya's ghostly presence, to hear Mother's voice singing in her office, or Father's reading to me, but the moon's light leaks in through the windows, turning it to a place of ghosts that don't belong to me. The house is a dead thing, musty and rotted and uncaring of who or what steps inside.

There's a table heavy with family portraits sitting in the entryway, but the paintings are of men and women I've never seen, someone else's family, someone else's memories. June steps up next to me, looking them over. "You know them?" she asks.

I shake my head. "I couldn't bear to see my own family anyway."

"You have to remember the good things." June's brow knots. "People . . . do the best they can."

Surprised, I look down at her. "You think?"

She shrugs. "The nice ones."

A board creaks in the next room, and June darts behind the table, pulling me down while I'm still looking in the direction it came from. We hold our breath while the creaks meander from one room to the next and, finally, toward us.

June's hand is around the gun's handle. She pulls it from my coat with her other finger to her lips. My muscles seem wound so tight it's a wonder they haven't torn. The footsteps draw near, June ready with the weapon, when a slippered foot appears just in my line of sight.

I put a hand on June's, pushing the gun down.

A second slipper appears, the woman wearing it wandering past us with slow, shuffling steps. Her breath rattles in her chest as if she's full of autumn leaves instead of a heart, lungs, and blood, and when her eyes turn toward us, they're milked over in white.

"Who's there?" she rasps, her eyes roving over exactly where we're crouched and missing us. "One of Lieutenant Hao's little runts? I've told you a hundred times, I'm not leaving my home."

On her crumpled hand, there are three white lines almost lost between the wrinkles.

"I've served here since I was a girl, and I won't let it go, no matter what you say about helis and supply lines and the General's Seph-bloodied son. I'll stay here and starve before I go down to the square."

The woman's hand fumbles along the top of the table, swiping toward us and upsetting two of the picture frames instead, sending one to the floor in a shatter of glass. "Yuan's ugly mistress!" she swears, takes another rasping breath.

June squeezes my shoulder, edging us away from the woman's groping hands as she tries to right the picture that didn't fall. We slip away from the table, and I lead her toward my old room, the floor thick with dust. The room itself is empty of anything that made it mine, the windows covered with a set of red curtains I would have hated as a child.

"Know her?" June whispers, looking back down the hall.

"No. If she cleaned the house when I was little . . ." I sigh, ashamed. "No, I don't know her." I kneel and pry up the floorboard with my fingernails.

Her secrets were now hidden in a place no one else could reach. That was the hint inside Mother's device. My stomach clenches, and I'm suddenly terrified that I was wrong, that it was a jump, that it was ridiculous. . . .

In the hole, under a coating of dust, there's a book.

A sleeping princess graces the cover, her form embossed so it sticks out from the dusty paper. It's too light in my hands, and when I open the book, instead of pages and words, there's a secret. The cover is glued around a box, and inside the box is a frail clutch of papers black with my mother's spiky hand. I look through them quickly, finding measurements. Diagrams. Howl's name. Dates. My name. *Encephalitis lethargica.* And next to it, a table that has been rewritten in perfect, clear characters with ingredients, amounts, directions I can't even begin to understand.

A hot flame ignites in my chest, warding off the moon's dead light. The only thing I understand is that this is what I came for. It's the cure.

June's hand snakes forward, plucking out a thicker sheet of paper, Mother's scrawl splashed across the back. "I love you both, so, so much," it says. June turns it over to find a painting of two little girls, their arms tight around each other.

Me and my sister, Aya.

Tears spill down my cheeks. Mother thought it would be both of us who found the cure. Maybe she thought we'd find it with Father's help, within a year even.

She sent me all the way to Port North, to her family and back again, somehow knowing that her secrets would never be safe in hands other than ours. A master of weiqi, more than I ever could have hoped to be, and finally here I am with the winning piece in my hand.

"Your sister?" June's voice is small.

"Yes."

She thinks for a moment, her lips pursed.

I give her hand a squeeze. "I'm glad I have more than one sister now."

Ducking her head, June hands the paper back, but if I didn't know better, I'd swear there was a smile on her face.

I tuck the papers back inside the box but slip the painting into my coat pocket. Then I hand the box to June. She regards it with narrowed eyes before taking it and looking up at me, her eyebrows raised.

"Yes. That's it. The cure."

Her fingers press into the box's cover, her knuckles turning white. She hands me the gun, then stuffs the box down her shirt and buttons her coat over it clear up to her chin.

I find my feet, putting a hand out to help June up, though she ignores it to push off the floor herself. Taking one last look at the room, I turn toward the door. It's finally time to leave this place behind.

CHAPTER 61
Sev

THE OLD WOMAN HAS TUCKED HERSELF INTO A cot in the room just off the main door, muttering to herself. I take extra care when I shut the front door behind us. June and I part ways when we come to the torch line, her scurrying through and heading back toward the gate, me running along the perimeter in the other direction toward the City Center.

That is, until I find a section of torches that have been hacked from their concrete blocks, the torch heads bleeding oil and chemicals on the cobblestones instead of burning. I slow to a stop, bending down to pick up the closest decapitated head, dropping it with a clatter when the metal burns my fingers. Still hot.

Goose bumps break out across my arms and down my neck as I remember the boy earlier reminding us to go to the People's Gate. That's not too far from here.

It wasn't just us who knew about the big gathering tonight.

I stare into the darkness, my legs shaking though I'm standing still. Behind me, a muted sort of roar erupts into the night from the lit area below. The sound of a crowd cheering. Like the ones at old City denunciation meetings, drunk on the idea of blood. Like the one Father watched from under the shadow of Traitor's Arch on the day of his execution, his wife standing over his head, her eyes closed. The same place my old friend Sister Shang met her end.

I can't change what was done in the past, but tonight it's Howl's head they mean to display. I will not lose one more person to that Arch.

Before I can finish this, though, there's one more thing I need to do. I take out the link and type, *I'm here. Are they ready for me?*

The reply comes immediately. *The Seconds farthest to the left of the City Center. Show them your birthmark and they'll let you in. Come fast. Dr. Yang is about to start.*

I have to weave in and out of the torch line more than once before I get to the People's Gate and the bridge that fords the river between the First Quarter and the People's Square. I keep watch but don't see anyone hiding in the streets or gathering under the gate. Long before I'm close, my view of the City Center seems to pulse, the whole square lit up for the last day of Guonian, paper lanterns softly glowing overhead.

The sight chills me even more than the frosty air, and I wonder once again whether the Port Northian heli that forced everyone to evacuate Dazhai is now here, hovering overhead, waiting for the right moment to strike. What good does it do to gather everyone together and then send up flares telling the enemy exactly where to find you?

As I draw nearer, the murmur of many voices speaking all together reaches me from below, benches set up in the shattered remains of the City Center. The building's roof is gone, the walls on the far side of the market reduced to a rubble of scorched marble blocks, and what used to be windows grin up at me in a gap-toothed smile, most of the panes broken out.

Traitor's Arch, however, is whole, even the stairs that lead up to where Mother's glass box used to sit, though the platform is now empty. Air seems to crackle around me as I sneak through the ruins of the People's Gate. Yuan Zhiwei's statue just below the square stands bereft, the lantern light catching on the blade of his ax.

A shadow detaches from an alleyway only a few feet away. For a split second I'm paralyzed with fear until the shadow resolves into Kasim's wide form. "Done sightseeing?" he asks.

In answer, I start down the hill toward the City Center and the guards ringing the square. Following the Chairman's instructions, Kasim leads me to the left side, the two of us coming out into the lantern light just as a sharp *crack* splinters the air. I duck, my heart startling into a gallop as I look around for the source of the shooting.

Instead, an echoing *boom* shudders through the air, and a bloom of red explodes in the sky above the square. Kasim and I freeze.

Guonian always ends this way, but simply knowing it was a fireworks display can't make me forget how close it sounded to chemical bombs. Another ground-shaking *boom* tears through the sky, and I duck down, flashing back to the day Menghu bombed the library, Tai-ge's father falling bloody at my feet.

"What is Dr. Yang playing at?" Kasim whispers. He puts a hand on my arm, walking close enough that it feels almost as if he's putting himself between me and the Reds.

There are some very terrible memories in my head dedicated to Kasim, but here he is, standing between me and City soldiers as if he can't help himself. An odd feeling comes over me, a memory of Howl's voice like an echo in my ear: *I just want to live through this.*

I guess we all do, and all of us have the blood on our hands to prove it. The gun feels cold, heavy, *wrong* where it's tucked inside my coat. I don't want to do this. But it's the only option.

"Weapons?" The guard closest to us looks up as we approach, his red stars looking muddy and tarnished at his collar. "Don't try to hold anything back. We've been instructed to search everyone who comes in, and if you attempt to bring a weapon, we'll have to assume you mean to use it."

I open the buckles at the side of my mask, pulling it down and baring the brown birthmark—no, *tattoo*—that has marked me as my mother's daughter my whole life. Butterflies churn in my belly as his eyes slide over the pigmentation in my skin.

One hand on his weapon, the Red meets my eyes. My stomach clenches when he doesn't say anything. Did we go to the wrong guard? Did the Chairman decide he doesn't want us at the execution after all? Or maybe he forgot to tell this man that, for the first time ever, he *wants* a Fourth to have a gun.

His muscles tense. So do mine, as if that will somehow stop a bullet when he decides to shoot me.

But then, he nods us in.

CHAPTER 62
Sev

MEMORIES ARE MADE UP OF FLASHES OF COLOR, pungent smells, and feelings strong enough to take you over. Entering the charred remains of my mother's former tomb—not to mention my own attempted murder by Dr. Yang—smells like the char of nightmares, the chemical tang of tubes and pipes that kept my mother alive until I disconnected her. There are benches set in front of the Arch filled with Firsts and Seconds on one side and Menghu on the other. All seem to have hands inside their coats, City- and Mountain-folk alike searching for the weapons that have been taken away from them. At the very front, standing at the base of the Arch like a dog at attention, Helix heads a group of Menghu who watch the crowd.

I'd be willing to bet *he* has a weapon.

Dr. Yang climbs up onto the Arch just as Kasim and I reach the benches, filtering in with the last stragglers from the Third Quarter and coming to rest in the place my mother once stared down at. Raising his hands, Dr. Yang's mouth opens to speak just as another gunpowder *boom* traces fire across the sky, lighting his face with gold.

"We are here together in a place long fought over," Dr. Yang begins once the firework's sound has faded from our ears. His voice, distorted by his gas mask, is amplified through the speakers set up to either side of the Arch. "We are here, old enemies, at a time when families should be together. We come mourning instead. Fathers, mothers, children. Gone."

I crane my neck, combing the audience for the people we seek. General Hong. The Chairman. *Howl.* From the back, it's hard to see much of anything. Kasim nudges me, inching to the side, but I'm not sure what he wants me to do. We can't walk up the aisles to get a better view of the room, not when everyone else is sitting so nicely, paying attention. Plus, shooting Dr. Yang now would mean that the Chairman and General Hong, wherever they are, would fly free. And who knows what would happen to Howl? We need to see all four before we can move.

I touch the gun inside my coat. I've always been a passable marksman. When I was young, I practiced until I could hit any target. Kasim tested me before we left, showing me a pinecone, a snowy branch, a knot in a tree, and asking me to shoot. I can still do it. It's just that shooting a human isn't quite the same thing.

"We come with war hanging on us like death." Dr. Yang holds a hand up as if to take in the destruction of the building, of the torches glowing hot in the night, and the eyes waiting on the other side. "Our old enemy has given us a disease we cannot fight. Rebels have taught those who could help us to keep the cure to themselves. And now even our refuges are threatened by helis carrying weapons that were outlawed during the Influenza War."

Dr. Yang looks up at the sky, the night reflected in his eyes. His speech is coming faster now, as if there's a timer on his words and he's about to run out. "Tonight, I want to show you what we—City and Mountain—could be if we worked together."

Which is when I hear it. Not the drone of a heli hovering above or the roar of one landing. Not the hiss and scream of chemical bombs pouring from the night sky. It's a sort of dry flapping sound, almost too quiet to register. But the Menghu around me begin to murmur the moment their ears capture the sound, some going as far as to stand and head for the edges of the lighted square.

"Stay where you are!" Dr. Yang's command raps out even as my stomach churns. What is it that has everyone so frightened?

Another firework hisses into the night sky, crowning over our heads in a red glory and lighting up the metal hull of a heli lurking in the sky.

"Don't be afraid." Dr. Yang smiles benevolently down on us. His light tenor voice is strained as he looks at the heli's black outline against the sky.

Kasim swears, grabbing my arm to haul me to my feet. "Maybe all he ever wanted was to kill us," he rasps. "Come on. We run."

Just as we clear the benches, a deeper *crack* than the cannon launching the fireworks tears through my ears, and then another and another in quick succession, blinding me with their light. I stumble, Kasim's hand around my arm tightening as he tries to drag me up from the ground.

The world seems imprinted in purple and ghostly white, all except for an angry orange *roar* in the air where the heli was, dribbling flames down as it careens to the ground out in the forest below. Something black flashed across the glow just before it fell, as if the occupants jumped out to avoid the flames. Would the fall be better than burning?

"Look at me," the doctor's voice purrs. "When we were separated

Outside and fending for ourselves, it took one heli to send us running. But here, with all of us together, it was easy to lure it. To
destroy it. The weapon was a combination of technology discovered
in the City and the Mountain, the execution of this plan facilitated
by good people on both sides." His voice rises even as a group
stands up from the front row of benches to stand next to him.
"With City walls, Menghu military expertise, with our engineers,
workers, medics, and researchers all working together, *look what we
are capable of!*"

My heart gallops back and forth in my chest, and I'm still
blinking away the afterimages of whatever it was they used to
shoot down the black heli. But even as my sight returns, all I can
see are flames on the forest floor.

Kasim tugs my arm, leading me farther up the benches, his
walk quick and intentional. My breath hitches in my chest as I see
why he's changed course so suddenly, and I match my stride to
his, ending up near the middle of the benches with a clear view of
the people at the front.

Just below the doctor, Chairman Sun and General Hong stand
to either side of the Arch.

My gut clenches as we slide onto the bench. Still no Howl.
Wasn't this supposed to be his execution?

The crowd doesn't respond to Dr. Yang's invitation to cheer. I
suppose it was obvious from the moment we stepped off the heli
that City and Mountain forces did not like the idea of sharing
space. It seems to be distilled into this moment, murmurs rum-
bling out from both sides of the room. *Why?* they seem to say.
Why invite Outsiders and murderers into our midst? from the Firsts and
Seconds, while the Mountain-folk seem to think the arrangement
that Dr. Yang had before—where they were taking everything they

wanted from the City without restraint—a much better plan.

"To demonstrate our goodwill, our first act as a united people will be to show you what happens to those who have worked so hard to keep us at odds." Dr. Yang raises one hand in invitation, and three Menghu muscle a fourth figure out into the gaping maw under the Arch. He looks thin. Pale. Complacent, though it seems his guards want him to put up a fight, pushing him roughly to his knees under Dr. Yang's feet.

Howl.

"We've got them," Kasim whispers. "Chairman's on the side with all the City-folk, so I'm guessing the Reds he said would cover us are there in front of him. Let's get close enough to finish this."

Dr. Yang continues once Howl is in front of him. "This young man spent years masquerading as the Chairman's own son, stealing vital information and supplies and giving them to the Mountain." His gleeful monologue sets the Firsts whispering to each other, the Seconds behind them standing to get a better look. "And Menghu have no love for this boy either. He was sent to spy because he'd become unpredictable. Leaving his own soldiers and friends exposed if it meant protecting himself. Even worse than that? When we had the cure to the horrible disease that plagues us, that makes our air poison and injects fear into every moment, he took it. He took it for himself."

Now it's the Menghu craning their necks to look at Howl, standing up in their chairs and making it easy for Kasim and me to creep closer. Memories of Mei's terrified recounting of Howl's story are enough for me to know that her beliefs about him didn't just belong to her. Never mind Dr. Yang knows just as I do that Howl didn't have any cure. That it was the doctor himself who

set SS loose on all of us, who destroyed the City, leaving even
the highest of the Firsts scrambling for existence and the lowest
Third forgotten entirely. Anger wires my jaw shut, my hand pressing hard against the gun.

Chairman's Sun's eyes catch our movement as we slink closer
to the front, and a grim smile cracks the stony expression on
his face.

Eight rows from the front. Seven. I'm ready to end this.

"And it isn't just Sun Howl who has betrayed us." Dr. Yang
snaps his fingers, and shouts fill the air as a group of soldiers
surround the Seconds backing the Chairman. Kasim and I slow
in shock, watching as the Seconds fight other Seconds. Surprise
from the Chairman's men makes this fight a quick one. Whispers
start at the back of the crowd, and I turn to find two Seconds
being frog-marched by their own comrades toward the Arch.

"There was a conspiracy here tonight to assassinate me and
General Hong, a pathetic grab at power by the Chairman to regain
the hold he had over all of you." Dr. Yang smiles as the last group
of armed Reds surround the Chairman, placing a gun to his head.
"He meant to keep the cure from us forever, as he, his father,
and his grandfathers all the way back to Yuan Zhiwei have done.
But that is not all. Look around you. You will find two people
here who do not belong. First, a traitor Menghu by the name of
Wu Kasim."

My heart stops even as Kasim barrels forward, gaining momen-
tum when his gun comes out. Howl's head jerks up, his mouth
open in protest, his eyes following Kasim down the aisle. Menghu
from Helix's team block Kasim's way, grabbing him by the shoulders and wrestling him to the ground. They extract the gun from
his fingers with an audible *crunch* of broken bones.

Dr. Yang continues as if nothing happened. "Our second traitor is a girl who, when joined with Sun Howl, holds the cure to
SS inside her." He glances down at Howl, who straightens from
his hunch, frantically looking out over the crowd. "These two
have done everything in their power to keep the cure from us, no
matter how many of our children die." Scanning the crowd, Dr.
Yang's eyes find me. "There you are."

"No!" Howl's voice rings out over the din as Menghu look
around, trying to figure out how to check under masks without
accidentally infecting friends.

Heart thumping, I pull out the gun, only to find a Menghu
blocking my way. She shies back from the gun's muzzle, but in
a practiced sort of way that makes me think she's running the
numbers in her head, deciding how best to disarm me. The crowd
swells around us, taking her attention away from me as people
all try to fit into the small space, and I lurch past her, stumbling
between two men in Yizhi's white coats into the empty bubble of
space just in front of the Arch. Howl's there on his knees, his eyes
a fearful swirl of terror and tears. "Sev," he chokes, "*no*. Please, no.
If you're here, then what was the point?"

Dr. Yang is directly above him. I point my gun between the old
snake's eyes. "You want to talk about betrayal? What about—"

Which is when three soldiers grab me from behind and knock
me over. My head hits the ground, cold stone gritty against
my cheek.

CHAPTER 63
Sev

THEY TAKE MY MASK, MY FACE NAKED FOR EVERYONE to see. From my spot next to the Arch, the crowd is infinitely clearer, Menghu captains with their collars embroidered in black whisper excitedly between rows at my appearance. Firsts and Seconds scowl in my direction, my traitorous blood proven long ago when they branded it into my very skin.

One face stands out from the others. Tai-ge is sitting at the front, his eyes horrified and his mouth sewn shut. As usual. Here to watch me die, just like we both always knew he would be. Untouched by his own actions, as if breaking into the southern garrison to free a traitor isn't enough to counteract the City red running through his veins.

Not untouched. A thread of ugly gratification strings my heartbeats together. He's not wearing a mask. At least Tai-ge's had a taste of what his mother and the doctor are doing to the rest of the world.

The General herself hovers next to me, though it's Helix's oily fingers that hold my wrists tight against the small of my back, my elbows twisted painfully behind me. She smiles, her fine-boned cheeks so delicate and yet so hard. "I've been waiting for the day I could finally get rid of you."

"I'm not a traitor." It comes out quiet the first time. The second it's more of a pained yell. "I'm not a traitor! I never wanted to destroy your son; I never wanted anyone to die! It's Dr. Yang who forced the Mountain to invade, it's him who set contagious SS loose, who manipulated me into—"

The crowd's garbled voice swells loud enough that no one can hear any of the words raking bloody lines inside my throat. Instead of listening, they're shouting at me, just like any good denunciation. Shouting at me, at Howl, even denouncing the Chairman, though the Firsts cluster off to the side as if they're not quite sure to whom their loyalties should fall. Kasim stands crooked at my side, his braced leg seeming to pain him, but he stares back at the crowd, making a rude gesture at the Menghu side when they begin to call out his name along with some choice obscenities, though it doesn't work very well because his broken fingers won't move. The crowd only seems to grow louder as Dr. Yang descends from his place atop the Arch to stand next to me.

He leans in, face only inches from mine. "This is your last chance, Jiang Sev. You know what your mother's note meant. Was it instructions on where to find her notes? A key code to bring back the erased information?" He waits a moment, his voice so low, I don't think even Helix can hear it over the din from where he's holding my arms. "If you don't tell me, you'll watch your friends here die one by one. You'll go back to Sleep. And if that still isn't enough, you'll die. You'll die alone, knowing you doomed every person left on this continent. You're leaving us all to SS."

"It wouldn't be that way if you hadn't *given* them all SS." My words come out through gritted teeth.

He smiles, a little chuckle escaping his throat. "Shall we see if you've grown a sense of shame since we last spoke?" He points at the Reds lined up, the Chairman a crisp exclamation point ending their ranks. The Chairman still fights against the Seconds holding him, issuing orders in a voice that sounds so strong and sure, and yet the Reds don't seem to hear.

"It was two of his own soldiers who came to me. Told me you were coming and when you arrived." Dr. Yang sighs. "*They* see that he has fallen. Why can't you?"

"I don't care what happens to the Chairman." A truth I don't like as it comes out of my mouth.

"He is helping you because you've found his son? Or promised to find him?" Dr. Yang nods at his own question. "What are you willing to sacrifice to keep your secrets, Jiang Sev?"

I shake my head. "There's nothing for me to tell you, Dr. Yang."

"These Seconds were going to help you." He points at the line of men and women, their uniforms dirty, fear in their eyes. The man who let me into the square stands at the end opposite the Chairman. "Just obeying orders, and now they're going to die because of *you*. One by one, until you tell me where your mother hid her notes. If you can stomach their deaths, it will be Kasim next." He puts a hand on the Menghu's shoulder and Kasim refuses to break eye contact, disgust curling at his mouth.

Swallowing hurts, the weight of all these lives feeling like stones enough to form a city on my shoulders. But I've seen more death. I've been responsible for so many already. I won't be responsible for *everyone* who would die, forgotten, under

Dr. Yang's unchallengeable authority if he got the cure away from June.

"After Kasim, it'll be Howl."

My stomach clenches, two hot tears burning down my cheeks. Howl kneels under the Arch, staring at me as if he means to light the whole room on fire with sheer anger.

"After Howl, I'll take you to where I hid the Chairman's son, and I'll slit his throat." I can't breathe, thinking of June and Yi-lai crouched outside the walls. He was supposed to be our insurance. Our way to make sure Chairman Sun got on the heli. But I've just brought him back to the man who put him to Sleep.

General Hong stands up, turning her back to the crowd and raising her weapon to point at the first Red's face. It's the man who let me into the square. I hardly register the shot, though it's louder than the taunts and anger roaring in my ears.

He falls, red painted between his eyes.

"After the Chairman's son, I'll hunt down your little blond Wood Rat friend."

The next Red in line falls. Dr. Yang's lips brush my ear, sending shivers of revulsion through me like waves of mud. "After her, we'll go after Sole and everyone she's got stashed under the Mountain."

Howl strains against the two Menghu holding him, his feet sliding across the floor. "At least tell me there's hope." Tears draw lines down his face, his voice choked.

"It's already done." I pull back from the doctor, my shoulders screaming with pain as Helix wrenches my arms to keep me in place. "We're jumping, Howl. You and me. It's the only thing that's going to give the rest of the world a chance."

All the breath seems to leave Howl's body, another shot going off, another Red slumping to the ground. But he squares his shoulders and gives me a firm nod. "You found the cure? Why come here?"

"You don't get to tell me when your life doesn't matter, Howl."

He stares back at me, his face crumpled. But his lips twitch up into a broken attempt at a smile. "We've won, then."

"That's right. We've *won*." Ejecting the word feels like a release. June's smart enough to already be running. No Red could find her in the forest. I turn my attention back to Dr. Yang, trying to find enough saliva to spit in his face, but my mouth is dry. "You can kill anyone you want, but you've already lost. These people will leave you at the first whisper of a cure once it's done."

Dr. Yang pushes away from me, an angry gesture that leaves me stumbling to the side, Helix moving to keep from wrenching my shoulders out of their sockets. "Put Howl up next."

The two soldiers holding Howl's arms jerk him up from the ground and lead him to the middle of the Arch. "Is this really what you want, Jiang Sev?" the doctor asks.

"I wanted you to be the one who lived!" Howl keeps his broken smile, and it knifes through me, leaving nothing but pain. "I wanted it to be you."

I bite my lip, my whole body seizing up. I think of June, probably already on her way out of the City. Sun Yi-lai, his whole life stolen. Peishan, Lihua, Sole, Aya . . . Dr. Yang standing there less than an inch away, his breath filtering through his mask in an ugly hiss. And I keep my mouth shut.

General Hong gestures for Tai-ge to come, and he obeys, feet dragging but unable to resist the string his mother always has had tied around his neck. She hands him the gun and steps back.

Closing my eyes feels dishonest, as if no one will witness

Howl's sacrifice, so I keep them open. For a moment, Tai-ge just stands there. General Hong shouts at Tai-ge to shoot, and still he does nothing. Delaying. Then he takes aim, and I bite my tongue to keep from screaming.

When the gun discharges, it blasts through me, though it's Howl who crumples to the ground, blood blooming on his leg. I pull against Helix's grasp on my wrists, falling to my knees when he jerks me back.

Another shot, this one to Howl's shoulder, the crisscross of scars still pink where they stick out from his shirt. He cries out in pain, and I can't stand to move, can't let myself look away as he keeps his eyes glued to mine.

"I love you!" I say it as loud as I can, though it only comes out in a rasp. A horribly inadequate, squeezed-together sob that means nothing and everything at once.

Howl holds my gaze. It's the end of the world, but I keep watching, staying with him.

The next shot shatters through us all, as if it's the sky itself cracking open. Everything around me seems to grind to a stop, the sound dying out, nothing but the hiss of masks and robotic, confused murmurs. Because the last shot didn't come from inside the square.

CHAPTER 64
Sev

IT HAPPENS SO QUICKLY, EVERYTHING SWEEPING
straight over me like a wave in the ocean. Tai-ge's voice is a horrible
yell that hardly penetrates the volley of gunfire cracking the night
into gaping fissures: "You have it? Sevvy, *where is the cure?*"

When I tear my eyes away from Howl where he's curled on the
ground, my heart begins to pound in time with the shouts coming
from the flood of people washing into the square. They're threadbare, missing shoes, and dusted over with ash and dirt, their ribs
showing through their torn clothing. Their fingers find masks,
tearing them from the crowd as they boil closer to the Arch.

"You ungrateful traitor for a son. . . ." I turn to find Tai-ge
with an arm around his own mother's neck. Reds who had been
sitting around Tai-ge form a wall between where he holds his
mother captive and the gobbled shouts and crushing mass of
humans. A Menghu peels out from the crowd, pulling her hood
back. It's Mei. She slides to a stop in front of General Hong,
training a gun on her forehead.

Tai-ge flinches, his forehead knotted. But he holds his mother still.

The second heli. Sole ignored me and sent Mei anyway. Orchestrated all of this with Tai-ge, only the timing came two shots too late.

I run to Howl, his guards fleeing into the crowds as the new-comers surround us. Howl's hand circles my wrist, clenching too tight. "Howl, look at me!" I yell it too loud, checking over him. His eyes are open but glazed even as he stares up at me. "I'm here. Just keep breathing."

"*Sevvy!*" Tai-ge yells, fighting his mother down as she bites at his arm. "*Do you have it?*"

"Not here! It's safe."

He tosses his gun toward me, sending it skittering across the floor to rest by Howl. "Don't let Dr. Yang get away. *Go!*"

I pick it up, the metal still warm from putting holes in Howl, but I can't turn away from the blood and death unfolding before me. I kneel, brandishing the gun like a flag. "Listen to me. *Listen to me!*" My scream falls like droplets of water on a raging bonfire, but still I continue. "I have the cure! We don't have to fight anymore!"

The few people in the crowd who look up at me seem hungry for more blood than what already decorates their hands and coats. One of the women starts toward me and Howl, but falls to her knees before she can come close, her hands twitching back and forth as she paws at the paving stones.

"*I have the cure.*" I'm almost whispering now, my throat hoarse as the crowd looks hungrily up at me. "And I'll give it to anyone. Anyone who will just *stop fighting.*"

Another shot rings out, zinging right past me to bury in Howl's chest.

For a moment, I can't process what just happened. "Howl?" I crouch over him, my voice rising to an unearthly shriek that tears my throat in two. *"Howl?"*

His eyes roll back into his head, his whole body going slack under me.

"No, you can't. . . ." The words won't come as I pull off my coat, ripping out the lining to cover the spot bubbling red. *"You can't. . . ."*

"Sevvy! He's above us!" Tai-ge's voice zips through my mind, leaving blood and fury. Because that's where the shot came from. Above us. From the ugly gap in the Arch where mother stood watch for so many years. Another bullet whips by me, and I duck out from Howl's arm to lay him flat on the floor. Once he's down, my feet slip out from under me in my race to get to the stairs.

The Arch runs parallel to the crumbling wall behind it, the platform balanced precariously with space behind the Arch in which a man could hide. The darkness seems to sing to me, warning that he's here, the man who killed my mother and put me to Sleep. The man who just shot Howl.

I run up the stairs to the back side of the Arch, my ears screaming one long, high-pitched note. He's here, I can feel it. Raising my gun, I point it behind the bend of the Arch closest to me. But there's nothing there. When I turn to check the other side, a body slams into my back. My head cracks against the Arch, and suddenly I'm on the floor and my arms and legs don't seem to work.

Cold washes across my body as Dr. Yang's shadow leaks across me, his silhouette burned into my brain. "You think you can use the cure against me?" he whispers. "When I've known who you were, who your mother was . . . when I've spent my whole life waiting to destroy this corrupt system and stop all the killing? You think you can steal it from *me*?"

He chuckles softly, the sound rusted and rotting through the filters of his gas mask. His hands latch onto my shoulders, fingers like claws piercing my skin as he rolls me over, the gun limp like a dead thing where it's caught in my coat.

"I know you wanted to give it to Sole. If she already has it, then I don't need you anymore." He coughs it out like a gore crowing over its prey, but his eyes seem to be smiling. "I can kill you. Howl. Sole. Anyone who helped you. You're all dead."

The air feels hot around me, pressing hard against my skin, slowing everything down to move centimeter by centimeter. Dr. Yang's voice is an unhealthy drone in my ears. The gun slips free of my coat, my sweaty hand gripping it too hard as it seems to swing by itself toward the doctor's chest.

But it's me, *my* finger, that pulls the trigger.

The sound flares in my ears, the awful *crack* of gunpowder. Dr. Yang falls forward onto me. Something warm leaks through my clothes and drips down my leg.

Awful stillness only lasts a split second before his hands snake up to my neck, thumbs jamming painfully into my throat as he tries to cut off my air. My muscles scream with the effort it takes to pull his strangling grasp from my neck. Dr. Yang's hands are shaking, and his breaths are coming in wet gasps that don't seem to be taking oxygen to his lungs. The bullet landed, even if it wasn't in his heart.

I push him off me, the gun heavier than it should be when I point it at his head. But before I can shoot, hands grab hold of me and wrench me back, pulling the gun from my hand. A Menghu steps into my vision, dragging the doctor up from the floor, the

whole ring of guards who were supposed to be protecting him
finally doing their job.

"This is where it stops, Jiang Sev," Dr. Yang gasps. "What
were you going to do with Sole and her pathetic operation under
the Mountain anyway? Sneak into our camps and inject us in our
sleep? Free the Sephs in the Mountain and hope they decided to
side with you? I have the resources and Firsts to make the cure.
Anyone who crosses me will die compulsing. Anyone who refuses
to do what I want will have nothing to look forward to but death.
All you have is a gun that's out of bullets."

He nods to the Menghu propping him up, so certain of obe-
dience he doesn't even make eye contact. Or maybe it's pain, his
mouth spewing all the things I've known were locked in his brain.
"Shoot her."

In a way, it's fitting that I die here, same as my mother. I close
my eyes, feel the waft of air as the Menghu raises the gun, and
wait for the air to splinter.

But nothing happens. Footsteps crinkle through my damaged
ears, and I open my eyes to find another Menghu stepping into
our circle wearing a mask with gore teeth painted across the filters.

Helix looks at me. "Dr. Yang really did infect the Mountain on
purpose? You have proof?" he asks quietly.

I nod.

"And you really do have a cure? Proof of that, too?"

I nod again.

He sighs, then points to the Menghu holding Dr. Yang. "Take
his mask and give him to the Sephs."

Dr. Yang's eyes go wide. "Captain Lan, you can't give
orders to—"

"You promised to make our lives better, Dr. Yang." Helix doesn't yell. He doesn't need to. His voice is so cold I shrink back. "You destroyed my home. Killed our real leaders. Let us starve, let us get shot. Sent us to the north in helis, every moment telling us you had the answer. *You* were the answer the whole time. You were the enemy. We were only waiting for the cure to appear before we killed you." He wipes his hands on his coat, turning away. "I'm glad it's finally done."

The Menghu around Dr. Yang hold him still while one wrestles the mask from his face. The doctor's face turns red as he fights, holding his breath once the filters are torn from his mouth and nose. His feet skid as he tries to pull himself free, blood dripping down from his side where I shot him. There are shots still sounding below. But the crowd pulls back as SS victims from outside the City Center slide up to meet the Menghu holding Dr. Yang. They take the doctor from them and drag him out into the shattered City, where his screams are lost in the chaos below.

CHAPTER 65
Sev

TAI-GE APPEARS ON THE STAIRS, KASIM AND MEI
flanking him on each side. Helix and his soldiers tense, Helix
looking from the two Menghu to Tai-ge's red stars, blood and horror in his eyes. But instead of shooting at them, Helix takes a step
forward, anger on his face that I don't understand. *"You?"* He sort
of laughs. "Mei told me there was a Red helping the Menghu stuck
here, but I didn't expect a Hong." His fingers flex around the gun.
"I think I owe you a good blow to the head."

Tai-ge holds himself straight. "I'm not just helping Menghu.
There are lots of people suffering out there." He points to the
still-fighting flood of people who washed into the square, some
still brandishing guns that seem to be out of bullets. "Mother
wanted to abandon all our people trapped here. Dr. Yang wanted
to abandon all the Menghu left behind. Now everyone who was
left behind gets to show how they feel about it."

Mei steps between them. "If we don't do something quick,
there won't be anyone left to save. It'll spread down to where the
soldiers who flew in are staying."

It strikes me that she didn't say *"Menghu."* She said *"soldiers."* The Reds, too.

Helix nods slowly, looking over at me. "You're working with Sole?"

I nod. "I don't know how complicated the cure will be to make, but we'll need help from everyone on both sides to get SS under control."

Tai-ge's smile rankles a bit, solid and assuming as if he never thought I'd do anything else. But then maybe that's trust. Even if I couldn't trust him to believe me, he's always known who I am and where I stand. Helix shakes his head as he goes down to join Tai-ge on the stairs, Mei a bridge between them. "I guess I was wrong about you, Jiang Sev. You're not as idiotic as I thought."

I don't have the energy to answer, every inch of me hurting as Kasim steps forward to pull me up from the ground. All that's left in me is one word: "Howl?"

He doesn't answer, letting me lean on him as I hobble down the stairs, my eyes on the tattered heap where I left Howl under the Arch. The Chairman kneels next to him on one side, two medics on the other inserting tubes and bandages into Howl as if they're trying to drain the last of his blood as a trophy. General Hong sits propped up against one of the Arch's base supports with her hands and feet tied together.

The Reds who were slated for execution cluster along the edge of the stage, keeping back the brawl, gunshots noticeably absent— I suppose the people surviving outside the square probably didn't have much ammunition to bring to this fight. Everyone else here wasn't allowed a gun per Dr. Yang's own orders. It makes me wonder if Tai-ge was a part of that conversation, pretending to have the new order's best interest in mind but planning his own takeover instead.

Kasim helps me to Howl's side, the Chairman's face inscrutable as he moves over to make room for me. "My son," he whispers. "You promised my son." The soldiers standing around us seem to bristle, Kasim's muscles going tense under my hands, where he holds me up.

"Back off." I push him away from Howl's still form. One of the medics looks up, his eyes bouncing between the two of us. "I keep my promises. Your son is safe, but you'll have to wait."

A firework's heavy *boom* ignites right over the crowd, the fighting jerking to a surprised pause. In the split second of silence, Helix steps up, shouting into the speakers Dr. Yang set for the rally. "Menghu, *attention!* Any man or woman still fighting will answer to me personally. Lower your fists, *now.*"

It seems a ridiculous command, but it gives Tai-ge the breath of silence he needs to step up next to the Menghu. "Captain Hao, Lieutenant Bai, rein in your soldiers. All of you who came to fight today. Listen for a moment, if you can."

The words ring oddly in my ears. *If you can?* The silence waxes a moment longer, broken only by ugly gasps and a few littered sounds of feet on stone. Not everyone in this crowd *can* listen with SS in their veins, but I don't think of Tai-ge as one who houses sympathy for something he's never experienced himself.

Except . . . he does have experience now.

Tai-ge takes a hesitant breath, his voice unclouded by filters. "My mother is officially stepping down from her post as General," he announces. "Firsts and Seconds, I came here to find a way to produce more masks, but it's an impossible job without raw materials from the farms. We don't have a safe way to transport food or water, much less continue with mining and factories. We don't have doctors or Mantis enough to meet SS victims' needs even here within our walls. You see what's left of our City." Tai-ge's voice is pained as he looks over the fractured ruin of the City Center around us and the broken graveyard of factories beyond. At the men and women who snuck in from beyond the torch line, their eyes hungry and their fingers clotted over with dirt. "We abandoned our own to die long before bombs started falling. We sent families to the farms to work until they withered away. The Chairman and my mother deserted even more of you at the first threat against them. That is not what it means to be a part of this City. We are all comrades. United with one purpose: to defeat SS." He looks at Helix. "We've been fighting over Mantis for so long it's hard to remember that sometimes fighting isn't the answer. If it's between settling old grudges and surviving, I know my choice."

Helix doesn't nod, prickly as he stands up next to Tai-ge, and I can hardly believe what I'm seeing, the two of them standing there shoulder to shoulder, even if Helix doesn't look very happy about it.

"I've fought my whole life, thinking safety was at the end of the road," Helix yells, his voice thick with emotion. "That if I killed just one more Red, if I stole one more case of Mantis, I was that much closer to carving out a space that might be safe enough for me to have a life." He blinks, one hand going to the sharp teeth painted across his mask. "That someday, the fighting would stop and I'd be able to sleep at night, not worried if my friends would die while my eyes were closed. That I'd be able to have my own family and know they would be safe." He raises a hand, his brow furrowed deep. "And every day the leaders I followed only took us deeper and deeper into the violence. There isn't any path to peace through fighting. There is only more fighting. We have to change."

They yell out instructions for City and Mountain to separate, then send soldiers out into the crowd to physically separate wrestling matches that aren't stopping. I can hardly pay attention or process the groups, people who listen to Helix or Tai-ge or anyone else, or *why*, because the medics won't let me touch Howl, the Chairman holding me back. Howl's skin is so pale, every inch of him motionless. A scream of anguish builds up like a geyser inside me, but I hold it back, watching.

If he were dead, the medics wouldn't care if I touched him. If he were dead, they'd have left him in a bloody heap on the stage, because there's no point to extracting bullets from a corpse.

We jumped together, so if he were dead, I'd be dead too.

CHAPTER 66
Tai-ge

THE CITY FEELS LIKE SOMETHING UNKNOWN AND familiar at once from my spot on the orphanage roof, the moon looming in the sky overhead. I shiver in the cold. Sevvy left almost before the shouting in the square stopped, hardly pausing for medics to make sure Howl was stable enough to move before wheeling him straight to a heli, the Chairman trailing behind her like a dog on a leash.

He didn't try to stop me from tying my own mother under the Arch or from stepping up to take control of the Seconds myself. The Chairman didn't look back even once as I watched him get on the heli with Sev. My guess is he didn't know what Sev had planned for him.

She was right all those weeks ago, when we were in the heli trying to plan what to do next. If things are going to work, we need a new start. New leaders. People who haven't lived with power clutched between their fists so long that the tiniest deviation feels like oppression.

Helix and I have had our share of difficulties, though he has agreed to keep his forces to a separate part of the City from mine until a more substantial peace agreement can be met. We've put up barriers, established talks. Lieutenant Hao's contacts among the Menghu who were left behind after the invasion have been instrumental in persuading Menghu from Outside to at least listen and see if we can work something out between us. Them and Mei.

They want Mantis. The cure. My own soldiers want it more than anything too, willing to look the other way when they see Menghu insignia within the City if it means no more masks. If it means bringing down the chemical torches entirely, letting people we love back into our lives.

Shots have been fired. More outside than inside the walls. But fewer than I would have expected. Everyone wants to believe the cure is real and is waiting for the first doses to arrive. And after that? Well, I guess we'll take it one step at a time.

The trapdoor leading downstairs squeaks, and I look back to find Mei climbing up the ladder. "What are you doing up here?" she aks.

I turn back to the lights dotting the City streets, so many more than when I first returned. "Just looking, I guess. It's almost like home again."

"Have you heard from Sev or Sole yet?"

I shake my head. "They asked for scientists and some supplies to be flown in from the labs. Some things we needed to get from the farms, but it was a good start to freeing people who have been incarcerated out there, though the Firsts left over weren't very happy about it. Our reach is sort of soft, but some of the people stayed on at the farms when we gave them the choice. More food. A promise of better living conditions, compensation, and the ability to stay or go in the future. I guess putting longtime workers in positions of authority and letting them take charge of their own bits of land helped." I scrub a hand through my overgrown hair. I'll have to find someone to cut it before it goes completely crazy. "Everyone seems much more . . . calm, now that we have a credible start on a cure."

Mei drops down next to me, kicking her heels over the edge of the roof. The light on her hair casts her over in silver. "After so many years of lies from Dr. Yang, it's hard to not feel a little worried."

"Sevvy doesn't lie. This is all she wanted. To give the cure to anyone who'd take it."

She narrows her eyes a bit, but nods after a moment. "You're going to be late for the meeting with Helix."

The way she says his name makes my hackles rise. "You don't like him."

It takes a second for her to answer. "It's hard to like anyone who is responsible for your life. If you screw up, then you screw everyone else over too. Leaders handle that differently, and the way he handled it when I was in his company was . . . bad." She smiles grimly, looking over at me. "But if there's one thing I'm sure of, it's that Helix wants the fighting to stop." Peeling herself up from the roof, she puts out a hand. "I don't think any of us thought *this* was how it would stop, but it seems kind of silly now, in retrospect, that I assumed we'd just kill all of you."

I let her help me up. "A little bit, I guess."

"I saw you gave Captain Bai's knife back." She doesn't look at me, opening the door to the stairs down. "I didn't realize you went back for it."

Captain Bai worked with Lieutenant Hao to clear the streets up to the Sanatorium, and we used the building as a place to set up a secure base. We were already planning a takeover of my mother's regime when Mei contacted me over the link to tell me Sev's plans. When I handed the knife back to Captain Bai, it didn't feel like a betrayal anymore that it had been used against a Second. It was more like a symbol of what I wanted to be. Even less, actually, because I no longer want things to be thrust under my nose before I believe they exist.

It doesn't come easily for me. But it's like those cots back at Dazhai. I shouldn't have to lie on one to know it's itchy. A good leader listens. Investigates. Changes, if necessary.

I let Mei go ahead of me down the stairs, trying not to think of that night, the blood, and everything wrong in the world that still needs to be fixed, contenting myself to say, "I went back for the knife because I didn't want Captain Bai to think I'd stolen it."

She nods, as if that somehow isn't nonsense. "I don't think your reputation could take another black mark." But then Mei looks at me out of the corner of her eye. "Hopefully, no one will have to use it again."

We walk toward the Sanatorium, passing through one of the padding zones between our armies: the less militant of our numbers—engineers, cooks, doctors, teachers, and scientists—who consented to be part of the barrier between guns. Those actively infected with SS have agreed to stay beyond the torch line now that they have access to our food stores. Every day we move the torches back a block as more and more have access to Mantis.

Their patience isn't only about having unspoiled food and clean water, though. Sev finding the cure changes everything. There's an end in sight. It's a lot easier to wait in line than it is to wait at the bottom of a hole, forgotten.

It's not that our wars against each other have really stopped.

But I'm hopeful this pause will be enough for everyone to seriously consider why they would want to go back to a life of hiding, shooting, worrying. I look at Mei, walking along beside me as if we aren't from opposite sides of this conflict. Proof that no matter how deeply rooted hatred is inside you, there's always hope to find some common ground.

Once we get to the City Center, Mei plops into a chair, growling at the person seated next to her until he moves to let me take the seat. I smile my thanks, and she shoots me an annoyed look, as if my noticing that she wants to sit next to me is impolite.

And, for all I've trained my whole life to deal with hostile forces, it seems like Mei so close beside me is a battle I'm not sure how to approach, much less win.

I think she likes it that way.

I think maybe I do too.

CHAPTER 67
Sev

IT WOULD BE RIDICULOUS TO HOPE FOR THE FIGHTING
to actually stop. Not when June hands Mother's precious box of
notes to a First who volunteered to come back to the Mountain
with us to work with Sole. Not when the primary cure trials are
ready, volunteers holding out their arms.

The first fractured moment of peace doesn't come until I'm
standing by Lihua in her bed, Sole drawing a dose of Mother's
cure into a syringe. Lihua's eyes scrunch shut as the needle pokes
her, a tear rolling down her cheek. Peishan crowds next to me to
hold Lihua's hand, using her elbows to move a First doctor out of
the way.

Lihua opens her brown eyes, her eyelashes so long it's a wonder
they don't weigh her eyelids closed. "Am I better now?" she whispers. "No more of those green pills? They're so hard to swallow."

Sole smiles, all her teeth showing. But she doesn't twitch.
"Yes. You're all better."

I lean down to hold Lihua close, to feel the flutter of her
heart and the steadiness of her breathing. She pushes away after

a moment, ready to be out of bed, to play, as if she never quite understood what was wrong with herself in the first place.

Peishan follows her, leaving me to go to the next bed alone. June doesn't mind, though, her eyes hungry on Sole's next syringe.

Once June's injection is done, she looks up at Sole. "Luokai next?"

Sole blinks once, twice. "We'll give it to everyone who gets in line so long as we have the materials to make it. We have to give priority to—"

June stands up, cutting Sole off. She turns to me, putting a hand on my shoulder. "You do it."

"Persuade her?" I ask. "She's right that there's a priority list. Skilled workers, like the people who agreed to stay out on the farms—"

"He's family." June squeezes my shoulder until I smile and push her off. "Dinner?"

I nod. "I'll see you then." I guess her ideas about who lives inside her circle of friends has expanded, June's family growing by one. I shake my head as she walks out, watching her diminutive form disappear down the hallway, wondering not for the first time what happened with June and Luokai on their way here.

Once she's out of earshot, I turn back to Sole, her hands full of things to do and reasons not to look at me. "You can't keep pulling special status to get the cure to the people you like most," she says. "If you only give it to your friends, then how are you different from the Chairman or Dr. Yang?"

"I've seen your lists of recipients for this first wave, and many of them are not friends of mine." I did see Aya's name on the list, the girl we brought down from the Sleep-infested Mountain above us. I know it's probably because she's well acquainted with the Heart and some of the Mountain's systems, but it's still nice to imagine the ghost of my sister with a cure. Brushing that image aside, I focus on Sole. "Do we have enough Mantis to last us while we manufacture more of the cure?"

She hedges, picking at her fingernails. "We should be able to maintain stability. Especially if we end up connected to City resources the way you keep saying we will be. And so long as those resources are responsibly produced. Not by slaves."

"It's happening. You know that from Mei and Kasim." I wait for a second. "So why are you trying to make sure Luokai doesn't get any of the cure? How is you *not* giving the cure to someone you *don't* like any different from Dr. Yang or the Chairman either?"

Sole sets down her tray of implements with a rattle.

"Didn't you just say yesterday that one of the Firsts has ideas on how to turn it into an aspirant, so it might not even be that difficult to fix the widespread infection?"

Sole walks toward the door, her hand still clenched around the plunger as if she can't quite let go. "That still has to be tested."

"Are we seriously refusing the *one* representative from Port North a cure?" I follow her toward the door, swallowing the lump in my throat at her icy expression. "They need to be a part of this . . . whatever it is we're building. We need to get out there as soon as possible to make sure they know we want to work with them so no more helis come this way. And because they deserve the cure same as we do."

"Luokai is not the only representative from Port North here." Sole shoves the syringe into a safe container in her medic bag. "And the cure might be a beginning, but it isn't going to end a hundred years of mistrust."

"That's why we need people like you not taking sides, Sole. You're a bridge. One of the few people interested in helping anyone who is sick rather than remembering who is supposed to be their enemy." Sighing when she won't look at me, I move to stand in front of her, willing her to meet my eyes. "You know that's exactly who Luokai is too. A bridge to a whole people who need you. Us."

She won't look at me, hands crunching the clean white fabric of her Yizhi coat "I'm not . . ." She sighs and looks up at me, her clear blue eyes piercing. "I'm not who I was when he left. I'm someone else, and so is he, and our lives aren't going to just snap back into place. Now, if you would please go away, I have work to do."

Something she said clicks into place in my mind as she walks out the door. "Wait—what do you mean Luokai isn't the only person here from Port North?"

Sole glances back. "My very next syringe full of cure is going to her, as a matter of fact." I follow her into the hall, and she pulls open the next door. A woman swathed in bandages lies inside, patches of ebony-dark skin showing between bandages. Tiny braids sit around her head like snakes on a pillow, though most of them seem to have been burned off at the ends. "She's from the heli."

"The heli?" I think back to the shadow jumping from the aircraft just before it fell from the sky. "The *black heli*? The one that was bombing—"

"Howl said if there were survivors, we needed to find them. I guess they're connected to Sun Yi-lai somehow." The woman's eyes twitch open at Sun Yi-lai's name, only to fall closed again. Sole gives me a pointed look as she begins undoing a bandage on the woman's arm. "Did I not ask you to go away?"

My throat is still clenched at Howl's name, my words suddenly gone. Howl is up? He's talking? He's *been* talking long enough to ask Sole to send people out to the heli in time to save this woman?

But I don't say any of that. Instead, my eyes drift down to the patient. "How is she supposed to be connected to Sun Yi-lai? What's her name, do you know?"

"Reifa something."

"Reifa . . . ?" It's like a question mark inside me, too frightening to look at. It can't be . . . can it? But I'm already pushing past Sole and running for the dorms.

If there's still a place in this world for hope, then I'm going to do everything I can to let it grow. Sun Yi-lai has a mother, and if there's a chance the woman in that room is her, I'm not going to keep them apart a moment longer.

CHAPTER 68
June

MY WORLD IS A CIRCLE, WITH LIGHT ABOVE AND dark underneath. Right now there's even food and a roof over my head, and a long hallway to sit in while I eavesdrop on Sole yelling at Luokai in the next room. He's pretty good at not wasting words when he wants to be.

Sev comes up the hall, Lihua skipping along at her side, the little girl's eyes widening at the loud voices. Sev's own eyes narrow, though. "You are just going to sit here and listen?"

I nod.

Lihua breaks from Sev to curl in at my side, the two of us pressed together like flowers on the same stalk. My gore seems to have shrunk back down so much that I barely notice him now. It's easy to ignore his grumbling when I have food in my mouth, warm clothes on my back, and my family here to remind me that I'm *wanted*. Now that I've let go of Dad, I can remember what life was like before he got so sick.

My wind, though. She's gone entirely. Maybe now that I've got my new family back, she knows I'm going to be okay. I look up

when Sev mentions something about the settlements, the farms—
where that stupid medic probably took my mother.

He's been smart enough to stay away from me.

"Tai-ige started a volunteer system that allows people to work
on the farms in exchange for an earlier dose of the cure. I guess
they're talking about splitting up the land and letting people own
smaller portions so they can trade crops for . . ." Sev stops when
she sees me thinking. "Your mother was on the farms, right?"

I tense a little. I'm not dumb the way Sev is, so full of hope
that there's no room left for sense. I know the chances of Mom
still being alive out there smaller than the grains of sand still
matted into my hair. But still . . . my wind had to go somewhere.
Maybe if she felt like I was safe enough for her to leave, it means
she went back to where she belonged. Back to Mom.

I stand up and brush myself off, holding my bowl close. Sole's
shouting has stopped, and now Luokai is talking, his voice low.
For a while I was worried that girl would cut him to pieces. She
knows a lot about needles and knives and stuff. But he seems
safe enough now that I feel okay leaving him to explain himself.
"Where's the medic?" I ask.

"Xuan?" Sev gets up, helping Lihua to follow. She doesn't ask
any more questions, leading me and Lihua down the halls until we
get to the hospital wing, one bed full of the Chairman's real son,
the one who isn't Howl, and the other unlucky enough to be holding up the medic. *Xuan.* His eyes widen a bit when I boost myself
up onto the foot of his bed, his mouth clamping shut, which I
happen to know is a first for him.

"You are going to take me to wherever they took my mother."

The medic puts down his half-eaten bun on a tray, keeping his
eyes focused on it. He'd rather I disappear, as if all the bad stuff

he's ever done in his life will disappear with me. But I'm done with disappearing. With hanging back and pretending. I'm done hiding.

Sev slides in next to me, her arm wrapping around me. I don't need her exactly, but it's nice that she's here. Xuan finally looks up, his eyebrows crunched together above his eyes. "I don't know how much hope there is, June."

"You're going to help me find out where she is. Even if she's dead." I look him in the eye, and it feels like power. "I deserve to know."

Xuan leans back an inch, but he doesn't break eye contact. "Yes, you do."

CHAPTER 69
Sev

I SIT DOWN IN THE CAFETERIA, STARING AT THE food in front of me, wondering if I can eat it. It smells good, which is better than when we first got back here. All I could smell was chemicals, blood, and that awful aftertaste of gunfire in my mouth. Now the eggs just smell like eggs. I spin the green apple around once, smiling as I remember the first time I saw Howl take a bite of raw apple and pretend to be poisoned by it.

But then I swallow that thought down, wishing I could see for myself that he's not dying now.

Sole and June sit next to me at the cafeteria table, June eyeing my full plate with interest. "Get your own." I scowl, pulling it closer. "All the food in the kitchen and you want *mine*?"

June smiles, grabbing the apple and taking a bite.

"You actually going to eat?" Kasim plops down next to me.

I pick up my plate, awkwardly sliding out from the bench with my hands full. The food might smell like food again, but I'm not in the mood for people right now. Not even ones that I like. "I have to go check on something."

"Contrary to popular belief, staring at someone's door won't heal them any quicker." He gives me a rakish smile. "And you know how cocky Howl is already. Don't make it worse." He links his free arm through mine. "You are going to eat, and then you are going to come help me."

Every time I end up sitting on the floor outside Howl's door, Kasim seems to find me, dragging me on excursions into the Mountain or Outside. He doesn't say much, the boyish smile that pulls at his cheeks almost seeming pasted on. It's still hard to look at him without seeing Xuan's blood on his hands. But the longer I spend with him, the more that image fades.

Xuan is out of bed now, preparing to be the official medic on Tai-ge and Helix's tour of the farms, and then to accompany them to the island for their first official visit. It was a good excuse to get him and June on the helis without a fuss. Sole says he's been helping with the wounded coming in from Outside. And that his girlfriend hasn't appeared yet, but Xuan still looks for her every time we bring in someone new.

Biting my lip, I unhook my arm and grab the apple from Kasim's plate. "If you want a buddy for your excursions, you'll have to catch me first." He protests as I walk away, but I ignore him.

"You're not even supposed to know where Howl is!" Sole calls after me, but she laughs as she's saying it. "Leave him alone!"

Her laugh makes me smile. It's real.

My fingers grip hard on the plate as I walk toward his stretch of hallway. It's not like I can bother him anyway. His door is still firmly closed and locked to everyone but Sole. I tell myself no one is allowed in because Sole wants to make sure no Menghu or City-folk try to take revenge on him for old grievances. I don't know if that's true, but it's easier than letting myself think too hard about the fact that he asked Sole to bar *me* from his room.

When I think about that, I only remember him yelling at me to go. Angry when I showed up in the City Center, gun limp in my hand.

After all the promises I made to myself, I'm still processing the things that have happened, like the feel of the gun in my hand as I stood over Dr. Yang, my finger on the trigger. I might not have been the one to kill him, but I tried. I meant to be the one to do it. And it wasn't the wrong choice.

I'm different. I'm not sure how I've changed or who I am anymore, and it's scary to think that I don't know where I fit. I thought I fit next to Howl, at least, but that doesn't mean much if he doesn't agree.

When I get to his door, I sit against the wall across from it, my feet out in front of me and my plate balanced on my lap. Fresh fruit. Eggs. Rice. It tastes good, as if the cooks took their time, not worried who would see the flames through the trees or if the smell of cooking food would attract predators.

"Sev?"

I look up, and my heart gives a surprised flail. Tai-ge's standing there, Mei a step behind him.

"I . . . didn't know . . . you were here." I look back down at my plate, wondering who held back that particular bit of information. If I'd known Hong Tai-ge was walking the halls, I would have found a less obvious place to be. Too much has happened between us to ever be fixed, and yet he *was* the one who organized the revolt against General Hong. It's too messy for me to want to deal with.

"I figured you'd have better things to do if I tried to set up a meeting with you." He shifts from foot to foot, his jaw clench-ing. Nervous.

"I probably would have."

"I heard you sit here a lot, so . . ." He glances at Mei, who rolls her eyes and makes a shooing motion with her hand. Tai-ge bends his knees, coming down to my level. "I just . . . I wanted to say that I'm sorry. You were right. I was wrong. I didn't listen when I should have." He bites his lip. "It's something I've realized I need to work on."

"You're . . . sorry?" I blink, not sure how the words can cover everything Tai-ge did to me to reach this point. There's just too much. More than I ever want to think about, and so nodding seems like the only thing to do. "I guess you came through in the end. After shooting Howl. Twice."

Tai-ge licks his lips. "I didn't know what else to do. Our sol-diers were *coming*. Mother would have shot me if I hadn't done it, and she wouldn't have chosen a place I'd recover from. I needed to be alive for it to work."

Unfortunately, I don't have to stretch my imagination far to think his mother would have been capable of shooting her own son, given the situation. She and his father had thrown him in prison before when they thought he was infected, the embarrass-ment of a sick son much more important in their estimation than Tai-ge was.

"I'm sorry," he says. I know it isn't enough to say it, but I mean it just the same."

I shake my head. "It's not enough. Maybe it never will be." Take a deep breath. "But thanks for saying it."

Watching him walk away isn't hard, but it feels odd. There are so many years of love between us, but it's strangely easy to let him go. I am who I am, Tai-ge is who he is, and I don't believe that we'll ever truly see eye-to-eye. But I appreciate that he's finally realized the world as something other than a Red fantasy land. I'll be watching him and Helix both. We all will.

But I have more hope than doubt, and that is a good enough start.

Mei is such an unlikely shadow to the former Red General's son, but the two of them seem to match their steps, and I smile a little as he ducks his head to tell her something. Mei's wrist is naked of bones, and she doesn't seem to miss them.

Maybe the world is bigger for everyone now, not just for me.

Once they've turned the corner, I go back to my staring contest with the door, as if I can make it open through sheer force of will, and that I'll find Howl alive and well inside, a smile catching his lips when he sees me.

But it doesn't open. The hallway stays cold and silent as a morgue.

CHAPTER 70
Howl

SOLE CONCENTRATES AS SHE PEELS THE LAST OF
the bandages away from my shoulder, inspecting the healing skin
underneath. She ties up all of her things and walks toward the
door, not bothering to speak.

We haven't spoken much. Just updates on what's happening
outside my room. She seems calmer now than when I first woke
up in this room. Every day her brow is a little less furrowed, as
if me getting better makes more of a difference to her than I
expected it would.

I look up when the doorknob turns, every inch of me going on
alert. "I thought no one was allowed in here."

Sole goes to the door and then steps back to let someone
through. A little blond someone with green glass eyes. I smile,
not sure where to put my thoughts or emotions. I'm so glad to
see June, but at the same time, I don't want anyone else I care
about anywhere near me. All I seem to do is hurt the people
I love.

How many times did I almost kill Sev? She came after me when she should have stayed safe. And now here I am, a monster in a new world where there isn't a place for monsters anymore.

June walks to the bed and hops up next to me without asking, leaning against me.

"You shouldn't be in here," I rasp, because what I really, really want is for her to be here.

She looks up at me, her eyes wide. "Shut up, Howl. Stop hiding."

Sole snorts, tamping down a laugh.

"I'm not hiding." I look at the door. "There are real people out there trying to build a better world. One I don't fit in anymore."

"You're my family." June's tousled curls are bright against my shoulder. "You're mine and Sev's. You don't get to say no."

"I'm not yours. I'm not anyone's. I've been on my own side my whole life, June, and people aren't going to understand that. They didn't before." When I close my eyes, I keep seeing Song Jie's helicopter diving through the night in a burst of flames. He was made for revenge. He was just like me, ready to take everything from those who stole from him.

And now he's dead.

I don't want that to be me. But it *is*, no matter how much I try to change. I never wanted to kill or hurt people. To spy, steal. Lie. But those things are what kept me alive, and no matter how much I want to change, I keep falling back on my old bad habits whenever life gets tough.

I'm not safe. I never was. I make the wrong choices again and again. I am broken.

"Hey." June pokes my chest, and I flinch, pain still a constant companion. "I got SS for you."

"Exactly. You got hurt because of me. Sev got hurt because of me. That's not family, or if it is, it's one you shouldn't want to be part of."

June just stares at me, unblinking. "Sev knew she would probably die."

My chest stills. Sev knew she would probably die and came after me anyway. Even after I begged her not to. I suppose things worked out this time. But what about next time, and the time after that?

June pulls my collar until I have to look at her again. "You don't get to take responsibility for the things Sev or I did to protect you. So stop being such a gore hole and let her see you."

Sole shifts by the door, her arms too tight around her medical bag. "Luokai was saying that choices are for us to make and others to forgive. That we can't control who forgives or who hurts us." She holds out a hand, as if she wants me out of the bed once and for all. "You and I know what it means to be afraid. For our lives, for our sanity. Our souls, if people have those." She looks down, concentrating on the hand extended toward me. "I used to think I was brave, facing down every day, but I realized I've been hiding this whole time, first behind a gun and then inside my lab. Controlling what happens next by deciding to be alone."

She looks up. "I said things I shouldn't have. I was scared that everything I said about you was true about *me*. That I wasn't a person worth saving." Sole slides over to the bed. "I don't think either of us can take back the things we've done, but we are in control of what comes next. And I don't want you to believe that you have to leave to keep the rest of us safe." Her voice is quiet. "We can still do good."

Tears blur my vision. "Not enough."

"Probably not. But that doesn't mean I don't want you here.

Why do you think I wasted so many bandages on you? I love you, Howl. And you already *have* changed. You aren't who you used to be any more than I am."

June curls closer to me, wrapping her arms around my rib cage. "I don't care what you deserve. We want you. Isn't that enough?"

Sole smiles a little. "It's not just about us anymore." She looks me up and down. "There are people out there waiting for us." She points to the door.

"That's what I'm afraid of. I'm not what she—"

Sole rolls her eyes. "Your existence is not validated by one person's opinion, Howl. If she doesn't get it, that doesn't erase you. Why don't you go ask her what she wants instead of sitting in here deciding for her?" She turns toward the door. "That's what Luokai did. Sat at the island alone, waiting to die. Believing— even after the SS restrictions lifted here at the Mountain—if he couldn't come back without SS, then no one would want him." Glancing over her shoulder, I see a glint of tear in Sole's eye. "When in reality, it would have made a world of difference for both of us to have him here."

I close my eyes, thinking of how I used to long to find my brother, how differently my life might have turned out if we'd been together.

June squeezes my hand and hops up from the bed. "You owe us." Then she skips out of the room.

And I can't deny that she's right.

CHAPTER 71
Sev

"ARE YOU READY TO GO IN?" I ASK.

Sun Yi-lai narrows his eyes at the door as June translates for me, my hand on the knob. Then he nods. Reifa stands close behind, bandages still across parts of her face, her hands gloved. But she moves forward to put a hand on his shoulder.

"Alone?" I ask. "Or do you want us with you?"

"I'll go in alone," June translates his whisper, as if being Asleep for so many years stripped him down to a ghostly presence, half of him still slumbering inside his head. "But stay close?"

Reifa nods, stepping back as I open the door to the line of cells, stifling a smile as General Hong's spluttering snore comes rushing out from behind one of the closed doors. Yi-lai smiles at Reifa, the two of them sharing something between them, as if I can see her propping him up, though she's the one who sags. He turns to stare down the hallway, the key to his father's cell in his hand, before glancing at me. His forehead puckers. "You aren't going to leave without me, are you? You'll take me with you back to Port North?" June translates.

"We'll hold the heli as long as you need." Tai-ge requested that I accompany the leaders touring the farms and visiting the island with Luokai. We are short on bridges, and if I can be one, I'm willing.

But there's still time for one visit. "I won't leave without you or Reifa." I look down the hallway. "The Chairman loves you, you know," I say. "But you don't have to say good-bye to him. You don't owe him anything."

"He's a bad person." Yi-lai looks at his feet as June interprets. His mannerisms and way of speaking are so childlike that it's hard to persuade myself he's supposed to be older than me.

Reifa says something in Port Northian. I squeeze June's arm, hating that I can't just understand. I'm determined to start learning Port Northian so I can talk for myself. "She says, 'He did a lot of bad things.'" June's brow crinkles. "'More bad things than good things. That's why he's in a cell instead of free like us. But that doesn't cancel out the fact that he loves you.'"

Yi-lai walks to the Chairman's cell door, fiddles with the key for a moment, and then slides it into the slot. I start to turn away, but Yi-lai calls my name, gesturing me to come into the Chairman's cell.

The Chairman looks more disheveled than I've ever seen him, wearing threadbare clothes and bearing dark circles beneath his eyes. When he sees his son, his eyes light up as if there's a soul inside him somwhere. I nod to Yi-lai, then go wait outside.

Inside the cell, June translates for Yi-lai and the Chairman, and I try not to listen. When they come out, Yi-lai has tears on his cheeks, but he doesn't look back. When I start to follow them, the Chairman's voice calls out after me. "Jiang Sev? I know you're still there."

Closing my eyes, I debate. He doesn't deserve my time any more than he deserves Yi-lai's. And yet, I let his voice, so familiar, pull me back into the cell. When I'm standing in the doorway, he looks me over. "How am I any different from your mother? She gave up everything to save you." He stares past me, up the hall, to where his son is disappearing, his eyes so tired that his indignant rage looks more like dull anger. Yi-lai's head bows, uncomfortable. "I did what I had to in order to save my son."

"My mother gave up everything she had." I take a step back, tempering my tone to smile at Yi-lai, like grown-ups pretending they aren't fighting when a child sits listening. "She gave up her family, her home, her position, her power—*everything* to save me, you're right." I hold his gaze for a moment. "*You* gave up every-one else."

June links her arm through mine as we walk back toward our quarters. It feels good to leave the Chairman, General Hong—*everything* that's happened—behind me. It isn't my decision what happens to them. Not my job to go find the doctor's dead body. And it's too exhausting to be upset or angry about them anymore. The tyrants who came before us might not change. Probably won't ever see things from any point of view but their own, convincing themselves that what they were doing was for the good of every-one despite abundant proof that was not the case. But I can walk away and leave it behind. Spite and arguing and spitting in old enemies' faces doesn't help me or anyone else, so I choose to think of other things.

I don't know if it's me or June who steers us down the back hallway that goes past Howl's room. At this point the route has become a habit.

When we get there, his door is open.

Surprise and nerves jolt in my stomach, warring with fear. June grips my arm hard, holding me in place as if she's afraid I'll bolt. Is someone in there? One of the people Howl worried would find him? Or is he well enough to be up and just hasn't gotten around to telling me?

The door swings the rest of the way open even as I watch, and an entire kaleidoscope of butterflies dance in my stomach as Howl steps out the doorway. The arm that was limp in a sling after the gore attack now hangs free by his side, thick red scars peeking out from his T-shirt where claws scored his shoulder. He leans on a crutch, and there's new-healing skin on his arm where the bullet went in.

He looks me up and down, swallowing over and over again as if he can't find the right words to say. When he finally speaks, it's with his familiar drawl. "Well, you look much healthier than the last time I saw you."

June groans and lets go of my arm. She gives Howl a meaningful glare before stalking up the hall and leaving the two of us alone.

"You seem healthy-ish too." My mouth dries up for a second as I look him over again, the way he stands curved around the crutch, his arm so red and blotched, much worse than any scars of mine. "How long have you been up?" Uncertainty boils up inside me. I'm suddenly noticing how far away he's standing, the way he isn't smiling even a little.

He shrugs, then flinches, touching the bandaging at his chest.

Is it because I left him in the southern garrison? Because he got shot and I didn't help him immediately? Did I do something else wrong to make him not want to see me? Or he could just be tired. . . . I firmly stop my brain before it goes any further. We're standing so far apart a passing medic walks right between us, hardly looking up from his clipboard of notes to notice that we're here. I stare at my toes, fire flooding my cheeks.

If this is how he wants it, then I'm not going to push him. "I'm going north," I say, taking a step down the hall after June. Toward our room, away from the awful awkwardness between me and Howl because it's almost worse than the blank door. Another step, and then another, and somehow Howl is limping along beside me. "I've got to get some things ready before we leave."

"Wait." His hand touches my shoulder, pulling me to a stop. My heart starts beating with a terrible goose step of a rhythm. "I . . . I want to come with you."

"You want to come tour the farms? See Port North again?"

He nods.

I finally look up and meet his eyes. "I can't really stop you. I mean, maybe that crutch could. I think I'd like it if you came. Depending on a few things."

"Like what?"

Nervous energy spirals through me as I make myself hold his gaze. But it's not just nervousness. Some of it is *anger*. Weeks of staring at that door, watching Sole go in and come out, reports of things he'd said to her, things he'd asked for. But no room for me. Not even to say good-bye, if that's what he wanted.

"I want you to tell me what the hell is wrong with you. Why wouldn't you let me come see you?"

Howl blinks once, then reaches out to pull one of my hands from my pocket. "Do you remember the story I told you that first night after we left the City? We were up on a ledge, you had dead guy caked on your shoes, and there was a gore trying to eat us."

"What does that have to do with—"

"I remember wondering how you could possibly survive. You seemed too young. Too frail. You were already persuaded you were broken."

Tears are burning behind my eyes. Whatever he's trying to say hurts, and I want it to be over. I want to run. "I remember. Zhinu and Niulang. The first story you ever told me about two people who loved each other ending up on opposite sides of the sky."

"Hey. You forgot the birds that let them hang out once a year."

My lips press together. I'm not willing to joke.

His hand on my arm rubs a thumb along the inside of my wrist. "Listen. Back then I was just telling stories so you'd follow me. Turns out it takes more than one lying, idiotic Menghu to break you. It takes more than a whole army. More than *two* of them." He laughs. "You found the cure. You tried to save me even when it was impossible. Believed in me when no one else in the entire world did. When I first met you, I thought I was the strong one, the one who had seen the world and knew how to survive in it. But I was just . . ." He smiles, grimacing at himself. "I'm not what you want. I'm not what you deserve."

The anger inside me *burns*. He's trying to make this decision *for* me when it's mine to decide. "Howl, do you remember the night I told you that you can't tell me what to do?"

"Which time?" He's smiling now, just a little. Bending closer as if there are magnets between us and it's all he can do to stop himself touching me.

But why stop? I don't understand. "If you're mad at me, fine. If you don't want to be around me anymore? Great. Maybe you fell madly in love with your pillow and need some more alone time? Go do that. But if you're trying to tell me to jump again, you're too late. I already did jump, that day at the Arch. And I jumped *with* you. You aren't any of the things you're pretending to be. A monster? A killer?" I throw my hands up in the air, my words coming faster and faster, anger building up like heat behind my lips. "I know you've had to make horrible decisions. We've all had to. I *shot* Dr. Yang, Howl! And I meant to kill him. I'm so sick of you telling me I'm supposed to sit up on my pedestal and keep my hands clean. So stop pretending that you're the only one who has had to do horrible things to survive and protect those you *love*."

Because I love Howl. The word feels like honey on my tongue, thick and sweet and impossible to say. I don't know why it's hard when I've said it before. Before, it was a potential good-bye, a last breath. A deathbed confession. But there is no death in this hallway, not that I can see. It's a start to something rather than an end. A start that I *want*. But before I can say it, he does.

"I love you, Sev. And it's terrifying." He grits his teeth when he says it, as if he expects me to laugh.

I close the space between us, threading my hands through his hair and pulling him close to me. "I love you too." My air seems stuck in my lungs. I'm too scared to speak or think or do anything but stare up at him because I know moving would disturb the cosmic forces that are allowing us to have this moment. "Also, you promised me a treehouse. I take promises very, very seriously."

A grin spreads across his face, the grin I didn't even know how much I'd missed until it's there and it's for me.

And before he gets the chance to kiss me, I kiss him first.

They say war isn't a dinner party, and I've decided I agree. At least, it's not any dinner party I'd want to have. I'd prefer my parties to leave less scarring.

It was war that took my family. It was also war that brought me the family I have now. A family made up of the most unlikely bits and pieces. June, Howl, Sole, maybe even Luokai and my aunt back at Port North. Things that have been so empty inside me are now full. The world that seemed so divided by what we look like, the sounds and syllables of our names, or the sizes and shapes of our scars is changing. It's growing. And even if not everyone agrees yet—some with guns still in their hands—there are voices arguing to make room, and that is the first step.

War is awful, evil, destructive. But it changed other things that were evil, awful, and destructive too. It gave us a chance at something better. I suppose that's the way things are. Nothing and no one is all the way good or all the way bad.

Life isn't a game of black and white stones. In life, you can only move forward.

The air nips at my skin as Howl and I walk to the newly cleared section of forest to wait for the heli, but every bite seems toothless, as if it's too tired to fight any longer. June comes next with Reifa, Xuan, and Yi-lai, the Chairman's real son and Howl looking at each other curiously as we wait for the whine of propellers to emerge from the frozen blue sky. Howl walks over after a moment, and it's sort of surreal to see the two of them standing opposite, a hint of the Chairman in both their features even while the man himself is already partially forgotten.

Sole comes next, Luokai a step behind her. They don't look at each other, but they're closer than I've seen them up until now. Luokai steps up to Howl, and when the two meet eyes, Howl nods to him. Not a wonderful beginning, but beginnings don't have to be wonderful. It's the end that counts.

When Howl comes back to stand by me, the world seems as if

it has gone truly quiet. Not the quiet of danger or of fear. Not the ugly silence of compulsion ready to strike, or the shocked stillness after a gunshot. It's the hush of calm, of peace, of the future waiting to be stepped into.

We took up our weapons and fought because the world was in the dead of winter. Now, though, outside in the open air, I swear I can smell a hint of spring.

PRONUNCIATION GUIDE

Baohujia	Bow (rhymes with "cow") hoo-jeeaha
Cai Ayi	Tsie (rhymes with "my") AH-yee
Cale	Cayl (rhymes with pale)
Bai	By (rhymes with "my")
Dazhai	Dah Jie (rhymes with "my")
Feng Liu	Fung Leo
Helix	Hee-lix
Hong Tai-ge	Hong (long o like in "tome") Tie (rhymes with "my") guh
Huifen	Hwey-fun
Jiang Gui-hua	Jee-ang GWAY-Hwa
Jiang Sev	Jee-ang Sev
Kasim	Kah-sim
Lihua	Lee-hwa
Mei	May
Menghu	Mung (rhymes with "rung") hoo
Peishan	Pay-shan
Song Jie	Sohng Jee-eh
Sun Howl	Soon Howl
Sun Luokai	Soon Loo-oh-kie (rhymes with "my")
Sun Yi-lai	Soon Ee-lie (rhymes with "my")
Xuan	Shwen (rhymes with "pen")
Yang He-ping	Yahng (long a as in "fawn") Huh-ping
Ze-ming	Zuh-ming